A SPECTRUM UNSEEN

A SPECTRUM UNSEEN

Invisible Men, Women, and Creatures in Classic Science Fiction and Fantasy

CHAD ARMENT, EDITOR

COACHWHIP PUBLICATIONS
Landisville, Pennsylvania

A Spectrum Unseen, edited by Chad Arment
Copyright © 2009 Coachwhip Publications

ISBN 1-61646-001-6
ISBN-13 978-1-61646-001-3

Cover: Spectrum © Giuseppe Ramos

Coachwhipbooks.com

CONTENTS

THE RING OF GYGES
Plato's *Republic*

Now that those who practise justice do so involuntarily and because they have not the power to be unjust will best appear if we imagine something of this kind: having given both to the just and the unjust power to do what they will, let us watch and see whither desire will lead them; then we shall discover in the very act the just and unjust man to be proceeding along the same road, following their interest, which all natures deem to be their good, and are only diverted into the path of justice by the force of law. The liberty which we are supposing may be most completely given to them in the form of such a power as is said to have been possessed by Gyges, the ancestor of Croesus the Lydian. According to the tradition, Gyges was a shepherd in the service of the king of Lydia; there was a great storm, and an earthquake made an opening in the earth at the place where he was feeding his flock. Amazed at the sight, he descended into the opening, where, among other marvels, he beheld a hollow brazen horse, having doors, at which he stooping and looking in saw a dead body of stature, as appeared to him, more than human, and having nothing on but a gold ring; this he took from the finger of the dead and reascended. Now the shepherds met together, according to custom, that they might send their monthly report about the flocks to the king; into their assembly he came having the ring on his finger, and as he was sitting among them he chanced to turn the collet of the ring inside his hand, when instantly he became invisible to the rest of the company and they began to speak of him as if he were no longer present. He was astonished at

7

this, and again touching the ring he turned the collet outwards and reappeared; he made several trials of the ring, and always with the same result—when he turned the collet inwards he became invisible, when outwards he reappeared. Whereupon he contrived to be chosen one of the messengers who were sent to the court; where as soon as he arrived he seduced the queen, and with her help conspired against the king and slew him, and took the kingdom. Suppose now that there were two such magic rings, and the just put on one of them and the unjust the other; no man can be imagined to be of such an iron nature that he would stand fast in justice. No man would keep his hands off what was not his own when he could safely take what he liked out of the market, or go into houses and lie with any one at his pleasure, or kill or release from prison whom he would, and in all respects be like a God among men. Then the actions of the just would be as the actions of the unjust; they would both come at last to the same point. And this we may truly affirm to be a great proof that a man is just, not willingly or because he thinks that justice is any good to him individually, but of necessity, for wherever any one thinks that he can safely be unjust, there he is unjust. For all men believe in their hearts that injustice is far more profitable to the individual than justice, and he who argues as I have been supposing, will say that they are right. If you could imagine any one obtaining this power of becoming invisible, and never doing any wrong or touching what was another's, he would be thought by the lookers-on to be a most wretched idiot, although they would praise him to one another's faces, and keep up appearances with one another from a fear that they too might suffer injustice. Enough of this.

WHAT WAS IT? A MYSTERY
Fitz-James O'Brien

It is, I confess, with considerable diffidence that I approach the strange narrative which I am about to relate. The events which I purpose detailing are of so extraordinary and unheard-of a character that I am quite prepared to meet with an unusual amount of incredulity and scorn. I accept all such beforehand. I have, I trust, the literary courage to face unbelief. I have, after mature consideration, resolved to narrate, in as simple and straightforward a manner as I can compass, some facts that passed under my observation in the month of July last, and which, in the annals of the mysteries of physical science, are wholly unparalleled.

I live at No. — Twenty-sixth Street, in this city. The house is in some respects a curious one. It has enjoyed for the last two years the reputation of being haunted. It is a large and stately residence, surrounded by what was once a garden, but which is now only a green enclosure used for bleaching clothes. The dry basin of what has been a fountain, and a few fruit-trees, ragged and unpruned, indicate that this spot, in past days, was a pleasant, shady retreat, filled with fruits and flowers and the sweet murmur of waters.

The house is very spacious. A hall of noble size leads to a vast spiral staircase winding through its centre, while the various apartments are of imposing dimensions. It was built some fifteen or twenty years since by Mr. A—, the well-known New York merchant, who five years ago threw the commercial world into convulsions by a stupendous bank fraud. Mr. A—, as every one knows, escaped to Europe, and died not long after of a broken heart. Almost immediately after the news of his decease reached this country, and was verified, the report spread in Twenty-sixth Street that No. — was haunted. Legal measures had dispossessed the widow of its former owner, and it was inhabited merely by a care-taker and his wife, placed there by the house-agent into whose hands it had passed for purposes of renting or sale. These people declared that they were troubled with unnatural noises. Doors were opened without any visible agency. The remnants of furniture scattered through the various rooms were, during the night, piled one upon the other by unknown hands. Invisible feet passed up and down the stairs in broad daylight, ac-companied by the rustle of unseen silk dresses, and the gliding of viewless hands along the massive balusters. The care-taker and his wife declared they would live there no longer. The house-agent laughed, dismissed them, and put others in their place. The noises and supernatural manifestations continued. The neighborhood caught up the story, and the house remained untenanted for three years. Several persons negotiated for it; but somehow, always be-fore the bargain was closed, they heard the unpleasant rumors, and declined to treat any further.

It was in this state of things that my landlady—who at that time kept a boarding-house in Bleecker Street, and who wished to move farther up town—conceived the bold idea of renting No. — Twenty-sixth Street. Happening to have in her house rather a plucky and philosophical set of boarders, she laid her scheme before us, stat-ing candidly everything she had heard respecting the ghostly quali-ties of the establishment to which she wished to remove us. With the exception of two timid persons,—a sea-captain and a returned Californian, who immediately gave notice that they would leave,—all of Mrs. Moffat's guests declared that they would accompany her in her chivalric incursion into the abode of spirits.

Our removal was effected in the month of May, and we were all charmed with our new residence. The portion of Twenty-sixth Street where our house is situated—between Seventh and Eighth Avenues—is one of the pleasantest localities in New York. The gar-dens back of the houses, running down nearly to the Hudson, form, in the summer time, a perfect avenue of verdure. The air is pure and invigorating, sweeping, as it does, straight across the river from the Weehawken heights, and even the ragged garden which surrounded the house on two sides, although displaying on washing days rather too much clothes-line, still gave us a piece of green sward to look at, and a cool retreat in the summer evenings, where we smoked our cigars in the dusk, and watched the fire-flies flashing their dark-lanterns in the long grass.

Of course we had no sooner established ourselves at No. — than we began to expect the ghosts. We absolutely awaited their advent with eagerness. Our dinner conversation was supernatural. One of the boarders, who had purchased Mrs. Crowe's "Night Side of Nature" for his own private delectation, was regarded as a public enemy by the entire household for not having bought twenty copies. The man led a life of supreme wretchedness while he was reading this volume. A system of espionage was established, of which he was the victim. If he incautiously laid the book down for an instant and left the room, it was immediately seized and read aloud in secret places to a select few. I found myself a person of immense importance, it having leaked out that I was tolerably well versed in the history of supernaturalism, and had once written a story, entitled "The Pot of Tulips," for *Harper's Monthly*, the foundation of which was a ghost. If a table or a wainscot panel happened to warp when we were assembled in the large drawing-room, there was an instant silence, and every one was prepared for an immediate clanking of chains and a spectral form.

After a month of psychological excitement, it was with the utmost dissatisfaction that we were forced to acknowledge that nothing in the remotest degree approaching the supernatural had manifested itself. Once the black butler asseverated that his candle had been blown out by some invisible agency while he was undressing himself for the night; but as I had more than once discovered this colored gentleman in a condition when one candle must have appeared to him like two, I thought it possible that, by going a step farther in his potations, he might have reversed this phenomenon, and seen no candle at all where he ought to have beheld one.

Things were in this state when an incident took place so awful and inexplicable in its character that my reason fairly reels at the bare memory of the occurrence. It was the tenth of July. After dinner was over I repaired, with my friend Dr. Hammond, to the garden to smoke my evening pipe. Independent of certain mental sympathies which existed between the Doctor and myself, we were linked together by a secret vice. We both smoked opium. We knew each other's secret, and respected it. We enjoyed together that wonderful expansion of thought, that marvellous intensifying of the perceptive faculties, that boundless feeling of existence when we seem to have points of contact with the whole universe,—in short, that unimaginable spiritual bliss, which I would not surrender for a throne, and which I hope you, reader, will never—never taste.

Those hours of opium happiness which the Doctor and I spent together in secret were regulated with a scientific accuracy. We did not blindly smoke the drug of Paradise, and leave our dreams to chance. While smoking, we carefully steered our conversation through the brightest and calmest channels of thought. We talked of the East, and endeavored to recall the magical panorama of its glowing scenery. We criticised the most sensuous poets, those who painted life ruddy with health, brimming with passion, happy in the possession of youth and strength and beauty. If we talked of Shakespeare's "Tempest," we lingered over Ariel, and avoided Caliban. Like the Gebers, we turned our faces to the east, and saw only the sunny side of the world.

This skilful coloring of our train of thought produced in our subsequent visions a corresponding tone. The splendors of Arabian fairy-land dyed our dreams. We paced that narrow strip of grass with the tread and port of kings. The song of the *rana arborea*, while he clung to the bark of the ragged plum-tree, sounded like the strains of divine orchestras. Houses, walls, and streets melted like rain-clouds, and vistas of unimaginable glory stretched away before us. It was a rapturous companionship. We enjoyed the vast delight more perfectly because, even in our most ecstatic moments, we were conscious of each other's presence. Our pleasures, while individual, were still twin, vibrating and moving in musical accord.

On the evening in question, the tenth of July, the Doctor and myself found ourselves in an unusually metaphysical mood. We lit our large meerschaums, filled with fine Turkish tobacco, in the core of which burned a little black nut of opium, that, like the nut in the fairy tale, held within its narrow limits wonders beyond the reach of kings; we paced to and fro, conversing. A strange perversity dominated the currents of our thought. They would *not* flow through the sun-lit channels into which we strove to divert them. For some unaccountable reason they constantly diverged into dark and lonesome beds, where a continual gloom brooded. It was in vain that, after our old fashion, we flung ourselves on the shores of the East, and talked of its gay bazaars, of the splendors of the time of Haroun, of harems and golden palaces. Black afreets continually arose from the depths of our talk, and expanded, like the one the fisherman released from the copper vessel, until they blotted everything bright from our vision. Insensibly, we yielded to the occult force that swayed us, and indulged in gloomy speculation. We had talked some time upon the proneness of the human mind to mysticism, and the almost universal love of the Terrible, when Hammond suddenly said to me, "What do you consider to be the greatest element of Terror?"

The question, I own, puzzled me. That many things were terrible, I knew. Stumbling over a corpse in the dark; beholding, as I once did, a woman floating down a deep and rapid river, with wildly-lifted arms, and awful, upturned face, uttering, as she sank, shrieks that rent one's heart, while we, the spectators, stood frozen at a window which overhung the river at a height of sixty feet, unable to make the slightest effort to save her, but dumbly watching her last supreme agony and her disappearance. A shattered wreck, with no life visible, encountered floating listlessly on the ocean, is a terrible object, for it suggests a huge terror, the proportions of which are veiled. But it now struck me for the first time that there must be one great and ruling embodiment of fear, a King of Terrors to which all others must succumb. What might it be? To what train of circumstances would it owe its existence?

"I confess, Hammond," I replied to my friend, "I never considered the subject before. That there must be one Something more terrible than any other thing, I feel. I cannot attempt, however, even the most vague definition."

"I am somewhat like you, Harry," he answered. "I feel my capacity to experience a terror greater than anything yet conceived by the human mind;—something combining in fearful and unnatural amalgamation hitherto supposed incompatible elements. The calling of the voices in Brockden Brown's novel of 'Wieland' is awful; so is the picture of the Dweller of the Threshold, in Bulwer's 'Zanoni'; but," he added, shaking his head gloomily, "there is something more horrible still than these."

"Look here, Hammond," I rejoined, "let us drop this kind of talk, for Heaven's sake! We shall suffer for it, depend on it."

"I don't know what's the matter with me to-night," he replied, "but my brain is running upon all sorts of weird and awful thoughts. I feel as if I could write a story like Hoffman, to-night, if I were only master of a literary style."

"Well, if we are going to be Hoffmanesque in our talk, I'm off to bed. Opium and nightmares should never be brought together. How sultry it is! Good-night, Hammond."

"Good-night, Harry. Pleasant dreams to you."

"To you, gloomy wretch, afreets, ghouls, and enchanters."

We parted, and each sought his respective chamber. I undressed quickly and got into bed, taking with me, according to my usual custom, a book, over which I generally read myself to sleep. I opened the volume as soon as I had laid my head upon the pillow, and instantly flung it to the other side of the room. It was Goudon's "History of Monsters"—a curious French work, which I had lately imported from Paris, but which, in the state of mind I had then reached, was anything but an agreeable companion. I resolved to go to sleep at once; so, turning down my gas until nothing but a little blue point of light glimmered on the top of the tube, I composed myself to rest.

The room was in total darkness. The atom of gas that still remained lighted did not illuminate a distance of three inches round the burner. I desperately drew my arm across my eyes, as if to shut out even the darkness, and tried to think of nothing. It was in vain. The confounded themes touched on by Hammond in the garden kept obtruding themselves on my brain. I battled against them. I erected ramparts of would-be blankness of intellect to keep them out. They still crowded upon me. While I was lying still as a corpse, hoping that by a perfect physical inaction I should hasten mental repose, an awful incident occurred. A Something dropped, as it seemed, from the ceiling, plumb upon my chest, and the next instant I felt two bony hands encircling my throat, endeavoring to choke me.

I am no coward, and am possessed of considerable physical strength. The suddenness of the attack, instead of stunning me, strung every nerve to its highest tension. My body acted from instinct, before my brain had time to realize the terrors of my position. In an instant I wound two muscular arms around the creature, and squeezed it, with all the strength of despair, against my chest. In a few seconds the bony hands that had fastened on my throat loosened their hold, and I was free to breathe once more. Then commenced a struggle of awful intensity. Immersed in the most profound darkness, totally ignorant of the nature of the Thing by which I was so suddenly attacked, finding my grasp slipping every moment, by reason, it seemed to me, of the entire nakedness of my assailant, bitten with sharp teeth in the shoulder, neck, and chest, having every moment to protect my throat against a pair of sinewy, agile hands, which my utmost efforts could not confine— these were a combination of circumstances to combat which required all the strength and skill and courage that I possessed.

At last, after a silent, deadly, exhausting struggle, I got my assailant under by a series of incredible efforts of strength. Once pinned, with my knee on what I made out to be its chest, I knew that I was victor. I rested for a moment to breathe. I heard the creature beneath me panting in the darkness, and felt the violent throbbing of a heart. It was apparently as exhausted as I was; that was one comfort. At this moment I remembered that I usually placed under my pillow, before going to bed, a large yellow silk pocket-handkerchief, for use during the night. I felt for it instantly; it was there. In a few seconds more I had, after a fashion, pinioned the creature's arms.

I now felt tolerably secure. There was nothing more to be done but to turn on the gas, and, having first seen what my midnight assailant was like, arouse the household. I will confess to being actuated by a certain pride in not giving the alarm before; I wished to make the capture alone and unaided.

Never losing my hold for an instant, I slipped from the bed to the floor, dragging my captive with me. I had but a few steps to make to reach the gas-burner; these I made with the greatest caution, holding the creature in a grip like a vice. At last I got within arm's-length of the tiny speck of blue light which told me where the gas-burner lay. Quick as lightning I released my grasp with one hand and let on the full flood of light. Then I turned to look at my captive.

I cannot even attempt to give any definition of my sensations the instant after I turned on the gas. I suppose I must have shrieked with terror, for in less than a minute afterward my room was crowded with the inmates of the house. I shudder now as I think of that awful moment. *I saw nothing!* Yes; I had one arm firmly clasped round a breathing, panting, corporeal shape, my other hand gripped with all its strength a throat as warm, and apparently fleshly, as my own; and yet, with this living substance in my grasp, with its body pressed against my own, and all in the bright glare of a large jet of gas, I absolutely beheld nothing! Not even an outline,—a vapor!

I do not, even at this hour, realize the situation in which I found myself. I cannot recall the astounding incident thoroughly. Imagination in vain tries to compass the awful paradox.

It breathed. I felt its warm breath upon my cheek. It struggled fiercely. It had hands. They clutched me. Its skin was smooth, like my own. There it lay, pressed close up against me, solid as stone,— and yet utterly invisible!

I wonder that I did not faint or go mad on the instant. Some wonderful instinct must have sustained me; for, absolutely, in place of loosening my hold on the terrible Enigma, I seemed to gain an additional strength in my moment of horror, and tightened my grasp with such wonderful force that I felt the creature shivering with agony.

Just then Hammond entered my room at the head of the household. As soon as he beheld my face—which, I suppose, must have been an awful sight to look at—he hastened forward, crying, "Great heaven, Harry! what has happened?"

"Hammond! Hammond!" I cried, "come here. Oh! this is awful! I have been attacked in bed by something or other, which I have hold of; but I can't see it—I can't see it!"

Hammond, doubtless struck by the unfeigned horror expressed in my countenance, made one or two steps forward with an anxious yet puzzled expression. A very audible titter burst from the remainder of my visitors. This suppressed laughter made me furious. To laugh at a human being in my position! It was the worst species of cruelty. *Now*, I can understand why the appearance of a man struggling violently, as it would seem, with an airy nothing, and calling for assistance against a vision, should have appeared ludicrous. *Then*, so great was my rage against the mocking crowd that had I the power I would have stricken them dead where they stood.

"Hammond! Hammond!" I cried again, despairingly, "for God's sake come to me. I can hold the—the Thing but a short while longer. It is overpowering me. Help me! Help me!"

"Harry," whispered Hammond, approaching me, "you have been smoking too much opium."

"I swear to you, Hammond, that this is no vision," I answered, in the same low tone. "Don't you see how it shakes my whole frame with its struggles? If you don't believe me, convince yourself. Feel it,—touch it."

Hammond advanced and laid his hand in the spot I indicated. A wild cry of horror burst from him. He had felt it!

In a moment he had discovered somewhere in my room a long piece of cord, and was the next instant winding it and knotting it about the body of the unseen being that I clasped in my arms.

"Harry," he said, in a hoarse, agitated voice, for, though he preserved his presence of mind, he was deeply moved, "Harry, it's all safe now. You may let go, old fellow, if you're tired. The Thing can't move."

I was utterly exhausted, and I gladly loosed my hold.

Hammond stood holding the ends of the cord that bound the Invisible, twisted round his hand, while before him, self-supporting as it were, he beheld a rope laced and interlaced, and stretching tightly round a vacant space. I never saw a man look so thoroughly stricken with awe. Nevertheless his face expressed all the courage and determination which I knew him to possess. His lips, although white, were set firmly, and one could perceive at a glance that, although stricken with fear, he was not daunted.

The confusion that ensued among the guests of the house who were witnesses of this extraordinary scene between Hammond and myself—who beheld the pantomime of binding this struggling Something,—who beheld me almost sinking from physical exhaustion when my task of jailer was over—the confusion and terror that took possession of the by-standers, when they saw all this, was beyond description. The weaker ones fled from the apartment. The few who remained clustered near the door, and could not be induced to approach Hammond and his Charge. Still incredulity broke out through their terror. They had not the courage to satisfy themselves, and yet they doubted. It was in vain that I begged of some of the men to come near and convince themselves by touch of the existence in that room of a living being which was invisible. They were incredulous, but did not dare to undeceive themselves. How could a solid, living, breathing body be invisible, they asked. My reply was this. I gave a sign to Hammond, and both of us— conquering our fearful repugnance to touch the invisible creature— lifted it from the ground, manacled as it was, and took it to my bed. Its weight was about that of a boy of fourteen.

"Now, my friends," I said, as Hammond and myself held the creature suspended over the bed, "I can give you self-evident proof that here is a solid, ponderable body which, nevertheless, you cannot see. Be good enough to watch the surface of the bed attentively."

I was astonished at my own courage in treating this strange event so calmly; but I had recovered from my first terror, and felt a sort of scientific pride in the affair which dominated every other feeling.

The eyes of the bystanders were immediately fixed on my bed. At a given signal Hammond and I let the creature fall. There was the dull sound of a heavy body alighting on a soft mass. The timbers of the bed creaked. A deep impression marked itself distinctly on the pillow, and on the bed itself. The crowd who witnessed this gave a sort of low, universal cry, and rushed from the room. Hammond and I were left alone with our Mystery.

We remained silent for some time, listening to the low, irregular breathing of the creature on the bed, and watching the rustle of the bed-clothes as it impotently struggled to free itself from confinement. Then Hammond spoke.

"Harry, this is awful."

"Ay, awful."

"But not unaccountable."

"Not unaccountable! What do you mean? Such a thing has never occurred since the birth of the world. I know not what to think, Hammond. God grant that I am not mad, and that this is not an insane fantasy! "

"Let us reason a little, Harry. Here is a solid body which we touch, but which we cannot see. The fact is so unusual that it strikes us with terror. Is there no parallel, though, for such a phenomenon? Take a piece of pure glass. It is tangible and transparent. A certain chemical coarseness is all that prevents its being so entirely transparent as to be totally invisible. It is not *theoretically impossible,* mind you, to make a glass which shall not reflect a single ray of light—a glass so pure and homogeneous in its atoms that the rays from the sun shall pass through it as they do through the air, refracted but not reflected. We do not see the air, and yet we feel it."

"That's all very well, Hammond, but these are inanimate substances. Glass does not breathe, air does not breathe. *This* thing has a heart that palpitates,—a will that moves it,—lungs that play, and inspire and respire."

"You forget the strange phenomena of which we have so often heard of late," answered the Doctor, gravely. "At the meetings called 'spirit circles,' invisible hands have been thrust into the hands of those persons round the table—warm, fleshly hands that seemed to pulsate with mortal life."

"What? Do you think, then, that this thing is—"

"I don't know what it is," was the solemn reply; "but please the gods I will, with your assistance, thoroughly investigate it."

We watched together, smoking many pipes, all night long, by the bedside of the unearthly being that tossed and panted until it was apparently wearied out. Then we learned by the low, regular breathing that it slept.

The next morning the house was all astir. The boarders congregated on the landing outside my room, and Hammond and myself were lions. We had to answer a thousand questions as to the state of our extraordinary prisoner, for as yet not one person in the house except ourselves could be induced to set foot in the apartment.

The creature was awake. This was evidenced by the convulsive manner in which the bed-clothes were moved in its efforts to escape. There was something truly terrible in beholding, as it were, those second-hand indications of the terrible writhings and agonized struggles for liberty which themselves were invisible.

Hammond and myself had racked our brains during the long night to discover some means by which we might realize the shape and general appearance of the Enigma. As well as we could make out by passing our hands over the creature's form, its outlines and lineaments were human. There was a mouth; a round, smooth head without hair; a nose, which, however, was little elevated above the cheeks; and its hands and feet felt like those of a boy. At first we thought of placing the being on a smooth surface and tracing its outline with chalk, as shoemakers trace the outline of the foot. This plan was given up as being of no value. Such an outline would give not the slightest idea of its conformation.

A happy thought struck me. We would take a cast of it in plaster of Paris. This would give us the solid figure, and satisfy all our wishes. But how to do it? The movements of the creature would disturb the setting of the plastic covering, and distort the mould. Another thought. Why not give it chloroform? It had respiratory organs—that was evident by its breathing. Once reduced to a state of insensibility, we could do with it what we would. Doctor X— was sent for; and after the worthy physician had recovered from the first shock of amazement, he proceeded to administer the chloro-form. In three minutes afterward we were enabled to remove the fetters from the creature's body, and a well-known modeler of this city was busily engaged in covering the invisible form with the moist clay. In five minutes more we had a mould, and before evening a rough *fac-simile* of the Mystery. It was shaped like a man,—distorted, uncouth, and horrible, but still a man. It was small, not over four feet and some inches in height, and its limbs revealed a muscular development that was unparalleled. Its face surpassed in hideousness anything I had ever seen. Gustave Doré, or Callot, or Tony Johannot, never conceived anything so horrible. There is a face in one of the latter's illustrations to *"Un Voyage où il vous plaira,"* which somewhat approaches the countenance of this creature, but does not equal it. It was the physiognomy of what I should have fancied a ghoul to be. It looked as if it was capable of feeding on human flesh.

Having satisfied our curiosity, and bound every one in the house to secrecy, it became a question, what was to be done with our Enigma? It was impossible that we should keep such a horror in our house; it was equally impossible that such an awful being should be let loose upon the world. I confess that I would have gladly voted for the creature's destruction. But who would shoul-der the responsibility? Who would undertake the execution of this horrible semblance of a human being? Day after day this question was deliberated gravely. The boarders all left the house. Mrs. Moffat was in despair, and threatened Hammond and myself with all sorts of legal penalties if we did not remove the Horror. Our answer was, "We will go if you like, but we decline taking this crea-ture with us. Remove it yourself if you please. It appeared in your house. On you the responsibility rests." To this there was, of course, no answer. Mrs. Moffat could not obtain for love or money a per-son who would even approach the Mystery.

The most singular part of the transaction was that we were entirely ignorant of what the creature habitually fed on. Everything in the way of nutriment that we could think of was placed before it, but was never touched. It was awful to stand by, day after day, and see the clothes toss, and hear the hard breathing, and know that it was starving.

Ten, twelve days, a fortnight passed, and it still lived. The pulsations of the heart, however, were daily growing fainter, and had now nearly ceased altogether. It was evident that the creature was dying for want of sustenance. While this terrible life-struggle was going on, I felt miserable. I could not sleep of nights. Horrible as the creature was, it was pitiful to think of the pangs it was suffering.

At last it died. Hammond and I found it cold and stiff one morning in the bed. The heart had ceased to beat, the lungs to inspire. We hastened to bury it in the garden. It was a strange funeral, the dropping of that viewless corpse into the damp hole. The cast of its form I gave to Doctor X—, who keeps it in his museum in Tenth Street.

As I am on the eve of a long journey from which I may not return, I have drawn up this narrative of an event the most singular that has ever come to my knowledge.

Note.

[It is rumored that the proprietors of a well-known museum in this city have made arrangements with Dr. X— to exhibit to the public the singular cast which Mr. Escott deposited with him. So extraordinary a history cannot fail to attract universal attention.]

MANMAT'HA
Charles De Kay

I

One day the breeze was talking of grand and simple things in the pines that look across the lower bay at Sandy Hook. The great water spaces were a delicious blue, dotted with the white tops of crushed waves; to the left, Coney Island lay mapped out in bleached surfaces, while beyond and seaward, from the purple sleeve formed by the hills of the Navesink, the Hook ran a brown finger eastward. A hawk which nests among the steep inclines of Todt Hill shot out from a neighboring ravine and hung motionless, but never quiet, in the middle distance.

Birds and beasts will make closer approach to a person clothed in dun-colored garments; therefore it was not odd that the hawk should not notice my presence on the pine needles near the crest of the hill. After steering without visible rustle of a feather through the lake of air before me, he stooped all at once, grasped a hedge-sparrow that had been shaking the top of a bush far down the slope, and, rising, bore it to the low branch of a pine not far from my resting-place.

The sun had fallen in a Titanic tragedy of color beyond Prince's Bay. The fierce bird, leisurely occupied in tearing to pieces the little twitterer, was a suitable accompaniment to the bloody drama in the clouds. Watching keenly, I gradually began to picture to myself the sensation of walking unseen to the murderous fowl and suddenly clasping his smooth back with both hands. How startled he would be! But in truth the thought was only a continuation of

23

another that had been floating through my mind while the hawk was wheeling. Unconsciously I had been mumbling to myself from the Nibelungen,—

"About the tameless dwarf-kin I have heard it said,
They dwell in hollow mountains; for safety are arrayed
In what is termed a tarn-kap, of wondrous quality;
Who hath it on his body preserved is said to be
From cuttings and from thrustings; of him is none aware
When he therein is clothed. Both see can he, and hear
According as he wishes, yet no one him perceives."

The magic cloak, the tarn-kap, I reasoned, with my eyes on the cruel bird, was only a symbol after all, something physical to make real that invisibility which we cannot readily conceive. But suddenly—could my wish have been felt?—the hawk gave a hoarse croak of fright, dropped his prey, and, springing heavily into the air, was gone.

He had not looked at me, he had not seen or heard me, nor could I see, far or near, the slightest cause for his terror. But I heard! Sh-sh-sh—I was aware of a light step in the needles under the tree he had left. Straining my eyes to watch the ground, surely, surely, in a line passing close to my couch, the needles and thin grass were pressed down, as if by a weight applied at even distances! I had remained motionless as a figure of stone, but when a tuft of hepatica, blooming late where the shade was deepest, fell crushed near my hand, I reached out. As luck would have it I was too conscious, too much ashamed at my own folly to act decisively. I did not grasp, I reached out—and touched a living thing.

On such occasions there comes at first the exuberance of joy; then doubt. I had long debated the possibility of invisibles. As far back as I can remember, elfin tales produced an awful wonderment upon my imagination. On long May nights have I not often stolen from the house to watch for elves? A moon after a rain was to my thinking the best for such mysterious beings, when everything was hazy with an imperceptible mist, when the dogwoods had flooded the landscape with sheets of reflected white, and somebody was drawing one veil after another slowly past a golden shield in the sky. On such nights, more than once, a boy might have been seen creeping on tiptoe through the open woods, over the great clearing, to the hilltop, where, if anywhere, brownies must play. But none did he espy, nor did the chance-flung cap ever fall upon his eager, outstretched hands. And if in later years the subject still fascinated me, it made me feel what the grown man realizes always more clearly, that fables and fairy tales rest on a solid groundwork of fact. Why, when so many other legends have been verified, should this universal tradition of vanishers and invisibles prove entirely false?

It occurs to one very soon that animal life does exist of so transparent a texture that to all intents and purposes it is invisible. The spawn of frogs, the larvæ of certain fresh-water insects, many marine animals, are of so clear a tissue that they are seen with difficulty. In the tropics a particular inhabitant of smooth seas is as invisible as a piece of glass, and can be detected only in the love season by the color which then mingles in its eyes. On reflection a thousand instances arise of assimilation of animal life to their surroundings, of mimicry of nature with a view to safety. Why, then, by survival of the most transparent, should not some invisible life of a high grade hold a secure position on the earth?

Pondering thus, I had been startled not a little by coming now and again on facts that seemed to bear this out. Strange tracks through untrodden grass suggested footsteps of the unseen. Flattened spaces of peculiar shape in the standing rye, where human beings could not have intruded, looked marvellously like human visitation. Or I lay concealed and watched the crows in a road-side field. What was it caused them to look up suddenly and flap away on sooty-fringed wings? No bird, beast, or man came. Then the rats, scampering about under a dock like so many gaunt Virginia swine: all at once came a flurry of whisking tails, and they were off! Yet I had not stirred, nor did anything move on the dock above. Nevertheless all seemed to realize a common danger, a noise of some kind,—perhaps a step? Again, you sit like a block while a snake basks unconscious in the sun, and may watch many hours without event; but sometimes it happens that he raises his head,

quivers for an instant his double tongue, and slides off the stump
into a bush. At such times put your ear to the earth. Do you not
distinguish—or is it all imagination—a sound, a brushing?

It availed me little, then, that I should have considered the subject, or have even gone the length of debating how a man might
attain invisibility. Now that I had a tangible proof of the existence
of such beings, I was crushed by misgivings. Like many a man before the supposed impossible, I questioned my own sanity. As to
the impression, however, the object I had touched or fancied I had
touched was at once hard and soft, smooth and rough; I recalled it
as each of these in turn, for it was moving, and at the moment of
contact bounded away as if at the shock of a galvanic current. To
my excited mind the dusky woods were becoming oppressive, and
so, like the hawk, but slowly and pondering, I betook myself home.

Who that has walked or run through autumn woods at night
has not sometimes looked curiously over his shoulder at the sound
of following steps? It always proves to be dry leaves whirled after
you in your rapid course; but this evening my gait was slow, and the
leaves of last year were hard to find; nor could I account, except
on the ground of nervous illusion, for the pattering that followed
in my rear. Yet there it was, albeit so gentle that had I not stretched
every sense to the utmost I am confident no sound would have
penetrated to my consciousness. And it was evident that I was thoroughly imposed upon by it, for when the small, irregular pond was
reached, which, with a cypress-scattered hillock, occupies the highest point of the main hill to the westward, I halted a moment and
considered. How, thought I, will this unseen attendant cross a piece
of water? Throwing off my shoes I waded over a shallow arm of the
pond, and sat down to watch. Presently in the twilight two wedges
of ruffled water were discerned advancing swiftly across the surface,—just such tracks as serpents make in swimming,—a light
touch was heard on the bank, and all was still. But then a sudden
disgust, unreasoning and childish, mastered me completely; a wave
of doubt greater than before filled me with disdain of my own im-
becility, and I hastened through the orchard to my home, and flung
myself into an arm-chair near the window.

The place I had selected long ago as a quiet refuge was a low veranda farm-house, hidden away from north winds under the crest of a hill, and crept over by many rods of honey-suckle. Events had so affected me that I considered nothing left in life but an alternation of hard work and of utter retreat from humanity, and had disposed me favorably toward the ancient apple orchard, and the meagre vegetable and flower garden, which alone remained of a former farm. The barns, the plowed lands, and the fences had disappeared. Only a heavy stone wall with flagged top, which protected the garden from the road, reminded one of a former powerful owner. From the veranda no house was visible; the eye had to travel many miles across the flat lower country to the bay before the distant ships recalled a busy world.

Here, beside myself, lived no one save Rachel, a woman whose Indian origin made it impossible to guess her age. Although she claimed for herself the purest descent from an Indian tribe of a headland a hundred miles to the eastward, and although her features were not without strong marks of her claim, yet in strict truth she was so much mixed with African blood that with most persons she would pass for a negress. Rachel had a talent for cooking breakfasts and suppers from little apparent supply; she was taciturn to speechlessness, hence our intercourse was never marred by discord; and while her box was kept supplied with strong tobacco, a slender meal of some kind was never wanting; and it was served in silence.

For two years Rachel and I had lived in this silent, limited partnership. My home was cool and soundless as the grave, a place in which the mind could stretch its shriveled wings, where everything could be done mechanically and without fear of a sudden jar into disagreeable reality. When of an afternoon I stepped from the hurrying world into the first quiet woods on the way to my home, a great door swung to behind me and another life began, in which Rachel's figure and swarthy, heavy-featured face had long ceased to interfere with my meditation.

This night, however, before the meal was served, the kitchen door opened and my housekeeper's inscrutable dull eyes rolled around the walls of the room; then it closed. What had happened? Why on this night had Rachel noticed my arrival? At supper I broke our unspoken compact and addressed her.

"Rachel, what made you look in just now? Has anything happened?"

The woman made no reply, yet there was evidence in her manner that she was groping for an answer. Presently to a second demand she made a reply that startled me:

"Heard two of you."

So, another ear had detected the steps as well as my own! Then the being, whatever it was, must be in the room, possibly at my elbow; or, seated perchance on that chair before me, was regarding me steadfastly! Except for the excitement bred of a new sensation, it was not a pleasant thought; nevertheless, I pulled a second chair to the table and filled a second plate with food; then, with my eyes fixed on the plate, continued the meal. It was all in vain. Nothing further was seen or heard.

This was my first definite encounter with that unseen which I would have called a spirit had I been a spiritualist. But I could not force myself to the gross materialism of calling this invisible existence a spirit, for tangibility was a quality I could not associate with pure spirit, and I had touched it.

Having once followed me, it seemed thenceforth to take up quarters in my house, at least for the evening and morning hours of the day, and strange as it was, I soon learned to regard the presence of a third person as an established fact; indeed, I came to believe that in some instances a faint breathing might be detected. Nevertheless I would not leave anything to the possibilities of imagination, but was always experimenting, with a view to prove still more clearly that there was no illusion possible. To this end a brass and steel rod, fitted between the floor and a projection from the wall, was connected with an indicator which moved in a large are when the slightest touch shook the floor. By this means my ears were reinforced by sight.

I also began systematically to conceal from the unknown guest the fact that I suspected its presence; but at last the point was reached where, to protect my own reason, it must be settled whether it was all a series of illusions or a sober truth.

For by dint of thought a scheme had been perfected, and on a Sunday morning, when as usual Rachel had disappeared, no man has ever known whither; when, according to its custom, the strange visitant had also, to all appearance, withdrawn,—on a Sunday morning I hastened to put my plan in action. On the main floor in the rear of the house was a chamber, into which the sounds had sometimes intruded, which was small, bare, and lighted by one deep window looking directly out on the orchard. This window I had grated strongly with heavy wire on the outside, where the orchard hill rose steeply from the house; and over against the window, in the wall between chamber and dining-room, was a high closet, in which I had stored a strong net, such as fishermen use for their seines. Fastening stout wires to the ceiling from one end of the room to the other, to be used for slides, and rigging several small blocks above the window and near the floor, I stretched the necessary ropes from closet to blocks and back again, laid everything ready for instant use, cleared the room of furniture, and awaited events.

There was no fear of interruption from Rachel, for during the years we had lived together I had never seen her on a Sabbath. Every Monday she was at her post, although laboring under some excitement, which showed itself in mutterings and a certain wild gesture that I had learned to attach no importance to. There was no fear that I should not have the invisible to myself.

Evening came to close a sultry day with growls of distant thunder and sudden flares of light behind Navesink Hills; the bushes drooped languidly; only the tree-toads were clamorous, and their jubilee was a mournful one on every side. I was sitting by the west window with my head on my breast, and, now that the crisis had come, almost apathetic to the presence itself, when its approach took place. It seemed to stop near my chair, as if it regarded me closely. I had been before in singular predicaments, but it seemed to me this was the most trying. I felt that I must look very pale, but with an affectation of indifference I arose, walked across the room and entered the bed-chamber. In a moment I understood that the unseen had likewise passed the sill and had entered the room; then I slammed the door, locked it, and put the key in my pocket.

Everything had been made ready to cope with a material and not a supernatural being; still it was purely a venture, and at no previous time had there seemed so little hope of success. Nevertheless not a moment was lost in hauling out the net and placing it in position across the room so that it hung straight, filling the space between wall and wall, and ceiling and floor. Then I began to draw it down the room by means of the ropes, and on the axis of the chamber, so that its edges passed smoothly along ceiling, walls, and floor. The anxious moment was at hand.

All the running gear had to be worked evenly; at the same time every nerve was strained in order to detect the slightest bulge in the upright net, should it come in contact with a tangible body.

Until three quarters of the room had been sifted nothing occurred. Then I saw the edge against the left-hand wall carefully drawn aside; to spring forward and close the opening was the instinctive work of a second. Terror combining with a fierce delight lent me an extraordinary force; I drew with convulsive power on the ropes. Every moment an invisible hand seemed to lift the net at some point, but each attempt was luckily frustrated. At last the movements ceased, and I drew the net flat against the farther wall. With feverish haste my hand travelled over its entire surface; the net was scanned in profile for the impression of a body, but there was none. The game had either escaped or withdrawn into the deep window-seat.

Now came a moment for breath, and for reflection. Again the cynical cloud of doubt folded me in. Dupe of my own morbid imagination, I should stand convicted of monomania in the eyes of any reasonable being who should see my actions. Then it was best, was it not? to tear the net away; or should I deliberately pursue to the utmost a plan begun? Never before had I so clearly felt a dual existence urging to opposite courses of action, as if the body's instinct commanded an advance, while the mind, assailing the whole proceeding with ridicule, was for giving up the game. But for all that

it was a good sign that I began to feel a slight awe at the near possibility of a discovery. For I retreated to the door, unlocked it,
and stood irresolute; then returned again to the window, without
strength to come to a decision.

But while I pondered, a low, chuckling noise startled me, and
Rachel stood by my side, erect and with features full of energy, her
dull eyes blazing, and her short straight hair tossed about; in her
hand she brandished with exultation a carved rod hung with bright
claws and shells, with lappets of fur and hair; and at her and it I
gazed with speechless amazement. Had she too gone mad? She took
a few steps, as if in a rude dance, and shook the stick, and while
her eyes glared into mine she nodded her head to the time.

"Bad spirit!" she muttered. "I have known, I have heard. But
this is strong Wabeno."

As she shook the talisman, which clinked and rattled like the
toy of a devil, I snatched the medicine stick from her hand and
motioned her to the door. Thither she retreated, muttering words
of an unknown tongue, and when it closed upon her I flung the
stick angrily on the floor. But hope had come, and decision as well,
although from a despised quarter; I was resolved to finish the under-
taking at all hazards.

The wild flames of the distant storm still lighted everything at
intervals with an intensity now greater and now less. When the
sheet lightning flashed strong, the square cage formed by the wire
outside the window-seat and the fish-net within stood out clear
against the northern sky. With dilated pupils I began to examine
the inclosed cube of air. During one particularly long and vivid
flash,—there, in that corner, was there not a heap, a translucent
shape, indistinguishable in quality or form? It was enough. Swiftly
as wild beasts when they spring, I raised the net, leaped into the
window, and grasped toward the corner where I thought I saw the
mass.

II

A thrill runs through the nerves of an entomologist when he
puts his hand on a specimen unknown, undescribed. The hunter

trembles when he espies in the thicket the royal hart whose existence has been called a fable. My emotion was all of this, intensi-
fied; nearer, perhaps, to the feeling of the elected mortal who has
discovered a new continent. For I had discovered a new world.

Had I not cause for exultation? I sat on the window-seat in the
alternate light and darkness, with one hand clenched, the other
arm curved in the air; my left held fast a slender wrist, while my
right was cast about a pair of delicate shoulders; the invisible but
tangible figure was crouched away into the smallest space in the
corner of the window.

With awe I now realized that my capture was a woman. The
delicate moulding of the shoulders and hand was proof enough,
but I also felt on my arm a light flood of the silkiest hair. This was
a shock to one who had lived apart from women for several years,
and had good cause to expect nothing but disaster from their influence. For a moment the impulse was strong to release the captive;
luckily reason prevailed, and I tightened my grip on the frail prize,
whose frame was shaken with sobs and whose bearing denoted the
most abject despair. I gave many timid reassurances by word and
hand before the sobs came slower and fear began to loose its hold.
As she raised her head I took occasion to pass my right hand lightly
over her face. Rendered sensitive by strong excitement, my palm
read her features as the blind read the raised print of their books,
and of this at least I was sure: the features were human, straight,
the eyes large; a full chin and a mouth of unspeakable fineness
were divined rather than felt by my flying touch; but I found no
trace of tears.

After this I do not know how long we sat. It seemed peaceful
and homelike, so that I wondered how it was possible so quickly to
forget wonder. A protective warmth toward the creature whose soft
breathing came and went; slower and slower near my face took a
quiet hold on all my senses. At last the gentle head drooped like a
tired child's, the delicate shoulders heaved in a long, peaceful sigh,
and to my amazement the strange captive fell asleep in my arms.

So while she slept I sat motionless and thinking, thinking. Who
was she? whence and of what order of beings? What was her language;

how and how long did she live. Was she really alive in our sense of
the word, that is, human with the exception of her transparency?
and was her shape like that of ordinary mortals, or did she end in
some monstrosity like a mermaid? Such were the questions agitating
me when interruption came with a knock at the door. My captive
awoke and instinctively started away, at the same time giving a
low, articulate cry; but I held her firmly, and called to Rachel to
bring me a certain relic of slavery which had been brought from
the South. I had profited by the discovery my prisoner's awakening furnished: the invisible, I argued, could articulate, then why
should she not understand and speak the language of the people
among whom she was found? Accordingly a few rapid questions
were put to her, which were unanswered. Then I bethought me of
a proof that at any rate she understood my words.

"My dear child, it is mere perverseness in you to refuse an answer. I am sure you understand. You are in my power for good or
evil, and if you refuse to speak I must consider you worthy of the
following treatment: you shall be made an example to the crowd
of the reality of invisible life."

Under cruel treatment of this kind, conjecture became certainty; I felt her shudder at the idea, and she laid her hand appeal-
ingly on mine. This was all I wanted; speech was now a mere affair
of time.

Rachel entered with the rusty handcuffs and handed them to
me as if she were conscious and acquiescent in what I did. Not a
feature moved, only her eyes shone with inner excitement, in a way
I had seen before, while I clasped one link about the unseen wrist.

"Pardon," I whispered, "I do not know you yet. I cannot trust
you."

My daily work ceased. To the few inquiries from the great city
Rachel had evasive answers ready; they were soon over, and I was
left to experience the fascination of a beautiful woman whom I had
never seen nor could hope ever to see. To be sure, in certain lights
and under certain angles of reflection an indistinct outline of a
not large, slender girl, which told of pure contours, could be made
out, but this was like following the glassy bells that pulsate far down

in the waves of northern seas, or the endeavor to catch the real surface of a mirror. Moreover, the slim captive herself resented any attempt to gain acquaintance with her through the eyes. But by degrees the reserve which had taken the place of her terror melted away before gentle and respectful management, and from her own lips I learned much concerning her marvelous race, before the love which presently overwhelmed us put an end to the cooler interests of reason. Thus she astonished me by speaking of her race as widely spread through almost every inhabited land. They never work or educate their children; their food, which is chiefly in liquid form, is taken from the stores laid up by human beings, and such education as they get is picked up by continual contact with mortals. While their passions would seem to be calm, their only laws relate to the observance of secrecy as to their presence on the earth. To secure this end they meet at stated periods and renew their solemn vows, keep a watch upon each other, and disperse again to a settled or wandering life, but one always dependent on the labors of other beings. This alone would explain the paramount importance attaching to secrecy. And as it is impossible to keep always all hint of their existence from human beings, the penalties for disclosure in the latest days have increased to far greater severity than was used in simpler ages; Manmat'ha could not be brought to tell me the fate which awaited her should it be discovered that she had revealed the great secret of her nation, and the very quiet with which she gave me to understand how vast was the danger impressed me more than the most violent words.

It must have been the pain that the thought of any harm befalling her produced in me, which opened my eyes to the strength of my passion. The time for questions had passed, and the days were long only that we might love. One day glided after another unheeded, while we strolled about the neighboring woody hills to catch a broad glimpse of the sea from this point, or to examine in that swampy valley the minute wonders of life in plants and insects. At an early stage of our intimacy I had begged to free her wrist from the handcuffs, but she had implored me to continue at least the appearance of slavery, to serve, in case of need, as a partial excuse for violation of her vows. This did not prevent her daily disappearance during the middle hours when the sun was strongest; but these absences only served to give a time for reflection on her beauties and to involve me deeper in the love which now mastered all my thoughts. There was one subject which was long in broaching, but when the necessary courage was summoned, found in Manmat'ha neither objection nor response. She did not comprehend its force. The subject was our marriage.

I had resolved on legal marriage, even if it were necessary to be content with only one witness to the ceremony; that witness could be no one except Rachel. My housekeeper had regarded my preparations and subsequent conduct with a consistent interest and without the least shadow of surprise, and once I remarked that she had caught sight in the twilight of a cup raised without hands; yet no hint fell from her lips to make me feel she was intruding on my affairs. The old blur was in her eyes; the only change in manner was her treatment of me: she regarded me with a kind of awe. And after it had proved abortive to tell her something and not all, because the pleasure of unbosoming myself of so much love was too great to restrain, I found Rachel not only full of faith, but even surpassing me. She looked upon Manmat'ha as a supernatural being, and plainly invested me with reflected holiness. Some sort of worship she thought due to Manmat'ha, whilst I, as high priest and mortal consort, was entitled to a share; and indeed it was with some difficulty that I persuaded her not to show her faith by uncouth rites. It was as if her life had been a preparation for some such affair as this, and found her enthusiastic, but not astonished.

Our favorite resort was the couch of pine needles looking south from the hillside where we first met. The same hawk, to me the most blessed of birds, would often sail as before in the middle distance, or night-hawks would cut their strange curves in the evening sky. Far out beyond, sea-gulls, mere specks of white, would wheel and plunge into the bay, and at our backs the woodcock, shy enough in any other presence, would whir fantastically through the woods. All nature was the same, but I was no longer its solitary admirer, for I held in my arms a gentle framework of delight such as no other man before or since has known. She was finer than the finest silk, smoother than the smoothest glass, as if the rays of light, falling on the amazing texture of her skin, found no inequalities from which to reflect.

One evening we had been drawing in long breaths of that delight of which the woods and the great bowl of landscape before us were so full, and I had been trying to convince Manmat'ha of the importance of the marriage ceremony. "What," I asked with some trouble in my heart, "what will they do to you in case members of your nation discover your position? I do not mean to ask you what you would not tell me before, but what would be their first step?"

"They would imprison me somewhere under a guard," said Manmat'ha. "It would be many months before a tribunal could be collected together, and still longer before I should be judged. What my fate would be then, it is not well to say."

Had I desired, there is little doubt that I could have compelled Manmat'ha to tell me all she knew, for I had found that my will was much the stronger. But what was curiosity compared with the delight of warming her into responsive love? When I now covered her delicious lips with kisses, she returned the pressure, instead of merely suffering me, as at first, with a mild surprise.

"My first love and my last!" I whispered. "They shall not get you from me while I am alive, if they will only give us warning; but if they rob me of you, I shall follow your trace and rescue you, if it be to the bottom of the sea!"

Manmat'ha laughed a pleased laugh. We both started at an echo, a moment after, which seemed to come from the lower hill, below where we sat. There was no echo possible in that direction.

"Manmat'ha!" I whispered, "tell me quickly! Is some one coming?"

She sat apparently unable to speak, but trembling and cold to the touch. I had enough presence of mind to take her up and place her on the other side of the pine, on the ground, and throw my coat carelessly over her. As once before I heard passing steps, but now my more practiced ear caught them distinctly. They came lightly up the steep hill and stopped a moment at a little distance from the tree. With eyes fixed on the ocean I waited in an agony of suspense, assuming the most unconscious air of which I was capable. The steps hesitated only a moment; then they passed lower and lower into the upper wood. For half an hour neither of us moved; at last, taking heart, we stole home.

The event set me thinking. If at any moment we were liable to be discovered and separated, the marriage must take place at once. A consumptive hastens his wedding, a wounded tree is quick to bear, and the night we had experienced taught me how slight was the thread on which my happiness hung; but Manmat'ha was calm with a maidenly content with little, which in my hasty resentment at even a suspicion of opposition to my plan, I was ready to call indifference.

When we entered I could tell by the unfailing sign of Rachel's eye that she was agitated. Later in the evening I heard her chanting in a discordant undertone an ancient formula of her savage ancestors, and therefore it was with some misgivings that I called and informed her that to-night she was to be the sole witness, by touch, if not by sight, of the lawful ceremony of wedlock between Manmat'ha and me. She listened in an awestruck silence, and left the room abruptly. As no calling was of any avail, we were compelled to wait her pleasure, which I did with great impatience; and when at last she did return, it was in a shape grotesque almost beyond recognition. Her face and arms were painted white and red in broad bands of coarse pigments; an old embroidered robe fastened over one shoulder, with a close-fitting skirt of buckskin, formed her whole attire. She had put feathers in her hair, and with flaming eyes shook her favorite talisman, the medicine-stick. At one bound she had returned to her ancient state of savagery.

Finding Manmat'ha regarding her with interest, I did not oppose the further proceedings. It struck me that it was not displeasing to my invisible love to receive divine honors even in this wild rite, so I held my peace. She seemed to receive them as her due.

The moon had risen, and gave light to the room through window and open door; flooded by its rays, Rachel moved slowly across the room, uttering in guttural tones a broken chant whose meaning I might have once interpreted, but could not now. On a different occasion I might not have been an entirely unsympathetic observer of the singular sight, but here passion had overcome curiosity. I was an impatient lover. With my arm about Manmat'ha, and filled with earnest emotions, I could not help a feeling of disgust at the monotonous discord and frantic gestures of the last of a superstitious race.

"This must end, Manmat'ha," I groaned. "I can wait no longer." As I spoke, the Indian woman grew ungovernable in wild excitement.

"They are on you! They are here!" she screamed.

I felt Manmat'ha stiffen in my arms with deadly terror. Resistless hands dragged us apart and held me absolutely motionless in spite of the deadly agony which filled me, while Manmat'ha's stifled shriek arose from midway across the room.

"Rachel!" I cried. "For God's sake, Rachel, bar the door!"

My cry roused the woman from a stupor; she sprang to the door. I heard the noise of many light feet, the sound of a blow, a heavy fall; then a deep silence came.

Bounding from the spot to which unseen hands up to that moment had pressed me, I sprang from the room and followed into the night. The earth reeled past me in my swift flight, until I suddenly stopped myself to ask where I was going. Where indeed? As well follow the wind. Wild as was the hope that moved me to return, I hurried back again to the house. Rachel alone, clad in her poor Indian finery, the medicine-stick broken by her side, lay stretched out dead in the moonlight.

THE CRYSTAL MAN
Edward Page Mitchell

I

Rapidly turning into the Fifth Avenue from one of the cross streets above the old reservoir, at quarter past eleven o'clock on the night of November 6, 1879, I ran plump into an individual coming the other way.

It was very dark on this corner. I could see nothing of the person with whom I had the honor to be in collision. Nevertheless, the quick habit of a mind accustomed to induction had furnished me with several well-defined facts regarding him before I fairly recovered from the shock of the encounter.

These were some of the facts: He was a heavier man than myself, and stiffer in the legs; but he lacked precisely three inches and a half of my stature. He wore a silk hat, a cape or cloak of heavy woolen material, and rubber overshoes or arctics. He was about thirty-five years old, born in America, educated at a German university, either Heidelberg or Freiburg, naturally of hasty temper, but considerate and courteous, in his demeanor to others. He was not entirely at peace with society: there was something in his life or in his present errand which he desired to conceal.

How did I know all this when I had not seen the stranger, and when only a single monosyllable had escaped his lips?

Well, I knew that he was stouter than myself, and firmer on his foot, because it was I, not he, who recoiled. I knew that I was just three inches and a half taller than he, for the tip of my nose was still tingling from its contact with the stiff, sharp brim of his hat.

My hand, involuntarily raised, had come under the edge of his cape. He wore rubber shoes, for I had not heard a footfall. To an observant ear; the indications of age are as plain in the tones of the voice as to the eye in the lines of the countenance. In the first moment of exasperation of my maladroitness, he had muttered "Ox!" a term that would occur to nobody except a German at such a time. The pronunciation of the guttural, however, told me that the speaker was an American German, not a German American, and that his German education had been derived south of the river Main. Moreover, the tone of the gentleman and scholar was manifest even in the utterance of wrath. That the gentleman was in no particular hurry, but for some reason anxious to remain unknown; was a conclusion drawn from the fact that, after listening in silence to my polite apology, he stooped to recover and restore to me my umbrella, and then passed on as noiselessly as he had approached.

I make it a point to verify my conclusions when possible. So I turned back into the cross street and followed the stranger toward a lamp part way down the block. Certainly, I was not more than five seconds behind him. There was no other road that he could have taken. No house door had opened and closed along the way. And yet, when we came into the light, the form that ought to have been directly in front of me did not appear. Neither man nor man's shadow was visible.

Hurrying on as fast as I could walk to the next gaslight, I paused under the lamp and listened. The street was apparently deserted. The rays from the yellow flame reached only a little way into the darkness. The steps and doorway, however, of the brownstone house facing the street lamp were sufficiently illuminated. The gilt figures above the door were distinct. I recognized the house: the number was a familiar one. While I stood under the gaslight, waiting, I heard a slight noise on these steps, and the click of a key in a lock. The vestibule door of the house was slowly opened, and then closed with a slam that echoed across the street. Almost immediately followed the sound of the opening and shutting of the inner door. Nobody had come out. As far as my eyes could be trusted to report an event hardly ten feet away and in broad light, nobody had gone in.

With a notion that here was scanty material for an exact application of the inductive process, I stood a long time wildly guessing at the philosophy of the strange occurrence. I felt that vague sense of the unexplainable which amounts almost to dread. It was a relief to hear steps on the sidewalk opposite, and turning, to see a policeman swinging his long black club and watching me.

II

This house of chocolate brown, whose front door opened and shut at midnight without indications of human agency, was, as I have said, well known to me. I had left it not more than ten minutes earlier, after spending the evening with my friend Bliss and his daughter Pandora. The house was of the sort in which each story constitutes a domicile complete in itself. The second floor, or flat, had been inhabited by Bliss since his return from abroad; that is to say, for a twelvemonth. I held Bliss in esteem for his excellent qualities of heart, while his deplorably illogical and unscientific mind commanded my profound pity. I adored Pandora.

Be good enough to understand that my admiration for Pandora Bliss was hopeless, and not only hopeless, but resigned to its hopelessness. In our circle of acquaintance there was a tacit covenant that the young lady's peculiar position as a flirt wedded to a memory should be at all times respected. We adored Pandora mildly, not passionately—just enough to feed her coquetry without excoriating the seared surface of her widowed heart. On her part, Pandora conducted herself with signal propriety. She did not sigh too obtrusively when she flirted: and she always kept her flirtations so well in hand that she could cut them short whenever the fond, sad recollections came.

It was considered proper for us to tell Pandora that she owed it to her youth and beauty to put aside the dead past like a closed book, and to urge her respectfully to come forth into the living present. It was not considered proper to press the subject after she had once replied that this was forever impossible.

The particulars of the tragic episode in Miss Pandora's European experience were not accurately known to us. It was understood, in a vague way, that she had loved while abroad, and trifled with her lover: that he had disappeared, leaving her in ignorance of his fate and in perpetual remorse for her capricious behavior. From Bliss I had gathered a few, sporadic facts, not coherent enough to form a history of the case. There was no reason to believe that Pandora's lover had committed suicide. His name was Flack. He was a scientific man. In Bliss's opinion he was a fool. In Bliss's opinion Pandora was a fool to pine on his account. In Bliss's opinion all scientific men were more or less fools.

III

That year I ate Thanksgiving dinner with the Blisses. In the evening I sought to astonish the company by reciting the mysterious events on the night of my collision with the stranger. The story failed to produce the expected sensation. Two or three odious people exchanged glances. Pandora, who was unusually pensive, listened with seeming indifference. Her father, in his stupid inability to grasp anything outside the commonplace, laughed outright, and even went so far as to question my trustworthiness as an observer of phenomena.

Somewhat nettled, and perhaps a little shaken in my own faith in the marvel, I made an excuse to withdraw early. Pandora accompanied me to the threshold. "Your story," said she, "interested me strangely. I, too, could report occurrences in and about this house which would surprise you. I believe I am not wholly in the dark. The sorrowful past casts a glimmer of light—but let us not be hasty. For my sake probe the matter to the bottom."

The young woman sighed as she bade me good night. I thought I heard a second sigh, in a deeper tone than hers, and too distinct to be a reverberation.

I began to go downstairs. Before I had descended half a dozen steps I felt a man's hand laid rather heavily upon my shoulder from behind. My first idea was that Bliss had followed me into the hall to apologize for his rudeness.

I turned around to meet his friendly overture. Nobody was in sight.

Again the hand touched my arm. I shuddered in spite of my philosophy.

This time the hand gently pulled at my coat sleeve, as if to invite me upstairs. I ascended a step or two, and the pressure on my arm was relaxed. I paused, and the silent invitation was repeated with an urgency that left no doubt as to what was wanted.

We mounted the stairs together, the presence leading the way, I following. What an extraordinary journey it was! The halls were bright with gaslight. By the testimony of my eyes there was no one but myself upon the stairway. Closing my eyes, the illusion, if illusion it could be called, was perfect. I could hear the creaking of the stairs ahead of me, the soft but distinctly audible footfalls synchronous with my own, even the regular breathing of my companion and guide. Extending my arm, I could touch and finger the skirt of his garment—a heavy woolen cloak lined with silk.

Suddenly I opened my eyes. They told me again that I was absolutely alone.

This problem then presented itself to mind: How to determine whether vision was playing me false, while the senses of hearing and feeling correctly informed me, or whether my ears and touch lied, while my eyes reported the truth. Who shall be arbiter when the senses contradict each other? The reasoning faculty? Reason was inclined to recognize the presence of an intelligent being, whose existence was flatly denied by the most trusted of the senses.

We reached the topmost floor of the house. The door leading out of the public hall opened for me, apparently of its own accord. A curtain within seemed to draw itself aside, and hold itself aside long enough to give me ingress to an apartment wherein every appointment spoke of good taste and scholarly habits. A wood fire was burning in the chimney place. The walls were covered with books and pictures. The lounging chairs were capacious and inviting. There was nothing in the room uncanny, nothing weird, nothing different from the furniture of everyday flesh and blood existence.

By this time I had cleared my mind of the last lingering suspicion of the supernatural. These phenomena were perhaps not inexplicable; all that I lacked was the key. The behavior of my unseen

host argued his amicable disposition. I was able to watch with perfect calmness a series of manifestations of independent energy on
the part of inanimate objects.

In the first place, a great Turkish easy chair wheeled itself out
of a corner of the room and approached the hearth. Then a square-
backed Queen Anne chair started from another corner, advancing
until it was planted directly opposite the first. A little tripod table
lifted itself a few inches above the floor and took a position between the two chairs. A thick octavo volume backed out of its place
on the shelf and sailed tranquilly through the air at the height of
three or four feet, landing neatly on top of the table. A finely
painted porcelain pipe left a hook on the wall and joined the volume.
A tobacco box jumped from the mantle-piece. The door of a cabinet
swung open, and a decanter and wineglass made the journey in
company, arriving simultaneously at the same destination. Everything in the room seemed instinct with the spirit of hospitality.

I seated myself in the easy chair, filled the wineglass, lighted
the pipe, and examined the volume. It was the *Handbuch der
Gewebelehre* of Bussius of Vienna. When I had replaced the book
upon the table, it deliberately opened itself at the four hundred
and forty-third page.

"You are not nervous?" demanded a voice, not four feet from
my tympanum.

IV

This voice had a familiar sound. I recognized it as the voice
that I heard in the street on the night of November 6, when it called
me an ox.

"No," I said. "I am not nervous. I am a man of science, accustomed to regard all phenomena as explainable by natural laws,
provided we can discover the laws. No, I am not frightened."

"So much the better. You are a man of science, like myself" —
here the voice groaned— "a man of nerve, and a friend of Pandora's."

"Pardon me," I interposed. "Since a lady's name is introduced
it would be well to know with whom or with what I am speaking."

"That is precisely what I desire to communicate," replied the voice, "before I ask you to render me a great service. My name is or was Stephen Flack. I am or have been a citizen of the United States. My exact status at present is as great a mystery to myself as it can possibly be to you. But I am, or was, an honest man and a gentleman, and I offer you my hand."

I saw no hand. I reached forth my own, however, and it met the pressure of warm, living fingers.

"Now," resumed the voice, after this silent pact of friendship, "be good enough to read the passage at which I have opened the book upon the table."

Here is a rough translation of what I read in German:

As the color of the organic tissues constituting the body depends upon the presence of certain proximate principles of the third class, all containing iron as one of the ultimate elements, it follows that the hue may vary according to well-defined chemico-physiological changes. An excess of hematin in the blood globules gives a ruddier tinge to every tissue. The melanin that colors the choroid of the eye, the iris, the hair, may be increased or diminished according to laws recently formulated by Schardt of Basel. In the epidermis the excess of melanin makes the Negro, the deficient supply the albino. The hematin and the melanin, together with the greenish-yellow biliverdine and the reddish-yellow urokacine, are the pigments which impart color character to tissues otherwise transparent, or nearly so. I deplore my inability to record the result of some highly interesting histological experiments conducted by that indefatigable investigator Fröliker in achieving success in the way of separating pink discoloration of the human body by chemical means.

"For five years," continued my unseen companion when I had finished reading, "I was Fröliker's student and laboratory assistant at Freiburg. Bussius only half guessed at the importance of our experiments. We reached results which were so astounding that public policy required they should not be published, even to the scientific world. Fröliker died a year ago last August.

"I had faith in the genius of this great thinker and admirable man. If he had rewarded my unquestioning loyalty with full confidence, I should not now be a miserable wretch. But his natural reserve, and the jealousy with which all savants guard their unverified results, kept me ignorant of the essential formulas governing our experiments. As his disciple I was familiar with the laboratory details of the work; the master alone possessed the radical secret. The consequence is that I have been led into a misfortune more appalling than has been the lot of any human being since the primal curse fell upon Cain.

"Our efforts were at first directed to the enlargement and variation of the quantity of pigmentary matter in the system. By increasing the proportion of melanin, for instance, conveyed in food to the blood, we were able to make a fair man dark, a dark man black as an African. There was scarcely a hue we could not impart to the skin by modifying and varying our combinations. The experiments were usually tried on me. At different times I have been copper-colored, violet blue, crimson, and chrome yellow. For one triumphant week I exhibited in my person all the colors of the rainbow. There still remains a witness to the interesting character of our work during this period."

The voice paused, and in a few seconds a hand bell upon the mantel was sounded. Presently an old man with a close-fitting skullcap shuffled into the room. "Käspar," said the voice, in German, "show the gentleman your hair."

Without manifesting any surprise, and as if perfectly accustomed to receive commands addressed to him out of vacancy, the old domestic bowed and removed his cap. The scanty locks thus discovered were of a lustrous emerald green. I expressed my astonishment.

"The gentleman finds your hair very beautiful," said the voice, again in German. "That is all, Käspar."

Replacing his cap, the domestic withdrew, with a look of grati-
fied vanity on his face.

"Old Käspar was Fröliker's servant, and is now mine. He was
the subject of one of our first applications of the process. The worthy man was so pleased with the result that he would never permit
us to restore his hair to its original red. He is a faithful soul, and
my only intermediary and representative in the visible world.

"Now," continued Flack, "to the story of my undoing. The great
histologist with whom it was my privilege to be associated, next
turned his attention to another and still more interesting branch
of the investigation. Hitherto he had sought merely to increase or
to modify the pigments in the tissues. He now began a series of
experiments as to the possibility of eliminating those pigments
altogether from the system by absorption, exudation, and the use
of the chlorides and other chemical agents acting on organic matter. He was only too successful!

"Again I was the subject of experiments which Fröliker super-
vised, imparting to me only so much of the secret of this process
as was unavoidable. For weeks at a time I remained in his private
laboratory, seeing no one and seen by no one excepting the professor and the trustworthy Käspar. Herr Friiliker proceeded with
caution, closely watching the effect of each new test, and advancing by degrees. He never went so far in one experiment that he
was unable to withdraw at discretion. He always kept open an easy
road for retreat. For that reason I felt myself perfectly safe in his
hands and submitted to whatever he required.

"Under the action of the etiolating drugs which the professor
administered in connection with powerful detergents, I became at
first pale, white, colorless as an albino, but without suffering in
general health. My hair and beard looked like spun glass and my
skin like marble. The professor was satisfied with his results, and
went no further at this time. He restored to me my normal color.

"In the next experiment, and in those succeeding, he allowed
his chemical agents to take firmer hold upon the tissues of my body.
I became not only white, like a bleached man, but slightly translucent, like a porcelain figure. Then again he paused for a while, giving

me back my color and allowing me to go forth into the world. Two
months later I was more than translucent. You have seen floating
those sea radiates, the medusa or jellyfish, their outlines almost
invisible to the eye. Well, I became in the air like a jellyfish in the
water. Almost perfectly transparent, it was only by close inspection that old Käspar could discover my whereabouts in the room
when he came to bring me food. It was Käspar who ministered to
my wants at times when I was cloistered."

"But your clothing?" I inquired, interrupting Flack's narrative.
"That must have stood out in strong contrast with the dim aspect
of your body."

"Ah, no," said Flack. "The spectacle of an apparently empty suit
of clothes moving about the laboratory was too grotesque even for
the grave professor. For the protection of his gravity he was obliged
to devise a way to apply his process to dead organic matter, such
as the wool of my cloak, the cotton of my shirts, and the leather of
my shoes. Thus I came to be equipped with the outfit which still
serves me.

"It was at this stage of our progress, when we had almost attained perfect transparency, and therefore complete invisibility,
that I met Pandora Bliss.

"A year ago last July, in one of the intervals of our experimenting, and at a time when I presented my natural appearance, I went
into the Schwarzwald to recuperate. I first saw and admired
Pandora at the little village of St. Blasien. They had come from the
Falls of the Rhine, and were traveling north; I turned around and
traveled north. At the Stern Inn I loved Pandora; at the summit of
the Feldberg I madly worshiped her. In the Höllenpass I was ready
to sacrifice my life for a gracious word from her lips. On
Hornisgrinde I besought her permission to throw myself from the
top of the mountain into the gloomy waters of the Mummelsee in
order to prove my devotion. You know Pandora. Since you know
her, there is no need to apologize for the rapid growth of my infatu-
ation. She flirted with me, laughed with me, laughed at me, drove
with me, walked with me through byways in the green woods,
climbed with me up aeclivities so steep that climbing together was

one delicious, prolonged embrace; talked science with me, and sentiment; listened to my hopes and enthusiasm, snubbed me, froze me, maddened me—all at her sweet will, and all while her matter-of-fact papa dozed in the coffee rooms of the inns over the financial columns of the latest New York newspapers. But whether she loved me I know not to this day.

"When Pandora's father learned what my pursuits were, and what my prospects, he brought our little idyl to an abrupt termination. I think he classed me somewhere between the professional jugglers and the quack doctors. In vain I explained to him that I should be famous and probably rich. 'When you are famous and rich,' he remarked with a grin, 'I shall be pleased to see you at my office in Broad street.' He carried Pandora off to Paris, and I returned to Freiburg.

"A few weeks later, one bright afternoon in August, I stood in Fröliker's laboratory unseen by four persons who were almost within the radius of my arm's length. Käspar was behind me, washing some test tubes. Fröliker, with a proud smile upon his face, was gazing intently at the place where he knew I ought to be. Two brother professors, summoned on some pretext, were unconsciously almost jostling me with their elbows as they discussed I know not what trivial question. They could have heard my heart beat. 'By the way, Herr Professor,' one asked as he was about to depart, 'has your assistant, Herr Flack, returned from his vacation?' This test was perfect.

"As soon as we were alone, Professor Fröliker grasped my invisible hand, as you have grasped it tonight. He was in high spirits.

"'My dear fellow,' he said, 'tomorrow crowns our work. You shall appear—or rather not appear—before the assembled faculty of the university. I have telegraphed invitations to Heidelberg, to Bonn, to Berlin. Schrotter, Haeckel, Steinmetz, Lavallo, will be here. Our triumph will be in presence of the most eminent physicists of the age. I shall then disclose those secrets of our process which I have hitherto withheld even from you, my colaborer and trusted friend. But you shall share the glory. What is this I hear about the forest bird that has flown? My boy, you shall be restocked with pigment and go to Paris to seek her with fame in your hands and the blessings of science on your head.'

"The next morning, the nineteenth of August, before I had arisen from my cot bed, Käspar hastily entered the laboratory.

"'Herr Flack! Herr Flack!' he gasped, 'the Herr Doctor Professor is dead of apoplexy.'"

V

The narrative had come to an end. I sat a long time thinking. What could I do? What could I say? In what shape could I offer consolation to this unhappy man?

Flack, the invisible, was sobbing bitterly.

He was the first to speak. "It is hard, hard, hard! For no crime in the eyes of man, for no sin in the sight of God, I have been condemned to a fate ten thousand times worse than hell. I must walk the earth, a man, living, seeing, loving, like other men, while between me and all that makes life worth having there is a barrier fixed forever. Even ghosts have shapes. My life is living death; my existence oblivion. No friend can look me in the face. Were I to clasp to my breast the woman I love, it would only be to inspire terror inexpressible. I see her almost every day. I brush against her skirts as I pass her on the stairs. Did she love me? Does she love me? Would not that knowledge make the curse still more cruel? Yet it was to learn the truth that I brought you here."

Then I made the greatest mistake of my life.

"Cheer up!" I said. "Pandora has always loved you."

By the sudden overturning of the table I knew with what vehemence Flack sprang to his feet. His two hands had my shoulders in a fierce grip.

"Yes," I continued; "Pandora has been faithful to your memory. There is no reason to despair. The secret of Fröliker's process died with him, but why should it not be rediscovered by experiment and induction *ab initio*, with the aid which you can render? Have courage and hope. She loves you. In five minutes you shall hear it from her own lips." No wail of pain that I ever heard was half so pathetic as his wild cry of joy.

I hurried downstairs and summoned Miss Bliss into the hall. In a few words I explained the situation. To my surprise, she neither fainted nor went into hysterics. "Certainly, I will accompany you," she said, with a smile which I could not then interpret.

She followed me into Flack's room, calmly scrutinizing every corner of the apartment, with the set smile still upon her face. Had she been entering a ballroom she could not have shown greater self-possession. She manifested no astonishment, no terror, when her hand was seized by invisible hands and covered with kisses from invisible lips. She listened with composure to the torrent of loving and caressing words which my unfortunate friend poured into her ears.

Perplexed and uneasy, I watched the strange scene.

Presently Miss Bliss withdrew her hand.

"Really, Mr. Flack," she said with a light laugh, "you are sufficiently demonstrative. Did you acquire the habit on the Continent?"

"Pandora!" I heard him say, "I do not understand."

"Perhaps," she calmly went on, "you regard it as one of the privileges of your invisibility. Let me congratulate you on the success of your experiment. What a clever man your professor—what is his name?—must be. You can make a fortune by exhibiting yourself."

Was this the woman who for months had paraded her inconsolable sorrow for the loss of this very man? I was stupefied. Who shall undertake to analyze the motives of a coquette? What science is profound enough to unravel her unconscionable whims?

"Pandora!" he exclaimed again, in a bewildered voice. "What does it mean? Why do you receive me in this manner? Is that all you have to say to me?"

"I believe that is all," she coolly replied, moving toward the door. "You are a gentleman, and I need not ask you to spare me any further annoyance."

"Your heart is quartz," I whispered, as she passed me in going out. "You are unworthy of him."

Flack's despairing cry brought Käspar into the room. With the instinct acquired by long and faithful service, the old man went straight to the place where his master was. I saw him clutch at the air, as if struggling with and seeking to detain the invisible man. He was flung violently aside. He recovered himself and stood an instant listening, his neck distended, his face pale. Then he rushed out of the door and down the stairs. I followed him.

The street door of the house was open. On the sidewalk Käspar hesitated a few seconds. It was toward the west that he finally turned, running down the street with such speed that I had the utmost difficulty to keep at his side.

It was near midnight. We crossed avenue after avenue. An inarticulate murmur of satisfaction escaped old Käspar's lips. A little way ahead of us we saw a man, standing at one of the avenue corners, suddenly thrown to the ground. We sped on, never relaxing our pace. I now heard rapid footfalls a short distance in advance of us. I clutched Käspar's arm. He nodded.

Almost breathless, I was conscious that we were no longer treading upon pavement, but on boards and amid a confusion of lumber. In front of us were no more lights; only blank vacancy. Käspar gave one mighty spring. He clutched, missed, and fell back with a cry of horror.

There was a dull splash in the black waters of the river at our feet.

THE HORLA
Guy de Maupassant

May 8. What a lovely day! I have spent all the morning lying on the grass in front of my house, under the enormous plantain tree which covers and shades and shelters the whole of it. I like this part of the country; I am fond of living here because I am attached to it by deep roots, the profound and delicate roots which attach a man to the soil on which his ancestors were born and died, to their traditions, their usages, their food, the local expressions, the peculiar language of the peasants, the smell of the soil, the hamlets, and to the atmosphere itself.

I love the house in which I grew up. From my windows I can see the Seine, which flows by the side of my garden, on the other side of the road, almost through my grounds, the great and wide Seine, which goes to Rouen and Havre, and which is covered with boats passing to and fro. On the left, down yonder, lies Rouen, populous Rouen with its blue roofs massing under pointed, Gothic towers. Innumerable are they, delicate or broad, dominated by the spire of the cathedral, full of bells which sound through the blue air on fine mornings, sending their sweet and distant iron clang to me, their metallic sounds, now stronger and now weaker, according as the wind is strong or light.

What a delicious morning it was! About eleven o'clock, a long line of boats drawn by a steam-tug, as big a fly, and which scarcely puffed while emitting its thick smoke, passed my gate.

After two English schooners, whose red flags fluttered toward the sky, there came a magnificent Brazilian three-master; it was

53

perfectly white and wonderfully clean and shining. I saluted it, I hardly know why, except that the sight of the vessel gave me great pleasure.

May 12. I have had a slight feverish attack for the last few days, and I feel ill, or rather I feel low-spirited.

Whence come those mysterious influences which change our happiness into discouragement, and our self-confidence into diffidence? One might almost say that the air, the invisible air, is full of unknowable Forces, whose mysterious presence we have to endure. I wake up in the best of spirits, with an inclination to sing in my heart. Why? I go down by the side of the water, and suddenly, after walking a short distance, I return home wretched, as if some misfortune were awaiting me there. Why? Is it a cold shiver which, passing over my skin, has upset my nerves and given me a fit of low spirits? Is it the form of the clouds, or the tints of the sky, or the colors of the surrounding objects which are so change-able, which have troubled my thoughts as they passed before my eyes? Who can tell? Everything that surrounds us, everything that we see without looking at it, everything that we touch without knowing it, everything that we handle without feeling it, everything that we meet without clearly distinguishing it, has a rapid, surprising, and inexplicable effect upon us and upon our organs, and through them on our ideas and on our being itself.

How profound that mystery of the Invisible is! We cannot fathom it with our miserable senses: our eyes are unable to perceive what is either too small or too great, too near to or too far from us; we can see neither the inhabitants of a star nor of a drop of water; our ears deceive us, for they transmit to us the vibrations of the air in sonorous notes. Our senses are fairies who work the miracle of changing that movement into noise, and by that metamorphosis give birth to music, which makes the mute agitation of nature a harmony. So with our sense of smell, which is weaker than that of a dog, and so with our sense of taste, which can scarcely distinguish the age of a wine!

Oh! If we only had other organs which could work other miracles in our favor, what a number of fresh things we might discover around us!

May 16. I am ill, decidedly! I was so well last month! I am feverish, horribly feverish, or rather I am in a state of feverish enerva-
tion, which makes my mind suffer as much as my body. I have without ceasing the horrible sensation of some danger threatening me,
the apprehension of some coming misfortune or of approaching
death, a presentiment which is no doubt, an attack of some illness
still unnamed, which germinates in the flesh and in the blood.

May 18. I have just come from consulting my medical man, for
I can no longer get any sleep. He found that my pulse was high, my
eyes dilated, my nerves highly strung, but no alarming symptoms.
I must have a course of shower baths and of bromide of potassium.

May 25. No change! My state is really very peculiar. As the
evening comes on, an incomprehensible feeling of disquietude
seizes me, just as if night concealed some terrible menace toward
me. I dine quickly, and then try to read, but I do not understand
the words, and can scarcely distinguish the letters. Then I walk up
and down my drawing-room, oppressed by a feeling of confused
and irresistible fear, a fear of sleep and a fear of my bed.

About ten o'clock I go up to my room. As soon as I have entered I lock and bolt the door. I am frightened—of what? Up till
the present time I have been frightened of nothing. I open my cupboards, and look under my bed; I listen—I listen—to what? How
strange it is that a simple feeling of discomfort, of impeded or
heightened circulation, perhaps the irritation of a nervous center,
a slight congestion, a small disturbance in the imperfect and delicate functions of our living machinery, can turn the most light-
hearted of men into a melancholy one, and make a coward of the
bravest? Then, I go to bed, and I wait for sleep as a man might
wait for the executioner. I wait for its coming with dread, and my
heart beats and my legs tremble, while my whole body shivers beneath the warmth of the bedclothes, until the moment when I suddenly fall asleep, as a man throws himself into a pool of stagnant
water in order to drown. I do not feel this perfidious sleep coming
over me as I used to, but a sleep which is close to me and watching
me, which is going to seize me by the head, to close my eyes and
annihilate me.

I sleep—a long time—two or three hours perhaps—then a dream—no—a nightmare lays hold on me. I feel that I am in bed and asleep—I feel it and I know it—and I feel also that somebody is coming close to me, is looking at me, touching me, is getting on to my bed, is kneeling on my chest, is taking my neck between his hands and squeezing it—squeezing it with all his might in order to strangle me.

I struggle, bound by that terrible powerlessness which paralyzes us in our dreams; I try to cry out—but I cannot; I want to move—I cannot; I try, with the most violent efforts and out of breath, to turn over and throw off this being which is crushing and suffocating me—I cannot!

And then suddenly I wake up, shaken and bathed in perspiration; I light a candle and find that I am alone, and after that crisis, which occurs every night, I at length fall asleep and slumber tranquilly till morning.

June 2. My state has grown worse. What is the matter with me? The bromide does me no good, and the shower-baths have no effect whatever. Sometimes, in order to tire myself out, though I am fatigued enough already, I go for a walk in the forest of Roumare. I used to think at first that the fresh light and soft air, impregnated with the odor of herbs and leaves, would instill new life into my veins and impart fresh energy to my heart. One day I turned into a broad ride in the wood, and then I diverged toward La Bouille, through a narrow path, between two rows of exceedingly tall trees, which placed a thick, green, almost black roof between the sky and me.

A sudden shiver ran through me, not a cold shiver, but a shiver of agony, and so I hastened my steps, uneasy at being alone in the wood, frightened stupidly and without reason, at the profound solitude. Suddenly it seemed as if I were being followed, that somebody was walking at my heels, close, quite close to me, near enough to touch me.

I turned round suddenly, but I was alone. I saw nothing behind me except the straight, broad ride, empty and bordered by high trees, horribly empty; on the other side also it extended until it was lost in the distance, and looked just the same—terrible.

I closed my eyes. Why? And then I began to turn round on one heel very quickly, just like a top. I nearly fell down, and opened my eyes; the trees were dancing round me and the earth heaved; I was obliged to sit down. Then, ah! I no longer remembered how I had come! What a strange idea! What a strange, strange idea! I did not the least know. I started off to the right, and got back into the avenue which had led me into the middle of the forest.

June 3. I have had a terrible night. I shall go away for a few weeks, for no doubt a journey will set me up again.

July 2. I have come back, quite cured, and have had a most delightful trip into the bargain. I have been to Mont Saint-Michel, which I had not seen before.

What a sight, when one arrives as I did, at Avranches toward the end of the day! The town stands on a hill, and I was taken into the public garden at the extremity of the town. I uttered a cry of astonishment. An extraordinarily large bay lay extended before me, as far as my eyes could reach, between two hills which were lost to sight in the mist; and in the middle of this immense yellow bay, under a clear, golden sky, a peculiar hill rose up, somber and pointed in the midst of the sand. The sun had just disappeared, and under the still flaming sky stood out the outline of that fantastic rock which bears on its summit a picturesque monument.

At daybreak I went to it. The tide was low, as it had been the night before, and I saw that wonderful abbey rise up before me as I approached it. After several hours' walking, I reached the enormous mass of rock which supports the little town, dominated by the great church. Having climbed the steep and narrow street, I entered the most wonderful Gothic building that has ever been erected to God on earth, large as a town, and full of low rooms which seem buried beneath vaulted roofs, and of lofty galleries supported by delicate columns.

I entered this gigantic granite jewel, which is as light in its effect as a bit of lace and is covered with towers, with slender belfries to which spiral staircases ascend. The flying buttresses raise strange heads that bristle with chimeras, with devils, with fantastic animals, with monstrous flowers, are joined together by finely carved arches, to the blue sky by day, and to the black sky by night.

When I had reached the summit. I said to the monk who accompanied me: "Father, how happy you must be here!" And he replied: "It is very windy, Monsieur"; and so we began to talk while watching the rising tide, which ran over the sand and covered it with a steel cuirass.

And then the monk told me stories, all the old stories belonging to the place—legends, nothing but legends.

One of them struck me forcibly. The country people, those belonging to the Mornet, declare that at night one can hear talking going on in the sand, and also that two goats bleat, one with a strong, the other with a weak voice. Incredulous people declare that it is nothing but the screaming of the sea birds, which occasionally resembles bleatings, and occasionally human lamentations; but belated fishermen swear that they have met an old shepherd, whose cloak covered head they can never see, wandering on the sand, between two tides, round the little town placed so far out of the world. They declare he is guiding and walking before a he-goat with a man's face and a she-goat with a woman's face, both with white hair, who talk incessantly, quarreling in a strange language, and then suddenly cease talking in order to bleat with all their might.

"Do you believe it?" I asked the monk. "I scarcely know," he replied; and I continued: "If there are other beings besides ourselves on this earth, how comes it that we have not known it for so long a time, or why have you not seen them? How is it that I have not seen them?"

He replied: "Do we see the hundred-thousandth part of what exists? Look here; there is the wind, which is the strongest force in nature. It knocks down men, and blows down buildings, uproots trees, raises the sea into mountains of water, destroys cliffs and casts great ships on to the breakers; it kills, it whistles, it sighs, it roars. But have you ever seen it, and can you see it? Yet it exists for all that."

I was silent before this simple reasoning. That man was a philosopher, or perhaps a fool; I could not say which exactly, so I held my tongue. What he had said had often been in my own thoughts.

July 3. I have slept badly; certainly there is some feverish influence here, for my coachman is suffering in the same way as I am. When I went back home yesterday, I noticed his singular paleness, and I asked him: "What is the matter with you, Jean?"

"The matter is that I never get any rest, and my nights devour my days. Since your departure, Monsieur, there has been a spell over me."

However, the other servants are all well, but I am very frightened of having another attack, myself.

July 4. I am decidedly taken again; for my old nightmares have returned. Last night I felt somebody leaning on me who was sucking my life from between my lips with his mouth. Yes, he was sucking it out of my neck like a leech would have done. Then he got up, satiated, and I woke up, so beaten, crushed, and annihilated that I could not move. If this continues for a few days, I shall certainly go away again.

July 5. Have I lost my reason? What has happened? What I saw last night is so strange that my head wanders when I think of it!

As I do now every evening, I had locked my door; then, being thirsty, I drank half a glass of water, and I accidentally noticed that the water-bottle was full up to the cut-glass stopper.

Then I went to bed and fell into one of my terrible sleeps, from which I was aroused in about two hours by a still more terrible shock. Picture to yourself a sleeping man who is being murdered, who wakes up with a knife in his chest, a gurgling in his throat, is covered with blood, can no longer breathe, is going to die and does not understand anything at all about it—there you have it.

Having recovered my senses, I was thirsty again, so I lighted a candle and went to the table on which my water-bottle was. I lifted it up and tilted it over my glass, but nothing came out. It was empty! It was completely empty! At first I could not understand it at all; then suddenly I was seized by such a terrible feeling that I had to sit down, or rather fall into a chair! Then I sprang up with a bound to look about me; then I sat down again, overcome by astonishment and fear, in front of the transparent crystal bottle! I looked at it with fixed eyes, trying to solve the puzzle, and my hands trembled! Some body had drunk the water, but who? I? I without any doubt. It could surely only be I? In that case I was a somnambulist—was living, without knowing it, that double, mysterious life which makes us doubt whether there are not two beings in us— whether a strange, unknowable, and invisible being does not, during our moments of mental and physical torpor, animate the inert body, forcing it to a more willing obedience than it yields to ourselves.

Oh! Who will understand my horrible agony? Who will understand the emotion of a man sound in mind, wide-awake, full of sense, who looks in horror at the disappearance of a little water while he was asleep, through the glass of a water-bottle! And I remained sitting until it was daylight, without venturing to go to bed again.

July 6. I am going mad. Again all the contents of my water-bottle have been drunk during the night; or rather I have drunk it!

But is it I? Is it I? Who could it be? Who? Oh! God! Am I going mad? Who will save me?

July 10. I have just been through some surprising ordeals. Undoubtedly I must be mad! And yet!

On July 6, before going to bed, I put some wine, milk, water, bread, and strawberries on my table. Somebody drank—I drank— all the water and a little of the milk, but neither the wine, nor the bread, nor the strawberries were touched.

On the seventh of July I renewed the same experiment, with the same results, and on July 8 I left out the water and the milk and nothing was touched.

Lastly, on July 9 I put only water and milk on my table, taking care to wrap up the bottles in white muslin and to tie down the stoppers. Then I rubbed my lips, my beard, and my hands with pencil lead, and went to bed.

Deep slumber seized me, soon followed by a terrible awakening. I had not moved, and my sheets were not marked. I rushed to the table. The muslin round the bottles remained intact; I undid the string, trembling with fear. All the water had been drunk, and so had the milk! Ah! Great God! I must start for Paris immediately.

July 12. Paris. I must have lost my head during the last few days! I must be the plaything of my enervated imagination, unless I am really a somnambulist, or I have been brought under the power of one of those influences—hypnotic suggestion, for example—which are known to exist, but have hitherto been inexplicable. In any case, my mental state bordered on madness, and twenty-four hours of Paris sufficed to restore me to my equilibrium.

Yesterday after doing some business and paying some visits, which instilled fresh and invigorating mental air into me, I wound up my evening at the *Théâtre-Français.* A drama by Alexander Dumas the Younger was being acted, and his brilliant and powerful play completed my cure. Certainly solitude is dangerous for active minds. We need men who can think and can talk, around us. When we are alone for a long time, we people space with phantoms.

I returned along the boulevards to my hotel in excellent spirits. Amid the jostling of the crowd I thought, not without irony, of my terrors and surmises of the previous week, because I believed, yes, I believed, that an invisible being lived beneath my roof. How weak our mind is; how quickly it is terrified and unbalanced as soon as we are confronted with a small, incomprehensible fact. Instead of dismissing the problem with: "We do not understand because we cannot find the cause," we immediately imagine terrible mysteries and supernatural powers.

July 14. Fête of the Republic. I walked through the streets, and the crackers and flags amused me like a child. Still, it is very foolish to make merry on a set date, by Government decree. People are like a flock of sheep, now steadily patient, now in ferocious revolt. Say to it: "Amuse yourself," and it amuses itself. Say to it: "Go and fight with your neighbor," and it goes and fights. Say to it: "Vote for the Emperor," and it votes for the Emperor; then say to it: "Vote for the Republic," and it votes for the Republic.

Those who direct it are stupid, too; but instead of obeying men they obey principles, a course which can only be foolish, ineffective, and false, for the very reason that principles are ideas which are considered as certain and unchangeable, whereas in this world one is certain of nothing, since light is an illusion and noise is deception.

July 16. I saw some things yesterday that troubled me very much. I was dining at my cousin's, Madame Sable, whose husband is colonel of the 76th Chasseurs at Limoges. There were two young women there, one of whom had married a medical man, Dr. Parent, who devotes himself a great deal to nervous diseases and to the extraordinary manifestations which just now experiments in hypnotism and suggestion are producing.

He related to us at some length the enormous results obtained by English scientists and the doctors of the medical school at Nancy, and the facts which he adduced appeared to me so strange, that I declared that I was altogether incredulous.

"We are," he declared, "on the point of discovering one of the most important secrets of nature, I mean to say, one of its most important secrets on this earth, for assuredly there are some up in the stars, yonder, of a different kind of importance. Ever since man has thought, since he has been able to express and write down his thoughts, he has felt himself close to a mystery which is impenetrable to his coarse and imperfect senses, and he endeavors to supplement the feeble penetration of his organs by the efforts of his intellect. As long as that intellect remained in its elementary stage, this intercourse with invisible spirits assumed forms which were commonplace though terrifying. Thence sprang the popular belief in the supernatural, the legends of wandering spirits, of fairies, of gnomes, of ghosts, I might even say the conception of God, for our ideas of the Workman-Creator, from whatever religion they may have come down to us, are certainly the most mediocre, the stupidest, and the most unacceptable inventions that ever sprang from the frightened brain of any human creature. Nothing is truer than what Voltaire says: 'If God made man in His own image, man has certainly paid Him back again.'

"But for rather more than a century, men seem to have had a presentiment of something new. Mesmer and some others have put us on an unexpected track, and within the last two or three years especially, we have arrived at results really surprising."

My cousin, who is also very incredulous, smiled, and Dr. Parent said to her: "Would you like me to try and send you to sleep, Madame?"

"Yes, certainly."

She sat down in an easy-chair, and he began to look at her fixedly, as if to fascinate her. I suddenly felt myself somewhat discomposed; my heart beat rapidly and I had a choking feeling in my throat. I saw that Madame Sable's eyes were growing heavy, her mouth twitched, and her bosom heaved, and at the end of ten minutes she was asleep.

"Go behind her," the doctor said to me; so I took a seat behind her. He put a visiting-card into her hands, and said to her: "This is a looking-glass; what do you see in it?"

She replied: "I see my cousin."

"What is he doing?"

"He is twisting his mustache."

"And now?"

"He is taking a photograph out of his pocket."

"Whose photograph is it?"

"His own."

That was true, for the photograph had been given me that same evening at the hotel.

"What is his attitude in this portrait?"

"He is standing up with his hat in his hand."

She saw these things in that card, in that piece of white pasteboard, as if she had seen them in a looking-glass.

The young women were frightened, and exclaimed: "That is quite enough! Quite, quite enough!"

But the doctor said to her authoritatively: "You will get up at eight o'clock to-morrow morning; then you will go and call on your cousin at his hotel and ask him to lend you the five thousand francs which your husband asks of you, and which he will ask for when he sets out on his coming journey."

Then he woke her up.

On returning to my hotel, I thought over this curious *séance* and I was assailed by doubts, not as to my cousin's absolute and

undoubted good faith, for I had known her as well as if she had
been my own sister ever since she was a child, but as to a possible
trick on the doctor's part. Had not he, perhaps, kept a glass hidden in his hand, which he showed to the young woman in her sleep
at the same time as he did the card? Professional conjurers do
things which are just as singular.

However, I went to bed, and this morning, at about half past
eight, I was awakened by my footman, who said to me: "Madame
Sable has asked to see you immediately, Monsieur." I dressed hastily and went to her.

She sat down in some agitation, with her eyes on the floor, and
without raising her veil said to me: "My dear cousin, I am going to
ask a great favor of you."

"What is it, cousin?"

"I do not like to tell you, and yet I must. I am in absolute want
of five thousand francs."

"What, you?"

"Yes, I, or rather my husband, who has asked me to procure
them for him."

I was so stupefied that I hesitated to answer. I asked myself
whether she had not really been making fun of me with Dr. Parent,
if it were not merely a very well-acted farce which had been got up
beforehand. On looking at her attentively, however, my doubts disappeared. She was trembling with grief, so painful was this step to
her, and I was sure that her throat was full of sobs.

I knew that she was very rich and so I continued: "What! Has
not your husband five thousand francs at his disposal? Come, think.
Are you sure that he commissioned you to ask me for them?"

She hesitated for a few seconds, as if she were making a great
effort to search her memory, and then she replied: "Yes—yes, I am
quite sure of it."

"He has written to you?"

She hesitated again and reflected, and I guessed the torture of
her thoughts. She did not know. She only knew that she was to borrow
five thousand francs of me for her husband. So she told a lie.

"Yes, he has written to me."

"When, pray? You did not mention it to me yesterday."

"I received his letter this morning."

"Can you show it to me?"

"No; no—no—it contained private matters, things too personal to ourselves. I burned it."

"So your husband runs into debt?"

She hesitated again, and then murmured: "I do not know."

Thereupon I said bluntly: "I have not five thousand francs at my disposal at this moment, my dear cousin."

She uttered a cry, as if she were in pair; and said: "Oh! oh! I beseech you, I beseech you to get them for me."

She got excited and clasped her hands as if she were praying to me! I heard her voice change its tone; she wept and sobbed, harassed and dominated by the irresistible order that she had received.

"Oh! oh! I beg you to—if you knew what I am suffering—I want them to-day."

I had pity on her: "You shall have them by and by, I swear to you."

"Oh! thank you! thank you! How kind you are."

I continued: "Do you remember what took place at your house last night?"

"Yes."

"Do you remember that Dr. Parent sent you to sleep?"

"Yes."

"Oh! Very well then; he ordered you to come to me this morning to borrow five thousand francs, and at this moment you are obeying that suggestion."

She considered for a few moments, and then replied: "But as it is my husband who wants them—"

For a whole hour I tried to convince her, but could not succeed, and when she had gone I went to the doctor. He was just going out, and he listened to me with a smile, and said: "Do you believe now?"

"Yes, I cannot help it."

"Let us go to your cousin's."

She was already resting on a couch, overcome with fatigue. The doctor felt her pulse, looked at her for some time with one hand raised toward her eyes, which she closed by degrees under the irresistible power of this magnetic influence. When she was asleep, he said:

"Your husband does not require the five thousand francs any longer! You must, therefore, forget that you asked your cousin to lend them to you, and, if he speaks to you about it, you will not understand him."

Then he woke her up, and I took out a pocket-book and said: "Here is what you asked me for this morning, my dear cousin." But she was so surprised, that I did not venture to persist; nevertheless, I tried to recall the circumstance to her, but she denied it vigorously, thought that I was making fun of her, and in the end, very nearly lost her temper.

There! I have just come back, and I have not been able to eat any lunch, for this experiment has altogether upset me.

July 19. Many people to whom I have told the adventure have laughed at me. I no longer know what to think. The wise man says: Perhaps?

July 21. I dined at Bougival, and then I spent the evening at a boatmen's ball. Decidedly everything depends on place and surroundings. It would be the height of folly to believe in the supernatural on the *île de la Grenouillière.* But on the top of Mont Saint-Michel or in India, we are terribly under the influence of our surroundings. I shall return home next week.

July 30. I came back to my own house yesterday. Everything is going on well.

August 2. Nothing fresh; it is splendid weather, and I spend my days in watching the Seine flow past.

August 4. Quarrels among my servants. They declare that the glasses are broken in the cupboards at night. The footman accuses the cook, she accuses the needlewoman, and the latter accuses the other two. Who is the culprit? It would take a clever person to tell.

August 6. This time, I am not mad. I have seen—I have seen—I have seen!—I can doubt no longer—I have seen it!

I was walking at two o'clock among my rose-trees, in the full sunlight—in the walk bordered by autumn roses which are beginning to fall. As I stopped to look at a *Géant de Bataille*, which had three splendid blooms, I distinctly saw the stalk of one of the roses bend close to me, as if an invisible hand had bent it, and then break, as if that hand had picked it! Then the flower raised itself, following the curve which a hand would have described in carrying it toward a mouth, and remained suspended in the transparent air, alone and motionless, a terrible red spot, three yards from my eyes. In desperation I rushed at it to take it! I found nothing; it had disappeared. Then I was seized with furious rage against myself, for it is not wholesome for a reasonable and serious man to have such hallucinations.

But was it a hallucination? I turned to look for the stalk, and I found it immediately under the bush, freshly broken, between the two other roses which remained on the branch. I returned home, then, with a much disturbed mind; for I am certain now, certain as I am of the alternation of day and night, that there exists close to me an invisible being who lives on milk and on water, who can touch objects, take them and change their places; who is, consequently, endowed with a material nature, although imperceptible to sense, and who lives as I do, under my roof—

August 7. I slept tranquilly. He drank the water out of my decanter, but did not disturb my sleep.

I ask myself whether I am mad. As I was walking just now in the sun by the riverside, doubts as to my own sanity arose in me; not vague doubts such as I have had hitherto, but precise and absolute doubts. I have seen mad people, and I have known some who were quite intelligent, lucid, even clear-sighted in every concern of life, except on one point. They could speak clearly, readily, profoundly on everything; till their thoughts were caught in the breakers of their delusions and went to pieces there, were dispersed and swamped in that furious and terrible sea of fogs and squalls which is called *madness*.

I certainly should think that I was mad, absolutely mad, if I were not conscious that I knew my state, if I could not fathom it and analyze it with the most complete lucidity. I should, in fact, be a reasonable man laboring under a hallucination. Some unknown disturbance must have been excited in my brain, one of those disturbances which physiologists of the present day try to note and to fix precisely, and that disturbance must have caused a profound gulf in my mind and in the order and logic of my ideas. Similar phenomena occur in dreams, and lead us through the most unlikely phantasmagoria, without causing us any surprise, because our verifying apparatus and our sense of control have gone to sleep, while our imaginative faculty wakes and works. Was it not possible that one of the imperceptible keys of the cerebral finger-board had been paralyzed in me? Some men lose the recollection of proper names, or of verbs, or of numbers, or merely of dates, in consequence of an accident. The localization of all the avenues of thought has been accomplished nowadays; what, then, would there be surprising in the fact that my faculty of controlling the unreality of certain hallucinations should be destroyed for the time being?

I thought of all this as I walked by the side of the water. The sun was shining brightly on the river and made earth delightful, while it filled me with love for life, for the swallows, whose swift agility is always delightful in my eyes, for the plants by the riverside, whose rustling is a pleasure to my ears.

By degrees, however, an inexplicable feeling of discomfort seized me. It seemed to me as if some unknown force were numbing and stopping me, were preventing me from going further and were calling me back. I felt that painful wish to return which comes on you when you have left a beloved invalid at home, and are seized by a presentiment that he is worse.

I, therefore, returned despite of myself, feeling certain that I should find some bad news awaiting me, a letter or a telegram. There was nothing, however, and I was surprised and uneasy, more so than if I had had another fantastic vision.

August 8. I spent a terrible evening, yesterday. He does not show himself any more, but I feel that He is near me, watching me, looking at me, penetrating me, dominating me, and more terrible to me when He hides himself thus than if He were to manifest his constant and invisible presence by supernatural phenomena. However, I slept.

August 9. Nothing, but I am afraid.

August 10. Nothing; but what will happen to-morrow?

August 11. Still nothing. I cannot stop at home with this fear hanging over me and these thoughts in my mind; I shall go away.

August 12. Ten o'clock at night. All day long I have been trying to get away, and have not been able. I contemplated a simple and easy act of liberty, a carriage ride to Rouen—and I have not been able to do it. What is the reason?

August 13. When one is attacked by certain maladies, the springs of our physical being seem broken, our energies destroyed, our muscles relaxed, our bones to be as soft as our flesh, and our blood as liquid as water. I am experiencing the same in my moral being, in a strange and distressing manner. I have no longer any strength, any courage, any self-control, nor even any power to set my own will in motion. I have no power left to *will* anything, but some one does it for me and I obey.

August 14. I am lost! Somebody possesses my soul and governs it! Somebody orders all my acts, all my movements, all my thoughts. I am no longer master of myself, nothing except an enslaved and terrified spectator of the things which I do. I wish to go out; I cannot. *He* does not wish to; and so I remain, trembling and distracted in the armchair in which he keeps me sitting. I merely wish to get up and to rouse myself, so as to think that I am still master of myself: I cannot! I am riveted to my chair, and my chair adheres to the floor in such a manner that no force of mine can move us.

Then suddenly, I must, I *must* go to the foot of my garden to pick some strawberries and eat them—and I go there. I pick the strawberries and I eat them! Oh! my God! my God! Is there a God? If there be one, deliver me! save me! succor me! Pardon! Pity! Mercy! Save me! Oh! what sufferings! what torture! what horror!

August 15. Certainly this is the way in which my poor cousin was possessed and swayed, when she came to borrow five thousand francs of me. She was under the power of a strange will which had entered into her, like another soul, a parasitic and ruling soul. Is the world coming to an end?

But who is he, this invisible being that rules me, this unknowable being, this rover of a supernatural race?

Invisible beings exist, then! how is it, then, that since the beginning of the world they have never manifested themselves in such a manner as they do to me? I have never read anything that resembles what goes on in my house. Oh! If I could only leave it, if I could only go away and flee, and never return, I should be saved; but I cannot.

August 16. I managed to escape to-day for two hours, like a prisoner who finds the door of his dungeon accidentally open. I suddenly felt that I was free and that He was far away, and so I gave orders to put the horses in as quickly as possible, and I drove to Rouen. Oh! how delightful to be able to say to my coachman: "Go to Rouen!"

I made him pull up before the library, and I begged them to lend me Dr. Herrmann Herestauss's treatise on the unknown inhabitants of the ancient and modern world. Then, as I was getting into my carriage, I intended to say: "To the railway station!" but instead of this I shouted—I did not speak; but I shouted—in such a loud voice that all the passers-by turned round: "Home!" and I fell back on to the cushion of my carriage, overcome by mental agony. He had found me out and regained possession of me.

August 17. Oh! What a night! what a night! And yet it seems to me that I ought to rejoice. I read until one o'clock in the morning! Herestauss, Doctor of Philosophy and Theogony, wrote the history and the manifestation of all those invisible beings which hover around man, or of whom he dreams. He describes their origin, their domains, their power; but none of them resembles the one which haunts me. One might say that man, ever since he has thought, has had a foreboding and a fear of a new being, stronger than himself, his successor in this world, and that, feeling him near, and not being able to foretell the nature of the unseen one, he has, in his terror, created the whole race of hidden beings, vague phantoms born of fear.

Having, therefore, read until one o'clock in the morning, I went and sat down at the open window, in order to cool my forehead and my thoughts in the calm night air. It was very pleasant and warm! How I should have enjoyed such a night formerly!

There was no moon, but the stars darted out their rays in the dark heavens. Who inhabits those worlds? What forms, what living beings, what animals are there yonder? Do those who are thinkers in those distant worlds know more than we do? What can they do more than we? What do they see which we do not? Will not one of them, some day or other, traversing space, appear on our earth to conquer it, just as formerly the Norsemen crossed the sea in order to subjugate nations feebler than themselves?

We are so weak, so powerless, so ignorant, so small—we who live on this particle of mud which revolves in liquid air.

I fell asleep, dreaming thus in the cool night air, and then, having slept for about three quarters of an hour, I opened my eyes without moving, awakened by an indescribably confused and strange sensation. At first I saw nothing, and then suddenly it appeared to me as if a page of the book, which had remained open on my table, turned over of its own accord. Not a breath of air had come in at my window, and I was surprised and waited. In about four minutes, I saw, I saw—yes I saw with my own eyes—another page lift itself up and fall down on the others, as if a finger had turned it over. My armchair was empty, appeared empty, but I knew that He was there, He, and sitting in my place, and that He was reading. With a furious bound, the bound of an enraged wild beast that wishes to disembowel its tamer, I crossed my room to seize him, to strangle him, to kill him! But before I could reach it, my chair fell over as if somebody had run away from me. My table rocked, my lamp fell and went out, and my window closed as if some thief had been surprised and had fled out into the night, shutting it behind him.

So He had run away; He had been afraid; He, afraid of me!

So to-morrow, or later—some day or other, I should be able to hold him in my clutches and crush him against the ground! Do not dogs occasionally bite and strangle their masters?

August 18. I have been thinking the whole day long. Oh! yes, I will obey Him, follow His impulses, fulfill all His wishes, show myself humble, submissive, a coward. He is the stronger; but an hour will come.

August 19. I know, I know, I know all! I have just read the following in the *Revue du Monde Scientifique*: "A curious piece of news comes to us from Rio de Janeiro. Madness, an epidemic of madness, which may be compared to that contagious madness which attacked the people of Europe in the Middle Ages, is at this moment raging in the Province of San-Paulo. The frightened inhabitants are leaving their houses, deserting their villages, abandoning their land, saying that they are pursued, possessed, governed like human cattle by invisible, though tangible beings, by a species of vampire, which feeds on their life while they are asleep, and which, besides, drinks water and milk without appearing to touch any other nourishment.

"Professor Don Pedro Henriques, accompanied by several medical savants, has gone to the Province of San-Paulo, in order to study the origin and the manifestations of this surprising madness on the spot, and to propose such measures to the Emperor as may appear to him to be most fitted to restore the mad population to reason."

Ah! Ah! I remember now that fine Brazilian three-master which passed in front of my windows as it was going up the Seine, on the eighth of last May! I thought it looked so pretty, so white and bright! That Being was on board of her, coming from there, where its race sprang from. And it saw me! It saw my house, which was also white, and He sprang from the ship on to the land. Oh! Good heavens!

Now I know, I can divine. The reign of man is over, and he has come. He whom disquieted priests exorcised, whom sorcerers evoked on dark nights, without seeing him appear, He to whom the imaginations of the transient masters of the world lent all the monstrous or graceful forms of gnomes, spirits, genii, fairies, and familiar spirits. After the coarse conceptions of primitive fear, men more enlightened gave him a truer form. Mesmer divined him, and ten years ago physicians accurately discovered the nature of his power, even before He exercised it himself. They played with that weapon of their new Lord, the sway of a mysterious will over the human soul, which had become enslaved. They called it mesmerism, hypnotism, suggestion, I know not what? I have seen them diverting themselves like rash children with this horrible power! Woe to us! Woe to man! He has come, the—the—what does He call himself—the—I fancy that he is shouting out his name to me and I do not hear him—the—yes—He is shouting it out—I am listening— I cannot—repeat—it—Horla—I have heard—the Horla—it is He— the Horla—He has come!—

Ah! the vulture has eaten the pigeon, the wolf has eaten the lamb; the lion has devoured the sharp-horned buffalo; man has killed the lion with an arrow, with a spear, with gunpowder; but the Horla will make of man what man has made of the horse and of the ox: his chattel, his slave, and his food, by the mere power of his will. Woe to us!

But, nevertheless, sometimes the animal rebels and kills the man who has subjugated it. I should also like—I shall be able to— but I must know Him, touch Him, see Him! Learned men say that eyes of animals, as they differ from ours, do not distinguish as ours do. And my eye cannot distinguish this newcomer who is oppressing me.

Why? Oh! Now I remember the words of the monk at Mont Saint-Michel: "Can we see the hundred-thousandth part of what exists? Listen; there is the wind which is the strongest force in nature; it knocks men down, blows down buildings, uproots trees, raises the sea into mountains of water, destroys cliffs, and casts great ships on to the breakers; it kills, it whistles, it sighs, it roars,— have you ever seen it, and can you see it? It exists for all that, however!"

And I went on thinking: my eyes are so weak, so imperfect, that they do not even distinguish hard bodies, if they are as transparent as glass! If a glass without quicksilver behind it were to bar my way, I should run into it, just like a bird which has flown into a room breaks its head against the windowpanes. A thousand things, moreover, deceive a man and lead him astray. How then is it surprising that he cannot perceive a new body which is penetrated and pervaded by the light?

A new being! Why not? It was assuredly bound to come! Why should we be the last? We do not distinguish it, like all the others created before us? The reason is, that its nature is more delicate, its body finer and more finished than ours. Our makeup is so weak, so awkwardly conceived; our body is encumbered with organs that are always tired, always being strained like locks that are too complicated; it lives like a plant and like an animal nourishing itself with difficulty on air, herbs, and flesh; it is a brute machine which is a prey to maladies, to malformations, to decay; it is broken-winded, badly regulated, simple and eccentric, ingeniously yet badly made, a coarse and yet a delicate mechanism, in brief, the outline of a being which might become intelligent and great.

There are only a few—so few—stages of development in this world, from the oyster up to man. Why should there not be one more, when once that period is accomplished which separates the successive products one from the other?

Why not one more? Why not, also, other trees with immense, splendid flowers, perfuming whole regions? Why not other elements beside fire, air, earth, and water? There are four, only four, nursing fathers of various beings! What a pity! Why should not there be forty, four hundred, four thousand! How poor everything is, how mean and wretched—grudgingly given, poorly invented, clumsily made! Ah! the elephant and the hippopotamus, what power! And the camel, what suppleness!

But the butterfly, you will say, a flying flower! I dream of one that should be as large as a hundred worlds, with wings whose shape, beauty, colors, and motion I cannot even express. But I see it—it flutters from star to star, refreshing them and perfuming them with the light and harmonious breath of its flight! And the people up there gaze at it as it passes in an ecstasy of delight!

What is the matter with me? It is He, the Horla who haunts me, and who makes me think of these foolish things! He is within me, He is becoming my soul; I shall kill him!

August 20. I shall kill Him. I have seen Him! Yesterday I sat down at my table and pretended to write very assiduously. I knew quite well that He would come prowling round me, quite close to me, so close that I might perhaps be able to touch him, to seize him. And then—then I should have the strength of desperation; I should have my hands, my knees, my chest, my forehead, my teeth to strangle him, to crush him, to bite him, to tear him to pieces. And I watched for him with all my overexcited nerves.

I had lighted my two lamps and the eight wax candles on my mantelpiece, as if, by this light I should discover Him.

My bed, my old oak bed with its columns, was opposite to me; on my right was the fireplace; on my left the door, which was carefully closed, after I had left it open for some time, in order to attract Him; behind me was a very high wardrobe with a looking-glass in it, which served me to dress by every day, and in which I was in the habit of inspecting myself from head to foot every time I passed it.

So I pretended to be writing in order to deceive Him, for He also was watching me, and suddenly I felt, I was certain, that He was reading over my shoulder, that He was there, almost touching my ear.

I got up so quickly, with my hands extended, that I almost fell. Horror! It was as bright as at midday, but I did not see myself in the glass! It was empty, clear, profound, full of light! But my figure was not reflected in it—and I, I was opposite to it! I saw the large, clear glass from top to bottom, and I looked at it with unsteady eyes. I did not dare advance; I did not venture to make a movement; feeling certain, nevertheless, that He was there, but that He would escape me again, He whose imperceptible body had absorbed my reflection.

How frightened I was! And then suddenly I began to see myself through a mist in the depths of the looking-glass, in a mist as it were, or through a veil of water; and it seemed to me as if this water were flowing slowly from left to right, and making my figure clearer every moment. It was like the end of an eclipse. Whatever hid me did not appear to possess any clearly defined outlines, but was a sort of opaque transparency, which gradually grew clearer.

At last I was able to distinguish myself completely, as I do every day when I look at myself. I had seen Him! And the horror of it remained with me, and makes me shudder even now.

August 21. How could I kill Him, since I could not get hold of Him? Poison? But He would see me mix it with the water; and then, would our poisons have any effect on His impalpable body? No—no—no doubt about the matter. Then?—then?

August 22. I sent for a blacksmith from Rouen and ordered iron shutters of him for my room, such as some private hotels in Paris have on the ground floor, for fear of thieves, and he is going to make me a similar door as well. I have made myself out a coward, but I do not care about that!

September 10. Rouen, Hotel Continental. It is done; it is done— but is He dead? My mind is thoroughly upset by what I have seen.

Well then, yesterday, the locksmith having put on the iron shutters and door, I left everything open until midnight, although it was getting cold.

Suddenly I felt that He was there, and joy, mad joy took possession of me. I got up softly, and I walked to the right and left for some time, so that He might not guess anything; then I took off my boots and put on my slippers carelessly; then I fastened the iron shutters and going back to the door quickly I double-locked it with a padlock, putting the key into my pocket.

Suddenly I noticed that He was moving restlessly round me, that in his turn He was frightened and was ordering me to let Him out. I nearly yielded, though I did not quite, but putting my back to the door, I half opened it, just enough to allow me to go out backward, and as I am very tall, my head touched the lintel. I was sure that He had not been able to escape, and I shut Him up quite alone, quite alone. What happiness! I had Him fast. Then I ran downstairs into the drawing-room which was under my bedroom. I took the two lamps and poured all the oil on to the carpet, the furniture, everywhere; then I set fire to it and made my escape, after having carefully double locked the door.

I went and hid myself at the bottom of the garden, in a clump of laurel bushes. How long it was! how long it was! Everything was dark, silent, motionless, not a breath of air and not a star, but heavy banks of clouds which one could not see, but which weighed, oh! so heavily on my soul.

I looked at my house and waited. How long it was! I already began to think that the fire had gone out of its own accord, or that He had extinguished it, when one of the lower windows gave way under the violence of the flames, and a long, soft, caressing sheet of red flame mounted up the white wall, and kissed it as high as the roof. The light fell on to the trees, the branches, and the leaves, and a shiver of fear pervaded them also! The birds awoke; a dog began to howl, and it seemed to me as if the day were breaking! Almost immediately two other windows flew into fragments, and I saw that the whole of the lower part of my house was nothing but a terrible furnace. But a cry, a horrible, shrill, heart-rending cry, a woman's cry, sounded through the night, and two garret windows were opened! I had forgotten the servants! I saw the terror-struck faces, and the frantic waving of their arms!

Then, overwhelmed with horror, I ran off to the village, shouting: "Help! help! fire! fire!" Meeting some people who were already coming on to the scene, I went back with them to see!

By this time the house was nothing but a horrible and magnificent funeral pile, a monstrous pyre which lit up the whole country, a pyre where men were burning, and where He was burning also, He, He, my prisoner, that new Being, the new Master, the Horla!

Suddenly the whole roof fell in between the walls, and a volcano of flames darted up to the sky. Through all the windows which opened on to that furnace, I saw the flames darting, and I reflected that He was there, in that kiln, dead.

Dead? Perhaps? His body? Was not his body, which was transparent, indestructible by such means as would kill ours?

If He were not dead? Perhaps time alone has power over that Invisible and Redoubtable Being. Why this transparent, unrecognizable body, this body belonging to a spirit, if it also had to fear ills, infirmities, and premature destruction?

Premature destruction? All human terror springs from that! After man the Horla. After him who can die every day, at any hour, at any moment, by any accident, He came, He who was only to die at his own proper hour and minute, because He had touched the limits of his existence!

No—no—without any doubt—He is not dead. Then—then—I suppose I must kill myself!

MY INVISIBLE FRIEND
Katharine Kip

When I first went to Mrs. Barker's boarding-house on Oak Street, I was greatly attracted by and interested in one boarder among the twelve. This was William Elliott, a tall, broad-shouldered man about thirty-five years old. During the day he was a bank cashier, while in his leisure hours he was an earnest and enthusiastic student of chemistry.

I had a hall bedroom on the fourth floor, while he occupied the large room next it, and had a good-sized closet fitted up as a laboratory.

Several nights during the late spring, when I had left my door open to create a draught, I had been forced to close it again because of the horrible odors from his vile chemicals that filled the hall. Once or twice I knocked on his door and complained, whereupon he immediately ceased his experiments for the evening. He told me, however, that the study was so fascinating that it was never out of his thoughts for an instant, and that his dream was to spend his whole life in the pursuit of it.

After awhile we became great friends, and soon it became my regular habit to go into his room each evening, and to sit there talking with him, or reading while he worked.

One night, about three months after the adoption of this program, Elliott was in a mood of unusual expansiveness. Instead of setting about work immediately in his laboratory, he drew up a chair near mine, sat down facing me, and looking at me seriously, said:—

79

"Look here, Emerson; I've taken a fancy to you, and I've a good mind to tell you what I'm trying for in all these experiments. You'll probably think me mad or a fool, but here goes:— "You know what wonderful things can be done with the Roëntgen rays? And you know they claim to be able to make glasses, by wearing which a surgeon can literally 'see through' his patients!

"Well, I say that somewhere in Nature, only waiting to be discovered, there is a certain something, by enveloping the human body in which, rays of light can pass directly through without obstacle; and which will therefore render the body absolutely invisible!"

He looked at me eagerly, his eyes bright, his face glowing.

"It sounds plausible," I said, but without enthusiasm, for the truth was that I had no idea what he meant, and regarded his schemes as little more than child's play.

"It is not only plausible, it is *so*," he answered, excitedly. "There is not in my mind the slightest doubt of the existence of that something, whatever it may prove to be. Its parts are about us somewhere—perhaps near at hand, only waiting for the right man to bring them together. And I intend to be that man! I know that it sounds like the wildest nonsense, the height of conceited assurance, to say so;—and yet, why *not* I?"

I hastened to assure him that there was no reason why he might not be the man, and I certainly meant it. I thought that he had just as good a chance as any other, but secretly I believed that no one could ever find that ridiculous "something."

Elliott talked to me of his work, his hopes, and struggles; and explained minutely many of his experiments, which were as Greek to me. It was midnight when I left his room.

"It's an expensive study," he said at last, with a half sigh. "My salary as cashier is a good one; and yet, here I am, on the top floor of a cheap boarding-house. I deny myself every luxury and many comforts, to buy the apparatus that I need, as well as the necessary books and pamphlets."

The next day I went away on my vacation, and three weeks passed before I returned to the boarding-house.

I had, however, received a postal from Elliott, two weeks after my departure, saying merely:—

"Dear Emerson: Am on the right track at last, I am sure.
"Elliott."

I arrived at the house just at dinner-time, and, going directly into the dining room, took my old seat at the table. Elliott came in a moment later and sat down opposite me. I was shocked at the change for the worse in his appearance. He looked thin, worn, and exhausted, while his eyes burned feverishly; but when he saw me his face brightened and he greeted me cordially.

He ate hardly anything, and, after taking a cup of black coffee, rose from the table.

"Come up to my den this evening, Emerson," he said as he passed out.

"Don't you think that Mr. Elliott looks terribly?" asked Mrs. Marvin, a pretty blonde. "The hot weather seems to have used him up completely; and I am sure he never sleeps, for he walks his room all night long. Mr. Marvin and I had the room under his, but we exchanged with Mr. Coleman and Mr. Gaines, and now are on the second floor. It really annoyed me so—the walking, you know—that I couldn't sleep."

I agreed with her that Elliott was looking badly, and secretly thought that the excitement of the chase bade fair to kill him, whether he were successful or not. Another half hour and I knocked at his door.

"Come in," he replied, in a high, strained voice. I opened the door and looked about me in surprise.

All the furniture had been pushed as far back in a corner as possible, while the center of the room was occupied by a small stone to which was fastened a long string.

"Shut the door!" he exclaimed. His cheeks burned with a hectic flush, and he glanced from me to the string, and back again. "Sit down—there, on the edge of the bed. That's it! Now look at this string. Do you see anything queer about it?"

I looked, and saw that it was jerked or blown about as if by the wind; and yet the doors and windows were closed. Then I thought my eyes must deceive me, for the string was pulled taut, *and jerked the stone about an inch!*

"Wh-what experiment is this, in Heaven's name?" I cried in amazement.

Elliott smiled triumphantly. "What do you see?" he asked.

"See? I *think* I see a string jerking a stone," I replied.

"Ah!" It was an exclamation of relief and delight.

He took a saucer from the, mantelpiece, filled it with milk from a pitcher, and holding it in one hand, said:—

"There happens to be a *cat* on the end of that string, my dear fellow, as I will demonstrate to you."

At that a disagreeable suspicion stirred in my mind. A chill crept along my spine, and my eyes turned toward the door.

"Don't be afraid, I'm not dangerous," he said, looking at me and smiling, as he placed the saucer on the floor. *The string moved toward it;* and I swear I saw the ripples on that milk, and watched it gradually disappear, while at the same time I heard a distinct purring sound!

The strain on my nerves was a little too severe, and I burst into a hoarse laugh.

"Ha, ha, ha!—forgive me, but it seems too ridiculous,—a phantom cat drinking milk!"

Elliott smiled abstractedly, but I don't think that he had heard a word that I said.

"Do you know what this means?" he asked, in a low voice. "It means a discovery as great as any that has ever been made. It means—Great Heavens, man! you don't know what it means,—that one could live his life in a crowded building, mix with hundreds of men, jostle them in the streets, eat with them, sleep with them, *murder* them, and never be seen by human vision!"

Elliott's eyes glittered, he trembled all over, and breathed heavily. He began a rapid march up and down the room, while he continued to enlighten me as to the wonderful effect this discovery would have, in case it proved as successful with human beings as it had with the invisible feline. I occupied as small a space as possible, for, in spite of his reassuring words of a short time before, I was afraid of him. I also tried to look enthusiastic and encouraging, but the effort was probably vain, for he suddenly stopped in his walk and said:—

"Here! get down and feel where that cat is."

I obeyed with alacrity, although I expected to find nothing, and was rewarded, as my fingers closed on something soft and furry, by hearing a maddened "*miaouw*" and by receiving a most realistic scratch from invisible claws.

"Damn it!" I exclaimed vigorously; and somehow, after that, the ghostly aspect of the whole affair was lost to me. "What on earth possessed you to tie the cat with a string?" I asked, nursing my injured hand.

"My dear fellow, will you tell me how I could locate her otherwise? You can't see the cat, which is carefully covered with—with the result of my experiments; and you *can* see the string, which has not been treated."

I stared at him in amazement. Somehow that simple idea had not occurred to me. "Why, then you *really* would be as invisible as air!" I exclaimed fatuously.

"Didn't I say so? Heavens, shall I take the stone to pound the idea into your head?" —in a vexed tone.

"No; I'll dispense with that crowning argument. You must remember that while you have had months to grow used to the idea, *I* have had it sprung on me with comparative suddenness. And it *is* a hard thing to credit! Even now—"

"Wait a minute!" he interrupted, his good humor restored. "I'll convince you." He stepped to the laboratory and brought out a small dish filled with a lead-colored liquid. He pulled the string toward him, and his fingers closed on the air, as far as I could see. He held his hand over the dish and thrust it downward. There was a wild mewing and spitting, a grand splash, and then—I saw before me a cat, wet and bedraggled, and with the string tied around her neck!

"And now," he said, after enjoying my astonishment for a while; "you can dig out, old fellow, and I'll get some sleep. I'll let you know when I'm ready for the next test. I want to try it on *myself* next, and it will take two weeks of hard work to make the necessary quantity."

I am not ashamed now to confess that, after that night's experience, when the great nature of the discovery had gradually dawned on me, I grew as nervous as any old woman. I started at the slightest sound; I never sat with my back to a door, and was never really satisfied unless I had Elliott within range of my vision. I saw him only at the table, for he told me that until two weeks had elapsed, and he had prepared for the great test, he didn't want me in his room.

I placed no reliance on what he had said, however, about the length of time required to prepare for it, but feared that he might at any time anoint himself with the mysterious compound and take me by surprise. For I was the only human being who knew of the discovery, and my terror showed to me, though my mind tried to deny, how thoroughly I believed in it.

Each night, after going to my room, I locked and bolted the door, and then gave the small room a thorough search. I poked under the bed and in the wardrobe with a cane; I stood in the middle of the floor and jabbed all around, quickly and scientifically. I had complained before because the place was so tiny; now it seemed too large for me. I understood thoroughly and sympathized with the nervous fears of those who believe in ghosts; and how much more reason had I to dread a "ha'nt" who, thin as he was, must weigh one hundred and seventy pounds, and who was possessed of the strength of a man mastered by one idea.

But one night, after two weeks of anxiety, Elliott stopped me in the hall after dinner, and said:—

"Come to my room to-night at nine. I'm ready for the great test."

The man looked positively wild. There were great hollows around his eyes, his cheeks were sunken, his hands like claws. I verily believe he had scarcely slept or eaten in a fortnight. He had, however, consumed enormous quantities of black coffee.

Well, I sat with Coleman and Gaines in their room until nine o'clock. Overhead I could hear Elliott's steady, rapid walk.

"Just hear that!" exclaimed Gaines. "I believe the fellow's cracked. Luckily Coleman and I have steady nerves, or that noise, kept up night after night, would drive us crazy."

At nine I left them and knocked at his door. He opened it quickly, then closed and locked it after me.

Everywhere was dust and disorder. The bed had been removed and had been replaced by a couch, over which was thrown a rug.

He waved his hand toward it. "Don't need a maid to make it up each morning," he said briefly. "Can't have a woman fooling around and upsetting things."

On a table near the couch was an immense glass jar, such as grocers use in their shop windows to display samples of preserves. It was about a foot in diameter and over two feet in height, and was tightly sealed. It was a faint yellow in color, but I could not then decide whether it was colored by the contents or not. Beside the table on the floor was a large porcelain tub, filled with the lead-colored liquid that I had seen before.

"There is my discovery," Elliott said, in a hushed voice, pointing to the jar. "And that," indicating the liquid in the tub, "you have seen before. To-morrow, if all goes well, the whole world will know of the great discovery. Think what it will mean! A man might travel the world over, unseen, unknown. He could penetrate the secrets of all lives. I dread to let the world share the knowledge with me, and yet it is too great to hide!"

Then, abruptly: "To-night I propose to make myself as invisible as that cat was. And I have asked you to be here, in case anything should go wrong, and I were to need help."

I sat spellbound in my chair, without the strength to speak. Elliott advanced to the table. He moistened his lips nervously, and his hands shook so that he could hardly grasp the jar. I saw, however, by the way he lifted it, that it was very light.

"My nerve is almost gone," he said, with a haggard smile. "Now I'll prepare myself in the laboratory,—while you wait here."

I sat there as he had directed, scarcely moving. My eyes were glued to the closed door of the laboratory. I could feel the hair rising on my scalp, and the chills running up and down my spine.

At last—whether in ten minutes or an hour, I do not know—the door was flung open. With a hoarse cry, I started to my feet, and retreated to the wall, holding my hands out to ward off—what? For, although a light burned in the laboratory, and I could see plainly around the little room, there was no one there!

"Quick! tell me, Emerson," exclaimed Elliott's strained voice *somewhere* in the room near me, "can you *see* me? Great Heavens,—you know what it means to me, man! Can't you speak—are you dumb?" The voice sounded nearer and threatening.

"No—no!" I fairly yelled, finding my voice suddenly, "I see no one. For God's sake, don't touch me, or I'll go mad."

A moment's pause, then the voice relaxed, and gently, and with a little happy laugh, murmured:—

"Don't be childish, Emerson! You know I'm *here*, don't you? Not only in voice, but in flesh. Why should you 'go mad' over your inability to see me, any more than because you can't see a friend when you can hear him through a telephone?"

Though a trifle reassured, I still shook with dread, and Elliott said good-humoredly:—

"Come here! Oh, I forgot," —with a really boyish laugh,— "you don't know where 'here' is! Well, I warn you. I'm coming to you, and to shake your hand," and I heard footsteps cross the floor, and felt the hearty grasp of his hand on mine.

"There—run your hand up my arm! It has the regular 'feel' of flesh, hasn't it?"

I admitted that it had. "And you really can see *no one*? Every article of furniture is as plain as if you were alone? Now I am between you and the laboratory door. How is it?"

"I see the laboratory, the light in it, the empty jar, and everything else, distinctly."

"Good!—but I *knew* that I must succeed!" and there was fairly a sob in his voice. Then, with a quick change, he asked gaily:—

"What do you think I intend to do now? I will enjoy myself like a schoolboy, for to-morrow I must be only a scientist. I will take a trip—go on a journey of exploration and adventure—through the house, and perhaps venture into the street."

"O Elliott, don't do that!—think of the risk! You've stood the test so far; just wash the stuff off now, go to bed and take some rest!"

"Nonsense!"—irritably. "As for risk, where is it? You're afraid of me, that's what's the matter!" This with a disagreeable laugh. "No, I intend to enjoy myself. The warm weather renders my lack of raiment very comfortable. Now, I'll say 'auf wiedersehen,' Emerson."

Unable to persuade him to abandon his plan, and, I admit, too cowardly, and too much overcome with the events of the past few moments, to say more, I sat in my chair, stupid with fright. The key turned in the lock, the door opened and closed, and I heard on the stairway the familiar creak of the third stair from the top.

Elliott had really gone!

Then, indeed, I regained my senses. Bounding from my seat, I rushed to the door, flung it open, and leaned over the banisters. The gas in the hall was burning low. Inspired by fright, I turned it on at full head, then resumed my position of leaning over the railing. All was quiet in the halls below. Suddenly the light in the second hall went out. Elliott was there, then! Perhaps he intended to play some trick on Coleman and Gaines;—no, they now had the room under Elliott's, and the Marvins had the second floor front.

"Well, he'll find it out as soon as he opens the door; and *they* can't see *him*," I murmured, realizing more than ever the advantages of invisibility.

A streak of light in the darkness of the second hall appeared and vanished.

"Their door opening and shutting," I decided.

There was complete silence for about five minutes. Then I heard a woman's scream, followed, after a slight pause, by another, and another, two pistol-shots, and the slamming of a door. I was rooted to the spot with fright and horror. The whole place seemed whirling around me, and I grasped at the railing to steady myself.

At the sound of the first scream, a door on the third hall had opened, and Gaines and Coleman had rushed for the stairway. Before they could reach it, the pistol-shots rang out, the door in the second hall slammed; and as Gaines placed his hand on the stair rail he paused, staggered, and fell heavily against the wall. Coleman, too, fell back; and then—then I heard the well-known creak of the stair near me—and the door of Elliott's room closed softly, and I heard the key turn in the lock.

With that sound, I was seized with a dread of being alone on the same floor with the madman; for such I now had fully decided him to be. I fled precipitately down the stairs, and reached the second hall almost simultaneously with Coleman and Gaines. We burst into the Marvins' room together.

There was only a dim lamplight in the room. Mrs. Marvin lay on a couch, unconscious. Over her, the revolver in hand and a look of frantic terror on his face, bent her husband. As we entered, he turned and looked wildly at us.

"Did you see any one—anything in the halls?" he demanded.

"No," answered Coleman and Gaines together. I slowly shook my head.

"What was all the shooting about?" asked Coleman suspiciously, "and why did Mrs. Marvin scream? Is she *shot?*"

"Shot? No!" replied Mr. Marvin, who had by this time put down the pistol. "I—I thought there was a burglar, and I shot," and he turned again to his wife and began chafing her hands.

By this time Mrs. Barker and the other boarders, all more or less in disarray, and all very much excited, were grouped at the door.

Mrs. Barker entered, and added her efforts to Mr. Marvin's and in a few minutes we had the satisfaction of seeing Mrs. Marvin's eyes open. Every one was clamoring for some explanation of the need for the shots; and in a short time we were in possession of the facts to which I listened with feelings of guilt and shame.

"Just before the disturbance Mr. and Mrs. Marvin were sitting by a table reading. The gas was lighted in the central chandelier and a lamp was burning on the table. The couple were sitting with their backs to the door, which was unlocked.

"Suddenly Mrs. Marvin was startled by hearing the door open. She turned just in time to see it close again, and noticed that the hall was dark.

"'Frank,' she exclaimed, 'some one opened the door and closed it again!'

"'Nonsense—the draught,' he replied, and continued reading.

"In another instant she noticed the light growing dimmer, and looking up saw that the gaslight was going out. At the same time she *felt* the presence of some stranger in the room, though she could see no one. She uttered an exclamation of alarm.

"'My dear Alice, what is it?' asked Mr. Marvin resignedly. (He was deeply interested in his book.)

"'Frank, the gas is going out—has *gone* out; and I feel that there is some one in the room. O Frank! I am so frightened—oh!" She stepped quickly toward her husband, and it was then that she uttered that first scream; for as she moved, she came into contact with some one—or something—although there was seemingly no one there.

"'By Heaven, there is something!' exclaimed her husband, as he, too, encountered the mysterious presence.

"Scream after scream issued from Mrs. Marvin's lips, and Mr. Marvin, utterly losing his head, rushed to the bureau, took out his revolver, and fired twice; as much to alarm the house, in his insane terror, as with the hope of hitting—hitting what? With a bewildered air, he acknowledged that he had seen no one.

"'And yet,' he said, when I fired the first shot, the door opened again, and I just had time to fire the second shot at the opening before it closed.'"

That ended Marvin's story. Marvin, himself, acted as if he did not expect to be believed. His listeners, for the most part, evidently thought that he had been under the influence of liquor. Mrs. Barker sniffed contemptuously, and said she only *hoped* the pistol-shots hadn't damaged the woodwork. One man even said consolingly:—

"You'll sleep it off, old fellow," while Mrs. Marvin wept hysterically.

But Coleman said slowly:—

"Well, it's deuced queer; but when I heard Mrs. Marvin scream, and started for the stairs, I had just reached them, when I got an awful shove that knocked me clean over against the wall. Yet I'll take my oath no one was there. And I hadn't had a drop to drink, either," with a fierce glare around.

Gaines listened open-mouthed.

"That was my experience to a T," he exclaimed. "I thought sure I 'had 'em.' Now *what* was it? I say, Emerson, did *you* see any one, or hear any one?"

"N-no," I replied articulating with difficulty, "n-nothing."

"Well, you've got a good case of rattles, anyhow," he said, laughing.

A few minutes more and the group had separated, Mrs. Marvin, tearful and still badly frightened, vowing that she would be up all night and leave in the morning; Marvin, pale and shaken, but a trifle shame-faced; Coleman and Gaines puzzled and looking angry; Mrs. Barker and others openly contemptuous; and the colored servants whispering of "ha'nts" and looking almost pale with fright.

I climbed slowly up to my room. No one had noticed Elliott's absence. I was thankful for that. I felt somehow like a fellow-conspirator. Should I go in and speak to him—ask him for his explanations of the affair, though I was sure how it had all happened?

No. I decided that what I needed was rest from Elliott! So I went cautiously into my own room, fearing to hear him call me. All was silent, however, and after going through my usual routine of search, I prepared for bed and was soon sound asleep.

The next morning, as I was dressing and reviewing the events of the evening before, the thought occurred to me for the first time that Elliott might have been wounded by one of those shots fired by Marvin. At this idea, I hurriedly opened my door and pounded on Elliott's. There was no reply.

"I knocked and knocked, Mr. Emerson," said the chambermaid who was passing, "and I couldn't wake him."

"Go down and ask Mr. Coleman if he's heard Mr. Elliott walking around this morning."

In a moment she was back. "No, sir."

"I—I'm certain he's ill," I said. My mind was dwelling on those shots. "Go and tell Mrs. Barker that we must force the door. Get James." James was the man-of-all-work.

Mrs. Barker came hurrying up, looking pale and worried.

"James is coming right up," she said; " but do you really think it's best to force the door?"

"I think Mr. Elliott must be ill. We can't wake him and delay is dangerous, you know."

"Yes, I know. It never rains but it pours, sir; and what with Mr. and Mrs. Marvin going at daybreak, and now *this!* I don't know what to do," and her eyes filled with tears.

James appeared at that moment, and the group was swelled by Coleman. James put his shoulder to the door, and quickly forced it open.

As it swung in we all started back in horror, for there, lying half in and half out of the porcelain tub, was the body of Elliott! His head was leaning back against the couch, his face was distorted, his hands clenched.

The physician who was hastily summoned said that life had been extinct for many hours.

"Chronic heart disease," he said. "The attack was probably brought on by some great excitement."

So it was not a bullet wound, after all! And I had a very decided idea as to what the "great excitement" was that had brought on the fatal attack of heart trouble. I did not make that idea public, however, and Coleman's theory, which differed very materially from mine, was generally accepted as true.

"It was the noise of all that screaming and of those shots that brought on the attack," said he. And it certainly sounded plausible enough.

No trace of the great discovery was left. I did venture to tell the relative who inherited all of Elliott's belongings that I had reason to believe that his cousin had made a very important discovery just before he died. I therefore urged upon him the advisability of having his papers examined by a competent person. But I learned that only a few disconnected notes, of no value whatsoever, had been found.

However, what one man has done another can do. And I confidently expect, and at no very distant time, to learn that Elliott's experiment has been made again, and has succeeded.

THE INVISIBLE MAN
H. G. Wells

1

THE STRANGE MAN'S ARRIVAL

The stranger came early in February one wintry day, through a biting wind and a driving snow, the last snowfall of the year, over the down, walking as it seemed from Bramblehurst railway station and carrying a little black portmanteau in his thickly gloved hand. He was wrapped up from head to foot, and the brim of his soft felt hat hid every inch of his face but the shiny tip of his nose; the snow had piled itself against his shoulders and chest, and added a white crest to the burden he carried. He staggered into the Coach and Horses, more dead than alive as it seemed, and flung his portmanteau down. "A fire," he cried, "in the name of human charity! A room and a fire!" He stamped and shook the snow from off himself in the bar, and followed Mrs. Hall into her guest parlour to strike his bargain. And with that much introduction, that and a ready acquiescence to terms and a couple of sovereigns flung upon the table, he took up his quarters in the inn.

Mrs. Hall lit the fire and left him there while she went to prepare him a meal with her own hands. A guest to stop at Iping in the winter-time was an unheard-of piece of luck, let alone a guest who was no "haggler," and she was resolved to show herself worthy of her good fortune. As soon as the bacon was well under way, and Millie, her lymphatic aid, had been brisked up a bit by a few deftly chosen expressions of contempt, she carried the cloth, plates, and glasses into the parlour and began to lay them with the utmost *éclat*. Although the fire was burning up briskly, she was surprised to see that her visitor still wore his hat and coat, standing with his back to her and staring out of the window at the falling snow in the yard. His gloved hands were clasped behind him, and he seemed to be lost in thought. She noticed that the melted snow that still sprinkled his shoulders dripped upon her carpet. "Can I take your hat and coat, sir," she said, "and give them a good dry in the kitchen?"

"No," he said without turning.

She was not sure she had heard him, and was about to repeat her question.

He turned his head and looked at her over his shoulder. "I prefer to keep them on," he said with emphasis, and she noticed that he wore big blue spectacles with side-lights and had a bushy side-whisker over his coat-collar that completely hid his face.

"Very well, sir," she said. "As you like. In a bit the room will be warmer."

He made no answer and had turned his face away from her again; and Mrs. Hall, feeling that her conversational advances were ill-timed, laid the rest of the table things in a quick staccato and whisked out of the room. When she returned he was still standing there like a man of stone, his back hunched, his collar turned up, his dripping hat-brim turned down, hiding his face and ears completely. She put down the eggs and bacon with considerable emphasis, and called rather than said to him, "Your lunch is served, sir."

"Thank you," he said at the same time, and did not stir until she was closing the door. Then he swung round and approached the table.

As she went behind the bar to the kitchen she heard a sound repeated at regular intervals. Chirk, chirk, chirk, it went, the sound of a spoon being rapidly whisked round a basin. "That girl!" she said. "There! I clean forgot it. It's her being so long!" And while she herself finished mixing the mustard, she gave Millie a few verbal stabs for her excessive slowness. She had cooked the ham and eggs, laid the table, and done everything, while Millie (help indeed!) had only succeeded in delaying the mustard. And him a new guest and wanting to stay! Then she filled the mustard pot, and, putting it with a certain stateliness upon a gold and black tea-tray, carried it into the parlour.

She rapped and entered promptly. As she did so her visitor moved quickly, so that she got but a glimpse of a white object disappearing behind the table. It would seem he was picking something from the floor. She rapped down the mustard pot on the table, and then she noticed the overcoat and hat had been taken off and put over a chair in front of the fire. A pair of wet boots threatened rust to her steel fender. She went to these things resolutely. "I suppose I may have them to dry now," she said in a voice that brooked no denial.

"Leave the hat," said her visitor in a muffled voice, and turning she saw he had raised his head and was sitting looking at her.

For a moment she stood gaping at him, too surprised to speak.

He held a white cloth—it was a serviette he had brought with him—over the lower part of his face, so that his mouth and jaws were completely hidden, and that was the reason of his muffled voice. But it was not that which startled Mrs. Hall. It was the fact that all his forehead above his blue glasses was covered by a white bandage, and that another covered his ears, leaving not a scrap of his face exposed excepting only his pink, peaked nose. It was bright pink, and shiny just as it had been at first. He wore a dark-brown velvet jacket with a high black linen lined collar turned up about his neck. The thick black hair, escaping as it could below and between the cross bandages, projected in curious tails and horns, giving him the strangest appearance conceivable. This muffled and bandaged head was so unlike what she had anticipated, that for a moment she was rigid.

He did not remove the serviette, but remained holding it, as she saw now, with a brown gloved hand, and regarding her with his inscrutable blue glasses. "Leave the hat," he said, speaking very distinctly through the white cloth.

Her nerves began to recover from the shock they had received. She placed the hat on the chair again by the fire. "I didn't know, sir," she began, "that—" and she stopped embarrassed.

"Thank you," he said drily, glancing from her to the door and then at her again.

"I'll have them nicely dried, sir, at once," she said, and carried his clothes out of the room. She glanced at his white-swathed head and blue goggles again as she was going out of the door; but his napkin was still in front of his face. She shivered a little as she closed the door behind her, and her face was eloquent of her surprise and perplexity. "I *never*," she whispered. "There!" She went quite softly to the kitchen, and was too preoccupied to ask Millie what she was messing about with now, when she got there.

The visitor sat and listened to her retreating feet. He glanced inquiringly at the window before he removed his serviette and resumed his meal. He took a mouthful, glanced suspiciously at the window, took another mouthful, then rose and, taking the serviette in his hand, walked across the room and pulled the blind down to the top of the white muslin that obscured the lower panes. This left the room in twilight. This done, he returned with an easier air to the table and his meal.

"The poor soul's had an accident or an op'ration or something," said Mrs. Hall. "What a turn them bandages did give me, to be sure!"

She put on some more coal, unfolded the clothes-horse, and extended the traveller's coat upon this. "And they goggles! Why, he looked more like a divin' helmet than a human man!" She hung his muffler on a corner of the horse. "And holding that handkerchief over his mouth all the time. Talkin' through it!... Perhaps his mouth was hurt too—maybe."

She turned round, as one who suddenly remembers. "Bless my soul alive!" she said, going off at a tangent; "ain't you done them taters *yet*, Millie?"

When Mrs. Hall went to clear away the stranger's lunch, her idea that his mouth must also have been cut or disfigured in the accident she supposed him to have suffered, was confirmed, for he was smoking a pipe, and all the time that she was in the room he never loosened the silk muffler he had wrapped round the lower part of his face to put the mouthpiece to his lips. Yet it was not forgetfulness, for she saw he glanced at it as it smouldered out. He sat in the corner with his back to the window-blind and spoke now, having eaten and drunk and being comfortably warmed through, with less aggressive brevity than before. The reflection of the fire lent a kind of red animation to his big spectacles they had lacked hitherto.

"I have some luggage," he said, "at Bramblehurst station," and he asked her how he could have it sent. He bowed his bandaged head quite politely in acknowledgment of her explanation. "To-morrow!" he said. "There is no speedier delivery?" and seemed quite disappointed when she answered "No." Was she quite sure? No man with a trap who would go over?

Mrs. Hall, nothing loath, answered his questions and developed a conversation. "It's a steep road by the down, sir," she said in answer to the question about a trap; and then, snatching at an opening said, "It was there a carriage was upsettled, a year ago and more. A gentleman killed, besides his coachman. Accidents, sir, happen in a moment, don't they?"

But the visitor was not to be drawn so easily. "They do," he said through his muffler, eyeing her quietly through his impen-etrable glasses.

"But they take long enough to get well, sir, don't they? ... There was my sister's son, Tom, jest cut his arm with a scythe, tumbled on it in the 'ayfield, and, bless me! he was three months tied up, sir. You'd hardly believe it. It's regular given me a dread of a scythe, sir."

"I can quite understand that," said the visitor.

"He was afraid, one time, that he'd have to have an op'ration—he was that bad, sir."

The visitor laughed abruptly, a bark of a laugh that he seemed to bite and kill in his mouth. "*Was* he?" he said.

"He was, sir. And no laughing matter to them as had the doing for him, as I had—my sister being took up with her little ones so much. There was bandages to do, sir, and bandages to undo. So that if I may make so bold as to say it, sir—"

"Will you get me some matches?" said the visitor, quite abruptly. "My pipe is out."

Mrs. Hall was pulled up suddenly. It was certainly rude of him, after telling him all she had done. She gasped at him for a moment, and remembered the two sovereigns. She went for the matches.

"Thanks," he said concisely, as she put them down, and turned his shoulder upon her and stared out of the window again. It was altogether too discouraging. Evidently he was sensitive on the topic of operations and bandages. She did not "make so bold as to say," however, after all. But his snubbing way had irritated her, and Millie had a hot time of it that afternoon.

The visitor remained in the parlour until four o'clock, without giving the ghost of an excuse for an intrusion. For the most part he was quite still during that time; it would seem he sat in the growing darkness smoking in the firelight, perhaps dozing.

Once or twice a curious listener might have heard him at the coals, and for the space of five minutes he was audible pacing the room. He seemed to be talking to himself. Then the armchair creaked as he sat down again.

2

MR. TEDDY HENFREY'S FIRST IMPRESSIONS

At four o'clock, when it was fairly dark and Mrs. Hall was screwing up her courage to go in and ask her visitor if he would take some tea, Teddy Henfrey, the clock-jobber, came into the bar. "My sakes! Mrs. Hall," said he, "but this is terrible weather for thin boots!" The snow outside was falling faster.

Mrs. Hall agreed with him, and then noticed he had his bag and hit upon a brilliant idea. "Now you're here, Mr. Teddy," said she, "I'd be glad if you'd give th' old clock in the parlour a bit of a look. 'Tis going, and it strikes well and hearty; but the hour-hand won't do nuthin' but point at six."

And leading the way, she went across to the parlour door and rapped and entered.

Her visitor, she saw as she opened the door, was seated in the armchair before the fire, dozing it would seem, with his bandaged head drooping on one side. The only light in the room was the red glow from the fire—which lit his eyes like adverse railway signals, but left his downcast face in darkness—and the scanty vestiges of the day that came in through the open door. Everything was ruddy, shadowy, and indistinct to her, the more so since she had just been lighting the bar lamp, and her eyes were dazzled. But for a second it seemed to her that the man she looked at had an enormous mouth wide open,—a vast and incredible mouth that swallowed the whole of the lower portion of his face. It was the sensation of a moment: the white-bound head, the monstrous goggle eyes, and this huge yawn below it. Then he stirred, started up in his chair, put up his hand. She opened the door wide, so that the room was lighter, and she saw him more clearly, with the muffler held to his face just as she had seen him hold the serviette before. The shadows, she fancied, had tricked her.

"Would you mind, sir, this man a-coming to look at the clock, sir?" she said, recovering from her momentary shock.

"Look at the clock?" he said, staring round in a drowsy manner and speaking over his hand, and then getting more fully awake, "certainly."

Mrs. Hall went away to get a lamp, and he rose and stretched himself. Then came the light, and Mr. Teddy Henfrey, entering, was confronted by this bandaged person. He was, he says, "taken aback."

"Good-afternoon," said the stranger, regarding him, as Mr. Henfrey says with a vivid sense of the dark spectacles, "like a lobster."

"I hope," said Mr. Henfrey, "that it's no intrusion."

"None whatever," said the stranger. "Though I understand," he said, turning to Mrs. Hall, "that this room is really to be mine for my own private use."

"I thought, sir," said Mrs. Hall, "you'd prefer the clock—" She was going to say "mended."

"Certainly," said the stranger, "certainly—but, as a rule, I like to be alone and undisturbed.

"But I'm really glad to have the clock seen to," he said, seeing a certain hesitation in Mr. Henfrey's manner. "Very glad." Mr. Henfrey had intended to apologise and withdraw, but this anticipation reassured him. The stranger stood round with his back to the fire-place and put his hands behind his back. "And presently," he said, "when the clock-mending is over, I think I should like to have some tea. But not until the clock-mending is over."

Mrs. Hall was about to leave the room,—she made no conversational advances this time, because she did not want to be snubbed in front of Mr. Henfrey,—when her visitor asked her if she had made any arrangements about his boxes at Bramblehurst. She told him she had mentioned the matter to the postman, and that the carrier could bring them over on the morrow. "You are certain that is the earliest?" he said.

She was certain, with a marked coldness.

"I should explain," he added, "what I was really too cold and fatigued to do before, that I am an experimental investigator."

"Indeed, sir," said Mrs. Hall, much impressed.

"And my baggage contains apparatus and appliances."

"Very useful things indeed they are, sir," said Mrs. Hall.

"And I'm naturally anxious to get on with my inquiries."

"Of course, sir."

"My reason for coming to Iping," he proceeded, with a certain deliberation of manner, "was—a desire for solitude. I do not wish to be disturbed in my work. In addition to my work, an accident—"

"I thought as much," said Mrs. Hall to herself.

"—necessitates a certain retirement. My eyes—are sometimes so weak and painful that I have to shut myself up in the dark for hours together. Lock myself up. Sometimes—now and then. Not at present, certainly. At such times the slightest disturbance, the entry of a stranger into the room, is a source of excruciating annoyance to me—it is well these things should be understood."

"Certainly, sir," said Mrs. Hall. "And if I might make so bold as to ask—"

"That, I think, is all," said the stranger, with that quietly irresistible air of finality he could assume at will. Mrs. Hall reserved her question and sympathy for a better occasion.

After Mrs. Hall had left the room, he remained standing in front of the fire, glaring, so Mr. Henfrey puts it, at the clock-mending.

Mr. Henfrey not only took off the hands of the clock, and the face, but extracted the works; and he tried to work in as slow and quiet and unassuming a manner as possible. He worked with the lamp close to him, and the green shade threw a brilliant light upon his hands, and upon the frame and wheels, and left the rest of the room shadowy. When he looked up, coloured patches swam in his eyes. Being constitutionally of a curious nature, he had removed the works—a quite unnecessary proceeding—with the idea of delaying his departure and perhaps falling into conversation with the stranger. But the stranger stood there, perfectly silent and still. So still, it got on Henfrey's nerves. He felt alone in the room and looked up, and there, grey and dim, was the bandaged head and huge blue lenses staring fixedly, with a mist of green spots drifting in front of them. It was so uncanny-looking to Henfrey that for a minute they remained staring blankly at one another. Then Henfrey looked down again. Very uncomfortable position! One would like to say something. Should he remark that the weather was very cold for the time of year? He looked up as if to take aim with that introductory shot. "The weather—" he began.

"Why don't you finish and go?" said the rigid figure, evidently in a state of painfully suppressed rage. "All you've got to do is to fix the hour-hand on its axle. You're simply humbugging—"

"Certainly, sir—one minute more, sir. I overlooked—" And Mr. Henfrey finished and went.

But he went off feeling excessively annoyed. "Damn it!" said Mr. Henfrey to himself, trudging down the village through the thawing snow; "a man must do a clock at times, sure-lie."

And again: "Can't a man look at you?—Ugly!"

And yet again: "Seemingly not. If the police was wanting you you couldn't be more wropped and bandaged."

At Gleeson's corner he saw Hall, who had recently married the stranger's hostess at the Coach and Horses, and who now drove the Iping conveyance, when occasional people required it, to Sidderbridge Junction, coming towards him on his return from that place. Hall had evidently been "stopping a bit" at Sidderbridge, to judge by his driving. "'Ow do, Teddy?" he said, passing.

"You got a rum un up home!" said Teddy.

Hall very sociably pulled up. "What's that?" he asked.

"Rum-looking customer stopping at the Coach and Horses," said Teddy. "My sakes!"

And he proceeded to give Hall a vivid description of his grotesque guest. "Looks a bit like a disguise, don't it? I'd like to see a man's face if I had him stopping in my place," said Henfrey. "But women are that trustful,—where strangers are concerned. He's took your rooms and he ain't even given a name, Hall."

"You don't say so!" said Hall, who was a man of sluggish apprehension.

"Yes," said Teddy. "By the week. Whatever he is, you can't get rid of him under the week. And he's got a lot of luggage coming tomorrow, so he says. Let's hope it won't be stones in boxes, Hall."

He told Hall how his aunt at Hastings had been swindled by a stranger with empty portmanteaux. Altogether he left Hall vaguely suspicious. "Get up, old girl," said Hall. "I s'pose I must see 'bout this."

Teddy trudged on his way with his mind considerably relieved.

Instead of "seeing 'bout it," however, Hall on his return was severely rated by his wife on the length of time he had spent in Sidderbridge, and his mild inquiries were answered snappishly and in a manner not to the point. But the seed of suspicion Teddy had sown germinated in the mind of Mr. Hall in spite of these discouragements. "You wim' don't know everything," said Mr. Hall, resolved to ascertain more about the personality of his guest at the earliest possible opportunity. And after the stranger had gone to bed, which he did about half-past nine, Mr. Hall went aggressively into the parlour and looked very hard at his wife's furniture, just to show that the stranger wasn't master there, and scrutinised closely and a little contemptuously a sheet of mathematical computation the stranger had left. When retiring for the night he instructed Mrs. Hall to look very closely at the stranger's luggage when it came next day.

"You mind your own business, Hall," said Mrs. Hall, "and I'll mind mine."

She was all the more inclined to snap at Hall because the stranger was undoubtedly an unusually strange sort of stranger, and she was by no means assured about him in her own mind. In the middle of the night she woke up dreaming of huge white heads like turnips, that came trailing after her at the end of interminable necks, and with vast black eyes. But being a sensible woman, she subdued her terrors and turned over and went to sleep again.

3
THE THOUSAND AND ONE BOTTLES

Thus it was that on the ninth day of February, at the beginning of the thaw, this singular person fell out of infinity into Iping Village. Next day his luggage arrived through the slush. And very remarkable luggage it was. There was a couple of trunks indeed, such as a rational man might need, but in addition there were a box of books,—big, fat books, of which some were just in an incomprehensible handwriting,—and a dozen or more crates, boxes, and cases, containing objects packed in straw, as it seemed to Hall, tugging with a casual curiosity at the straw—glass bottles. The stranger, muffled in hat, coat, gloves, and wrapper, came out impatiently to meet Fearenside's cart, while Hall was having a word or so of gossip preparatory to helping bring them in. Out he came, not noticing Fearenside's dog, who was sniffing in a *dilettante* spirit at Hall's legs. "Come along with those boxes," he said. "I've been waiting long enough."

And he came down the steps towards the tail of the cart as if to lay hands on the smaller crate.

No sooner had Fearenside's dog caught sight of him, however, than it began to bristle and growl savagely, and when he rushed down the steps it gave an undecided hop, and then sprang straight at his hand. "Whup!" cried Hall, jumping back, for he was no hero with dogs, and Fearenside howled, "Lie down!" and snatched his whip.

They saw the dog's teeth had slipped the hand, heard a kick, saw the dog execute a flanking jump and get home on the stranger's leg, and heard the rip of his trousering. Then the finer end of

Fearenside's whip reached his property, and the dog, yelping with dismay, retreated under the wheels of the waggon. It was all the business of a half-minute. No one spoke, every one shouted. The stranger glanced swiftly at his torn glove and at his leg, made as if he would stoop to the latter, then turned and rushed up the steps into the inn. They heard him go headlong across the passage and up the uncarpeted stairs to his bedroom.

"You brute, you!" said Fearenside, climbing off the waggon with his whip in his hand, while the dog watched him through the wheel. "Come here!" said Fearenside— "You'd better."

Hall had stood gaping. "He wuz bit," said Hall. "I'd better go and see to en," and he trotted after the stranger. He met Mrs. Hall in the passage. "Carrier's darg," he said, "bit en."

He went straight upstairs, and the stranger's door being ajar, he pushed it open and was entering without any ceremony, being of a naturally sympathetic turn of mind.

The blind was down and the room dim. He caught a glimpse of a most singular thing, what seemed a handless arm waving towards him, and a face of three huge indeterminate spots on white, very like the face of a pale pansy. Then he was struck violently in the chest, hurled back, and the door slammed in his face and locked, all so rapidly that he had no time to observe. A waving of indecipherable shapes, a blow, and a concussion. There he stood on the dark little landing, wondering what it might be that he had seen.

After a couple of minutes he rejoined the little group that had formed outside the Coach and Horses. There was Fearenside telling about it all over again for the second time; there was Mrs. Hall saying his dog didn't have no business to bite her guests; there was Huxter, the general dealer from over the road, interrogative; and Sandy Wadgers from the forge, judicial; besides women and children,— all of them saying fatuities: "Wouldn't let en bite *me*, I knows"; "'Tasn't right *have* such dargs"; "Whad '*e* bite 'n for then?" and so forth.

Mr. Hall, staring at them from the steps and listening, found it incredible that he had seen anything very remarkable happen upstairs. Besides, his vocabulary was altogether too limited to express his impressions.

"He don't want no help, he says," he said in answer to his wife's enquiry. "We'd better be a-takin' of his luggage in."

"He ought to have it cauterised at once," said Mr. Huxter; "especially if it's at all inflamed."

"I'd shoot en, that's what I'd do," said a lady in the group.

Suddenly the dog began growling again.

"Come along," cried an angry voice in the doorway, and there stood the muffled stranger with his collar turned up, and his hat-brim bent down. "The sooner you get those things in the better I'll be pleased." It is stated by an anonymous bystander that his trousers and gloves had been changed.

"Was you hurt, sir?" said Fearenside. "I'm rare sorry the darg—"

"Not a bit," said the stranger. "Never broke the skin. Hurry up with those things."

He then swore to himself, so Mr. Hall asserts.

Directly the first crate was carried into the parlour, in accordance with his directions, the stranger flung himself upon it with extraordinary eagerness, and began to unpack it, scattering the straw with an utter disregard of Mrs. Hall's carpet. And from it he began to produce bottles—little fat bottles containing powders, small and slender bottles containing coloured and white fluids, fluted blue bottles labelled Poison, bottles with round bodies and slender necks, large green-glass bottles, large white-glass bottles, bottles with glass stoppers and frosted labels, bottles with fine corks, bottles with bungs, bottles with wooden caps, wine bottles, salad-oil bottles—putting them in rows on the chiffonier, on the mantel, on the table under the window, round the floor, on the book-shelf—everywhere. The chemist's shop in Bramblehurst could not boast half so many. Quite a sight it was. Crate after crate yielded bottles, until all six were empty and the table high with straw; the only things that came out of these crates besides the bottles were a number of test-tubes and a carefully packed balance.

And directly the crates were unpacked, the stranger went to the window and set to work, not troubling in the least about the litter of straw, the fire which had gone out, the box of books outside, nor for the trunks and other luggage that had gone upstairs.

When Mrs. Hall took his dinner in to him, he was already so absorbed in his work, pouring little drops out of the bottles into test-tubes, that he did not hear her until she had swept away the bulk of the straw and put the tray on the table, with some little emphasis perhaps, seeing the state that the floor was in. Then he half turned his head and immediately turned it away again. But she saw he had removed his glasses; they were beside him on the table, and it seemed to her that his eye sockets were extraordinarily hollow. He put on his spectacles again, and then turned and faced her. She was about to complain of the straw on the floor when he anticipated her.

"I wish you wouldn't come in without knocking," he said in the tone of abnormal exasperation that seemed so characteristic of him.

"I knocked, but seemingly—"

"Perhaps you did. But in my investigations—my really very urgent and necessary investigations—the slightest disturbance, the jar of a door—I must ask you—"

"Certainly, sir. You can turn the lock if you're like that, you know—any time."

"A very good idea," said the stranger.

"This stror, sir, if I might make so bold as to remark—"

"Don't. If the straw makes trouble put it down in the bill." And he mumbled at her—words suspiciously like curses.

He was so odd, standing there, so aggressive and explosive, bottle in one hand and test-tube in the other, that Mrs. Hall was quite alarmed. But she was a resolute woman. "In which case, I should like to know, sir, what you consider—"

"A shilling. Put down a shilling. Surely a shilling's enough?"

"So be it," said Mrs. Hall, taking up the tablecloth and beginning to spread it over the table. "If you're satisfied, of course—"

He turned and sat down, with his coat-collar towards her.

All the afternoon he worked with the door locked and, as Mrs. Hall testifies, for the most part in silence. But once there was a concussion and a sound of bottles ringing together as though the table had been hit, and the smash of a bottle flung violently down, and then a rapid pacing athwart the room. Fearing "something was the matter," she went to the door and listened, not caring to knock.

"I can't go on," he was raving. "I *can't* go on. Three hundred thousand, four hundred thousand! The huge multitude! Cheated! All my life it may take me! Patience! Patience indeed! Fool and liar!"

There was a noise of hobnails on the bricks in the bar, and Mrs. Hall very reluctantly had to leave the rest of his soliloquy. When she returned the room was silent again, save for the faint crepitation of his chair and the occasional clink of a bottle. It was all over. The stranger had resumed work.

When she took in his tea she saw broken glass in the corner of the room under the concave mirror, and a golden stain that had been carelessly wiped. She called attention to it.

"Put it down in the bill," snapped her visitor. "For God's sake don't worry me. If there's damage done, put it down in the bill"; and he went on ticking a list in the exercise book before him.

"I'll tell you something," said Fearenside mysteriously. It was late in the afternoon, and they were in the little beer-shop of Iping Hanger.

"Well?" said Teddy Henfrey.

"This chap you're speaking of, what my dog bit. Well—he's black. Leastways, his legs are. I seed through the tear of his glove. You'd have expected a sort of pinky to show, wouldn't you? Well— there wasn't none. Just blackness. I tell you, he's as black as my hat."

"My sakes!" said Henfrey. "It's a rummy case altogether. Why, his nose is as pink as paint!"

"That's true," said Fearenside. "I knows that. And I tell 'ee what I'm thinking. That marn's a piebald, Teddy. Black here and white there—in patches. And he's ashamed of it. He's a kind of half-breed, and the colour's come off patchy instead of mixing. I've heard of such things before. And it's the common way with horses, as anyone can see."

4

MR. CUSS INTERVIEWS THE STRANGER

I have told the circumstances of the stranger's arrival in Iping with a certain fulness of detail, in order that the curious impression he created may be understood by the reader. But excepting two odd incidents, the circumstances of his stay until the extraordinary day of the Club Festival may be passed over very cursorily. There were a number of skirmishes with Mrs. Hall on matters of domestic discipline, but in every case until late in April, when the first signs of penury began, he over-rode her by the easy expedient of an extra payment. Hall did not like him, and whenever he dared he talked of the advisability of getting rid of him; but he showed his dislike chiefly by concealing it ostentatiously, and avoiding his visitor as much as possible. "Wait till the summer," said Mrs. Hall, sagely, "when the artisks are beginning to come. Then we'll see. He may be a bit overbearing, but bills settled punctual is bills settled punctual, whatever you like to say."

The stranger did not go to church, and indeed made no difference between Sunday and the irreligious days, even in costume. He worked, as Mrs. Hall thought, very fitfully. Some days he would come down early and be continuously busy. On others he would rise late, pace his room, fretting audibly for hours together, smoke, sleep in the armchair by the fire. Communication with the world beyond the village he had none. His temper continued very uncertain; for the most part his manner was that of a man suffering under almost unendurable provocation, and once or twice things were snapped, torn, crushed, or broken in spasmodic gusts of violence. He seemed under a chronic irritation of the greatest intensity. His habit of talking to himself in a low voice grew steadily upon him, but though Mrs. Hall listened conscientiously she could make neither head nor tail of what she heard.

He rarely went abroad by daylight, but at twilight he would go out muffled up enormously, whether the weather were cold or not, and he chose the loneliest paths and those most overshadowed by trees and banks. His goggling spectacles and ghastly bandaged face under the penthouse of his hat, came with a disagreeable suddenness out of the darkness upon one or two home-going labourers; and Teddy Henfrey, tumbling out of the Scarlet Coat one night at half-past nine, was scared shamefully by the stranger's skull-like head (he was walking hat in hand) lit by the sudden light of the opened door. Such children as saw him at nightfall dreamt of bogies, and it seemed doubtful whether he disliked boys more than they disliked him, or the reverse—but there was certainly a vivid enough dislike on either side.

It was inevitable that a person of so remarkable an appearance and bearing should form a frequent topic in such a village as Iping. Opinion was greatly divided about his occupation. Mrs. Hall was sensitive on the point. When questioned, she explained very carefully that he was an "experimental investigator," going gingerly over the syllables as one who dreads pitfalls. When asked what an experimental investigator was, she would say with a touch of superiority that most educated people knew that, and would then explain that he "discovered things." Her visitor had had an accident, she said, which temporarily discoloured his face and hands; and being of a sensitive disposition, he was averse to any public notice of the fact.

Out of her hearing there was a view largely entertained that he was a criminal trying to escape from justice by wrapping himself up so as to conceal himself altogether from the eye of the police. This idea sprang from the brain of Mr. Teddy Henfrey. No crime of any magnitude dating from the middle or end of February was known to have occurred. Elaborated in the imagination of Mr. Gould, the probationary assistant in the National School, this theory took the form that the stranger was an Anarchist in disguise, preparing explosives, and he resolved to undertake such detective operations as his time permitted. These consisted for the most part in looking very hard at the stranger whenever they met, or in asking people who had never seen the stranger leading questions about him. But he detected nothing.

Another school of opinion followed Mr. Fearenside, and either accepted the piebald view or some modification of it; as, for instance, Silas Durgan, who was heard to assert that "if he choses to show enself at fairs he'd make his fortune in no time," and being a bit of a theologian, compared the stranger to the man with the one talent. Yet another view explained the entire matter by regarding the stranger as a harmless lunatic. That had the advantage of accounting for everything straight away.

Between these main groups there were waverers and compro-misers. Sussex folk have few superstitions, and it was only after the events of early April that the thought of the supernatural was first whispered in the village. Even then it was only credited among the women folks.

But whatever they thought of him, people in Iping on the whole agreed in disliking him. His irritability, though it might have been comprehensible to an urban brain-worker, was an amazing thing to these quiet Sussex villagers. The frantic gesticulations they sur-prised now and then, the headlong pace after nightfall that swept him upon them round quiet corners, the inhuman bludgeoning of all the tentative advances of curiosity, the taste for twilight that led to the closing of doors, the pulling down of blinds, the extinc-tion of candles and lamps—who could agree with such goings on? They drew aside as he passed down the village, and when he had gone by, young humorists would up with coat-collars and down with hat-brims, and go pacing nervously after him in imitation of his occult bearing. There was a song popular at that time called the "Bogey Man"; Miss Statchell sang it at the schoolroom concert (in aid of the church lamps), and thereafter whenever one or two of the villagers were gathered together and the stranger appeared, a bar or so of this tune, more or less sharp or flat, was whistled in the midst of them. Also belated little children would call "Bogey Man!" after him, and make off tremulously elated.

Cuss, the general practitioner, was devoured by curiosity. The bandages excited his professional interest, the report of the thou-sand and one bottles aroused his jealous regard. All through April and May he coveted an opportunity of talking to the stranger; and at last, towards Whitsuntide, he could stand it no longer, and hit upon the subscription-list for a village nurse as an excuse. He was surprised to find that Mr. Hall did not know his guest's name. "He give a name," said Mrs. Hall—an assertion which was quite un-founded— "but I didn't rightly hear it." She thought it seemed so silly not to know the man's name.

Cuss rapped at the parlour door and entered. There was a fairly audible imprecation from within. "Pardon my intrusion," said Cuss, and then the door closed and cut Mrs. Hall off from the rest of the conversation.

She could hear the murmur of voices for the next ten minutes, then a cry of surprise, a stirring of feet, a chair flung aside, a bark of laughter, quick steps to the door, and Cuss appeared, his face white, his eyes staring over his shoulder. He left the door open behind him, and without looking at her strode across the hall and went down the steps, and she heard his feet hurrying along the road. He carried his hat in his hand. She stood behind the door, looking at the open door of the parlour. Then she heard the stranger laughing quietly, and then his footsteps came across the room. She could not see his face where she stood. The parlour door slammed, and the place was silent again.

Cuss went straight up the village to Bunting the vicar. "Am I mad?" Cuss began abruptly, as he entered the shabby little study. "Do I look like an insane person?"

"What's happened?" said the vicar, putting the ammonite on the loose sheets of his forthcoming sermon.

"That chap at the inn—"

"Well?"

"Give me something to drink," said Cuss, and he sat down.

When his nerves had been steadied by a glass of cheap sherry—the only drink the good vicar had available—he told him of the interview he had just had. "Went in," he gasped, "and began to demand a subscription for that Nurse Fund. He'd stuck his hands in his pockets as I came in, and he sat down lumpily in his chair. Sniffed. I told him I'd heard he took an interest in scientific things. He said yes. Sniffed again. Kept on sniffing all the time; evidently recently caught an infernal cold. No wonder, wrapped up like that! I developed the nurse idea, and all the while kept my eyes open. Bottles—chemicals—everywhere. Balance, test-tubes in stands, and a smell of—evening primrose. Would he subscribe? Said he'd consider it. Asked him, point-blank, was he researching. Said he was. A long research? Got quite cross. 'A damnable long research,' said he, blowing the cork out, so to speak. 'Oh,' said I. And out came the grievance. The man was just on the boil, and my question boiled him over. He had been given a prescription, most valuable pre-scription—what for he wouldn't say. Was it medical? 'Damn you! What are you fishing after?' I apologised. Dignified sniff and cough. He resumed. He'd read it. Five ingredients. Put it down; turned his head. Draught of air from window lifted the paper. Swish, rustle. He was working in a room with an open fireplace, he said. Saw a flicker, and there was the prescription burning and lifting chimneyward. Rushed towards it just as it whisked up chimney. So! Just at that point, to illustrate his story, out came his arm."

"Well?"

"No hand—just an empty sleeve. Lord! I thought, *that's* a de-formity! Got a cork arm, I suppose, and has taken it off. Then, I thought, there's something odd in that. What the devil keeps that sleeve up and open, if there's nothing in it? There was nothing in it, I tell you. Nothing down it, right down to the joint. I could see right down it to the elbow, and there was a glimmer of light shin-ing through a tear of the cloth. 'Good God!' I said. Then he stopped. Stared at me with those black goggles of his, and then at his sleeve."

"Well?"

"That's all. He never said a word; just glared, and put his sleeve back in his pocket quickly. 'I was saying,' said he, 'that there was the prescription burning, wasn't I?' Interrogative cough. 'How the devil,' said I, 'can you move an empty sleeve like that?' 'Empty sleeve?' 'Yes,' said I, 'an empty sleeve.'

"'It's an empty sleeve, is it? You saw it was an empty sleeve?' He stood up right away. I stood up too. He came towards me in three very slow steps, and stood quite close. Sniffed venomously. I didn't flinch, though I'm hanged if that bandaged knob of his, and those blinkers, aren't enough to unnerve any one, coming quietly up to you.

"'You said it was an empty sleeve?' he said. 'Certainly,' I said. At staring and saying nothing a barefaced man, unspectacled, starts scratch. Then very quietly he pulled his sleeve out of his pocket again, and raised his arm towards me as though he would show it to me again. He did it very, very slowly. I looked at it. Seemed an age. 'Well?' said I, clearing my throat, 'there's nothing in it.' Had to say something. I was beginning to feel frightened. I could see right down it. He extended it straight towards me, slowly, slowly—just like that—until the cuff was six inches from my face. Queer thing to see an empty sleeve come at you like that! And then—"

"Well?"

"Something—exactly like a finger and thumb it felt—nipped my nose."

Bunting began to laugh.

"There wasn't anything there!" said Cuss, his voice running up i nto a shriek at the "there." "It's all very well for you to laugh, but I tell you I was so startled, I hit his cuff hard, and turned round, and cut out of the room—I left him—"

Cuss stopped. There was no mistaking the sincerity of his panic. He turned round in a helpless way and took a second glass of the excellent vicar's very inferior sherry.

"When I hit his cuff," said Cuss, "I tell you, it felt exactly like hitting an arm. And there wasn't an arm! There wasn't the ghost of an arm!"

Mr. Bunting thought it over. He looked suspiciously at Cuss. "It's a most remarkable story," he said. He looked very wise and grave indeed. "It's really," said Mr. Bunting with judicial emphasis, "a most remarkable story."

5

THE BURGLARY AT THE VICARAGE

The facts of the burglary at the vicarage came to us chiefly through the medium of the vicar and his wife. It occurred in the small hours of Whit-Monday—the day devoted in Iping to the Club festivities. Mrs. Bunting, it seems, woke up suddenly in the stillness that comes before the dawn, with the strong impression that the door of their bedroom had opened and closed. She did not arouse her husband at first, but sat up in bed listening. She then distinctly heard the pad, pad, pad of bare feet coming out of the adjoining dressing-room and walking along the passage towards the staircase. As soon as she felt assured of this, she aroused the Rev. Mr. Bunting as quietly as possible. He did not strike a light, but putting on his spectacles, her dressing-gown, and his bath slippers, he went out on the landing to listen. He heard quite distinctly a fumbling going on at his study desk downstairs, and then a violent sneeze.

At that he returned to his bedroom, armed himself with the most obvious weapon, the poker, and descended the staircase as noiselessly as possible. Mrs. Bunting came out on the landing.

The hour was about four, and the ultimate darkness of the night was past. There was a faint shimmer of light in the hall, but the study doorway yawned impenetrably black. Everything was still except the faint creaking of the stairs under Mr. Bunting's tread, and the slight movements in the study. Then something snapped, the drawer was opened, and there was a rustle of papers. Then came an imprecation, and a match was struck and the study was flooded with yellow light. Mr. Bunting was now in the hall, and through the crack of the door he could see the desk and the open drawer and a candle burning on the desk. But the robber he could not see. He stood there in the hall undecided what to do, and Mrs. Bunting, her face white and intent, crept slowly downstairs after him. One thing kept up Mr. Bunting's courage: the persuasion that this burglar was a resident in the village.

They heard the chink of money, and realised that the robber had found the housekeeping reserve of gold—two pounds ten in half-sovereigns altogether. At that sound Mr. Bunting was nerved to abrupt action. Gripping the poker firmly, he rushed into the room, closely followed by Mrs. Bunting. "Surrender!" cried Mr. Bunting, fiercely, and then stopped amazed. Apparently the room was perfectly empty.

Yet their conviction that they had, that very moment, heard somebody moving in the room had amounted to a certainty. For half a minute, perhaps, they stood gaping, then Mrs. Bunting went across the room and looked behind the screen, while Mr. Bunting, by a kindred impulse, peered under the desk. Then Mrs. Bunting turned back the window-curtains, and Mr. Bunting looked up the chimney and probed it with the poker. Then Mrs. Bunting scrutinised the waste-paper basket and Mr. Bunting opened the lid of the coal-scuttle. Then they came to a stop and stood with eyes in-terrogating each other.

"I could have sworn—" said Mr. Bunting.

"The candle!" said Mr. Bunting. "Who lit the candle?"

"The drawer!" said Mrs. Bunting. "And the money's gone!"

She went hastily to the doorway.

"Of all the extraordinary occurrences—"

There was a violent sneeze in the passage. They rushed out, and as they did so the kitchen door slammed. "Bring the candle," said Mr. Bunting, and led the way. They both heard a sound of bolts being hastily shot back.

As he opened the kitchen door he saw through the scullery that the back door was just opening, and the faint light of early dawn displayed the dark masses of the garden beyond. He is certain that nothing went out of the door. It opened, stood open for a moment, and then closed with a slam. As it did so, the candle Mrs. Bunting was carrying from the study flickered and flared. It was a minute or more before they entered the kitchen.

The place was empty. They refastened the back door, exam-ined the kitchen, pantry, and scullery thoroughly, and at last went down into the cellar. There was not a soul to be found in the house, search as they would.

Daylight found the vicar and his wife, a quaintly-costumed little couple, still marvelling about on their own ground floor by the unnecessary light of a guttering candle.

6

THE FURNITURE THAT WENT MAD

Now it happened that in the early hours of Whit-Monday, be-fore Millie was hunted out for the day, Mr. Hall and Mrs. Hall both rose and went noiselessly down into the cellar. Their business there was of a private nature, and had something to do with the specific gravity of their beer. They had hardly entered the cellar when Mrs. Hall found she had forgotten to bring down a bottle of sarsaparilla from their joint-room. As she was the expert and principal opera-tor in this affair, Hall very properly went upstairs for it.

On the landing he was surprised to see that the stranger's door was ajar. He went on into his own room and found the bottle as he had been directed.

But returning with the bottle, he noticed that the bolts of the front door had been shot back, that the door was in fact simply on the latch. And with a flash of inspiration he connected this with the stranger's room upstairs and the suggestions of Mr. Teddy Henfrey. He distinctly remembered holding the candle while Mrs. Hall shot those bolts overnight. At the sight he stopped, gaping, then with the bottle still in his hand went upstairs again. He rapped at the stranger's door. There was no answer. He rapped again; then pushed the door wide open and entered.

It was as he expected. The bed, the room also, was empty. And what was stranger, even to his heavy intelligence, on the bedroom chair and along the rail of the bed were scattered the garments, the only garments so far as he knew, and the bandages of their guest. His big slouch hat even was cocked jauntily over the bed-post.

As Hall stood there he heard his wife's voice coming out of the depth of the cellar, with that rapid telescoping of the syllables and interrogative cocking up of the final words to a high note, by which the West Sussex villager is wont to indicate a brisk impatience. "Gearge! You gart what a wand?"

At that he turned and hurried down to her. "Janny," he said, over the rail of the cellar steps, "'tas the truth what Henfrey sez. 'E's not in uz room, 'e ent. And the front door's unbolted."

At first Mrs. Hall did not understand, and as soon as she did she resolved to see the empty room for herself. Hall, still holding the bottle, went first. "If 'e ent there," he said, "his close are. And what's 'e doin' without his close, then? 'Tas a most curious basness."

As they came up the cellar steps, they both, it was afterwards ascertained, fancied they heard the front door open and shut, but seeing it closed and nothing there, neither said a word to the other about it at the time. Mrs. Hall passed her husband in the passage and ran on first upstairs. Some one sneezed on the staircase. Hall, following six steps behind, thought that he heard her sneeze. She, going on first, was under the impression that Hall was sneezing. She flung open the door and stood regarding the room. "Of all the curious!" she said.

She heard a sniff close behind her head as it seemed, and, turning, was surprised to see Hall a dozen feet off on the top-most stair. But in another moment he was beside her. She bent forward and put her hand on the pillow and then under the clothes.

"Cold," she said. "He's been up this hour or more."

As she did so, a most extraordinary thing happened—the bed-clothes gathered themselves together, leapt up suddenly into a sort of peak, and then jumped headlong over the bottom rail. It was exactly as if a hand had clutched them in the centre and flung them aside. Immediately after, the stranger's hat hopped off the bed-post, describing a whirling flight in the air through the better part of a circle, and then dashed straight at Mrs. Hall's face. Then as swiftly came the sponge from the washstand; and then the chair, flinging the stranger's coat and trousers carelessly aside, and laughing dryly in a voice singularly like the stranger's, turned it-self up with its four legs at Mrs. Hall, seemed to take aim at her for a moment, and charged at her. She screamed and turned, and then the chair legs came gently but firmly against her back and impelled her and Hall out of the room. The door slammed violently and was locked. The chair and bed seemed to be executing a dance of tri-umph for a moment, and then abruptly everything was still.

Mrs. Hall was left almost in a fainting condition in Mr. Hall's arms on the landing. It was with the greatest difficulty that Mr. Hall and Millie, who had been roused by her scream of alarm, suc-ceeded in getting her downstairs, and applying the restoratives customary in these cases.

"'Tas sperrits," said Mrs. Hall. "I know 'tas sperrits. I've read in papers of en. Tables and chairs leaping and dancing..."

"Take a drop more, Janny," said Hall. "'Twill steady ye."

"Lock him out," said Mrs. Hall. "Don't let him come in again. I half guessed—I might ha' known. With them goggling eyes and bandaged head, and never going to church of a Sunday. And all they bottles—more'n it's right for any one to have. He's put the sperrits into the furniture. My good old furniture! 'Twas in that very chair my poor dear mother used to sit when I was a little girl. To think it should rise up against me now!"

"Just a drop more, Janny," said Hall. "Your nerves is all upset."

They sent Millie across the street through the golden five o'clock sunshine to rouse up Mr. Sandy Wadgers, the blacksmith. Mr. Hall's compliments and the furniture upstairs was behaving most extraordinary. Would Mr. Wadgers come round? He was a knowing man, was Mr. Wadgers, and very resourceful. He took quite a grave view of the case. "Arm darmed ef thet ent witchcraft," was the view of Mr. Sandy Wadgers. "You warnt horseshoes for such gentry as he."

He came round greatly concerned. They wanted him to lead the way upstairs to the room, but he didn't seem to be in any hurry. He preferred to talk in the passage. Over the way Huxter's apprentice came out and began taking down the shutters of the tobacco window. He was called over to join the discussion. Mr. Huxter naturally followed in the course of a few minutes. The Anglo-Saxon genius for parliamentary government asserted itself; there was a great deal of talk and no decisive action. "Let's have the facts first," insisted Mr. Sandy Wadgers. "Let's be sure we'd be acting perfectly right in bustin' that there door open. A door onbust is always open to bustin', but ye can't onbust a door once you've busted en."

And suddenly and most wonderfully the door of the room upstairs opened of its own accord, and as they looked up in amazement, they saw descending the stairs the muffled figure of the stranger staring more blackly and blankly than ever with those unreasonably large blue glass eyes of his. He came down stiffly and slowly, staring all the time; he walked across the passage staring, then stopped.

"Look there!" he said, and their eyes followed the direction of his gloved finger and saw a bottle of sarsaparilla hard by the cellar door. Then he entered the parlour, and suddenly, swiftly, viciously slammed the door in their faces.

Not a word was spoken until the last echoes of the slam had died away. They stared at one another. "Well, if that don't lick everything!" said Mr. Wadgers, and left the alternative unsaid.

"I'd go in and ask'n 'bout it," said Wadgers, to Mr. Hall. "I'd d'mand an explanation."

It took some time to bring the landlady's husband up to that pitch. At last he rapped, opened the door, and got as far as, "Excuse me—"

"Go to the devil!" said the stranger in a tremendous voice, and "Shut that door after you." So that brief interview terminated.

7

THE UNVEILING OF THE STRANGER

The stranger went into the little parlour of the Coach and Horses about half-past five in the morning, and there he remained until near midday, the blinds down, the door shut, and none, after Hall's repulse, venturing near him.

All that time he must have fasted. Thrice he rang his bell, the third time furiously and continuously, but no one answered him. "Him and his 'go to the devil' indeed!" said Mrs. Hall. Presently came an imperfect rumour of the burglary at the vicarage, and two and two were put together. Hall, assisted by Wadgers, went off to find Mr. Shuckleforth, the magistrate, and take his advice. No one ventured upstairs.

How the stranger occupied himself is unknown. Now and then he would stride violently up and down, and twice came an outburst of curses, a tearing of paper, and a violent smashing of bottles.

The little group of scared but curious people increased. Mrs. Huxter came over; some gay young fellows resplendent in black ready-made jackets and piqu paper ties, for it was Whit-Monday, joined the group with confused interrogations. Young Archie Harker distinguished himself by going up the yard and trying to peep under the window-blinds. He could see nothing, but gave reason for supposing that he did, and others of the Iping youth presently joined him.

It was the finest of all possible Whit-Mondays, and down the village street stood a row of nearly a dozen booths and a shooting gallery, and on the grass by the forge were three yellow and chocolate waggons and some picturesque strangers of both sexes putting up a cocoanut shy. The gentlemen wore blue jerseys, the ladies white aprons and quite fashionable hats with heavy plumes. Wodger of the Purple Fawn and Mr. Jaggers the cobbler, who also sold second-hand ordinary bicycles, were stretching a string of union-jacks and royal ensigns (which had originally celebrated the Jubilee) across the road...

And inside, in the artificial darkness of the parlour, into which only one thin jet of sunlight penetrated, the stranger, hungry we must suppose, and fearful, hidden in his uncomfortable hot wrappings, pored through his dark glasses upon his paper or chinked his dirty little bottles, and occasionally swore savagely at the boys, audible if invisible, outside the windows. In the corner by the fireplace lay the fragments of half a dozen smashed bottles, and a pungent tang of chlorine tainted the air. So much we know from what was heard at the time and from what was subsequently seen in the room.

About noon he suddenly opened his parlour door and stood glaring fixedly at the three or four people in the bar. "Mrs. Hall," he said. Somebody went sheepishly and called for Mrs. Hall.

Mrs. Hall appeared after an interval, a little short of breath, but all the fiercer for that. Hall was still out. She had deliberated over the scene, and she came holding a little tray with an unsettled bill upon it. "Is it your bill you're wanting, sir?" she said.

"Why wasn't my breakfast laid? Why haven't you prepared my meals and answered my bell? Do you think I live without eating?"

"Why isn't my bill paid?" said Mrs. Hall. "That's what I want to know."

"I told you three days ago I was awaiting a remittance—"

"I told you two days ago I wasn't going to await no remittances. You can't grumble if your breakfast waits a bit, if my bill's been waiting these five days, can you?"

The stranger swore briefly but vividly.

"Nar, nar!" from the bar.

"And I'd thank you kindly, sir, if you'd keep your swearing to yourself, sir," said Mrs. Hall.

The stranger stood looking more like an angry diving-helmet than ever. It was universally felt in the bar that Mrs. Hall had the better of him. His next words showed as much.

"Look here, my good woman—" he began.

"Don't good woman *me*," said Mrs. Hall.

"I've told you my remittance hasn't come—"

"Remittance indeed!" said Mrs. Hall.

"Still, I daresay in my pocket—"

"You told me two days ago that you hadn't anything but a sovereign's worth of silver upon you—"

"Well, I've found some more—"

"'Ul-lo!" from the bar.

"I wonder where you found it!" said Mrs. Hall.

That seemed to annoy the stranger very much. He stamped his foot. "What do you mean?" he said.

"That I wonder where you found it," said Mrs. Hall. "And before I take any bills or get any breakfasts, or do any such things whatsoever, you got to tell me one or two things I don't understand, and what nobody don't understand, and what everybody is very anxious to understand. I want know what you been doing t' my chair upstairs, and I want know how 'tis your room was empty, and how you got in again. Them as stops in this house comes in by the doors—that's the rule of the house, and that you *didn't* do, and what I want know is how you *did* come in. And I want know—"

Suddenly the stranger raised his gloved hands clenched, stamped his foot, and said, "Stop!" with such extraordinary violence that he silenced her instantly.

"You don't understand," he said, "who I am or what I am. I'll show you. By Heaven! I'll show you." Then he put his open palm over his face and withdrew it. The centre of his face became a black cavity. "Here," he said. He stepped forward and handed Mrs. Hall something which she, staring at his metamorphosed face, accepted automatically. Then, when she saw what it was, she screamed loudly, dropped it, and staggered back. The nose—it was the stranger's nose! pink and shining—rolled on the floor.

Then he removed his spectacles, and every one in the bar gasped. He took off his hat, and with a violent gesture tore at his whiskers and bandages. For a moment they resisted him. A flash of horrible anticipation passed through the bar. "Oh, my Gard!" said some one. Then off they came.

It was worse than anything. Mrs. Hall, standing open-mouthed and horror-struck, shrieked at what she saw, and made for the door of the house. Every one began to move. They were prepared for scars, disfigurements, tangible horrors, but nothing! The bandages and false hair flew across the passage into the bar, making a hobbledehoy jump to avoid them. Every one tumbled on every one else down the steps. For the man who stood there shouting some incoherent explanation, was a solid gesticulating figure up to the coat-collar of him, and then—nothingness, no visible thing at all!

People down the village heard shouts and shrieks, and looking up the street saw the Coach and Horses violently firing out its humanity. They saw Mrs. Hall fall down and Mr. Teddy Henfrey jump to avoid tumbling over her, and then they heard the frightful screams of Millie, who, emerging suddenly from the kitchen at the noise of the tumult, had come upon the headless stranger from behind.

Forthwith every one all down the street, the sweet-stuff seller, cocoanut shy proprietor and his assistant, the swing man, little boys and girls, rustic dandies, smart wenches, smocked elders and aproned gipsies, began running towards the inn; and in a miraculously short space of time a crowd of perhaps forty people, and rapidly increasing, swayed and hooted and inquired and exclaimed and suggested, in front of Mrs. Hall's establishment. Every one seemed eager to talk at once, and the result was babel. A small group supported Mrs. Hall, who was picked up in a state of collapse. There was a conference, and the incredible evidence of a vociferous eyewitness. "O'Bogey!" "What's he been doin', then?" "Ain't hurt the girl, 'as 'e?" "Run at en with a knife, I believe." "No 'ed, I tell ye. I don't mean no manner of speaking, I mean *marn without a 'ed!"* "Narnsense! 'tas some conjuring trick." "Fetched off 'is wrappin's, 'e did—"

In its struggles to see in through the open door, the crowd formed itself into a straggling wedge, with the more adventurous apex nearest the inn. "He stood for a moment, I heerd the gal scream, and he turned. I saw her skirts whisk, and he went after her. Didn't take ten seconds. Back he comes with a knife in uz hand and a loaf; stood just as if he was staring. Not a moment ago. Went in that there door. I tell 'e, 'e ain't gart no 'ed 't all. You just missed en—"

There was a disturbance behind, and the speaker stopped to step aside for a little procession that was marching very resolutely towards the house—first Mr. Hall, very red and determined, then Mr. Bobby Jaffers, the village constable, and then the wary Mr. Wadgers. They had come now armed with a warrant.

People shouted conflicting information of the recent circumstances. "'Ed or no 'ed," said Jaffers, "I got to 'rest en, and 'rest en I *will.*"

Mr. Hall marched up the steps, marched straight to the door of the parlour and flung it open. "Constable," he said, "do your duty."

Jaffers marched in, Hall next, Wadgers last. They saw in the dim light the headless figure facing them, with a gnawed crust of bread in one gloved hand and a chunk of cheese in the other.

"That's him!" said Hall.

"What the devil's this?" came in a tone of angry expostulation from above the collar of the figure.

"You're a damned rum customer, mister," said Mr. Jaffers. "But 'ed or no 'ed, the warrant says 'body,' and duty's duty—"

"Keep off!" said the figure, starting back.

Abruptly he whipped down the bread and cheese, and Mr. Hall just grasped the knife on the table in time to save it. Off came the stranger's left glove and was slapped in Jaffers' face. In another moment Jaffers, cutting short some statement concerning a warrant, had gripped him by the handless wrist and caught his invisible throat. He got a sounding kick on the shin that made him shout, but he kept his grip. Hall sent the knife sliding along the table to

Wadgers, who acted as goal-keeper for the offensive, so to speak, and then stepped forward as Jaffers and the stranger swayed and staggered towards him, clutching and hitting in. A chair stood in the way, and went aside with a crash as they came down together.

"Get the feet," said Jaffers between his teeth.

Mr. Hall, endeavoring to act on instructions, receiving a sounding kick in the ribs that disposed of him for a moment, and Mr. Wadgers, seeing the decapitated stranger had rolled over and got the upper side of Jaffers, retreated towards the door, knife in hand, and so collided with Mr. Huxter and the Siddermorton carter coming to the rescue of law and order. At the same moment down came three or four bottles from the chiffonier and shot a web of pungency into the air of the room.

"I'll surrender," cried the stranger, though he had Jaffers down, and in another moment he stood up panting, a strange figure, headless and handless—for he had pulled off his right glove now as well as his left. "It's no good," he said, as if sobbing for breath.

It was the strangest thing in the world to hear that voice coming as if out of empty space, but the Sussex peasants are perhaps the most matter-of-fact people under the sun. Jaffers got up also and produced a pair of handcuffs. Then he started.

"I say!" said Jaffers, brought up short by a dim realisation of the incongruity of the whole business. "Darm it! Can't use 'em as I can see."

The stranger ran his arm down his waistcoat, and as if by a miracle the buttons to which his empty sleeve pointed became undone. Then he said something about his shin, and stooped down. He seemed to be fumbling with his shoes and socks.

"Why!" said Huxter, suddenly, "that's not a man at all. It's just empty clothes. Look! You can see down his collar and the linings of his clothes. I could put my arm—"

He extended his hand; it seemed to meet something in midair, and he drew it back with a sharp exclamation. "I wish you'd keep your fingers out of my eye," said the aerial voice, in a tone of savage expostulation. "The fact is, I'm all here: head, hands, legs, and all the rest of it, but it happens I'm invisible. It's a confounded nuisance, but I am. That's no reason why I should be poked to pieces by every stupid bumpkin in Iping, is it?"

The suit of clothes, now all unbuttoned and hanging loosely upon its unseen supports, stood up, arms akimbo.

Several other of the men folks had now entered the room, so that it was closely crowded. "Invisible, eigh?" said Huxter, ignoring the stranger's abuse. "Who ever heard the likes of that?"

"It's strange, perhaps, but it's not a crime. Why am I assaulted by a policeman in this fashion?"

"Ah! that's a different matter," said Jaffers. "No doubt you are a bit difficult to see in this light, but I got a warrant, and it's all correct. What I'm after ain't no invisibility—it's burglary. There's a house been broken into and money took."

"Well?"

"And circumstances certainly point—"

"Stuff and nonsense!" said the Invisible Man.

"I hope so, sir; but I've got my instructions."

"Well," said the stranger, "I'll come. I'll *come*. But no handcuffs."

"It's the regular thing," said Jaffers.

"No handcuffs," stipulated the stranger.

"Pardon me," said Jaffers.

Abruptly the figure sat down, and before any one could realise what was being done, the slippers, socks, and trousers had been kicked off under the table. Then he sprang up again and flung off his coat.

"Here, stop that," said Jaffers, suddenly realising what was happening. He gripped the waist-coat; it struggled, and the shirt slipped out of it and left it limp and empty in his hand. "Hold him!" said Jaffers loudly. "Once he gets they things off—!"

"Hold him!" cried every one, and there was a rush at the fluttering white shirt which was now all that was visible of the stranger.

The shirt-sleeve planted a shrewd blow in Hall's face that stopped his open-armed advance, and sent him backward into old Toothsome the sexton, and in another moment the garment was lifted up and became convulsed and vacantly flapping about the arms, even as a shirt that is being thrust over a man's head. Jaffers clutched at it, and only helped to pull it off; he was struck in the mouth out of the air, and incontinently drew his truncheon and smote Teddy Henfrey savagely upon the crown of his head.

"Look out!" said everybody, fencing at random and hitting at nothing. "Hold him! Shut the door! Don't let him loose! I got something! Here he is!" A perfect babel of noises they made. Everybody, it seemed, was being hit all at once, and Sandy Wadgers, knowing as ever and his wits sharpened by a frightful blow in the nose, reopened the door and led the rout. The others, following incontinently, were jammed for a moment in the corner by the doorway. The hitting continued. Phipps, the Unitarian, had a front tooth broken, and Henfrey was injured in the cartilage of his ear. Jaffers was struck under the jaw, and, turning, caught at something that intervened between him and Huxter in the mêlée, and prevented their coming together. He felt a muscular chest, and in another moment the whole mass of struggling, excited men shot out into the crowded hall.

"I got him!" shouted Jaffers, choking and reeling through them all, and wrestling with purple face and swelling veins against his unseen enemy.

Men staggered right and left as the extraordinary conflict swayed swiftly towards the house door, and went spinning down the half-dozen steps of the inn. Jaffers cried in a strangled voice—holding tight, nevertheless, and making play with his knee—spun round, and fell heavily undermost with his head on the gravel. Only then did his fingers relax.

There were excited cries of "Hold him!" "Invisible!" and so forth, and a young fellow, a stranger in the place whose name did not come to light, rushed in at once, caught something, missed his hold, and fell over the constable's prostrate body. Halfway across the road, a woman screamed as something pushed by her; a dog, kicked apparently, yelped and ran howling into Huxter's yard, and with that the transit of the Invisible Man was accomplished. For a space people stood amazed and gesticulating, and then came Panic, and scattered them abroad through the village as a gust scatters dead leaves.

But Jaffers lay quite still, face upward and knees bent.

8
In Transit

The eighth chapter is exceedingly brief, and relates that Gibbins, the amateur naturalist of the district, while lying out on the spacious open downs without a soul within a couple of miles of him, as he thought, and almost dozing, heard close to him the sound as of a man coughing, sneezing, and then swearing savagely to himself; and looking, beheld nothing. Yet the voice was indisputable. It continued to swear with that breadth and variety that distinguishes the swearing of a cultivated man. It grew to a climax, diminished again, and died away in the distance, going as it seemed to him in the direction of Adderdean. It lifted to a spasmodic sneeze and ended. Gibbins had heard nothing of the morning's occurrences, but the phenomenon was so striking and disturbing that his philosophical tranquility vanished; he got up hastily, and hurried down the steepness of the hill towards the village, as fast as he could go.

9
Mr. Thomas Marvel

You must picture Mr. Thomas Marvel as a person of copious, flexible visage, a nose of cylindrical protrusion, a liquorish, ample, fluctuating mouth, and a beard of bristling eccentricity. His figure inclined to embonpoint; his short limbs accentuated this inclination. He wore a furry silk hat, and the frequent substitution of twine and shoe-laces for buttons, apparent at critical points of his costume, marked a man essentially bachelor.

Mr. Thomas Marvel was sitting with his feet in a ditch by the roadside over the down toward Adderdean, about a mile and a half out of Iping. His feet, save for socks of irregular openwork, were bare, his big toes were broad, and pricked like the ears of a watchful dog. In a leisurely manner—he did everything in a leisurely manner—he was contemplating trying on a pair of boots. They were the soundest boots he had come across for a long time, but too large for him; whereas the ones he had were, in dry weather, a very comfortable fit, but too thin-soled for damp. Mr. Thomas Marvel hated roomy boots, but then he hated damp. He had never properly thought out which he hated most, and it was a pleasant day, and there was nothing better to do. So he put the four boots in a graceful group on the turf and looked at them. And seeing them there among the grass and springing agrimony, it suddenly occurred to him that both pairs were exceedingly ugly to see. He was not at all startled by a voice behind him.

"They're boots, anyhow," said the voice.

"They are—charity boots," said Mr. Thomas Marvel, with his head on one side regarding them distastefully; "and which is the ugliest pair in the whole blessed universe, I'm darned if I know!"

"H'm," said the voice.

"I've worn worse—in fact, I've worn none. But none so owdacious ugly—if you'll allow the expression. I've been cadging boots—in particular—for days. Because I was sick of them. They're sound enough, of course. But a gentleman on tramp sees such a thundering lot of his boots. And if you'll believe me, I've raised nothing in the whole blessed county, try as I would, but them. Look at 'em! And a good county for boots, too, in a general way. But it's just my promiscuous luck. I've got my boots in this county ten years or more. And then they treat you like this."

"It's a beast of a county," said the voice. "And pigs for people."

"Ain't it?" said Mr. Thomas Marvel. "Lord! But them boots! It beats it."

He turned his head over his shoulder to the right, to look at the boots of his interlocutor with a view to comparisons, and lo! where the boots of his interlocutor should have been were neither legs nor boots. He turned his head over his shoulder to the left, and there also were neither legs nor boots. He was irradiated by the dawn of a great amazement. "Where are yar?" said Mr. Thomas Marvel over his shoulder and coming round on all fours. He saw a stretch of empty downs with the wind swaying and remote green-pointed furze bushes.

"Am I drunk?" said Mr. Marvel. "Have I had visions? Was I talking to myself? What the—"

"Don't be alarmed," said a voice.

"None of your ventriloquising *me*," said Mr. Thomas Marvel, rising sharply to his feet. "Where *are* yer? Alarmed, indeed!"

"Don't be alarmed," repeated the voice.

"*You'll* be alarmed in a minute, you silly fool," said Mr. Thomas Marvel. "Where *are* yer? Lemme get my mark on yer—"

"Are you *buried*?" said Mr. Thomas Marvel, after an interval.

There was no answer. Mr. Thomas Marvel stood bootless and amazed, his jacket nearly thrown off.

"Peewit," said a peewit, very remote.

"Peewit, indeed!" said Mr. Thomas Marvel. "This ain't no time for foolery." The down was desolate, east and west, north and south; the road with its shallow ditches and white bordering stakes, ran smooth and empty north and south, and, save for that peewit, the blue sky was empty too. "So help me," said Mr. Thomas Marvel, shuffling his coat on to his shoulders again. "It's the drink! I might ha' known."

"It's not the drink," said the voice. "You keep your nerves steady."

"Ow!" said Mr. Marvel, and his face grew white amidst its patches. "It's the drink," his lips repeated noiselessly. He remained staring about him, rotating slowly backwards. "I could have *swore* I heard a voice," he whispered.

"Of course you did."

"It's there again," said Mr. Marvel, closing his eyes and clasping his hand on his brow with a tragic gesture. He was suddenly taken by the collar and shaken violently and left more dazed than ever. "Don't be a fool," said the voice.

"I'm—off—my—blooming—chump," said Mr. Marvel. "It's no good. It's fretting about them blarsted boots. I'm off my blessed blooming chump. Or it's spirits."

"Neither one thing nor the other," said the voice. "Listen!"

"Chump," said Mr. Marvel.

"One minute," said the voice penetratingly,—tremulous with self-control.

"Well?" said Mr. Thomas Marvel, with a strange feeling of having been dug in the chest by a finger.

"You think I'm just imagination? Just imagination?"

"What else can you be?" said Mr. Thomas Marvel, rubbing the back of his neck.

"Very well," said the voice, in a tone of relief. "Then I'm going to throw flints at you till you think differently."

"But where *are* yer?"

The voice made no answer. Whiz came a flint, apparently out of the air, and missed Mr. Marvel's shoulder by a hair's breadth. Mr. Marvel, turning, saw a flint jerk up into the air, trace a complicated path, hang for a moment, and then fling at his feet with almost invisible rapidity. He was too amazed to dodge. Whiz it came, and ricocheted from a bare toe into the ditch. Mr. Thomas Marvel jumped a foot and howled aloud. Then he started to run, tripped over an unseen obstacle, and came head over heels into a sitting position.

"Now," said the voice, as a third stone curved upward and hung in the air above the tramp. "Am I imagination?"

Mr. Marvel by way of reply struggled to his feet, and was immediately rolled over again. He lay quiet for a moment. "If you struggle any more," said the voice, "I shall throw the flint at your head."

"It's a fair do," said Mr. Thomas Marvel, sitting up, taking his wounded toe in hand and fixing his eye on the third missle. "I don't understand it. Stones flinging themselves. Stones talking. Put yourself down. Rot away. I'm done."

The third flint fell.

"It's very simple," said the voice. "I'm an invisible man."

"Tell us something I don't know," said Mr. Marvel, gasping with pain. "Where you've hid—how you do it—I *don't* know, I'm beat."

"That's all," said the voice. "I'm invisible. That's what I want you to understand."

"Any one could see that. There is no need for you to be so confounded impatient, mister. *Now* then. Give us a notion. How are you hid?"

"I'm invisible. That's the great point. And what I want you to understand is this—"

"But whereabouts?" interrupted Mr. Marvel.

"Here! Six yards in front of you."

"Oh, *come!* I ain't blind. You'll be telling me next you're just thin air. I'm not one of your ignorant tramps—"

"Yes, I am—thin air. You're looking through me."

"What! Ain't there any stuff to you? *Vox et*—what is it?—jabber. Is it that?

"I am just a human being—solid, needing food and drink, needing covering too—But I'm invisible. You see? Invisible. Simple idea. Invisible."

"What, real like?"

"Yes, real."

"Let's have a hand of you," said Marvel, "if you *are* real. It won't be so darn out-of-the-way like, then—*Lord!*" he said, "how you made me jump!—gripping me like that!"

He felt the hand that had closed round his wrist with his disengaged fingers, and his touch went timorously up the arm, patted a muscular chest, and explored a bearded face. Marvel's face was astonishment.

"I'm dashed!" he said. "If this don't beat cock-fighting! Most remarkable!—And there I can see a rabbit clean through you, 'arf a mile away! Not a bit of you visible—except—"

He scrutinised the apparently empty space keenly. "You 'aven't been eatin' bread and cheese?" he asked, holding the invisible arm.

"You're quite right, and it's not quite assimilated into the system."

"Ah!" said Mr. Marvel. "Sort of ghostly, though."

"Of course, all this isn't so wonderful as you think."

"It's quite wonderful enough for *my* modest wants," said Mr. Thomas Marvel. "Howjer manage it? How the dooce is it done?"

"It's too long a story. And besides—"

"I tell you, the whole business fair beats me," said Mr. Marvel.

"What I want to say at present is this: I need help. I have come to that—I came upon you suddenly. I was wandering, mad with rage, naked, impotent. I could have murdered. And I saw you—"

"*Lord!*" said Mr. Marvel.

"I came up behind you—hesitated—went on—"

Mr. Marvel's expression was eloquent.

"—then stopped. 'Here,' I said, 'is an outcast like myself. This is the man for me.' So I turned back and came to you—you. And—"

"*Lord!*" said Mr. Marvel. "But I'm all in a dizzy. May I ask— How is it? And what you may be requiring in the way of help?— Invisible!"

"I want you to help me get clothes—and shelter—and then, with other things. I've left them long enough. If you won't—well! But you *will—must.*"

"Look here," said Mr. Marvel. "I'm too flabbergasted. Don't knock me about any more. And leave me go. I must get steady a bit. And you've pretty near broken my toe. It's all so unreasonable. Empty downs, empty sky. Nothing visible for miles except the bosom of Nature. And then comes a voice. A voice out of heaven! And stones! And a fist—Lord!"

"Pull yourself together," said the voice, "for you have to do the job I've chosen for you."

Mr. Marvel blew out his cheeks, and his eyes were round.

"I've chosen you," said the voice. "You are the only man, except some of those fools down there, who knows there is such a thing as an invisible man. You have to be my helper. Help me— and I will do great things for you. An invisible man is a man of power." He stopped for a moment to sneeze violently.

"But if you betray me," he said, "if you fail to do as I direct you—"

He paused and tapped Mr. Marvel's shoulder smartly. Mr. Marvel gave a yelp of terror at the touch. "I don't want to betray you," said Mr. Marvel, edging away from the direction of the fingers. "Don't you go a-thinking that, whatever you do. All I want to do is to help you—just tell me what I got to do. (Lord!) Whatever you want done, that I'm most willing to do."

10
MR. MARVEL'S VISIT TO IPING

After the first gusty panic had spent itself Iping became argumentative. Scepticism suddenly reared its head—rather nervous

scepticism, not at all assured of its back, but scepticism nevertheless. It is so much easier not to believe in an invisible man; and
those who had actually seen him dissolve into air, or felt the
strength of his arm, could be counted on the fingers of two hands.
And of these witnesses Mr. Wadgers was presently missing, having
retired impregnably behind the bolts and bars of his own house,
and Jaffers was lying stunned in the parlour of the Coach and
Horses. Great and strange ideas transcending experience often
have less effect upon men and women than smaller, more tangible
considerations. Iping was gay with bunting, and everybody was in
gala dress. Whit-Monday had been looked forward to for a month
or more. By the afternoon even those who believed in the Unseen
were beginning to resume their little amusements in a tentative
fashion, on the supposition that he had quite gone away, and with
the sceptics he was already a jest. But people, sceptics and believ-
ers alike, were remarkably sociable all that day.

Haysman's meadow was gay with a tent, in which Mrs. Bunting
and other ladies were preparing tea, while, without, the Sunday-
school children ran races and played games under the noisy guidance of the curate and the Misses Cuss and Sackbut. No doubt there
was a slight uneasiness in the air, but people for the most part had
the sense to conceal whatever imaginative qualms they experienced. On the village green an inclined string, down which, clinging the while to a pulley-swung handle, one could be hurled violently against a sack at the other end, came in for considerable
favour among the adolescent. There were swings and cocoanut
shies and promenading, and the steam organ attached to the swings
filled the air with a pungent flavour of oil and with equally pungent
music. Members of the Club, who had attended church in the morning, were splendid in badges of pink and green, and some of the
gayer-minded had also adorned their bowler hats with brilliant-
coloured favours of ribbon. Old Fletcher, whose conceptions of
holiday-making were severe, was visible through the jasmine about
his window or through the open door (whichever way you chose to
look), poised delicately on a plank supported on two chairs, and
whitewashing the ceiling of his front room.

About four o'clock a stranger entered the village from the direction of the downs. He was a short, stout person in an extraordinarily shabby top hat, and he appeared to be very much out of breath. His cheeks were alternately limp and tightly puffed. His mottled face was apprehensive, and he moved with a sort of reluctant alacrity. He turned the corner by the church, and directed his way to the Coach and Horses. Among others old Fletcher remembers seeing him, and indeed the old gentleman was so struck by his peculiar agitation that he inadvertently allowed a quantity of whitewash to run down the brush into the sleeve of his coat while regarding him.

This stranger, to the perceptions of the proprietor of the cocoanut shy, appeared to be talking to himself, and Mr. Huxter remarked the same thing. He stopped at the foot of the Coach and Horses steps, and, according to Mr. Huxter, appeared to undergo a severe internal struggle before he could induce himself to enter the house. Finally he marched up the steps, and was seen by Mr. Huxter to turn to the left and open the door of the parlour. Mr. Huxter heard voices from within the room and from the bar apprising the man of his error. "That room's private!" said Hall, and the stranger shut the door clumsily and went into the bar.

In the course of a few minutes he reappeared, wiping his lips with the back of his hand with an air of quiet satisfaction that somehow impressed Mr. Huxter as assumed. He stood looking about him for some moments, and then Mr. Huxter saw him walk in an oddly furtive manner towards the gates of the yard, upon which the parlour window opened. The stranger, after some hesitation, leant against one of the gate-posts, produced a short clay pipe, and prepared to fill it. His fingers trembled while doing so. He lit it clumsily, and folding his arms began to smoke in a languid attitude, an attitude which his occasional quick glances up the yard altogether belied.

All this Mr. Huxter saw over the canisters of the tobacco window, and the singularity of the man's behaviour prompted him to maintain his observation.

Presently the stranger stood up abruptly and put his pipe in his pocket. Then he vanished into the yard. Forthwith Mr. Huxter, conceiving he was witness of some petty larceny, leapt round his

counter and ran out into the road to intercept the thief. As he did
so, Mr. Marvel reappeared, his hat askew, a big bundle in a blue
table-cloth in one hand, and three books tied together—as it proved
afterwards with the Vicar's braces—in the other. Directly he saw
Huxter he gave a sort of gasp, and turning sharply to the left, began
to run. "Stop thief!" cried Huxter, and set off after him. Mr. Huxter's sensations were vivid but brief. He saw the man just before
him and spurting briskly for the church corner and the hill road.
He saw the village flags and festivities beyond, and a face or so
turned towards him. He bawled, "Stop!" again. He had hardly gone
ten strides before his shin was caught in some mysterious fashion,
and he was no longer running, but flying with inconceivable rapidity through the air. He saw the ground suddenly close to his
face. The world seemed to splash into a million whirling specks of
light, and subsequent proceedings interested him no more.

11

IN THE COACH AND HORSES

Now in order clearly to understand what had happened in the
inn, it is necessary to go back to the moment when Mr. Marvel first
came into view of Mr. Huxter's window. At that precise moment
Mr. Cuss and Mr. Bunting were in the parlour. They were seriously
investigating the strange occurrences of the morning, and were,
with Mr. Hall's permission, making a thorough examination of the
Invisible Man's belongings. Jaffers had partially recovered from
his fall and had gone home in the charge of his sympathetic friends.
The stranger's scattered garments had been removed by Mrs. Hall
and the room tidied up. And on the table under the window where
the stranger had been wont to work, Cuss had hit almost at once
on three big books in manuscript labelled "Diary."

"Diary!" said Cuss, putting the three books on the table. "Now,
at any rate, we shall learn something." The Vicar stood with his
hands on the table.

"Diary," repeated Cuss, sitting down, putting two volumes to
support the third, and opening it. "H'm—no name on the fly-leaf.
Bother!—cypher. And figures."

The Vicar came round to look over his shoulder.

Cuss turned the pages over with a face suddenly disappointed. "I'm—dear me! It's all cypher, Bunting."

"There are no diagrams?" asked Mr. Bunting. "No illustrations throwing light—"

"See for yourself," said Mr. Cuss. "Some of it's mathematical and some of it's Russian or some such language (to judge by the letters), and some of it's Greek. Now the Greek I thought you—"

"Of course," said Mr. Bunting, taking out and wiping his spectacles and feeling suddenly very uncomfortable,—for he had no Greek left in his mind worth talking about; "yes—the Greek, of course, may furnish a clue."

"I'll find you a place."

"I'd rather glance through the volumes first," said Mr. Bunting, still wiping. "A general impression first, Cuss, and *then*, you know, we can go looking for clues."

He coughed, put on his glasses, arranged them fastidiously, coughed again, and wished something would happen to avert the seemingly inevitable exposure. Then he took the volume Cuss handed him in a leisurely manner. And then something did happen.

The door opened suddenly.

Both gentlemen started violently, looked around, and were relieved to see a sporadically rosy face beneath a furry silk hat. "Tap?" asked the face, and stood staring.

"No," said both gentlemen at once.

"Over the other side, my man," said Mr. Bunting. And "Please shut that door," said Mr. Cuss irritably.

"All right," said the intruder, as it seemed, in a low voice curiously different from the huskiness of its first enquiry. "Right you are," said the intruder in the former voice. "Stand clear!" and he vanished and closed the door.

"A sailor, I should judge," said Mr. Bunting. "Amusing fellows they are. Stand clear! indeed. A nautical term referring to his getting back out of the room, I suppose."

"I daresay so," said Cuss. "My nerves are all loose to-day. It quite made me jump—the door opening like that."

Mr. Bunting smiled as if he had not jumped. "And now," he said with a sigh, "these books."

"One minute," said Cuss, and went and locked the door. "Now I think we are safe from interruption."

Some one sniffed as he did so.

"One thing is indisputable," said Bunting, drawing up a chair next to that of Cuss. "There certainly have been very strange things happen in Iping during the last few days—very strange. I cannot of course believe in this absurd invisibility story—"

"It's incredible," said Cuss, "—incredible. But the fact remains that I saw—I certainly saw right down his sleeve—"

"But did you—are you sure? Suppose a mirror, for instance,—hallucinations are so easily produced. I don't know if you have ever seen a really good conjuror—"

"I won't argue again," said Cuss. "We've thrashed that out, Bunting. And just now there's these books—Ah! here's some of what I take to be Greek! Greek letters certainly."

He pointed to the middle of the page. Mr. Bunting flushed slightly and brought his face nearer, apparently finding some difficulty with his glasses. Suddenly he became aware of a strange feeling at the nape of his neck. He tried to raise his head, and encountered an immovable resistance. The feeling was a curious pressure, the grip of a heavy, firm hand, and it bore his chin irresistibly to the table. "Don't move, little men," whispered a voice, "or I'll brain you both!" He looked into the face of Cuss, close to his own, and each saw a horrified reflection of his own sickly astonishment.

"I'm sorry to handle you roughly," said the Voice, "but it's unavoidable.

"Since when did you learn to pry into an investigator's private memoranda?" said the Voice; and two chins struck the table simultaneously and two sets of teeth rattled.

"Since when did you learn to invade the private rooms of a man in misfortune?" and the concussion was repeated.

"Where have they put my clothes?

"Listen," said the Voice. "The windows are fastened and I've taken the key out of the door. I am a fairly strong man, and I have the poker handy—besides being invisible. There's not the slightest doubt that I could kill you both and get away quite easily if I wanted to—do you understand? Very well. If I let you go will you promise not to try any nonsense and do what I tell you?"

The Vicar and the Doctor looked at one another, and the Doctor pulled a face. "Yes," said Mr. Bunting, and the Doctor repeated it. Then the pressure on the necks relaxed, and the Doctor and the Vicar sat up, both very red in the face and wriggling their heads.

"Please keep sitting where you are," said the Invisible Man. "Here's the poker, you see.

"When I came into this room," continued the Invisible Man, after presenting the poker to the tip of the nose of each of his visitors, "I did not expect to find it occupied, and I expected to find, in addition to my books of memoranda, an outfit of clothing. Where is it? No,—don't rise. I can see it's gone. Now, just at present, though the days are quite warm enough for an invisible man to run about stark, the evenings are chilly. I want clothing—and other accommodation; and I must also have those three books."

12

THE INVISIBLE MAN LOSES HIS TEMPER

It is unavoidable that at this point the narrative should break off again, for a certain very painful reason that will presently be apparent. While these things were going on in the parlour, and while Mr. Huxter was watching Mr. Marvel smoking his pipe against the gate, not a dozen yards away were Mr. Hall and Teddy Henfrey discussing in a state of cloudy puzzlement the one Iping topic.

Suddenly there came a violent thud against the door of the parlour, a sharp cry, and then—silence.

"Hul—lo!" said Teddy Henfrey.

"Hul—lo!" from the Tap.

Mr. Hall took things in slowly but surely. "That ain't right," he said, and came round from behind the bar towards the parlour door.

He and Teddy approached the door together, with intent faces. Their eyes considered. "Summat wrong," said Hall, and Henfrey nodded agreement. Whiffs of an unpleasant chemical odour met them, and there was a muffled sound of conversation, very rapid and subdued.

"You all raight thur?" asked Hall, rapping.

The muttered conversation ceased abruptly, for a moment silence, then the conversation was resumed in hissing whispers, then a sharp cry of "No! no, you don't!" There came a sudden motion and the oversetting of a chair, a brief struggle. Silence again.

"What the dooce?" exclaimed Henfrey, *sotto voce.*

"You—all—raight thur?" asked Mr. Hall sharply, again.

The Vicar's voice answered with a curious jerking intonation: "Quite ri-ight. Please don't—interrupt."

"Odd!" said Mr. Henfrey.

"Odd!" said Mr. Hall.

"Says, 'Don't interrupt,'" said Henfrey.

"I heerd'n," said Hall.

"And a sniff," said Henfrey.

They remained listening. The conversation was rapid and subdued. "I *can't*," said Mr. Bunting, his voice rising; "I tell you, sir, I *will* not."

"What was that?" asked Henfrey.

"Says he wi' nart," said Hall. "Warn't speakin' to us, wuz he?"

"Disgraceful!" said Mr. Bunting, within.

"'Disgraceful,'" said Mr. Henfrey. "I heard it—distinct."

"Who's that speaking now?" asked Henfrey.

"Mr. Cuss, I s'pose," said Hall. "Can you hear—anything?"

Silence. The sounds within indistinct and perplexing.

"Sounds like throwing the table-cloth about," said Hall.

Mrs. Hall appeared behind the bar. Hall made gestures of silence and invitation. This roused Mrs. Hall's wifely opposition. "What yer listenin' there for, Hall?" she asked. "Ain't you nothin' better to do—busy day like this?"

Hall tried to convey everything by grimaces and dumb show, but Mrs. Hall was obdurate. She raised her voice. So Hall and Henfrey, rather crestfallen, tip-toed back to the bar, gesticulating to explain to her.

At first she refused to see anything in what they had heard at all. Then she insisted on Hall keeping silence, while Henfrey told her his story. She was inclined to think the whole business non-sense—perhaps they were just moving the furniture about. "I heerd'n say 'disgraceful'; that I did," said Hall.

"*I* heerd that, Mis' Hall," said Henfrey.

"Like as not—" began Mrs. Hall.

"Hsh!" said Mr. Teddy Henfrey. "Didn't I hear the window?"

"What window?" asked Mrs. Hall.

"Parlour window," said Henfrey.

Every one stood listening intently. Mrs. Hall's eyes, directed straight before her, saw without seeing the brilliant oblong of the inn door, the road white and vivid, and Huxter's shop-front blistering in the June sun. Abruptly Huxter's door opened and Huxter appeared, eyes staring with excitement, arms gesticulating. "Yap!" cried Huxter. "Stop thief!" and he ran obliquely across the oblong towards the yard gates, and vanished.

Simultaneously came a tumult from the parlour, and a sound of windows being closed.

Hall, Henfrey, and the human contents of the Tap rushed out at once pell-mell into the street. They saw some one whisk round the corner towards the down road, and Mr. Huxter executing a complicated leap in the air that ended on his face and shoulder. Down the street people were standing astonished or running towards them.

Mr. Huxter was stunned. Henfrey stopped to discover this, but Hall and the two labourers from the Tap rushed at once to the corner, shouting incoherent things, and saw Mr. Marvel vanishing by the corner of the church wall. They appear to have jumped to the impossible conclusion that this was the Invisible Man suddenly become visible, and set off at once along the lane in pursuit. But Hall had hardly run a dozen yards before he gave a loud shout of astonishment and went flying headlong sideways, clutching one of the labourers and bringing him to the ground. He had been charged just as one charges a man at football. The second labourer came round in a circle, stared, and conceiving that Hall had tumbled over of his own accord, turned to resume the pursuit, only to be tripped by the ankle just as Huxter had been. Then, as the first labourer struggled to his feet, he was kicked sideways by a blow that might have felled an ox.

As he went down, the rush from the direction of the village green came round the corner. The first to appear was the proprietor of the cocoanut shy, a burly man in a blue jersey. He was astonished to see the lane empty save for three men sprawling absurdly on the ground. And then something happened to his rear-most foot, and he went headlong and rolled sideways just in time to graze the feet of his brother and partner, following headlong. The two were then kicked, knelt on, fallen over, and cursed by quite a number of over-hasty people.

Now when Hall and Henfrey and the labourers ran out of the house, Mrs. Hall, who had been disciplined by years of experience, remained in the bar next the till. And suddenly the parlour door was opened, and Mr. Cuss appeared, and without glancing at her rushed at once down the steps towards the corner. "Hold him!" he cried. "Don't let him drop that parcel! You can see him so long as he holds the parcel." He knew nothing of the existence of Marvel. For the Invisible Man had handed over the books and bundle in the yard. The face of Mr. Cuss was angry and resolute, but his costume was defective, a sort of limp white kilt that could only have passed muster in Greece. "Hold him!" he bawled. "He's got my trousers! And every stitch of the Vicar's clothes!

"'Tend to him in a minute!" he cried to Henfrey as he passed the prostrate Huxter, and coming round the corner to join the tumult, was promptly knocked off his feet into an indecorous sprawl. Somebody in full flight trod heavily on his finger. He yelled, struggled to regain his feet, was knocked against and thrown on all fours again, and became aware that he was involved not in a capture, but a rout. Every one was running back to the village. He rose again and was hit severely behind the ear. He staggered and set off back to the Coach and Horses forthwith, leaping over the deserted Huxter, who was now sitting up, on his way.

Behind him as he was halfway up the inn steps he heard a sudden yell of rage, rising sharply out of the confusion of cries, and a sounding smack in some one's face. He recognised the voice as that

of the Invisible Man, and the note was that of a man suddenly infuri-
ated by a painful blow.

In another moment Mr. Cuss was back in the parlour. "He's
coming back, Bunting!" he said, rushing in. "Save yourself! He's
gone mad!"

Mr. Bunting was standing in the window engaged in an attempt
to clothe himself in the hearth-rug and a *West Surrey Gazette*.
"Who's coming?" he said, so startled that his costume narrowly
escaped disintegration.

"Invisible Man," said Cuss, and rushed to the window. "We'd
better clear out from here! He's fighting mad! Mad!"

In another moment he was out in the yard.

"Good heavens!" said Mr. Bunting, hesitating between two horrible alternatives. He heard a frightful struggle in the passage of
the inn, and his decision was made. He clambered out of the window, adjusted his costume hastily, and fled up the village as fast
as his fat little legs would carry him.

From the moment when the Invisible Man screamed with rage
and Mr. Bunting made his memorable flight up the village, it became impossible to give a consecutive account of affairs in Iping.
Possibly the Invisible Man's original intention was simply to cover
Marvel's retreat with the clothes and books. But his temper, at no
time very good, seems to have gone completely at some chance
blow, and forthwith he set to smiting and overthrowing, for the
mere satisfaction of hurting.

You must figure the street full of running figures, of doors slamming and fights for hiding-places. You must figure the tumult suddenly striking on the unstable equilibrium of old Fletcher's planks and
two chairs,—with cataclysmal results. You must figure an appalled
couple caught dismally in a swing. And then the whole tumultuous
rush has passed and the Iping streets with its gauds and flags is
deserted save for the still raging Unseen, and littered with cocoa-
nuts, overthrown canvas screens, and the scattered stock in trade of
a sweetstuff stall. Everywhere there is a sound of closing shutters
and shoving bolts, and the only visible humanity is an occasional
flitting eye under a raised eyebrow in the corner of a window pane.

The Invisible Man amused himself for a little while by breaking all the windows in the Coach and Horses, and then he thrust a street lamp through the parlour window of Mrs. Gribble. He it must have been who cut the telegraph wire to Adderdean just beyond Higgins' cottage on the Adderdean road. And after that, as his peculiar qualities allowed, he passed out of human perceptions altogether, and he was neither heard, seen, nor felt in Iping any more. He vanished absolutely.

But it was the best part of two hours before any human being ventured out again into the desolation of Iping Street.

13
MR. MARVEL DISCUSSES HIS RESIGNATION

When the dusk was gathering and Iping was just beginning to peep timorously forth again upon the shattered wreckage of its Bank Holiday, a short, thick-set man in a shabby silk hat was marching painfully through the twilight behind the beechwoods on the road to Bramblehurst.

He carried three books bound together by some sort of ornamental elastic ligature, and a bundle wrapped in a blue tablecloth. His rubicund face expressed consternation and fatigue; he appeared to be in a spasmodic sort of hurry. He was accompanied by a Voice other than his own, and ever and again he winced under the touch of unseen hands.

"If you give me the slip again," said the Voice; "if you attempt to give me the slip again—"

"Lord!" said Mr. Marvel. "That shoulder's a mass of bruises as it is."

"—on my honour," said the Voice, "I will kill you."

"I didn't try to give you the slip," said Marvel, in a voice that was not far remote from tears. "I swear I didn't. I didn't know the blessed turning, that was all! How the devil was I to know the blessed turning? As it is, I've been knocked about—"

"You'll get knocked about a great deal more if you don't mind," said the Voice, and Mr. Marvel abruptly became silent. He blew out his cheeks, and his eyes were eloquent of despair.

"It's bad enough to let these floundering yokels explode my little secret, without your cutting off with my books. It's lucky for some of them they cut and ran when they did! Here am I—No one knew I was invisible! And now what am I to do?"

"What am *I* to do?" asked Marvel, *sotto voce*.

"It's all about. It will be in the papers! Everybody will be looking for me; everyone on their guard—" The Voice broke off into vivid curses and ceased.

The despair of Mr. Marvel's face deepened, and his pace slacked.

"Go on!" said the Voice.

Mr. Marvel's face assumed a greyish tint between the ruddier patches.

"Don't drop those books, stupid," said the Voice, sharply—overtaking him.

"The fact is," said the Voice, "I shall have to make use of you. You're a poor tool, but I must."

"I'm a *miserable* tool," said Marvel.

"You are," said the Voice.

"I'm the worst possible tool you could have," said Marvel.

"I'm not strong," he said after a discouraging silence.

"I'm not over strong," he repeated.

"No?"

"And my heart's weak. That little business—I pulled it through, of course—but bless you! I could have dropped."

"Well?"

"I haven't the nerve and strength for the sort of thing you want."

"*I'll* stimulate you."

"I wish you wouldn't. I wouldn't like to mess up your plans, you know. But I might,—out of sheer funk and misery."

"You'd better not," said the Voice, with quiet emphasis.

"I wish I was dead," said Marvel. "It ain't justice," he said; "you must admit—It seems to me I've a perfect right—"

"*Get* on!" said the Voice.

Mr. Marvel mended his pace, and for a time they went in silence again.

"It's devilish hard," said Mr. Marvel.

This was quite ineffectual. He tried another tack. "What do I make by it?" he began again in a tone of unendurable wrong.

"Oh! *shut up!*" said the Voice, with sudden amazing vigour. "I'll see to you all right. You do what you're told. You'll do it all right. You're a fool and all that, but you'll do—"

"I tell you, sir, I'm not the man for it. Respectfully—but it *is* so—"

"If you don't shut up I shall twist your wrist again," said the Invisible Man. "I want to think."

Presently two oblongs of yellow light appeared through the trees, and the square tower of a church loomed through the gloaming. "I shall keep my hand on your shoulder," said the Voice, "all through the village. Go straight through and try no foolery. It will be the worse for you if you do."

"I know that," sighed Mr. Marvel, "I know all that."

The unhappy-looking figure in the obsolete silk hat passed up the street of the little village with his burdens, and vanished into the gathering darkness beyond the lights of the windows.

14

AT PORT STOWE

Ten o'clock the next morning found Mr. Marvel, unshaven, dirty, and travel-stained, sitting with the books beside him and his hands deep in his pockets, looking very weary, nervous, and uncomfortable, and inflating his cheeks at frequent intervals, on the bench outside a little inn on the outskirts of Port Stowe. Beside him were the books, but now they were tied with string. The bundle had been abandoned in the pinewoods beyond Bramblehurst, in accordance with a change in the plans of the Invisible Man. Mr. Marvel sat on the bench, and although no one took the slightest notice of him, his agitation remained at fever heat. His hands would go ever and again to his various pockets with a curious nervous fumbling.

When he had been sitting for the best part of an hour, however, an elderly mariner, carrying a newspaper, came out of the inn and sat down beside him. "Pleasant day," said the mariner.

Mr. Marvel glanced about him with something very like terror. "Very," he said.

"Just seasonable weather for the time of year," said the mariner, taking no denial.

"Quite," said Mr. Marvel.

The mariner produced a toothpick, and (saving his regard) was engrossed thereby for some minutes. His eyes meanwhile were at liberty to examine Mr. Marvel's dusty figure and the books beside him. As he had approached Mr. Marvel he had heard a sound like the dropping of coins into a pocket. He was struck by the contrast of Mr. Marvel's appearance with this suggestion of opulence. Thence his mind wandered back again to a topic that had taken a curiously firm hold of his imagination.

"Books?" he said suddenly, noisily finishing with the toothpick.

Mr. Marvel started and looked at them. "Oh, yes," he said. "Yes, they're books."

"There's some extra-ordinary things in books," said the mariner.

"I believe you," said Mr. Marvel.

"And some extra-ordinary things out of 'em," said the mariner.

"True likewise," said Mr. Marvel. He eyed his interlocutor, and then glanced about him.

"There's some extra-ordinary things in newspapers, for example," said the mariner.

"There are."

"In *this* newspaper," said the mariner.

"Ah!" said Mr. Marvel.

"There's a story," said the mariner, fixing Mr. Marvel with an eye that was firm and deliberate; "there's a story about an Invisible Man, for instance."

Mr. Marvel pulled his mouth askew and scratched his cheek and felt his ears glowing. "What will they be writing next?" he asked faintly. "Ostria, or America?"

"Neither," said the mariner. "*Here!*"

"Lord!" said Mr. Marvel, starting.

"When I say *here*," said the mariner, to Mr. Marvel's intense relief, "I don't of course mean here in this place, I mean hereabouts."

"An Invisible Man!" said Mr. Marvel. "And what's *he* been up to?"

"Everything," said the mariner, controlling Marvel with his eye, and then amplifying: "Every Blessed Thing."

"I ain't seen a paper these four days," said Marvel.

"Iping's the place he started at," said the mariner.

"In-*deed!*" said Mr. Marvel.

"He started there. And where he came from, nobody don't seem to know. Here it is: Pe Culiar Story from Iping. And it says in this paper that the evidence is extra-ordinary strong—extra-ordinary."

"Lord!" said Mr. Marvel.

"But then, it's a extra-ordinary story. There is a clergyman and a medical gent witnesses,—saw 'im all right and proper—or least-ways, didn't see 'im. He was staying, it says, at the Coach an' Horses, and no one don't seem to have been aware of his misfortune, it says, aware of his misfortune, until in an Alteration in the inn, it says, his bandages on his head was torn off. It was then observed that his head was invisible. Attempts were At Once made to secure him, but casting off his garments, it says, he succeeded in escaping, but not until after a desperate struggle, In Which he had inflicted serious injuries, it says, on our worthy and able constable, Mr. J.A. Jaffers. Pretty straight story, eigh? Names and everything."

"Lord!" said Mr. Marvel, looking nervously about him, trying to count the money in his pockets by his unaided sense of touch, and full of a strange and novel idea. "It sounds most astonishing."

"Don't it? Extra-ordinary, *I* call it. Never heard tell of Invisible Men before, I haven't, but nowadays one hears such a lot of extra-ordinary things—that—"

"That all he did?" asked Marvel, trying to seem at his ease.

"It's enough, ain't it?" said the mariner.

"Didn't go *back* by any chance?" asked Marvel. "Just escaped and that's all, eh?"

"All!" said the mariner. "Why!—ain't it enough?"

"Quite enough," said Marvel.

"I should think it was enough," said the mariner. "I should think it was enough."

"He didn't have any pals—it don't say he had any pals, does it?" asked Mr. Marvel, anxious.

"Ain't one of a sort enough for you?" asked the mariner. "No, thank Heaven, as one might say, he didn't."

He nodded his head slowly. "It makes me regular uncomfortable, the bare thought of that chap running about the country! He is at present At Large, and from certain evidence it is supposed that he has—taken—*took*, I suppose they mean—the road to Port Stowe. You see we're right *in* it! None of your American wonders, this time. And just think of the things he might do! Where'd you be, if he took a drop over and above, and had a fancy to go for you? Suppose he wants to rob—who can prevent him? He can trespass, he can burgle, he could walk through a cordon of policemen as easy as me or you could give the slip to a blind man! Easier! For these here blind chaps hear uncommon sharp, I'm told. And wherever there was liquor he fancied—"

"He's got a tremenjous advantage, certainly," said Marvel. "And—well."

"You're right," said the mariner. "He *has*."

All this time Mr. Marvel had been glancing about him intently, listening for faint footfalls, trying to detect imperceptible movements. He seemed on the point of some great resolution. He coughed behind his hand.

He looked about him again, listened, bent towards to the mariner, and lowered his voice: "The fact of it is—I happen—to know just a thing or two about this Invisible Man. From private sources."

"Oh!" said the mariner, interested. "*You?*"

"Yes," said Mr. Marvel. "Me."

"Indeed!" said the mariner. "And may I ask—"

"You'll be astonished," said Mr. Marvel behind his hand. "It's tremenjous."

"Indeed!" said the mariner.

"The fact is," began Mr. Marvel eagerly in a confidential undertone. Suddenly his expression changed marvellously. "Ow!" he said. He rose stiffly in his seat. His face was eloquent of physical suffering. "Wow!" he said.

"What's up?" said the mariner, concerned.

"Toothache," said Mr. Marvel, and put his hand to his ear. He caught hold of his books. "I must be getting on, I think," he said. He edged in a curious way along the seat away from his interlocutor. "But you was just agoing to tell me about this here Invisible Man!" protested the mariner. Mr. Marvel seemed to consult with himself. "Hoax," said a voice. "It's a hoax," said Mr. Marvel.

"But it's in the paper," said the mariner.

"Hoax all the same," said Marvel. "I know the chap that started the lie. There ain't no Invisible Man whatsoever—Blimey."

"But how 'bout this paper? D'you mean to say—?"

"Not a word of it," said Marvel, stoutly.

The mariner stared, paper in hand. Mr. Marvel jerkily faced about. "Wait a bit," said the mariner, rising and speaking slowly. "D'you mean to say—?"

"I do," said Mr. Marvel.

"Then why did you let me go on and tell you all this blarsted stuff, then? What d'yer mean by letting a man make a fool of himself like that for? Eigh?"

Mr. Marvel blew out his cheeks. The mariner was suddenly very red indeed; he clenched his hands. "I been talking here this ten minutes," he said; "and you, you little pot-bellied, leathery-faced son of an old boot, couldn't have the elementary manners—"

"Don't you come bandying words with *me*," said Mr. Marvel.

"Bandying words! I'm a jolly good mind—"

"Come up," said a voice, and Mr. Marvel was suddenly whirled about and started marching off in a curious spasmodic manner. "You'd better move on," said the mariner. "Who's moving on?" said Mr. Marvel. He was receding obliquely with a curious hurrying gait, with occasional violent jerks forward. Some way along the road he began a muttered monologue, protests and recriminations.

"Silly devil!" said the mariner, legs wide apart, elbows akimbo, watching the receding figure. "I'll show you, you silly ass,—hoaxing *me!* It's here—on the paper!"

Mr. Marvel retorted incoherently and, receding, was hidden by a bend in the road, but the mariner still stood magnificent in the midst of the way, until the approach of a butcher's cart dislodged him. Then he turned himself towards Port Stowe. "Full of extraordinary asses," he said softly to himself. "Just to take me down a bit—that was his silly game—It's on the paper!"

And there was another extraordinary thing he was presently to hear, that had happened quite close to him. And that was a vision of a "fist full of money" (no less) travelling without visible agency, along by the wall at the corner of St. Michael's Lane. A brother mariner had seen this wonderful sight that very morning. He had snatched at the money forthwith and had been knocked headlong, and when he had got to his feet the butterfly money had vanished. Our mariner was in the mood to believe anything, he declared, but that was a bit *too* stiff. Afterwards, however, he began to think things over.

The story of the flying money was true. And all about that neighbourhood, even from the august London and Country Banking Company, from the tills of shops and inns—doors standing that sunny weather entirely open—money had been quietly and dexterously making off that day in handfuls and rouleaux, floating quietly along by walls and shady places, dodging quickly from the approaching eyes of men. And it had, though no man had traced it, invariably ended its mysterious flight in the pocket of that agitated gentleman in the obsolete silk hat, sitting outside the little inn on the outskirts of Port Stowe.

It was ten days after—and indeed only when the Burdock story was already old—that the mariner collated these facts and began to understand how near he had been to the wonderful Invisible Man.

15

THE MAN WHO WAS RUNNING

In the early evening time Doctor Kemp was sitting in his study in the belvedere on the hill overlooking Burdock. It was a pleasant little room, with three windows, north, west, and south, and bookshelves crowded with books and scientific publications, and a broad writing-table, and, under the north window, a microscope, glass slips, minute instruments, some cultures, and scattered bottles of reagents. Doctor Kemp's solar lamp was lit, albeit the sky was still bright with the sunset light, and his blinds were up because there was no offence of peering outsiders to require them pulled down. Doctor Kemp was a tall and slender young man, with flaxen hair and a moustache almost white, and the work he was upon would earn him, he hoped, the fellowship of the Royal Society, so highly did he think of it.

And his eye presently wandering from his work caught the sunset blazing at the back of the hill that is over against his own. For a minute perhaps he sat, pen in mouth, admiring the rich golden colour above the crest, and then his attention was attracted by the little figure of a man, inky black, running over the hill-brow towards him. He was a shortish little man, and he wore a high hat, and he was running so fast that his legs verily twinkled.

"Another of those fools," said Doctor Kemp. "Like that ass who ran into me this morning round a corner, with his "Visible Man a-coming, sir!' I can't imagine what possesses people. One might think we were in the thirteenth century."

He got up, went to the window, and stared at the dusky hillside and the dark little figure tearing down it. "He seems in a confounded hurry," said Doctor Kemp, "but he doesn't seem to be getting on. If his pockets were full of lead, he couldn't run heavier.

"Spurted, sir," said Doctor Kemp.

In another moment the higher of the villas that had clambered up the hill from Burdock had occulted the running figure. He was visible again for a moment, and again, and then again, three times between the three detached houses that came next, and then the terrace hid him.

"Asses!" said Doctor Kemp, swinging round on his heel and walking back to his writing-table.

But those who saw the fugitive nearer, and perceived the abject terror on his perspiring face, being themselves in the open roadway, did not share in the doctor's contempt. By the man pounded, and as he ran he chinked like a well-filled purse that is tossed to and fro. He looked neither to the right nor the left, but his dilated eyes stared straight downhill to where the lamps were being lit, and the people were crowded in the street. And his ill-shaped mouth fell apart, and a glairy foam lay on his lips, and his breath came hoarse and noisy. All he passed stopped and began staring up the road and down, and interrogating one another with an inkling of discomfort for the reason of his haste.

And then presently, far up the hill, a dog playing in the road yelped and ran under a gate, and as they still wondered something—a wind—a pad, pad, pad,—a sound like a panting breathing,—rushed by.

People screamed. People sprang off the pavement. It passed in shouts, it passed by instinct down the hill. They were shouting in the street before Marvel was halfway there. They were bolting into houses and slamming the doors behind them, with the news. He heard it and made one last desperate spurt. Fear came striding by, rushed ahead of him, and in a moment had seized the town.

"The Invisible Man is coming! The Invisible Man!"

16

IN THE JOLLY CRICKETERS

The Jolly Cricketers is just at the bottom of the hill, where the tram-lines begin. The barman leant his fat red arms on the counter and talked of horses with an anaemic cabman, while a black-bearded man in grey snapped up biscuit and cheese, drank Burton, and conversed in American with a policeman off duty.

"What's the shouting about?" said the anaemic cabman going off at a tangent, trying to see up the hill over the dirty yellow blind in the low window of the inn. Somebody ran by outside. "Fire, perhaps," said the barman.

Footsteps approached, running heavily, the door was pushed open violently, and Marvel, weeping and dishevelled, his hat gone, the neck of his coat torn open, rushed in, made a convulsive turn, and attempted to shut the door. It was held half open by a strap.

"Coming!" he bawled, his voice shrieking with terror. "He's coming. The 'Visible Man! After me! For Gawd's sake! Elp! Elp! Elp!"

"Shut the doors," said the policeman. "Who's coming? What's the row?" He went to the door, released the strap, and it slammed. The American closed the other door.

"Lemme go inside," said Marvel, staggering and weeping, but still clutching the books. "Lemme go inside. Lock me in—somewhere. I tell you he's after me. I give him the slip. He said he'd kill me and he will."

"*You're* safe," said the man with the black beard. "The door's shut. What's it all about?"

"Lemme go inside," said Marvel, and shrieked aloud as a blow suddenly made the fastened door shiver and was followed by a hurried rapping and a shouting outside.

"Hullo," cried the policeman, "who's there?"

Mr. Marvel began to make frantic dives at panels that looked like doors. "He'll kill me—he's got a knife or something. For Gawd's sake!"

"Here you are," said the barman. "Come in here." And he held up the flap of the bar.

Mr. Marvel rushed behind the bar as the summons outside was repeated. "Don't open the door," he screamed. "*Please* don't open the door. *Where* shall I hide?"

"This, this Invisible Man, then?" asked the man with the black beard, with one hand behind him. "I guess it's about time we saw him."

The window of the inn was suddenly smashed in, and there was a screaming and running to and fro in the street. The policeman had been standing on the settee staring out, craning to see who was at the door. He got down with raised eyebrows. "It's that," he said. The barman stood in front of the bar-parlour door which was now locked on Mr. Marvel, stared at the smashed window and came round to the two other men.

Everything was suddenly quiet. "I wish I had my truncheon," said the policeman, going irresolutely to the door. "Once we open, in he comes. There's no stopping him."

"Don't you be in too much hurry about that door," said the anaemic cabman, anxiously.

"Draw the bolts," said the man with the black beard, "and if he comes—" He showed a revolver in his hand.

"That won't do," said the policeman; "that's murder."

"I know what country I'm in," said the man with the beard. "I'm going to let off at his legs. Draw the bolts."

"Not with that thing going off behind me," said the barman, craning over the blind.

"Very well," said the man with the black beard, and stooping down, revolver ready, drew them himself. Barman, cabman, and police-man faced about.

"Come in," said the bearded man in an undertone, standing back and facing the unbolted doors with his pistol behind him. No one came in, the door remained closed. Five minutes afterwards when a second cabman pushed his head in cautiously, they were still waiting, and an anxious face peered out of the bar-parlour and supplied information. "Are all the doors of the house shut?" asked Marvel. "He's going round—prowling round. He's as artful as the devil."

"Good Lord!" said the burly barman. "There's the back! Just watch them doors! I say!—" He looked about him helplessly. The bar-parlour door slammed and they heard the key turn. "There's the yard door and the private door. The yard door—"

He rushed out of the bar.

In a minute he reappeared with a carving-knife in his hand. "The yard door was open!" he said, and his fat underlip dropped.

"He may be in the house now!" said the first cabman.

"He's not in the kitchen," said the barman. "There's two women there, and I've stabbed every inch of it with this little beef slicer. And they don't think he's come in. They haven't noticed—"

"Have you fastened it?" asked the first cabman.

"I'm out of frocks," said the barman.

The man with the beard replaced his revolver. And even as he did so the flap of the bar was shut down and the bolt clicked, and then with a tremendous thud the catch of the door snapped and the bar-parlour door burst open. They heard Marvel squeal like a caught leveret, and forthwith they were clambering over the bar to his rescue. The bearded man's revolver cracked and the looking-glass at the back of the parlour was starred brightly and came smashing and tinkling down.

As the barman entered the room he saw Marvel, curiously crumpled up and struggling against the door that led to the yard and kitchen. The door flew open while the barman hesitated, and Marvel was dragged into the kitchen. There was a scream and a clatter of pans. Marvel, head down, and lugging back obstinately, was forced to the kitchen door, and the bolts were drawn.

Then the policeman, who had been trying to pass the barman, rushed in, followed by one of the cabmen, gripped the wrist of the invisible hand that collared Marvel, was hit in the face and went reeling back. The door opened, and Marvel made a frantic effort to obtain a lodgment behind it. Then the cabman clutched something. "I got him," said the cabman. The barman's red hands came clawing at the unseen. "Here he is!" said the barman.

Mr. Marvel, released, suddenly dropped to the ground and made an attempt to crawl behind the legs of the fighting men. The struggle blundered round the edge of the door. The voice of the Invisible Man was heard for the first time, yelling out sharply, as the policeman trod on his foot. Then he cried out passionately and his fists flew round like flails. The cabman suddenly whooped and doubled up, kicked under the diaphragm. The door into the bar-parlour from the kitchen slammed and covered Mr. Marvel's retreat. The men in the kitchen found themselves clutching at and struggling with empty air.

"Where's he gone?" cried the man with the beard. "Out?"

"This way," said the policeman, stepping into the yard and stopping. A piece of tile whizzed by his head and smashed among the crockery on the kitchen table.

"I'll show him," shouted the man with the black beard, and suddenly a steel barrel shone over the policeman's shoulder, and five bullets had followed one another into the twilight whence the missle had come. As he fired, the man with the beard moved his hand in a horizontal curve, so that his shots radiated out into the narrow yard like spokes from a wheel.

A silence followed. "Five cartridges," said the man with the black beard. "That's the best of all. Four aces and the joker. Get a lantern, some one, and come and feel about for his body."

17
DOCTOR KEMP'S VISITOR

Doctor Kemp had continued writing in his study until the shots aroused him. Crack, crack, crack, they came one after the other.

"Hello!" said Doctor Kemp, putting his pen into his mouth again and listening. "Who's letting off revolvers in Burdock? What are the asses at now?"

He went to the south window, threw it up, and leaning out stared down on the network of windows, beaded gas-lamps and shops with black interstices of roof and yard that made up the town at night. "Looks like a crowd down the hill," he said, "by the Cricketers," and remained watching. Thence his eyes wandered over the town to far away where the ships' lights shone, and the pier glowed, a little illuminated pavilion like a gem of yellow light. The moon in its first quarter hung over the western hill, and the stars were clear and almost tropically bright.

After five minutes, during which his mind had travelled into a remote speculation of social conditions of the future, and lost itself at last over the time dimension, Doctor Kemp roused himself with a sigh, pulled down the window again, and returned to his writing-desk.

It must have been about an hour after this that the front-door bell rang. He had been writing slackly and with intervals of abstraction, since the shots. He sat listening. He heard the servant answer the door, and waited for her feet on the staircase, but she did not come.

"Wonder what that was," said Doctor Kemp.

He tried to resume his work, failed, got up, went downstairs from his study to the landing, rang, and called over the balustrade to the housemaid as she appeared in the hall below. "Was that a letter?" he asked.

"Only a runaway ring, sir," she answered.

"I'm restless to-night," he said to himself. He went back to his study, and this time attacked his work resolutely. In a little while he was hard at work again, and the only sounds in the room were the ticking of the clock and the subdued shrillness of his quill, hurrying in the very centre of the circle of light his lamp-shade threw on his table.

It was two o'clock before Doctor Kemp had finished his work for the night. He rose, yawned, and went downstairs to bed. He had already removed his coat and vest, when he noticed that he was thirsty. He took a candle and went down to the dining-room in search of a siphon and whisky.

Doctor Kemp's scientific pursuits had made him a very observant man, and as he recrossed the hall, he noticed a dark spot on the linoleum near the mat at the foot of the stairs. He went on upstairs, and then it suddenly occurred to him to ask himself what the spot on the linoleum might be. Apparently some subconscious element was at work. At any rate, he turned with his burden, went back to the hall, put down the siphon and whisky, and bending down, touched the spot. Without any great surprise he found it had the stickiness and colour of drying blood.

He took up his burden again, and returned upstairs, looking about him and trying to account for the blood-spot. On the landing he saw something and stopped astonished. The door-handle of his own room was blood-stained.

He looked at his own hand. It was quite clean, and then he remembered that the door of his room had been open when he came down from his study, and that consequently he had not touched the handle at all. He went straight into his room, his face quite calm—perhaps a trifle more resolute that usual. His glance, wandering inquisitively, fell on the bed. On the counterpane was a mess of blood, and the sheet had been torn. He had not noticed this before because he had walked straight to the dressing-table. On the further side the bed-clothes were depressed as if some one had been recently sitting there.

Then he had an odd impression that he had heard a loud voice say, "Good Heavens!—Kemp!"

But Doctor Kemp was no believer in Voices.

He stood staring at the tumbled sheets. Was that really a voice? He looked about again, but noticed nothing further than the disordered and blood-stained bed. Then he distinctly heard a movement across the room, near the wash-hand stand. All men, however highly educated, retain some superstitious inklings. The feeling that is called "eerie" came upon him. He closed the door of the room, came forward to the dressing-table, and put down his burdens. Suddenly, with a start, he perceived a coiled and blood-stained bandage of linen rag hanging in mid-air, between him and the wash-hand stand.

He stared at this in amazement. It was an empty bandage, a bandage properly tied but quite empty. He would have advanced to grasp it, but a touch arrested him, and a voice speaking quite close to him. "Kemp!" said the Voice.

"Eigh?" said Kemp, with his mouth open.

"Keep your nerve," said the Voice. "I'm an Invisible Man."

Kemp made no answer for a space, simply stared at the bandage. "Invisible Man," he said.

"I'm an Invisible Man," repeated the Voice.

The story he had been active to ridicule only that morning rushed through Kemp's brain. He does not appear to have been either very much frightened or very greatly surprised at the moment. Realisation came later.

"I thought it was all a lie," he said. The thought uppermost in his mind was the reiterated arguments of the morning. "Have you a bandage on?" he asked.

"Yes," said the Invisible Man.

"Oh!" said Kemp, and then roused himself. "I say!" he said. "But this is nonsense. It's some trick." He stepped forward suddenly, and his hand, extended towards the bandage, met invisible fingers.

He recoiled at the touch and his colour changed.

"Keep steady, Kemp, for God's sake! I want help badly. Stop!"

The hand gripped his arm. He struck at it.

"Kemp!" cried the Voice. "Kemp! Keep steady!" and the grip tightened.

A frantic desire to free himself took possession of Kemp. The hand of the bandaged arm gripped his shoulder, and he was suddenly tripped and flung backwards upon the bed. He opened his mouth to shout, and the corner of the sheet was thrust between his teeth. The Invisible Man had him down grimly, but his arms were free and he struck and tried to kick savagely.

"Listen to reason, will you?" said the Invisible Man, sticking to him in spite of a pounding in the ribs. "By Heaven! you'll madden me in a minute!

"Lie still, you fool!" bawled the Invisible Man in Kemp's ear.

Kemp struggled for another moment and then lay still.

"If you shout I'll smash your face," said the Invisible Man, relieving his mouth.

"I'm an Invisible Man. It's no foolishness, and no magic. I really am an Invisible Man. And I want your help. I don't want to hurt you, but if you behave like a frantic rustic, I must. Don't you remember me, Kemp?—Griffin, of University College?"

"Let me get up," said Kemp. "I'll stop where I am. And let me sit quiet for a minute." He sat up and felt his neck.

"I am Griffin, of University College, and I have made myself invisible. I am just an ordinary man—a man you have known—made invisible."

"Griffin?" said Kemp.

"Griffin," answered the Voice— "a younger student, almost an albino, six feet high, and broad, with a pink and white face and red eyes—who won the medal for chemistry."

"I am confused," said Kemp. "My brain is rioting. What has this to do with Griffin?"

"I *am* Griffin."

Kempt thought. "It's horrible," he said. "But what devilry must happen to make a man invisible?"

"It's no devilry. It's a process, sane and intelligible enough—"

"It's horrible!" said Kemp. "How on earth—?"

"It's horrible enough. But I'm wounded an in pain, and tired— Great God! Kemp, you are a man. Take it steady. Give me some food and drink, and let me sit down here."

Kemp stared at the bandage as it moved across the room, then saw a basket chair dragged across the floor and come to rest near the bed. It creaked, and the seat was depressed the quarter of an inch or so. He rubbed his eyes and felt his neck again. "This beats ghosts," he said, and laughed stupidly.

"That's better. Thank Heaven, you're getting sensible!"

"Or silly," said Kemp, and knuckled his eyes.

"Give me some whisky. I'm near dead."

"It didn't feel so. Where are you? If I get up shall I run into you? *There!* all right. Whisky? Here. Where shall I give it you?"

The chair creaked and Kemp felt the glass drawn away from him. He let go by an effort; his instinct was all against it. It came to rest poised twenty inches above the front edge of the seat of the chair. He stared at it in infinite perplexity. "This is—this must be—hypnotism. You must have suggested you are invisible."

"Nonsense," said the Voice.

"It's frantic."

"Listen to me."

"I demonstrated conclusively this morning," began Kemp, "that invisibility—"

"Never mind what you've demonstrated!—I'm starving," said the Voice, "and the night is—chilly to a man without clothes."

"Food!" said Kemp.

The tumbler of whisky tilted itself. "Yes," said the Invisible Man, rapping it down. "Have you got a dressing gown?"

Kemp made some exclamation in an undertone. He walked to a wardrobe and produced a robe of dingy scarlet. "This do?" he asked. It was taken from him. It hung limp for a moment in mid-air, fluttered weirdly, stood full and decorous buttoning itself, and sat down in his chair. "Drawers, socks, slippers would be a comfort," said the Unseen, curtly. "And food."

"Anything. But this is the insanest thing I ever was in, in my life!"

He turned out his drawers for the articles, and then went downstairs to ransack his larder. He came back with some cold cutlets and bread, pulled up a light table, and placed them before his guest.

"Never mind knives," said his visitor, and a cutlet hung in mid-air, with a sound of gnawing.

"Invisible!" said Kemp, and sat down on a bedroom chair.

"I always like to get something about me before I eat," said the Invisible Man, with a full mouth, eating greedily. "Queer fancy!"

"I suppose that wrist is all right," said Kemp.

"Trust me," said the Invisible Man.

"Of all the strange and wonderful—"

"Exactly. But it's odd I should blunder into your house to get my bandaging. My first stroke of luck. Anyhow I meant to sleep in this house to-night. You must stand that! It's a filthy nuisance, my blood showing, isn't it? Quite a clot over there. Gets visible as it coagulates, I see. I've been in the house three hours."

"But how's it done?" began Kemp, in a tone of exasperation. "Confound it! The whole business—it's unreasonable from beginning to end."

"Quite reasonable," said the Invisible Man. "Perfectly reasonable."

He reached over and secured the whisky bottle. Kemp stared at the devouring dressing-gown. A ray of candle-light penetrating a torn patch in the right shoulder, made a triangle of light under the left ribs. "What were the shots?" he asked. "How did the shooting begin?"

"There was a fool of a man—a sort of confederate of mine—curse him!—who tried to steal my money. *Has* done so."

"Is *he* invisible too?"

"No."

"Well?"

"Can't I have some more to eat before I tell you all that? I'm hungry—in pain. And you want me to tell stories!"

Kemp got up. "*You* didn't do any shooting?" he asked.

"Not me," said his visitor. "Some fool I'd never seen fired at random. A lot of them got scared. They all got scared at me. Curse them!—I say—I want more to eat than this, Kemp."

"I'll see what there is more to eat downstairs," said Kemp. "Not much, I'm afraid."

After he had done eating, and he made a heavy meal, the Invisible Man demanded a cigar. He bit the end savagely before Kemp could find a knife, and cursed when the outer leaf loosened. It was strange to see him smoking; his mouth and throat, pharynx and nares, became visible as a sort of whirling smoke cast.

"This blessed gift of smoking!" he said, and puffed vigorously. "I'm lucky to have fallen upon you, Kemp. You must help me. Fancy tumbling on you just now! I'm in a devilish scrape. I've been mad, I think. The things I have been through! But we will do things yet. Let me tell you—"

He helped himself to more whisky and soda. Kemp got up, looked about him, and fetched himself a glass from his spare room. "It's wild—but I suppose I may drink."

"You haven't changed much, Kemp, these dozen years. You fair men don't. Cool and methodical—after the first collapse. I must tell you. We will work together!"

"But how was it all done?" said Kemp, "and how did you get like this?"

"For God's sake, let me smoke in peace for a little while! And then I will begin to tell you."

But the story was not told that night. The Invisible Man's wrist was growing painful, he was feverish, exhausted, and his mind came round to brood upon his chase down the hill and the struggle about the inn. He spoke in fragments of Marvel, he smoked faster, his voice grew angry. Kemp tried to gather what he could.

"He was afraid of me, I could see he was afraid of me," said the Invisible Man many times over. "He meant to give me the slip—he was always casting about! What a fool I was!"

"The cur!"

"I should have killed him—"

"Where did you get the money?" asked Kemp, abruptly.

The Invisible Man was silent for a space. "I can't tell you to-night," he said. He groaned suddenly and leant forward, supporting his invisible head on invisible hands. "Kemp," he said, "I've had no sleep for near three days—except a couple of dozes of an hour or so. I must sleep soon."

"Well, have my room—have this room."

"But how can I sleep? If I sleep—he will get away. Ugh! What does it matter?"

"What's the shot-wound?" asked Kemp, abruptly.

"Nothing—scratch and blood. Oh, God! How I want sleep!"

"Why not?"

The Invisible Man appeared to be regarding Kemp. "Because I've a particular objection to being caught by my fellow-men," he said slowly.

Kemp started.

"Fool that I am!" said the Invisible Man, striking the table smartly. "I've put the idea into your head."

18
THE INVISIBLE MAN SLEEPS

Exhausted and wounded as the Invisible Man was, he refused to accept Kemp's word that his freedom should be respected. He examined the two windows of the bedroom, drew up the blinds, and opened the sashes to confirm Kemp's statement that a retreat by them would be possible. Outside the night was very quiet and still, and the new moon was setting over the down. Then he examined the keys of the bedroom and the two dressing-room doors, to satisfy himself that these also could be made an assurance of freedom. Finally he expressed himself satisfied. He stood on the hearth-rug and Kemp heard the sound of a yawn.

"I'm sorry," said the Invisible Man, "if I cannot tell you all that I have done to-night. But I am worn out. It's grotesque, no doubt. It's horrible! But believe me, Kemp, it is quite a possible thing. I have made a discovery. I meant to keep it to myself. I can't. I must have a partner. And you—We can do such things—But to-morrow. Now, Kemp, I feel as though I must sleep or perish."

Kemp stood in the middle of the room staring at the headless garment. "I suppose I must leave you," he said. "It's—incredible. Three things happening like this, overturning all my preconceptions, would make me insane. But it's real! Is there anything more that I can get you?"

"Only bid me good-night," said Griffin.

"Good-night," said Kemp, and shook an invisible hand. He walked sideways to the door. Suddenly the dressing-gown walked quickly towards him. "Understand me!" said the dressing-gown. "No attempts to hamper me, or capture me! Or—"

Kemp's face changed a little. "I thought I gave you my word," he said.

Kemp closed the door softly behind him, and the key was turned upon him forthwith. Then, as he stood with an expression of passive amazement on his face, the rapid feet came to the door of the dressing-room and that too was locked. Kemp slapped his brow with his hand. "Am I dreaming? Has the world gone mad—or have I?"

He laughed, and put his hand to the locked door. "Barred out of my own bedroom, by a flagrant absurdity!" he said.

He walked to the head of the staircase, turned, and stared at the locked doors. "It's fact," he said. He put his fingers to his slightly bruised neck. "Undeniable fact!

"But—"

He shook his head hopelessly, turned, and went downstairs.

He lit the dining-room lamp, got out a cigar, and began pacing the room, ejaculating. Now and then he would argue with himself.

"Invisible!" he said.

"Is there such a thing as an invisible animal? In the sea, yes. Thousands! millions! All the larvae, all the little nauplii and tornarias, all the microscopic things, the jelly-fish. In the sea there are more things invisible than visible! I never thought of that before. And in the ponds too! All those little pond-life things—specks of colourless translucent jelly! But in air? No!

"It can't be.

"But after all—why not?

"If a man was made of glass he would still be visible."

His meditation became profound. The bulk of three cigars had passed into the invisible or diffused as a white ash over the carpet before he spoke again. Then it was merely an exclamation. He turned aside, walked out of the room, and went into his little consulting-room and lit the gas there. It was a little room, because

Dr. Kemp did not live by practice, and in it were the day's newspapers. The morning's paper lay carelessly opened and thrown aside. He caught it up, turned it over, and read the account of a "Strange Story from Iping" that the Mariner at Port Stowe had spelt over so painfully to Mr. Marvel. Kemp read it swiftly.

"Wrapped up!" said Kemp. "Disguised! Hiding it! 'No one seems to have been aware of his misfortune.' What the devil *is* his game?"

He dropped the paper, and his eye went seeking. "Ah!" he said, and caught up the *St. James' Gazette*, lying folded up as it arrived. "Now we shall get at the truth," said Dr. Kemp. He rent the paper open; a couple of columns confronted him. "An Entire Village in Sussex goes Mad" was the heading.

"Good Heavens!" said Kemp, reading eagerly an incredulous account of the events in Iping the previous afternoon, that have already been described. Over the leaf the report in the morning paper had been reprinted.

He re-read it. "Ran through the streets striking right and left. Jaffers insensible. Mr. Huxter in great pain—still unable to describe what he saw. Painful humiliation—vicar. Women ill with terror! Windows smashed. This extraordinary story probably a fabrication. Too good not to print—*cum grano!*"

He dropped the paper and stared blankly in front of him. "Probably a fabrication!"

He caught up the paper again, and re-read the whole business. "But where does the Tramp come in? Why the deuce was he chasing a Tramp?"

He sat down abruptly on the surgical couch. "He's not only invisible," he said, "but he's mad! Homicidal!"

When dawn came to mingle its pallor with the lamp-light and cigar smoke of the dining-room, Kemp was still pacing up and down, trying to grasp the incredible.

He was altogether too excited to sleep. His servants, descending sleepily, discovered him, and were inclined to think that overstudy had worked this ill on him. He gave them extraordinary but quite explicit instructions to lay breakfast for two in the belvedere study—and then to confine themselves to the basement and ground-floor. Then he continued to pace the dining-room until the morning's paper came. That had much to say and little to tell, beyond the confirmation of the evening before and a very baldly written account of another remarkable tale from Port Burdock. This gave Kemp the essence of the happenings at the Jolly Cricketers, and the name of Marvel. "He has made me keep with him twenty-four hours," Marvel testified. Certain minor facts were added to the Iping story, notably the cutting of the village telegraph-wire. But there was nothing to throw light on the connection between the Invisible Man and the Tramp; for Mr. Marvel had supplied no information about the three books, or the money with which he was lined. The incredulous tone had vanished and a shoal of reporters and inquirers were already at work elaborating the matter.

Kemp read every scrap of the report and sent his housemaid out to get every one of the morning papers she could. These also he devoured.

"He is invisible!" he said. "And it reads like rage growing to mania! The things he may do! The things he may do! And he's upstairs free as the air. What on earth ought I to do?

"For instance, would it be a breach of faith if—? No."

He went to a little untidy desk in the corner, and began a note. He tore this up half written, and wrote another. He read it over and considered it. Then he took an envelope and addressed it to "Colonel Adye, Port Burdock."

The Invisible Man awoke even as Kemp was doing this. He awoke in an evil temper, and Kemp, alert for every sound, heard his pattering feet rush suddenly across the bedroom overhead. Then a chair was flung over and the wash-hand stand tumbler smashed. Kemp hurried upstairs and rapped eagerly.

19

CERTAIN FIRST PRINCIPLES

"What's the matter?" asked Kemp, when the Invisible Man admitted him.

"Nothing," was the answer.

"But, confound it! The smash?"

"Fit of temper," said the Invisible Man. "Forgot this arm; and it's sore."

"You're rather liable to that sort of thing."

"I am."

Kemp walked across the room and picked up the fragments of broken glass. "All the facts are out about you," said Kemp, standing up with the glass in his hand; "all that happened in Iping, and down the hill. The world has become aware of its invisible citizen. But no one knows you are here."

The Invisible Man swore.

"The secret's out. I gather it was a secret. I don't know what your plans are, but of course I'm anxious to help you."

The Invisible Man sat down on the bed.

"There's breakfast upstairs," said Kemp, speaking as easily as possible, and he was delighted to find his strange guest rose willingly. Kemp led the way up the narrow staircase to the belvedere.

"Before we can do anything else," said Kemp, "I must understand a little more about this invisibility of yours." He had sat down, after one nervous glance out of the window, with the air of a man who has talking to do. His doubts of the sanity of the entire business flashed and vanished again as he looked across to where Griffin sat at the breakfast-table,—a headless, handless dressing-gown, wiping unseen lips on a miraculously held serviette.

"It's simple enough—and credible enough," said Griffin, putting the serviette aside and leaning the invisible head on an invisible hand.

"No doubt, to you, but—" Kemp laughed.

"Well, yes; to me it seemed wonderful at first, no doubt. But now, great God!—But we will do great things yet! I came on the stuff first at Chesilstowe."

"Chesilstowe?"

"I went there after I left London. You know I dropped medicine and took up physics? No? well, I did. *Light* fascinated me."

"Ah!"

"Optical density! The whole subject is a network of riddles—a network with solutions glimmering elusively through. And being but two-and-twenty and full of enthusiasm, I said, 'I will devote my life to this. This is worth while.' You know what fools we are at two-and-twenty?"

"Fools then or fools now," said Kemp.

"As though Knowing could be any satisfaction to a man!

"But I went to work—like a nigger. And I had hardly worked and thought about the matter six months before light came through one of the meshes suddenly—blindingly! I found a general principle of pigments and refraction,—a formula, a geometrical expression involving four dimensions. Fools, common men, even common mathematicians, do not know anything of what some general expression may mean to the student of molecular physics. In the books—the books that Tramp has hidden—there are marvels, miracles! But this was not a method, it was an idea that might lead to a method by which it would be possible, without changing any other property of matter,—except, in some instances, colours,—to lower the refractive index of a substance, solid or liquid, to that of air—so far as all practical purposes are concerned."

"Phew!" said Kemp. "That's odd! But still I don't see quite—I can understand that thereby you could spoil a valuable stone, but personal invisibility is a far cry."

"Precisely," said Griffin. "But consider: Visibility depends on the action of the visible bodies on light. Either a body absorbs light, or it reflects or refracts it, or does all these things. If it neither reflects nor refracts nor absorbs light, it cannot of itself be visible. You see an opaque red box, for instance, because the colour absorbs some of the light and reflects the rest, all the red part of the light, to you. If it did not absorb any particular part of the light, but reflected it all, then it would be a shining white box. Silver! A diamond box would neither absorb much of the light nor reflect much from the general surface, but just here and there where the surfaces were favourable the light would be reflected and refracted, so that you would get a brilliant appearance of flashing reflections and translucencies,—a sort of skeleton of light. A glass box would not be so brilliant, not so clearly visible, as a diamond box, because there would be less refraction and reflection. See that? From certain points of view you would see quite clearly through it. Some kinds of glass would be more visible than others, a box of flint glass would be brighter than a box of ordinary window glass. A box of very thin common glass would be hard to see in a bad light, because it would absorb hardly any light and refract and reflect very little. And if you put a sheet of common white glass in water, still more if you put it in some denser liquid than water, it would vanish almost altogether, because light passing from water to glass is only slightly refracted or reflected or indeed affected in any way. It is almost as invisible as a jet of coal gas or hydrogen is in air. And for precisely the same reason!"

"Yes," said Kemp, "that is pretty plain sailing."

"And here is another fact you will know to be true. If a sheet of glass is smashed, Kemp, and beaten into a powder, it becomes much more visible while it is in the air; it becomes at last an opaque white powder. This is because the powdering multiplies the surfaces of the glass at which refraction and reflection occur. In the sheet of glass there are only two surfaces; in the powder the light is reflected or refracted by each grain it passes through, and very little gets right through the powder. But if the white powdered glass is put into water, it forthwith vanishes. The powdered glass and water have much the same refractive index; that is, the light undergoes very little refraction or reflection in passing from one to the other.

"You make the glass invisible by putting it into a liquid of nearly the same refractive index; a transparent thing becomes invisible if it is put in any medium of almost the same refractive index. And if you will consider only a second, you will see also that the powder of glass might be made to vanish in air, if its refractive index could be made the same as that of air; for then there would be no refraction or reflection as the light passed from glass to air."

"Yes, yes," said Kemp. "But a man's not powdered glass!"

"No," said Griffin. "He's more transparent!"

"Nonsense!"

"That from a doctor! How one forgets! Have you already forgotten your physics, in ten years? Just think of all the things that are transparent and seem not to be so. Paper, for instance, is made up of transparent fibres, and it is white and opaque only for the same reason that a powder of glass is white and opaque. Oil white paper, fill up the interstices between the particles with oil so that there is no longer refraction or reflection except at the surfaces, and it becomes as transparent as glass. And not only paper, but cotton fibre, linen fibre, wool fibre, woody fibre, and *bone*, Kemp, *flesh*, Kemp, *hair*, Kemp, *nails* and *nerves*, Kemp, in fact the whole fabric of a man except the red of his blood and the black pigment of hair, are all made up of transparent, colourless tissue. So little suffices to make us visible one to the other. For the most part the fibres of a living creature are no more opaque than water."

"Great Heavens!" cried Kemp. "Of course, of course! I was thinking only last night of the sea larvae and all jelly-fish!"

"*Now* you have me! And all that I knew and had in mind a year after I left London—six years ago. But I kept it to myself. I had to do my work under frightful disadvantages. Oliver, my professor, was a scientific bounder, a journalist by instinct, a thief of ideas,— he was always prying! And you know the knavish system of the scientific world. I simply would not publish, and let him share my credit. I went on working. I got nearer and nearer making my for- mula into an experiment, a reality. I told no living soul, because I meant to flash my work upon the world with crushing effect,—to become famous at a blow. I took up the question of pigments to fill up certain gaps. And suddenly, not by design but by accident, I made a discovery in physiology."

"Yes?"

"You know the red colouring matter of blood; it can be made white—colourless—and remain with all the functions it has now!"

Kemp gave a cry of incredulous amazement.

The Invisible Man rose and began pacing the little study. "You may well exclaim. I remember that night. It was late at night,—in the daytime one was bothered with the gaping, silly students,— and I worked then sometimes till dawn. It came suddenly, splen- did and complete into my mind. I was alone; the laboratory was still, with the tall lights burning brightly and silently. In all my great moments I have been alone. 'One could make an animal—a tissue—transparent! One could make it invisible! All except the pigments. I could be invisible!' I said, suddenly realising what it meant to be an albino with such knowledge. It was overwhelming. I left the filtering I was doing, and went and stared out of the great window at the stars. 'I could be invisible!' I repeated.

"To do such a thing would be to transcend magic. And I beheld, unclouded by doubt, a magnificent vision of all that invisibility might mean to a man,—the mystery, the power, the freedom. Drawbacks I saw none. You have only to think! And I, a shabby, poverty-struck, hemmed-in demonstrator, teaching fools in a provincial college, might suddenly become—this. I ask you, Kemp, if *you*... Anyone, I tell you, would have flung himself upon that research. And I worked three years, and every mountain of difficulty I toiled over showed another from its summit. The infinite details! And the exasperation,—a professor, a provincial professor, always prying. 'When are you going to publish this work of yours?' was his everlasting question. And the students, the cramped means! Three years I had of it—

"And after three years of secrecy and exasperation, I found that to complete it was impossible,—impossible."

"How?" asked Kemp.

"Money," said the Invisible Man, and went again to stare out of the window.

He turned round abruptly. "I robbed the old man—robbed my father.

"The money was not his, and he shot himself."

20
At the House in Great Portland Street

For a moment Kemp sat in silence, staring at the back of the headless figure at the window. Then he started, struck by a thought, rose, took the Invisible Man's arm, and turned him away from the outlook.

"You are tired," he said, "and while I sit, you walk about. Have my chair."

He placed himself between Griffin and the nearest window.

For a space Griffin sat silent, and then he resumed abruptly:

"I had left the Chesilstowe cottage already," he said, "when that happened. It was last December. I had taken a room in London, a large unfurnished room in a big ill-managed lodging-house in a slum near Great Portland Street. The room was soon full of the appliances I had bought with his money; the work was going on steadily, successfully, drawing near an end. I was like a man emerging from a thicket, and suddenly coming on some unmeaning tragedy. I went to bury him. My mind was still on this research, and I did not lift a finger to save his character. I remember the funeral, the cheap hearse, the scant ceremony, the windy frost-bitten hillside, and the old college friend of his who read the service over him,—a shabby, black, bent old man with a snivelling cold.

"I remember walking back to the empty home, through the place that had once been a village and was now patched and tinkered by the jerry builders into the ugly likeness of a town. Every way the roads ran out at last into the desecrated fields and ended in rubble heaps and rank wet weeds. I remember myself as a gaunt black figure, going along the slippery, shiny pavement, and the strange sense of detachment I felt from the squalid respectability, the sordid commercialism of the place.

"I did not feel a bit sorry for my father. He seemed to me to be the victim of his own foolish sentimentality. The current cant required my attendance at his funeral, but it was really not my affair.

"But going along the High Street, my old life came back to me for a space, for I met the girl I had known ten years since. Our eyes met.

"Something moved me to turn back and talk to her. She was a very ordinary person.

"It was all like a dream, that visit to the old places. I did not feel then that I was lonely, that I had come out from the world into a desolate place. I appreciated my loss of sympathy, but I put it down to the general inanity of things. Re-entering my room seemed like the recovery of reality. There were the things I knew and loved. There stood the apparatus, the experiments arranged and waiting. And now there was scarcely a difficulty left, beyond the planning of details.

"I will tell you, Kemp, sooner or later, all the complicated processes. We need not go into that now. For the most part, saving certain gaps I chose to remember, they are written in cypher in those books that tramp has hidden. We must hunt him down. We must get those books again. But the essential phase was to place the transparent object whose refractive index was to be lowered between two radiating centres of a sort of ethereal vibration, of which I will tell you more fully later. No, not these Röntgen vibrations—I don't know that these others of mine have been described. Yet they are obvious enough. I needed two little dynamos, and these I worked with a cheap gas engine. My first experiment was with a bit of white wool fabric. I was the strangest thing in the world to see it in the flicker of the flashes soft and white, and then to watch it fade like a wreath of smoke and vanish.

"I could scarcely believe I had done it. I put my hand into the emptiness, and there was the thing as solid as ever. I felt it awkwardly, and threw it on the floor. I had a little trouble finding it again.

"And then came a curious experience. I heard a miaow behind me, and turning, saw a lean white cat, very dirty, on the cistern cover outside the window. A thought came into my head. 'Everything ready for you,' I said, and went to the window, opened it, and called softly. She came in, purring,—the poor beast was starving,— and I gave her some milk. All my food was in a cupboard in the corner of the room. After that she went smelling round the room,— evidently with the idea of making herself at home. The invisible rag upset her a bit; you should have seen her spit at it! But I made her comfortable on the pillow of my truckle-bed. And I gave her butter to get her to wash."

"And you processed her?"

"I processed her. But giving drugs to a cat is no joke, Kemp! And the process failed."

"Failed!"

"In two particulars. These were the claws and the pigment stuff—what is it?—at the back of the eye in a cat. You know?"

"*Tapetum.*"

"Yes, the *tapetum*. It didn't go. After I'd given the stuff to bleach the blood and done certain other things to her, I gave the beast opium, and put her and the pillow she was sleeping on, on the apparatus. And after all the rest had faded and vanished, there remained two little ghosts of her eyes."

"Odd!"

"I can't explain it. She was bandaged and clamped, of course,—so I had her safe; but she woke while she was still misty, and miaowed dismally, and some one came knocking. It was an old woman from downstairs, who suspected me of vivisecting,—a drink-sodden old creature, with only a white cat to care for in all the world. I whipped out some chloroform, and applied it, and answered the door. 'Did I hear a cat?' she asked. 'My cat?' 'Not here,' said I, very politely. She was a little doubtful and tried to peer past me into the room; strange enough to her no doubt,—bare walls, uncurtained windows, truckle-bed, with the gas engine vibrating, and the seethe of the radiant points, and that faint ghastly stinging of chloroform in the air. She had to be satisfied at last and went away again."

"How long did it take?" asked Kemp.

"Three or four hours—the cat. The bones and sinews and the fat were the last to go, and the tips of the coloured hairs. And, as I say, the back part of the eye, tough iridescent stuff it is, wouldn't go at all.

"It was night outside long before the business was over, and nothing was to be seen but the dim eyes and the claws. I stopped the gas engine, felt for and stroked the beast, which was still insensible, and then, being tired, left it sleeping on the invisible pillow and went to bed. I found it hard to sleep. I lay awake thinking weak aimless stuff, going over the experiment over and over again, or dreaming feverishly of things growing misty and vanishing about me, until everything, the ground I stood on, vanished, and so I came to that sickly falling nightmare one gets. About two, the cat began miaowing about the room. I tried to hush it by talking to it, and then I decided to turn it out. I remember the shock I had when striking a light—there were just the round eyes shining green—and nothing round them. I would have given it milk, but I hadn't any. It wouldn't be quiet, it just sat down and miaowed at the door. I tried to catch it, with an idea of putting it out of the window, but it wouldn't be caught, it vanished. Then it began miaowing in different parts of the room. At last I opened the window and made a bustle. I suppose it went out at last. I never saw any more of it.

"Then—Heaven knows why—I fell thinking of my father's funeral again, and the dismal windy hillside, until the day had come. I found sleeping was hopeless, and, locking my door after me, wandered out into the morning streets."

"You don't mean to say there's an invisible cat at large!" said Kemp.

"If it hasn't been killed," said the Invisible Man. "Why not?"

"Why not?" said Kemp. "I didn't mean to interrupt."

"It's very probably been killed," said the Invisible Man. "It was alive four days after, I know, and down a grating in Great Titchfield Street; because I saw a crowd round the place, trying to see whence the miaowing came."

He was silent for the best part of a minute. Then he resumed abruptly:

"I remember that morning before the change very vividly. I must have gone up Great Portland Street. I remember the barracks in Albany Street, and the horse soldiers coming out, and at last I found myself sitting in the sunshine and feeling very ill and strange, on the summit of Primrose Hill. It was a sunny day in January,— one of those sunny, frosty days that came before the snow this year. My weary brain tried to formulate the position, to plot out a plan of action.

"I was surprised to find, now that my prize was within my grasp, how inconclusive its attainment seemed. As a matter of fact I was worked out; the intense stress of nearly four years' continuous work left me incapable of any strength of feeling. I was apathetic, and I tried in vain to recover the enthusiasm of my first inquiries, the passion of discovery that had enabled me to compass even the downfall of my father's grey hairs. Nothing seemed to matter. I saw pretty clearly this was a transient mood, due to overwork and want of sleep, and that either by drugs or rest it would be possible to recover my energies.

"All I could think clearly was that the thing had to be carried through; the fixed idea still ruled me. And soon, for the money I had was almost exhausted. I looked about me at the hillside, with children playing and girls watching them, and tried to think of all the fantastic advantages an invisible man would have in the world. After a time I crawled home, took some food and a strong dose of strychnine, and went to sleep in my clothes on my unmade bed. Strychnine is a grand tonic, Kemp, to take the flabbiness out of a man."

"It's the devil," said Kemp. "It's the palaeolithic in a bottle."

"I awoke vastly invigorated and rather irritable. You know?"

"I know the stuff."

"And there was some one rapping at the door. It was my land-lord with threats and inquiries, an old Polish Jew in a long grey coat and greasy slippers. I had been tormenting a cat in the night he was sure,—the old woman's tongue had been busy. He insisted on knowing all about it. The laws of this country against vivisec-tion were very severe,—he might be liable. I denied the cat. Then the vibration of the little gas engine could be felt all over the house, he said. That was true, certainly. He edged round me into the room, peering about over his German-silver spectacles, and a sudden dread came into my mind that he might carry away something of my secret. I tried to keep between him and the concentrating ap-paratus I had arranged, and that only made him more curious. What was I doing? Why was I always alone and secretive? Was it legal? Was it dangerous? I paid nothing but the usual rent. His had always been a most respectable house—in a disreputable neighbourhood. Suddenly my temper gave way. I told him to get out. He began to protest, to jabber of his right of entry. In a mo-ment I had him by the collar; something ripped, and he went spin-ning out into his own passage. I slammed and locked the door and sat down quivering.

"He made a fuss outside, which I disregarded, and after a time he went away.

"But this brought matters to a crisis. I did not know what he would do, nor even what he had power to do. To move to fresh apartments would have meant delay; altogether I had barely twenty pounds left in the world,—for the most part in the bank,—and I could not afford that. Vanish! It was irresistible. Then there would be an inquiry, the sacking of my room—

"At the thought of the possibility of my work being exposed or interrupted at its very climax, I became angry and active. I hurried out with my three books of notes, my cheque-book,—the tramp has them now,—and directed them from the nearest Post Office to a house of call for letters and parcels in Great Portland Street. I tried to go out noiselessly. Coming in, I found my landlord going quietly upstairs; he had heard the door close, I suppose. You would have laughed to see him jump aside on the landing as I came tearing after him. He glared at me as I went by him, and I made the house quiver with the slamming of my door. I heard him come shuffling up to my floor, hesitate, and go down. I set to work upon my preparations forthwith.

"It was all done that evening and night. While I was still sitting under the sickly, drowsy influence of the drugs that decolourise blood, there came a repeated knocking at the door. It ceased, footsteps went away and returned, and the knocking was resumed. There was an attempt to push something under the door—a blue paper. Then in a fit of irritation I rose and went and flung the door wide open. 'Now then?' said I.

"It was my landlord, with a notice of ejectment or something. He held it out to me, saw something odd about my hands, I expect, and lifted his eyes to my face.

"For a moment he gaped. Then he gave a sort of inarticulate cry, dropped candle and writ together, and went blundering down the dark passage to the stairs. I shut the door, locked it, and went to the looking-glass. Then I understood his terror. My face was white—like white stone.

"But it was all horrible. I had not expected the suffering. A night of racking anguish, sickness and fainting. I set my teeth, though my skin was presently afire; all my body afire; but I lay there like grim death. I understood now how it was the cat had howled until I chloroformed it. Lucky it was I lived alone and untended in my room. There were times when I sobbed and groaned and talked. But I stuck to it. I became insensible and woke languid in the darkness.

"The pain had passed. I thought I was killing myself and I did not care. I shall never forget that dawn, and the strange horror of seeing that my hands had become as clouded glass, and watching them grow clearer and thinner as the day went by, until at last I could see the sickly disorder of my room through them, though I closed my transparent eyelids. My limbs became glassy, the bones and arteries faded, vanished, and the little white nerves went last. I ground my teeth and stayed there to the end. At last only the dead tips of the finger-nails remained, pallid and white, and the brown stain of some acid upon my fingers.

"I struggled up. At first I was as incapable as a swathed infant,— stepping with limbs I could not see. I was weak and very hungry. I went and stared at nothing in my shaving-glass, at nothing save where an attenuated pigment still remained behind the retina of my eyes, fainter than mist. I had to hang on to the table and press my forehead to the glass.

"It was only by a frantic effort of will that I dragged myself back to the apparatus and completed the process.

"I slept during the forenoon, pulling the sheet over my eyes to shut out the light, and about midday I was awakened again by a knocking. My strength had returned. I sat up and listened and heard a whispering. I sprang to my feet and as noiselessly as possible began to detach the connections of my apparatus, and to distribute it about the room, so as to destroy the suggestions of its arrangement. Presently the knocking was renewed and voices called, first my landlord's, and then two others. To gain time I answered them. The invisible rag and pillow came to hand and I opened the window and pitched them out on to the cistern cover. As the window opened, a heavy crash came at the door. Some one had charged it with the idea of smashing the lock. But the stout bolts I had screwed up some days before stopped him. That startled me, made me angry. I began to tremble and do things hurriedly.

"I tossed together some loose paper, straw, packing paper and so forth, in the middle of the room, and turned on the gas. Heavy blows began to rain upon the door. I could not find the matches. I beat my hands on the wall with rage. I turned down the gas again, stepped out of the window on the cistern cover, very softly lowered the sash, and sat down, secure and invisible, but quivering with anger, to watch events. They split a panel, I saw, and in another moment they had broken away the staples of the bolts and stood in the open doorway. It was the landlord and his two stepsons, sturdy young men of three or four and twenty. Behind them fluttered the old hag of a woman from downstairs.

"You may imagine their astonishment on finding the room empty. One of the younger men rushed to the window at once, flung it up and stared out. His staring eyes and thick-lipped bearded face came a foot from my face. I was half minded to hit his silly countenance, but I arrested my doubled fist. He stared right through me. So did the others as they joined him. The old man went and peered under the bed, and then they all made a rush for the cupboard. They had to argue about it at length in Yiddish and Cockney English. They concluded I had not answered them, that their imagination had deceived them. A feeling of extraordinary elation took the place of my anger as I sat outside the window and watched these four people—for the old lady came in, glancing suspiciously about her like a cat, trying to understand the riddle of my behaviour.

"The old man, so far as I could understand his patois, agreed with the old lady that I was a vivisectionist. The sons protested in garbled English that I was an electrician, and appealed to the dynamos and radiators. They were all nervous against my arrival, although I found subsequently that they had bolted the front door. The old lady peered into the cupboard and under the bed, and one of the young men pushed up the register and stared up the chimney. One of my fellow lodgers, a costermonger who shared the opposite room with a butcher, appeared on the landing, and he was called in and told incoherent things.

"It occurred to me that the radiators, if they fell into the hands of some acute well-educated person, would give me away too much, and watching my opportunity, I came into the room and tilted one of the little dynamos off its fellow on which it was standing, and smashed both apparatus. Then, while they were trying to explain the smash, I dodged out of the room and went softly downstairs.

"I went into one of the sitting-rooms and waited until they came down, still speculating and argumentative, all a little disappointed at finding no 'horrors,' and all a little puzzled how they stood with regard to me. Then I slipped up again with a box of matches, fired my heap of paper and rubbish, put the chairs and bedding thereby, led the gas to the affair, by means of an india-rubber tube, and waving a farewell to the room left it for the last time."

"You fired the house!" exclaimed Kemp.

"Fired the house. It was the only way to cover my trail—and no doubt it was insured. I slipped the bolts of the front door quietly and went out into the street. I was invisible, and I was only just beginning to realise the extraordinary advantage my invisibility gave me. My head was already teeming with plans of all the wild and wonderful things I had now impunity to do."

21

IN OXFORD STREET

"In going downstairs the first time I found an unexpected difficulty because I could not see my feet; indeed I stumbled twice, and there was an unaccustomed clumsiness in gripping the bolt. By not looking down, however, I managed to walk on the level passably well.

"My mood, I say, was one of exaltation. I felt as a seeing man might do, with padded feet and noiseless clothes, in a city of the blind. I experienced a wild impulse to jest, to startle people, to clap men on the back, fling people's hats astray, and generally revel in my extraordinary advantage.

"But hardly had I emerged upon Great Portland Street, however (my lodgings was close to the big draper's shop there), when I heard a clashing concussion and was hit violently behind, and turning saw a man carrying a basket of soda-water siphons, and looking in amazement at his burden. Although the blow had really hurt me, I found something so irresistible in his astonishment that I laughed aloud. 'The devil's in the basket,' I said, and suddenly twisted it out of his hand. He let go incontinently, and I swung the whole weight into the air.

"But a fool of a cabman, standing outside a public house, made a sudden rush for this, and his extending fingers took me with excruciating violence under the ear. I let the whole down with a smash on the cabman, and then, with shouts and the clatter of feet about me, people coming out of shops, vehicles pulling up, I realised what I had done for myself, and cursing my folly, backed against a shop window and prepared to dodge out of the confusion. In a moment I should be wedged into a crowd and inevitably discovered. I pushed by the butcher boy, who luckily did not turn to see the nothingness that shoved him aside, and dodged behind the cabman's four-wheeler. I do not know how they settled the business. I hurried straight across the road, which was happily clear, and hardly heeding which way I went, in the fright of detection the incident had given, plunged into the afternoon throng of Oxford Street.

"I tried to get into the stream of people, but they were too thick for me, and in a moment my heels were being trodden upon. I took to the gutter, the roughness of which I found painful to my feet, and forthwith the shaft of a crawling hansom dug me forcibly under the shoulder blade, reminding me that I was already bruised severely. I staggered out of the way of the cab, avoided a perambulator by a convulsive movement, and found myself behind the hansom. A happy thought saved me, and as this drove slowly along I followed in its immediate wake, trembling and astonished at the turn of my adventure. And not only trembling, but shivering. It was a bright day in January and I was stark naked and the thin slime of mud that covered the road was freezing. Foolish as it seems to me now, I had not reckoned that, transparent or not, I was still amenable to the weather and all its consequences.

"Then suddenly a bright idea came into my head. I ran round and got into the cab. And so, shivering, scared, and sniffing with the first intimations of a cold, and with the bruises in the small of my back growing upon my attention. I drove slowly along Oxford Street and past Tottenham Court Road. My mood was as different from that in which I had sallied forth ten minutes ago as it is possible to imagine. This invisibility indeed! The one thought that possessed me was—how was I to get out of the scrape I was in.

"We crawled past Mudie's, and there a tall woman with five or six yellow-labelled books hailed my cab, and I sprang out just in time to escape her, shaving a railway van narrowly in my flight. I made off up the roadway to Bloomsbury Square, intending to strike north past the Museum and so get into the quiet district. I was not cruelly chilled, and the strangeness of my situation so unnerved me that I whimpered as I ran. At the northward corner of the Square a little white dog ran out of the Pharmaceutical Society's offices, and incontinently made for me, nose down.

"I had never realised it before, but the nose is to the mind of a dog what the eye is to the mind of a seeing man. Dogs perceive the scent of a man moving as men perceive his vision. This brute began barking and leaping, showing, as it seemed to me, only too plainly that he was aware of me. I crossed Great Russell Street, glancing over my shoulder as I did so, and went some way along Montague Street before I realised what I was running towards.

"Then I became aware of a blare of music, and looking along the street saw a number of people advancing out of Russell Square, red shirts, and the banner of the Salvation Army to the fore. Such a crowd, chanting in the roadway and scoffing on the pavement, I could not hope to penetrate, and dreading to go back and farther from home again, and deciding on the spur of the moment, I ran up the white steps of a house facing the Museum railings, and stood there until the crowd should have passed. Happily the dog stopped at the noise of the band too, hesitated, and turned tail, running back to Bloomsbury Square again.

"On came the band, bawling with unconscious irony some hymn about 'When shall we see his Face?' and it seemed an interminable time to me before the tide of the crowd washed along the pavement by me. Thud, thud, thud, came the drum with a vibrating resonance, and for the moment I did not notice two urchins stopping at the railings by me. 'See 'em,' said one. 'See what?' said the other. 'Why—them footmarks—bare. Like what you makes in mud.'

"I looked down and saw the youngsters had stopped and were gaping at the muddy footmarks I had left behind me up the newly whitened steps. The passing people elbowed and jostled them, but their confounded intelligence was arrested. 'Thud, thud, thud, When, thud, shall we see, thud, his face, thud, thud.' 'There's a barefoot man gone up them steps, or I don't know nothing,' said one. 'And he ain't never come down again. And his foot was a-bleeding.'

"The thick of the crowd had already passed. 'Looky there, Ted,' quoth the younger of the detectives, with the sharpness of surprise in his voice, and pointed straight to my feet. I looked down and saw at once the dim suggestion of their outline sketched in splashes of mud. For a moment I was paralysed.

"'Why, that's rum,' said the elder. 'Dashed rum! It's just like the ghost of a foot, ain't it?' He hesitated and advanced with outstretched hand. A man pulled up short to see what he was catching, and then a girl. In another moment he would have touched me. Then I saw what to do. I made a step, the boy started back with an exclamation, and with a rapid movement I swung myself over into the portico of the next house. But the smaller boy was sharp-eyed enough to follow the movement and before I was well down the steps and upon the pavement, he had recovered from his momentary astonishment and was shouting out that the feet had gone over the wall.

"They rushed round and saw my new footmarks flash into being on the lower step and upon the pavement. 'What's up?' asked some one. 'Feet! Look! Feet running!' Everybody in the road, except my three pursuers, was pouring along after the Salvation Army, and this not only impeded me but them. There was an eddy of surprise and interrogation. At the cost of bowling over one young fellow I got through, and in another moment I was rushing headlong round the circuit of Russell Square, with six or seven astonished people following my footmarks. There was no time for explanation, or else the whole host would have been after me.

"Twice I doubled round corners, thrice I crossed the road and came back on my tracks, and then, as my feet grew hot and dry, the damp impressions began to fade. At last I had a breathing space and rubbed my feet clean with my hands, and so got away altogether. The last I saw of the chase was a little group of a dozen people perhaps, studying with infinite perplexity a slowly drying footprint that had resulted from a puddle in Travistock Square—a footprint as isolated and incomprehensible to them as Crusoe's solitary discovery.

"This running warmed me to a certain extent, and I went on with a better courage through the maze of less frequented roads that runs hereabouts. My back had now become very stiff and sore, my tonsils were painful from the cabman's fingers, and the skin of my neck had been scratched by his nails; my feet hurt exceedingly and I was lame from a little cut on one foot. I saw in time a blind man approaching me, and fled limping, for I feared his subtle intuitions. Once or twice accidental collisions occurred and I left people amazed, with unaccountable curses ringing in their ears. Then came something silent and quiet against my face, and across the Square fell a thin veil of slowly falling flakes of snow. I had caught a cold, and do as I would I could not avoid an occasional sneeze. And every dog that came in sight, with its pointing nose and curious sniffing, was a terror to me.

"Then came men and boys running, first one and then others, and shouting as they ran. It was a fire. They ran in the direction of my lodging, and looking back down a street I saw a mass of black smoke streaming up above the roofs and telephone wires. It was my lodging burning; my clothes, my apparatus, all my resources indeed, except my cheque-book and the three volumes of memoranda that awaited me in Great Portland Street, were there. Burning! I had burnt my boats—if ever a man did! The place was blazing."

The Invisible Man paused and thought. Kemp glanced nervously out of the window. "Yes?" he said. "Go on."

22

IN THE EMPORIUM

"So last January, with the beginning of a snowstorm in the air about me—and if it settled on me it would betray me!—weary, cold, painful, inexpressibly wretched, and still but half convinced of my invisible quality, I began this new life to which I am committed. I had no refuge, no appliances, no human being in the world in whom I could confide. To have told my secret would have given me away—made a mere show and rarity of me. Nevertheless, I was half minded to accost some passer-by and throw myself upon his mercy. But I knew too clearly the terror and brutal cruelty my advances would evoke. I made no plans in the street. My sole object was to get shelter from the snow, to get myself covered and warm; then I might hope to plan. But even to me, an Invisible Man, the rows of London houses stood latched, barred, and bolted impregnably.

"Only one thing could I see clearly before me, the cold exposure and misery of the snowstorm and the night.

"And then I had a brilliant idea. I turned down one of the roads leading from Gower Street to Tottenham Court Road, and found myself outside Omniums, the big establishment where everything is to be bought—you know the place—meat, grocery, linen, furniture, clothing, oil paintings even—a huge meandering collection of shops rather than a shop. I had thought I should find the doors open, but they were closed, and as I stood in the wide entrance a carriage stopped outside, and a man in uniform—you know the kind of personage with 'Omnium' on his cap—flung open the door. I contrived to enter, and walking down the shop—it was a department where they were selling ribbons and gloves and stockings and that kind of thing—came to a more spacious region devoted to picnic baskets and wicker furniture.

"I did not feel safe there, however; people were going to and fro, and I prowled restlessly about until I came upon a huge section in an upper floor containing scores and hundreds of bedsteads, and beyond these I found a resting-place at last among a huge pile of folded flock mattresses. The place was already lit up and aggreeably warm, and I decided to remain where I was, keeping a cautious eye on the two or three sets of shopmen and customers who were meandering through the place until closing time came. Then I should be able, I thought, to rob the place for food and clothing, and disguised, prowl through it and examine its resources, perhaps sleep on some of the bedding. That seemed an acceptable plan. My idea was to procure clothing to make myself a muffled but acceptable figure, to get money, and then to recover my books and parcels where they awaited me, take a lodging somewhere and elaborate plans for the complete realisation of the advantages my invisibility gave me (as I still imagined) over my fellow-men.

"Closing time arrived quickly enough; it could not have been more than an hour after I took up my position on the mattresses before I noticed the blinds of the windows being drawn, and customers being marched doorward. And then a number of brisk young men began with remarkable alacrity to tidy up the goods that remained disturbed. I left my lair as the crowds diminished, and prowled cautiously out into the less desolate parts of the shop. I was really surprised to observe how rapidly the young men and women whipped away the goods displayed for sale during the day. All the boxes of goods, the hanging fabrics, the festoons of lace, the boxes of sweets in the grocery section, the displays of this and that, were being whipped down, folded up, slapped into tidy receptacles, and everything that could not be taken down and put away had sheets of some coarse stuff like sacking flung over it. Finally all the chairs were turned up on to the counters, leaving the floor clear. Directly each of these young people had done, he or she made promptly for the door with such an expression of animation as I have rarely observed in a shop assistant before. Then came a lot of youngsters scattering sawdust and carrying pails and brooms. I had to dodge to get out of the way, and as it was, my ankle got stung with the sawdust. For some time, wandering through the swathed and darkened departments, I could hear the brooms at work. And at last a good hour or more after the shop had been closed, came a noise of locking doors. Silence came upon the place, and I found myself wandering through the vast and intricate shops, galleries and showrooms of the place, alone. It was very still; in one place I remember passing near one of the Tottenham Court Road entrances and listening to the tapping of bootheels of the passers-by.

"My first visit was to the place where I had seen stockings and gloves for sale. It was dark, and I had the devil of a hunt after matches, which I found at last in the drawer of the little cash desk. Then I had to get a candle. I had to tear down wrappings and ransack a number of boxes and drawers, but at last I managed to turn out what I sought; the box label called them lambswool pants, and lambswool vests. Then socks, a thick comforter, and then I went to the clothing place and got trousers, a lounge jacket, an overcoat and a slouch hat—a clerical sort of hat with the brim turned down. I began to feel a human being again, and my next thought was food.

"Upstairs was a refreshment department, and there I got cold meat. There was coffee still in the urn, and I lit the gas and warmed it up again, and altogether I did not do badly. Afterwards, prowling through the place in search of blankets—I had to put up at last with a heap of down quilts—I came upon a grocery section with a lot of chocolate and candied fruits, more than was good for me indeed—and some white burgundy. And near that was a toy department, and I had a brilliant idea. I found some artificial noses—dummy noses, you know, and I thought of dark spectacles. But Omniums had no optical department. My nose had been a difficulty indeed—I had thought of paint. But the discovery set my mind running on wigs and masks and the like. Finally I went to sleep on a heap of down quilts, very warm and comfortable.

"My last thoughts before sleeping were the most agreeable I had had since the change. I was in a state of physical serenity, and that was reflected in my mind. I thought that I should be able to slip out unobserved in the morning with my clothes upon me, muffling my face with a white wrapper I had taken, purchase, with the money I had taken, spectacles and so forth, and so complete my disguise. I lapsed into disorderly dreams of all the fantastic things that had happened during the last few days. I saw the ugly little Jew of a landlord vociferating in his rooms; I saw his two sons marvelling, and the wrinkled old woman's gnarled face as she asked for her cat. I experienced again the strange sensation of seeing the cloth disappear, and so I came round to the windy hillside and the sniffing old clergyman mumbling 'Dust to dust, earth to earth,' and my father's open grave.

"'You also,' said a voice, and suddenly I was being forced towards the grave. I struggled, shouted, appealed to the mourners, but they continued stonily following the service; the old clergyman, too, never faltered droning and sniffing through the ritual. I realised I was invisible and inaudible, that overwhelming forces had their grip on me. I struggled in vain, I was forced over the brink, the coffin rang hollow as I fell upon it, and the gravel came flying after me in spadefuls. Nobody heeded me, nobody was aware of me. I made convulsive struggles and awoke.

"The pale London dawn had come, the place was full of a chilly grey light that filtered round the edges of the window blinds. I sat up, and for a time I could not think where this ample apartment, with its counters, its piles of rolled stuff, its heaps of quilts and cushions, its iron pillars, might be. Then, as recollection came back to me, I heard voices in conversation.

"Then far down the place, in the brighter light of some department which had already raised its blinds, I saw two men approaching. I scrambled to my feet, looking about me for some way of escape, and even as I did so the sound of my movement made them aware of me. I suppose they saw merely a figure moving quietly and quickly away. 'Who's that?' cried one, and 'Stop there,' shouted the other. I dashed round a corner and came full tilt—a faceless figure, mind you!—on a lanky lad of fifteen. He yelled and I bowled him over, rushed past him, turned another corner, and by a happy inspiration threw myself flat behind a counter. In another moment feet went running past and I heard voices shouting, 'All hands to the doors!' asking what was 'up,' and giving one another advice how to catch me.

"Lying on the ground, I felt scared out of my wits. But—odd as it may seem—it did not occur to me at the moment to take off my clothes as I should have done. I had made up my mind, I suppose, to get away in them, and that ruled me. And then down the vista of the counters came a bawling of 'Here he is!'

"I sprang to my feet, whipped a chair off the counter, and sent it whirling at the fool who had shouted, turned, came into another round a corner, sent him spinning, and rushed up the stairs. He kept his footing, gave a view hallo! and came up the staircase hot after me. Up the staircase were piled a multitude of those bright-coloured pot things—what are they?"

"Art pots," suggested Kemp.

"That's it! Art pots. Well, I turned at the top step and swung round, plucked one out of a pile and smashed it on his silly head as he came at me. The whole pile of pots went headlong, and I heard shouting and footsteps running from all parts. I made a mad rush for the refreshment place, and there was a man in white like a man cook, who took up the chase. I made one last desperate turn and found myself among lamps and ironmongery. I went behind the counter of this, and waited for my cook, and as he bolted in at the head of the chase, I doubled him up with a lamp. Down he went, and I crouched behind the counter and began whipping off my clothes as fast as I could. Coat, jacket, trousers, shoes were all right, but a lambswool vest fits a man like a skin. I heard more men coming, my cook was lying quiet on the other side of the counter, stunned or scared speechless, and I had to make another dash for it, like a rabbit hunted out of a wood-pile.

"'This way, policeman!' I heard some one shouting. I found myself in my bedstead store-room again, and at the end a wilderness of wardrobes. I rushed among them, went flat, got rid of my vest after infinite wriggling, and stood a free man again, panting and scared, as the policeman and three of the shopmen came round the corner. They made a rush for the vest and pants, and collared the trousers. 'He's dropping his plunder,' said one of the young men. 'He must be somewhere here.'

"But they did not find me all the same.

"I stood watching them hunt for me for a time, and cursing my ill-luck in losing the clothes. Then I went into the refreshment-room, drank a little milk I found there, and sat down by the fire to consider my position.

"In a little while two assistants came and began to talk over the business very excitedly and like the fools they were. I heard a magnified account of my depredations, and other speculations as to my whereabouts. Then I fell to scheming again. The insurmountable difficulty of the place, especially now it was alarmed, was to get any plunder out of it. I went down into the warehouse to see if there was any chance of packing and addressing a parcel, but I could not understand the system of checking. About eleven o'clock, the snow having thawed as it fell, and the day being finer and a little warmer than the previous one, I decided that the Emporium was hopeless, and went out again, exasperated at my want of success, with only the vaguest plans of action in my mind."

23

IN DRURY LANE

"But you begin to realise now," said the Invisible Man, "the full disadvantage of my condition. I had no shelter, no covering. To get clothing was to forego all my advantage, to make of myself a strange and terrible thing. I was fasting; for to eat, to fill myself with unassimilated matter, would be to become grotesquely visible again."

"I never thought of that," said Kemp.

"Nor had I. And the snow had warned me of other dangers. I could not go abroad in snow—it would settle on me and expose me. Rain, too, would make me a watery outline, a glistening surface of a man—a bubble. And fog—I should be like a fainter bubble in a fog, a surface, a greasy glimmer of humanity. Moreover, as I went abroad—in the London air—I gathered dirt about my ankles, floating smuts and dust upon my skin. I did not know how long it would be before I should become visible from that cause also. But I saw clearly it could not be for long.

"Not in London at any rate.

"I went into the slums towards Great Portland Street, and found myself at the end of the street in which I had lodged. I did not go that way, because of the crowd halfway down it opposite to the still smoking ruins of the house I had fired. My most immediate problem was to get clothing. What to do with my face puzzled me. Then I saw in one of those little miscellaneous shops—news, sweets, toys, stationery, belated Christmas tomfoolery, and so forth—an array of masks and noses. I realised that problem was solved. In a flash I saw my course. I turned about, no longer aimless, and went—circuitously in order to avoid the busy ways, towards the back streets north of the Strand; for I remembered, though not very distinctly where, that some theatrical costumiers had shops in that district.

"The day was cold, with a nipping wind down the northward running streets. I walked fast to avoid being overtaken. Every crossing was a danger, every passenger a thing to watch alertly. One man as I was about to pass him at the top of Bedford Street, turned upon me abruptly and came into me, sending me into the road and almost under the wheel of a passing hansom. The verdict of the cab-rank was that he had had some sort of stroke. I was so unnerved by this encounter that I went into Covent Garden Market and sat down for some time in a quiet corner by a stall of violets, panting and trembling. I found I had caught a fresh cold, and had to turn out after a time lest my sneezes should attract attention.

"At last I reached the object of my quest, a dirty fly-blown little shop in a byway near Drury Lane, with a window full of tinsel robes, sham jewels, wigs, slippers, dominoes and theatrical photographs. The shop was old-fashioned and low and dark, and the house rose above it for four storeys, dark and dismal.

"I peered through the window and, seeing no one within, entered. The opening of the door set a clanking bell ringing. I left it open, and walked round a bare costume stand, into a corner behind a cheval glass. For a minute or so no one came. Then I heard heavy feet striding across a room, and a man appeared down the shop.

"My plans were now perfectly definite. I proposed to make my way into the house, secrete myself upstairs, watch my opportunity, and when everything was quiet, rummage out a wig, mask, spectacles, and costume, and go into the world, perhaps a grotesque but still a credible figure. And incidentally of course I could rob the house of any available money.

"The man who had entered the shop was a short, slight, hunched, beetle-browed man, with long arms and very short bandy legs. Apparently I had interrupted a meal. He stared about the shop with an expression of expectation. This gave way to surprise, and then anger, as he saw the shop empty. 'Damn the boys!' he said. He went to stare up and down the street. He came in again in a minute, kicked the door to with his foot spitefully, and went muttering back to the house door.

"I came forward to follow him, and at the noise of my movement he stopped dead. I did so too, startled by his quickness of ear. He slammed the house door in my face.

"I stood hesitating. Suddenly I heard his quick footsteps returning, and the door reopened. He stood looking about the shop like one who was still not satisfied. Then, murmuring to himself, he examined the back of the counter and peered behind some fixtures. Then he stood doubtful. He had left the house door open and I slipped into the inner room.

"It was a queer little room, poorly furnished and with a number of big masks in the corner. On the table was his belated breakfast, and it was a confoundedly exasperating thing for me, Kemp, to have to sniff his coffee and stand watching while he came in and resumed his meal. And his table manners were irritating. Three doors opened into the little room, one going upstairs and one down, but they were all shut. I could not get out of the room while he was there, I could scarcely move because of his alertness, and there was draught down my back. Twice I strangled a sneeze just in time.

"The spectacular quality of my sensations was curious and novel, but for all that I was heartily tired and angry long before he had done his eating. But at last he made an end and putting his beggarly crockery on the black tin tray upon which he had had his teapot, and gathering all the crumbs up on the mustard-stained cloth, he took the whole lot of things after him. His burden prevented his shutting the door behind him—as he would have done; I never saw such a man for shutting doors—and I followed him into a very dirty underground kitchen and scullery. I had the pleasure of seeing him begin to wash up, and then, finding no good in keeping down there, and the brick floor being cold to my feet, I returned upstairs and sat in his chair by the fire. It was burning low, and scarcely thinking, I put on a little coal.

"The noise of this brought him up at once, and he stood aglare. He peered about the room and was within an ace of touching me. Even after that examination, he scarcely seemed satisfied. He stopped in the doorway and took a final inspection before he went down.

"I waited in the little parlour for an age, and at last he came up and opened the upstairs door. I just managed to get by him.

"On the staircase he stopped suddenly, so that I very nearly blundered into him. He stood looking back right into my face and listening. 'I could have sworn,' he said. His long hairy hand pulled at his lower lip. His eye went up and down the staircase. Then he grunted and went on up again.

"His hand was on the handle of a door, and then he stopped again with the same puzzled anger on his face. He was becoming aware of the faint sounds of my movements about him. The man must have had diabolically acute hearing. He suddenly flashed into rage. 'If there's any one in this house,' he cried with an oath, and left the threat unfinished. He put his hand in his pocket, failed to find what he wanted, and rushing past me went blundering noisily and pugnaciously downstairs. But I did not follow him. I sat on the head of the staircase until his return.

"Presently he came up again, still muttering. He opened the door of the room, and before I could enter, slammed it in my face.

"I resolved to explore the house, and spent some time in doing so as noiselessly as possible. The house was very old and tumble-down, damp so that the paper in the attics was peeling from the walls, and rat-infested. Some of the door handles were stiff and I was afraid to turn them. Several rooms I did inspect were unfur-nished, and others were littered with theatrical lumber, bought second-hand, I judged, from its appearance. In one room next to his I found a lot of old clothes. I began routing among these, and in my eagerness forgot again the evident sharpness of his ears. I heard a stealthy footstep and, looking up just in time, saw him peering in at the tumbled heap and holding an old-fashioned revolver in his hand. I stood perfectly still while he stared about open-mouthed and suspicious. 'It must have been her,' he said slowly. 'Damn her!'

"He shut the door quietly, and immediately I heard the key turn in the lock. Then his footsteps retreated. I realised abruptly that I was locked in. For a minute a did not know what to do. I walked from door to window and back, and stood perplexed. A gust of anger came upon me. But I decided to inspect the clothes before I did anything further, and my first attempt brought down a pile from an upper shelf. This brought him back, more sinister than ever. That time he actually touched me, jumped back with amazement and stood astonished in the middle of the room.

"Presently he calmed a little. 'Rats,' he said in an undertone, fingers on lip. He was evidently a little scared. I edged quietly out of the room, but a plank creaked. Then the infernal little brute started going all over the house, revolver in hand and locking door after door and pocketing the keys. When I realised what he was up to I had a fit of rage—I could hardly control myself sufficiently to watch my opportunity. By this time I knew he was alone in the house, and so I made no more ado, but knocked him on the head."

"Knocked him on the head!" exclaimed Kemp.

"Yes—stunned him—as he was going downstairs. Hit him from behind with a stool that stood on the landing. He went downstairs like a bag of old boots."

"But—! I say! The common conventions of humanity—"

"Are all very well for common people. But the point was, Kemp, that I had to get out of that house in a disguise without his seeing me. I couldn't think of any other way of doing it. And then I gagged him with a Louis Quatorze vest and tied him up in a sheet."

"Tied him up in a sheet!"

"Made a sort of bag of it. It was rather a good idea to keep the idiot scared and quiet, and a devilish hard thing to get out of—head away from the string. My dear Kemp, it's no good your sitting and glaring as though I was a murderer. It had to be done. He had his revolver. If once he saw me he would be able to describe me—"

"But still," said Kemp, "in England—to-day. And the man was in his own house, and you were—well, robbing."

"Robbing! Confound it! You'll call me a thief next! Surely, Kemp, you're not fool enough to dance on the old strings. Can't you see my position?"

"And his too," said Kemp.

The Invisible Man stood up sharply. "What do you mean to say?"

Kemp's face grew a trifle hard. He was about to speak and checked himself. "I suppose, after all," he said with a sudden change of manner, "the thing had to be done. You were in a fix. But still—"

"Of course I was in a fix—an infernal fix. And he made me wild too—hunting me about the house, fooling about with his revolver, locking and unlocking doors. He was simply exasperating. You don't blame me, do you? You don't blame me?"

"I never blame any one," said Kemp. "It's quite out of fashion. What did you do next?"

"I was hungry. Downstairs I found a loaf and some rank cheese—more than sufficient to satisfy my hunger. I took some brandy and water, and then went up past my impromptu bag—he was lying quite still—to the room containing the old clothes. This looked out upon the street, two lace curtains brown with dirt guarding the window. I went and peered out through their interstices. Outside the day was bright—by contrast with the brown shadows of the dismal house in which I found myself, dazzlingly bright. A brisk traffic was going by, fruit carts, a hansom, a four-wheeler with a pile of boxes, a fishmonger's cart. I turned with spots of colour swimming before my eyes to the shadowy fixtures behind me. My excitement was giving place to a clear apprehension of my position again. The room was full of a faint scent of benzoline, used, I suppose, in cleaning the garments.

"I began a systematic search of the place. I should judge the hunchback had been alone in the house for some time. He was a curious person. Everything that could possibly be of service to me I collected in the clothes storeroom, and then I made a deliberate selection. I found a handbag I thought a suitable possession, and some powder, rouge, and sticking-plaster.

"I had thought of painting and powdering my face and all that there was to show of me, in order to render myself visible, but the disadvantage of this lay in the fact that I should require turpentine and other appliances and a considerable amount of time before I could vanish again. Finally I chose a mask of the better type, slightly grotesque but not more so than many human beings, dark glasses, greyish whiskers, and a wig. I could find no underclothing, but that I could buy subsequently, and for the time I swathed myself in calico dominoes and some white cashmere scarfs. I could find no socks, but the hunchback's boots were rather a loose fit and sufficed. In a desk in the shop were three sovereigns and about thirty shillings' worth of silver, and in a locked cupboard I burst in the inner room were eight pounds in gold. I could go forth into the world again, equipped.

"Then came a curious hesitation. Was my appearance really— credible? I tried myself with a little bedroom looking-glass, inspecting myself from every point of view to discover any forgotten chink, but it all seemed sound. I was grotesque to the theatrical pitch, a stage miser, but I was certainly not a physical impossibility. Gathering confidence, I took my looking-glass down into the shop, pulled down the shop blinds, and surveyed myself from every point of view with the help of the cheval glass in the corner.

"I spent some minutes screwing up my courage and then unlocked the shop door and marched out into the street, leaving the little man to get out of his sheet again when he liked. In five minutes a dozen turnings intervened between me and the costumier's shop. No one appeared to notice me very pointedly. My last difficulty seemed overcome."

He stopped again.

"And you troubled no more about the hunchback?" said Kemp.

"No," said the Invisible Man. "Nor have I heard what became of him. I suppose he untied himself or kicked himself out. The knots were pretty tight."

He became silent, and went to the window and stared out.

"What happened when you went out into the Strand?"

"Oh!—disillusionment again. I thought my troubles were over. Practically I thought I had impunity to do whatever I chose, everything—save to give away my secret. So I thought. Whatever I did, whatever the consequences might be, was nothing to me. I had merely to fling aside my garments and vanish. No person could hold me. I could take my money where I found it. I decided to treat myself to a sumptuous feast, and then put up at a good hotel, and accumulate a new outfit of property. I felt amazingly confident—it's not particularly pleasant recalling that I was an ass. I went into a place and was already ordering a lunch, when it occurred to me that I could not eat unless I exposed my invisible face. I finished ordering the lunch, told the man I should be back in ten minutes, and went out exasperated. I don't know if you have ever been disappointed in your appetite."

"Not quite so badly," said Kemp, "but I can imagine it."

"I could have smashed the silly devils. At last, faint with the desire for tasteful food, I went into another place and demanded a private room. 'I am disfigured,' I said. 'Badly.' They looked at me curiously, but of course it was not their affair—and so at last I got my lunch. It was not particularly well served, but it sufficed; and when I had had it, I sat over a cigar, trying to plan my line of action. And outside a snowstorm was beginning.

"The more I thought it over, Kemp, the more I realised what a helpless absurdity an Invisible Man was—in a cold and dirty climate and a crowded civilised city. Before I made this mad experiment I had dreamt of a thousand advantages. That afternoon it seemed all disappointment. I went over the heads of the things a man reckons desirable. No doubt invisibility made it possible to get them, but it made it impossible to enjoy them when they are got. Ambition—what is the good of pride of place when you cannot appear there? What is the good of the love of woman when her name must needs be Delilah? I have no taste for politics, for the blackguardisms of fame, for philanthropy, for sport. What was I to do? And for this I had become a wrapped-up mystery, a swathed and bandaged caricature of a man!"

He paused, and his attitude suggested a roving glance at the window.

"But how did you get to Iping?" said Kemp, anxious to keep his guest busy talking.

"I went there to work. I had one hope. It was a half idea! I have it still. It is a full blown idea now. A way of getting back! Of restoring what I have done. When I choose. When I have done all I mean to do invisibly. And that is what I chiefly want to talk to you about now."

"You went straight to Iping?"

"Yes. I had simply to get my three volumes of memoranda and my cheque-book, my luggage and underclothing, order a quantity of chemicals to work out this idea of mine—I will show you the calculations as soon as I get my books—and then I started. Jove! I remember the snowstorm now, and the accursed bother it was to keep the snow from damping my pasteboard nose."

"At the end," said Kemp, "the day before yesterday, when they found you out, you rather—to judge by the papers—"

"I did. Rather. Did I kill that fool of a constable?"

"No," said Kemp. "He's expected to recover."

"That's his luck, then. I clean lost my temper, the fools! Why couldn't they leave me alone? And that grocer lout?"

"There are no deaths expected," said Kemp.

"I don't know about that tramp of mine," said the Invisible Man, with an unpleasant laugh.

"By Heaven, Kemp, you don't know what rage *is!* To have worked for years, to have planned and plotted, and then to get some fumbling purblind idiot messing across your course! Every conceivable sort of silly creature that has ever been created has been sent to cross me.

"If I have much more of it, I shall go wild—I shall start mowing 'em.

"As it is, they've made things a thousand times more difficult."

"No doubt it's exasperating," said Kemp, dryly.

24

THE PLAN THAT FAILED

"But now," said Kemp, with a side glance out of the window, "what are we to do?"

He moved nearer his guest as he spoke in such a manner as to prevent the possibility of a glimpse of the three men who were advancing up the hill road—with an intolerable slowness, as it seemed to Kemp.

"What were you planning to do when you were heading for Port Burdock? *Had* you any plan?"

"I was going to clear out of the country. But I have altered that plan rather since seeing you. I thought it would be wise, now the weather is hot and invisibility possible, to make for the South. Especially as my secret was known, and every one would be on the lookout for a masked and muffled man. You have a line of steamers from here to France. My idea was to get aboard one and run the risks of the passage. Thence I could go by train into Spain, or else get to Algiers. It would not be difficult. There a man might always be invisible—and yet live. And do things. I was using that tramp as a money box and luggage carrier, until I decided how to get my books and things sent over to meet me."

"That's clear."

"And then the filthy brute must needs try and rob me! He has hidden my books, Kemp. Hidden my books! If I can lay my hands on him!"

"Best plan to get the books out of him first."

"But where is he? Do you know?"

"He's in the town police station, locked up, by his own request, in the strongest cell in the place."

"Cur!" said the Invisible Man.

"But that hangs up your plans a little."

"We must get those books; those books are vital."

"Certainly," said Kemp, a little nervously, wondering if he heard footsteps outside. "Certainly we must get those books. But that won't be difficult, if he doesn't know they're for you."

"No," said the Invisible Man, and thought.

Kemp tried to think of something to keep the talk going, but the Invisible Man resumed of his own accord.

"Blundering into your house, Kemp," he said, "changes all my plans. For you are a man that can understand. In spite of all that has happened, in spite of this publicity, of the loss of my books, of what I have suffered, there still remain great possibilities, huge possibilities—

"You have told no one I am here?" he asked abruptly.

Kemp hesitated.

"That was implied," he said.

"No one?" insisted Griffin.

"Not a soul."

"Ah! Now—" The Invisible Man stood up, and sticking his arms akimbo began to pace the study.

"I made a mistake, Kemp, a huge mistake, in carrying this thing through alone. I have wasted strength, time, opportunities. Alone— it is wonderful how little a man can do alone! To rob a little, to hurt a little, and there is the end.

"What I want, Kemp, is a goal-keeper, a helper, and a hiding-place, an arrangement whereby I can sleep and eat and rest in peace, and unsuspected. I must have a confederate. With a confederate, with food and rest—a thousand things are possible.

"Hitherto I have gone on vague lines. We have to consider all that invisibility means, all that it does not mean. It means little advantage for eavesdropping and so forth—one makes sounds. It's of little help, a little help perhaps—in housebreaking and so forth. Once you've caught me you could easily imprison me. But on the other hand I am hard to catch. This invisibility, in fact, is only good in two cases: It's useful in getting away, it's useful in approaching. It's particularly useful, therefore, in killing. I can walk round a man, whatever weapon he has, choose my point, strike as I like. Dodge as I like. Escape as I like."

Kemp's hand went to his moustache. Was that a movement downstairs?

"And it is killing we must do, Kemp."

"It is killing we must do," repeated Kemp. "I'm listening to your plan, Griffin, but I'm not agreeing, mind. *Why* killing?"

"Not wanton killing but a judicious slaying. The point is they know there is an Invisible Man—as well as we know there is an Invisible Man. And that Invisible Man, Kemp, must now establish a Reign of Terror. Yes—no doubt it's startling. But I mean it. A Reign of Terror. He must take some town like your Burdock and terrify and dominate it. He must issue his orders. He can do that in a thousand ways—scraps of paper thrust under doors would suffice. And all who disobey his orders he must kill, and kill all who would defend the disobedient."

"Humph!" said Kemp, no longer listening to Griffin but to the sound of his front door opening and closing.

"It seems to me, Griffin," he said, to cover his wandering attention, "that your confederate would be in a difficult position."

"No one would know he was a confederate," said the Invisible Man, eagerly. And then suddenly, "Hush! What's that downstairs?"

"Nothing," said Kemp, and suddenly began to speak loud and fast. "I don't agree to this, Griffin," he said. "Understand me, I don't agree to this. Why dream of playing a game against the race? How can you hope to gain happiness? Don't be a lone wolf. Publish your results; take the world—take the nation at least—into your confidence. Think what you might do with a million helpers—"

The Invisible Man interrupted Kemp. "There are footsteps coming upstairs," he said in a low voice.

"Nonsense," said Kemp.

"Let me see," said the Invisible Man, and advanced, arm extended, to the door.

Kemp hesitated for a second and then moved to intercept him. The Invisible Man started and stood still. "Traitor!" cried the Voice, and suddenly the dressing-gown opened, and sitting down the Unseen began to disrobe. Kemp made three swift steps to the door, and forthwith the Invisible Man—his legs had vanished—sprang to his feet with a shout. Kemp flung the door open.

As it opened, there came a sound of hurrying feet downstairs and voices.

With a quick movement Kemp thrust the Invisible Man back, sprang aside, and slammed the door. The key was outside and ready. In another moment Griffin would have been alone in the belvedere study, a prisoner. Save for one little thing. The key had been slipped in hastily that morning. As Kemp slammed the door it fell noisily upon the carpet.

Kemp's face became white. He tried to grip the door handle with both hands. For a moment he stood lugging. Then the door gave six inches. But he got it closed again. The second time it was jerked a foot wide, and the dressing-gown came wedging itself into the opening. His throat was gripped by invisible fingers, and he left his hold on the handle to defend himself. He was forced back, tripped and pitched heavily into the corner of the landing. The empty dressing-gown was flung on the top of him.

Halfway up the staircase was Colonel Adye, the recipient of Kemp's letter, the chief of the Burdock police. He was staring aghast at the sudden appearance of Kemp, followed by the extraordinary sight of clothing tossing empty in the air. He saw Kemp felled, and struggling to his feet. He saw him rush forward, and go down again, felled like an ox.

Then suddenly he was struck violently. By nothing! A vast weight, it seemed, leapt upon him, and he was hurled headlong down the staircase, with a grip at his throat and a knee in his groin. An invisible foot trod on his back, a ghostly patter passed downstairs, he heard the two police officers in the hall shout and run, and the front door of the house slammed violently.

He rolled over and sat up staring. He saw, staggering down the staircase, Kemp, dusty and dishevelled, one side of his face white from a blow, his lip bleeding, holding a pink dressing-gown and some underclothing in his arms.

"My God!" cried Kemp, "the game's up! He's gone!"

25
THE HUNTING OF THE INVISIBLE MAN

For a space Kemp was too inarticulate to make Adye understand the swift things that had just happened. The two men stood on the landing, Kemp speaking swiftly, the grotesque swathings of Griffin still on his arm. But presently Adye began to grasp something of the situation.

"He's mad," said Kemp; "inhuman. He is pure selfishness. He thinks of nothing but his own advantage, his own safety. I have listened to such a story this morning of brutal self-seeking! He has wounded men. He will kill them unless we can prevent him. He will create a panic. Nothing can stop him. He is going out now—furious!"

"He must be caught," said Adye. "That is certain."

"But how?" cried Kemp, and suddenly became full of ideas. "You must begin at once. You must set every available man to work. You must prevent his leaving this district. Once he gets away he may go through the countryside as he wills, killing and maiming. He dreams of a reign of terror! A reign of terror, I tell you. You must set a watch on trains and roads and shipping. The garrison must help. You must wire for help. The only thing that may keep him here is the thought of recovering some books of notes he counts of value. I will tell you of that! There is a man in your police station—Marvel."

"I know," said Adye, "I know. Those books—yes."

"And you must prevent him from eating or sleeping; day and night the country must be astir for him. Food must be locked up and secured, all food, so that he will have to break his way to it. The houses everywhere must be barred against him. Heaven send us cold nights and rain! The whole countryside must begin hunting and keep hunting. I tell you, Adye, he is a danger, a disaster; unless he is pinned and secured, it is frightful to think of the things that may happen."

"What else can we do?" said Adye. "I must go down at once and begin organising. But why not come? Yes—you come too! Come, and we must hold a sort of council of war,—get Hopps to help—and the railway managers. By jove! it's urgent. Come along—tell me as we go. What else is there we can do? Put that stuff down."

In another moment Adye was leading the way downstairs. They found the front door open and the policemen standing outside staring at empty air. "He's got away, sir," said one.

"We must go to the central station at once," said Adye. "One of you go on down and get a cab to come up and meet us—quickly. And now, Kemp, what else?"

"Dogs," said Kemp. "Get dogs. They don't see him, but they wind him. Get dogs."

"Good," said Adye. "It's not generally known, but the prison officials over at Halstead know a man with bloodhounds. Dogs. What else?"

"Bear in mind," said Kemp, "his food shows. After eating, his food shows until it is assimilated. So that he has to hide after eating. You must keep on beating—every thicket, every quiet corner.

And put all weapons, all implements that might be weapons, away. He can't carry such things for long. And what he can snatch up and strike men with must be hidden away."

"Good again," said Adye. "We shall have him yet!"

"And on the roads," said Kemp, and hesitated.

"Yes?" said Adye.

"Powdered glass," said Kemp. "It's cruel, I know. But think of what he may do!"

Adye drew the air in between his teeth sharply. "It's unsportsmanlike. I don't know. But I'll have powdered glass got ready. If he goes too far—"

"The man's become inhuman, I tell you," said Kemp. "I am as sure he will establish a reign of terror—so soon as he has got over the emotions of this escape—as I am sure I am talking to you. Our only chance is to be ahead. He has cut himself off from his kind. His blood be upon his own head."

26

THE WICKSTEED MURDER

The Invisible Man seems to have rushed out of Kemp's house in a state of blind fury. A little child playing near Kemp's gateway was violently caught up and thrown aside, so that its ankle was broken, and thereafter for some hours the Invisible Man passed out of human perceptions. No one knows where he went nor what he did. But one can imagine him hurrying through the hot June forenoon, up the hill and on to the open downland behind Port Burdock, raging and despairing at his intolerable fate, and sheltering at last, heated and weary, amid the thickets of Hintondean, to piece together again his shattered schemes against his species. That seems the most probable refuge for him, for there it was he reasserted himself in a grimly tragical manner about two in the afternoon.

One wonders what his state of mind may have been during that time, and what plans he devised. No doubt he was almost ecstatically exasperated by Kemp's treachery, and though we may be able to understand the motives that led to that deceit, we may still imagine and even sympathise a little with the fury the attempted surprise must have occasioned. Perhaps something of the stunned astonishment of his Oxford Street experiences may have returned to him, for evidently he had counted on Kemp's co-operation in his brutal dream of a terrorised world. At any rate he vanished from human ken about midday, and no living witness can tell what he did until about half-past two. It was a fortunate thing, perhaps, for humanity, but for him it was a fatal inaction.

During that time a growing multitude of men scattered over the countryside were busy. In the morning he had still been simply a legend, a terror; in the afternoon, by virtue chiefly of Kemp's drily worded proclamation, he was presented as a tangible antagonist, to be wounded, captured, or overcome, and the countryside began organising itself with inconceivable rapidity. By two o'clock even he might still have removed himself out of the district by getting aboard a train, but after two that became impossible. Every passenger train along the lines on a great parallelogram between Southampton, Manchester, Brighton, and Horsham, travelled with locked doors, and the goods traffic was almost entirely suspended. And in a great circle of twenty miles round Port Burdock, men armed with guns and bludgeons were presently setting out in groups of three and four, with dogs, to beat the roads and fields.

Mounted policemen rode along the country lanes, stopping at every cottage and warning the people to lock up their houses, and keep indoors unless they were armed, and all the elementary schools had broken up by three o'clock, and the children, scared and keeping together in groups, were hurrying home. Kemp's proclamation—signed indeed by Adye—was posted over almost the whole district by four or five o'clock in the afternoon. It gave briefly but clearly all the conditions of the struggle, the necessity of keeping the Invisible Man from food and sleep, the necessity for incessant watchfulness and for a prompt attention to any evidence of his movements. And so swift and decided was the action of the authorities, so prompt and universal was the belief in this strange being, that before nightfall an area of several hundred square miles was in a stringent state of siege. And before nightfall, too, a thrill of horror went through the whole watching nervous countryside. Going from whispering mouth to mouth, swift and certain over the length and breadth of the county, passed the story of the murder of Mr. Wicksteed.

If our supposition that the Invisible Man's refuge was the Hintondean thickets, then we must suppose that in the early afternoon he sallied out again bent upon some project that involved the use of a weapon. We cannot know what the project was, but the evidence that he had the iron rod in hand before he met Wicksteed is to me at least overwhelming.

We can know nothing of the details of the encounter. It occurred on the edge of a gravel pit, not two hundred yards from Lord Burdock's Lodge gate. Everything points to a desperate struggle,— the trampled ground, the numerous wounds Mr. Wicksteed received, his splintered walking-stick; but why the attack was made— save in a murderous frenzy—it is impossible to imagine. Indeed the theory of madness is almost unavoidable. Mr. Wicksteed was a man of forty-five or forty-six, steward to Lord Burdock, of inoffensive habits and appearance, the very last person in the world to provoke such a terrible antagonist. Against him it would seem the Invisible Man used an iron rod dragged from a broken piece of fence. He stopped this quiet man, going quietly home to his midday meal, attacked him, beat down his feeble defences, broke his arm, felled him, and smashed his head to a jelly.

He must have dragged this rod out of the fencing before he met his victim; he must have been carrying it ready in his hand. Only two details beyond what has already been stated seem to bear on the matter. One is the circumstance that the gravel pit was not in Mr. Wicksteed's direct path home, but nearly a couple of hundred yards out of his way. The other is the assertion of a little girl to the effect that, going to her afternoon school, she saw the murdered man "trotting" in a peculiar manner across a field towards the gravel pit. Her pantomime of his action suggests a man pursuing something on the ground before him and striking at it ever and again with his walking-stick. She was the last person to see him alive. He passed out of her sight to his death, the struggle being hidden from her only by a clump of beech trees and a slight depression in the ground.

Now this, to the present writer's mind at least, lifts the murder out of the realm of the absolutely wanton. We may imagine that Griffin had taken the rod as a weapon indeed, but without any deliberate intention of using it in murder. Wicksteed may then have come by and noticed this rod inexplicably moving through the air. Without any thought of the Invisible Man—for Port Burdock is ten miles away—he may have pursued it. It is quite conceivable that he may not even have heard of the Invisible Man. One can then imagine the Invisible Man making off—quietly in order to avoid discovering his presence in the neighbourhood, and Wicksteed, excited and curious, pursuing this unaccountably locomotive object—finally striking at it.

No doubt the Invisible Man could easily have distanced his middle-aged pursuer under ordinary circumstances, but the position in which Wicksteed's body was found suggests that he had the ill luck to drive his quarry into a corner between a drift of stinging nettles and the gravel pit. To those who appreciate the extraordinary irascibility of the Invisible Man, the rest of the encounter will be easy to imagine.

But this is pure hypothesis. The only undeniable facts—for stories of children are often unreliable—are the discovery of Wicksteed's body, done to death, and of the blood-stained iron rod flung among the nettles. The abandonment of the rod by Griffin, suggests that in the emotional excitement of the affair, the purpose for which he took it—if he had a purpose—was abandoned. He was certainly an intensely egotistical and unfeeling man, but the sight of his victim, his first victim, bloody and pitiful at his feet, may have released some long pent fountain of remorse to flood for a time whatever scheme of action he had contrived.

After the murder of Mr. Wicksteed, he would seem to have struck across the country towards the downland. There is a story of a voice heard about sunset by a couple of men in a field near Fern Bottom. It was wailing and laughing, sobbing and groaning, and ever and again it shouted. It must have been queer hearing. It drove up across the middle of a clover field and died away towards the hills.

That afternoon the Invisible Man must have learnt something of the rapid use Kemp had made of his confidences. He must have found houses locked and secured; he may have loitered about railway stations and prowled about inns, and no doubt he read the proclamations and realised something of the nature of the campaign against him. And as the evening advanced, the fields became dotted here and there with groups of three or four men, and noisy with the yelping of dogs. These men-hunters had particular instructions as to the way they should support one another in the case of an encounter. He avoided them all. We may understand something of his exasperation, and it could have been none the less because he himself had supplied the information that was being used so remorselessly against him. For that day at least he lost heart; for nearly twenty-four hours, save when he turned on Wicksteed, he was a hunted man. In the night, he must have eaten and slept; for in the morning he was himself again, active, powerful, angry, and malignant, prepared for his last great struggle against the world.

27
THE SIEGE OF KEMP'S HOUSE

Kemp read a strange missive, written in pencil on a greasy sheet of paper.

"You have been amazingly energetic and clever," this letter ran, "though what you stand to gain by it I cannot imagine. You are against me. For a whole day you have chased me; you have tried to rob me of a night's rest. But I have had food in spite of you, I have slept in spite of you, and the game is only beginning. The game is only beginning. There is nothing for it, but to start the Terror. This announces the first day of the Terror. Port Burdock is no longer under the Queen tell your Colonel of Police, and the rest of them; it is under me—the Terror! This is day one of year one of the new epoch—the Epoch of the Invisible Man. I am Invisible Man the First. To begin with the rule will be easy. The first day there will be one execution for the sake of example—a man named Kemp.

Death starts for him to-day. He may lock himself away, hide himself away, get guards about him, put on armour if he likes; Death, the unseen Death, is coming. Let him take precautions; it will impress my people. Death starts from the pillar-box by midday. The letter will fall in as the postman comes along, then off! The game begins. Death starts. Help him not, my people, lest Death fall upon you also. To-day Kemp is to die."

Kemp read this letter twice. "It's no hoax," he said. "That's his voice! And he means it."

He turned the folded sheet over and saw on the addressed side of it the postmark Hintondean, and the prosaic detail, "2d. to pay."

He got up, leaving his lunch unfinished—the letter had come by the one o'clock post—and went into his study. He rang for his housekeeper, and told her to go round the house at once, examine all the fastenings of the windows, and close all the shutters. He closed the shutters of his study himself. From a locked drawer in his bedroom he took a little revolver, examined it carefully, and put it into the pocket of his lounge jacket. He wrote a number of brief notes, one to Colonel Adye, gave them to his servant to take, with explicit instructions as to her way of leaving the house. "There is no danger," he said, and added a mental reservation, "to you." He remained meditative for a space after doing this, and then returned to his cooling lunch.

He ate with gaps of thought. Finally he struck the table sharply. "We will have him!" he said; "and I am the bait. He will come too far."

He went up to the belvedere, carefully shutting every door after him. "It's a game," he said, "an odd game—but the chances are all for me, Mr. Griffin, in spite of your invisibility. Griffin *contra mundum*... with a vengeance!"

He stood at the window staring at the hot hillside. "He must get food every day—and I don't envy him. Did he really sleep last night? Out in the open somewhere—secure from collisions. I wish we could get some good cold wet weather instead of the heat.

"He may be watching me now."

He went close to the window. Something rapped smartly against the brickwork over the frame, and made him start violently.

"I'm getting nervous," said Kemp. But it was five minutes before he went to the window again. "It must have been a sparrow," he said.

Presently he heard the front-door bell ringing, and hurried downstairs. He unbolted and unlocked the door, examined the chain, put it up, and opened cautiously without showing himself. A familiar voice hailed him. It was Adye.

"Your servant's been assaulted, Kemp," he said round the door.

"What!" exclaimed Kemp.

"Had that note of yours taken away from her. He's close about here. Let me in."

Kemp released the chain, and Adye entered through as narrow an opening as possible. He stood in the hall, looking with infinite relief at Kemp refastening the door. "Note was snatched out of her hand. Scared her horribly. She's down at the station. Hysterics. He's close here. What was it about?"

Kemp swore.

"What a fool I was," said Kemp. "I might have known. It's not an hour's walk from Hintondean. Already!"

"What's up?" said Adye.

"Look here!" said Kemp, and led the way into his study. He handed Adye the Invisible Man's letter. Adye read it and whistled softly. "And you—?" said Adye.

"Proposed a trap—like a fool," said Kemp, "and sent my proposal out by a maid servant. To him."

Adye followed Kemp's profanity.

"He'll clear out," said Adye.

"Not he," said Kemp.

A resounding smash of glass came from upstairs. Adye had a silvery glimpse of a little revolver half out of Kemp's pocket. "It's a window, upstairs!" said Kemp, and led the way up. There came a second smash while they were still on the staircase. When they reached the study they found two of the three windows smashed, half the room littered with splintered glass, and one big flint lying on the writing table. The two men stopped in the doorway, contemplating the wreckage. Kemp swore again, and as he did so the third window went with a snap like a pistol, hung starred for a moment, and collapsed in jagged, shivering triangles into the room.

"What's this for?" said Adye.

"It's a beginning," said Kemp.

"There's no way of climbing up here?"

"Not for a cat," said Kemp.

"No shutters?"

"Not here. All the downstairs rooms—Hullo!"

Smash, and then whack of boards hit hard came from downstairs. "Confound him! said Kemp. "That must be—yes—it's one of the bedrooms. He's going to do all the house. But he's a fool. The shutters are up, and the glass will fall outside. He'll cut his feet."

Another window proclaimed its destruction. The two men stood on the landing perplexed. "I have it!" said Adye. "Let me have a stick or something, and I'll go down to the station and get the bloodhounds put on. That ought to settle him! They're hard by—not ten minutes—"

Another window went the way of its fellows.

"You haven't a revolver?" asked Adye.

Kemp's hand went to his pocket. Then he hesitated. "I haven't one—at least to spare."

"I'll bring it back," said Adye, "you'll be safe here."

Kemp handed him the weapon.

"Now for the door," said Adye.

As they stood hesitating in the hall, they heard one of the first-floor bedroom windows crack and clash. Kemp went to the door and began to slip the bolts as silently as possible. His face was a little paler than usual. "You must step straight out," said Kemp. In another moment Adye was on the doorstep and the bolts were dropping back into the staples. He hesitated for a moment, feeling more comfortable with his back against the door. Then he marched, upright and square, down the steps. He crossed the lawn and approached the gate. A little breeze seemed to ripple over the grass. Something moved near him. "Stop a bit," said a Voice, and Adye stopped dead and his hand tightened on the revolver.

"Well?" said Adye, white and grim, and every nerve tense.

"Oblige me by going back to the house," said the Voice, as tense and grim as Adye's.

"Sorry," said Adye a little hoarsely, and moistened his lips with his tongue. The Voice was on his left front, he thought. Suppose he were to take his luck with a shot?

"What are you going for?" said the Voice, and there was a quick movement of the two, and a flash of sunlight from the open lip of Adye's pocket.

Adye desisted and thought. "Where I go," he said slowly, "is my own business." The words were still on his lips, when an arm came round his neck, his back felt a knee, and he was sprawling backward. He drew clumsily and fired absurdly, and in another moment he was struck in the mouth and the revolver wrested from his grip. He made a vain clutch at a slippery limb, tried to struggle up and fell back. "Damn!" said Adye. The Voice laughed. "I'd kill you now if it wasn't the waste of a bullet," it said. He saw the revolver in mid-air, six feet off, covering him.

"Well?" said Adye, sitting up.

"Get up," said the Voice.

Adye stood up.

"Attention" said the Voice, and then fiercely, "Don't try any games. Remember I can see your face if you can't see mine. You've got to go back to the house."

"He won't let me in," said Adye.

"That's a pity," said the Invisible Man. "I've got no quarrel with you."

Adye moistened his lips again. He glanced away from the barrel of the revolver and saw the sea far off very blue and dark under the midday sun, the smooth green down, the white cliff of the Head, and the multitudinous town, and suddenly he knew that life was very sweet. His eyes came back to this little metal thing hanging between heaven and earth, six yards away. "What am I to do?" he said sullenly.

"What am I to do?" asked the Invisible Man. "You will get help. The only thing is for you to go back."

"I will try. If he lets me in will you promise not to rush the door?"

"I've got no quarrel with you," said the Voice.

Kemp had hurried upstairs after letting Adye out, and now crouching among the broken glass and peering cautiously over the edge of the study window-sill, he saw Adye stand parleying with the Unseen. "Why doesn't he fire?" whispered Kemp to himself. Then the revolver moved a little and the glint of the sunlight flashed in Kemp's eyes. He shaded his eyes and tried to see the source of the blinding beam.

"Surely!" he said. "Adye has given up the revolver."

"Promise not to rush the door," Adye was saying. "Don't push a winning game too far. Give a man a chance."

"You go back to the house. I tell you flatly I will not promise anything."

Adye's decision seemed suddenly made. He turned towards the house, walking slowly with his hands behind him. Kemp watched him—puzzled. The revolver vanished, flashed again into sight, vanished again, and became evident on a closer scrutiny as a little dark object following Adye. Then things happened very quickly. Adye leapt backwards, swung round, clutched at this little object, missed it, threw up his hands and fell forward on his face, leaving a little puff of blue in the air. Kemp did not hear the sound of the shot. Adye writhed, raised himself on one arm, fell forward, and lay still.

For a space Kemp remained staring at the quiet carelessness of Adye's attitude. The afternoon was very hot and still, nothing seemed stirring in all the world save a couple of yellow butterflies chasing each other through the shrubbery between the house and the road gate. Adye lay on the lawn near the gate. The blinds of all the villas down the hill-road were drawn, but in one little green summer-house was a white figure, apparently an old man asleep. Kemp scrutinised the surroundings of the house for a glimpse of the revolver, but it had vanished. His eyes came back to Adye. The game was opening well.

Then came a ringing and knocking at the front door, that grew at last tumultuous, but pursuant to Kemp's instructions the servants had locked themselves into their rooms. This was followed by a silence. Kemp sat listening and then began peering cautiously out of the three windows, one after another. He went to the staircase head and stood listening uneasily. He armed himself with his bedroom poker, and went to examine the interior fastenings of the ground-floor windows again. Everything was safe and quiet. He returned to the belvedere. Adye lay motionless over the edge of the gravel just as he had fallen. Coming along the road by the villas were the housemaid and two policemen.

Everything was deadly still. The three people seemed very slow in approaching. He wondered what his antagonist was doing.

He started. There was a smash from below. He hesitated and went downstairs again. Suddenly the house resounded with heavy blows and the splintering of wood. He heard a smash and the destructive clang of the iron fastenings of the shutters. He turned the key and opened the kitchen door. As he did so, the shutters, split and splintering, came flying inward. He stood aghast. The window frame, save for one cross bar, was still intact, but only little teeth of glass remained in the frame. The shutters had been driven in with an axe, and now the axe was descending in sweeping blows upon the window frame and the iron bars defending it. Then suddenly it leapt aside and vanished. He saw the revolver lying on the path outside, and then the little weapon sprang into the air. He dodged back. The revolver cracked just too late, and a splinter from the edge of the closing door flashed over his head. He slammed and locked the door, and as he stood outside he heard Griffin shouting and laughing. Then the blows of the axe, with their splitting and smashing accompaniments, were resumed.

Kemp stood in the passage trying to think. In a moment the Invisible Man would be in the kitchen. This door would not keep him a moment, and then—

A ringing came at the front door again. It would be the policemen. He ran into the hall, put up the chain, and drew the bolts. He made the girl speak before he dropped the chain, and the three people blundered into the house in a heap, and Kemp slammed the door again.

"The Invisible Man!" said Kemp. "He has a revolver, with two shots—left. He's killed Adye. Shot him anyhow. Didn't you see him on the lawn? He's lying there."

"Who?" said one of the policemen.

"Adye," said Kemp.

"We came round the back way," said the girl.

"What's that smashing?" asked one of the policemen.

"He's in the kitchen—or will be. He has found an axe—"

Suddenly the house was full of the Invisible Man's resounding blows on the kitchen door. The girl stared towards the kitchen, shuddered, and retreated into the dining-room. Kemp tried to explain in broken sentences. They heard the kitchen door give.

"This way," cried Kemp, starting into activity, and bundled the policemen into the dining-room doorway.

"Poker," said Kemp, and rushed to the fender. He handed a poker to each policeman. He suddenly flung himself backward.

"Whup!" said one policeman, ducked, and caught the axe on his poker. The pistol snapped its penultimate shot and ripped a valuable Sidney Cooper. The second policeman brought his poker down on the little weapon, as one might knock down a wasp, and sent it rattling to the floor.

At the first clash the girl screamed, stood screaming for a moment by the fireplace, and then ran to open the shutters—possibly with an idea of escaping by the shattered window.

The axe receded into the passage, and fell to a position about two feet from the ground. They could hear the Invisible Man breathing. "Stand away, you two," he said. "I want that man Kemp."

"We want you," said the first policeman, making a quick step forward and wiping with his poker at the Voice. The Invisible Man must have started back. He blundered into the umbrella stand. Then, as the policeman staggered with the swing of the blow he had aimed, the Invisible Man countered with the axe, the helmet crumpled like paper, and the blow sent the man spinning to the floor at the head of the kitchen stairs. But the second policeman, aiming behind the axe with his poker, hit something soft that snapped. There was a sharp exclamation of pain and the axe fell to the ground. The policeman wiped again at vacancy and hit nothing; he put his foot on the axe, and struck again. Then he stood, poker clubbed, listening intent for the slightest movement.

He heard the dining-room window open, and a quick rush of feet within. His companion rolled over and sat up with the blood running down between his eye and ear. "Where is he?" asked the man on the floor.

"Don't know. I've hit him. He's standing somewhere in the hall. Unless he's slipped past you. Doctor Kemp—sir."

Pause.

"Doctor Kemp," cried the policeman again.

The second policeman struggled to his feet. He stood up. Suddenly the faint pad of bare feet on the kitchen stairs could be heard. "Yap!" cried the first policeman and incontinently flung his poker. It smashed a little gas bracket.

He made as if he would pursue the Invisible Man downstairs. Then he thought better of it and stepped into the dining-room.

"Doctor Kemp," he began, and stopped short—

"Doctor Kemp's in here," he said, as his companion looked over his shoulder.

The dining-room window was wide open, and neither housemaid nor Kemp was to be seen.

The second policeman's opinion of Kemp was terse and vivid.

28

THE HUNTER HUNTED

Mr. Heelas, Mr. Kemp's nearest neighbour among the villa holders, was asleep in his summer house when the siege of Kemp's house began. Mr. Heelas was one of the sturdy minority who refused to believe "in all this nonsense" about an Invisible Man. His wife, however, as he was to be reminded subsequently, did. He insisted upon walking about his garden just as if nothing was the matter, and he went to sleep in the afternoon in accordance with the custom of years. He slept through the smashing of the windows, and then woke up suddenly with a curious persuasion of something wrong. He looked across at Kemp's house, rubbed his eyes and looked again. Then he put his feet to the ground, and sat listening. He said he was damned, and still the strange thing was visible. The house looked as though it had been deserted for weeks—after a violent riot. Every window was broken, and every window, save those of the belvedere study, was blinded by the internal shutters.

"I could have sworn it was all right"—he looked at his watch—"twenty minutes ago."

He became aware of a measured concussion and the clash of glass, far away in the distance. And then, as he sat open-mouthed, came a still more wonderful thing. The shutters of the drawing-room window were flung open violently, and the housemaid in her outdoor hat and garments, appeared struggling in a frantic manner to throw up the sash. Suddenly a man appeared beside her, helping her—Dr. Kemp! In another moment the window was open, and the housemaid was struggling out; she pitched forward and vanished among the shrubs. Mr. Heelas stood up, exclaiming vaguely and vehemently at all these wonderful things. He saw Kemp stand on the sill, spring from the window, and reappear almost instantaneously running along a path in the shrubbery and stooping as he ran, like a man who evades observation. He vanished behind a laburnum, and appeared again clambering a fence that abutted on the open down. In a second he had tumbled over and was running at a tremendous pace down the slope towards Mr. Heelas.

"Lord!" cried Mr. Heelas, struck with an idea; "it's that Invisible Man brute! It's right, after all!"

With Mr. Heelas to think things like that was to act, and his cook watching him from the top window was amazed to see him come pelting towards the house at a good nine miles an hour. "Thought he wasn't afraid," said the cook. "Mary, just come here!" There was a slamming of doors, a ringing of bells, and the voice of Mr. Heelas bellowing like a bull. "Shut the doors, shut the windows, shut everything! the Invisible Man is coming!" Instantly the house was full of screams and directions, and scurrying feet. He ran to shut the French windows himself that opened on the veranda; as he did so Kemp's head and shoulders and knee appeared over the edge of the garden fence. In another moment Kemp had ploughed through the asparagus, and was running across the tennis lawn to the house.

"You can't come in," said Mr. Heelas, shutting the bolts. "I'm very sorry if he's after you, but you can't come in!"

Kemp appeared with a face of terror close to the glass, rapping and then shaking frantically at the French window. Then, seeing his efforts were useless, he ran along the veranda, vaulted the end, and went to hammer at the side door. Then he ran round by the side gate to the front of the house, and so into the hill-road. And Mr. Heelas staring from his window—a face of horror—had scarcely witnessed Kemp vanish, ere the asparagus was being trampled this way and that by feet unseen. At that Mr. Heelas fled precipitately upstairs, and the rest of the chase is beyond his purview. But as he passed the staircase window, he heard the side gate slam.

Emerging into the hill-road, Kemp naturally took the downward direction, and so it was he came to run in his own person the very race he had watched with such a critical eye from the belvedere study only four days ago. He ran it well for a man out of training; and though his face was white and wet, his wits were cool to the last. He ran with wide strides, and wherever a patch of rough ground intervened, wherever there came a patch of raw flints, or a bit of broken glass shone dazzling, he crossed it and left the bare invisible feet that followed to take what line they would.

For the first time in his life Kemp discovered that the hill-road was indescribably vast and desolate, and that the beginnings of the town far below at the hill foot were strangely remote. Never had there been a slower or more painful method of progression than running. All the gaunt villas, sleeping in the afternoon sun, looked locked and barred; no doubt they were locked and barred— by his own orders. But at any rate they might have kept a lookout for an eventuality like this! The town was rising up now, the sea had dropped out of sight behind it, and people down below were stirring. A tram was just arriving at the hill foot. Beyond that was the police station. Was that footsteps he heard behind him? Spurt.

The people below were staring at him, one or two were running, and his breath was beginning to saw in his throat. The tram was quite near now, and the Jolly Cricketers was noisily barring its doors. Beyond the tram were posts and heaps of gravel—the drainage works. He had a transitory idea of jumping into the tram and slamming the doors, and then he resolved to go to the police station. In another moment he had passed the door of the Jolly Cricketers, and was in the blistering fag end of the street, with human beings about him. The tram driver and his helper—arrested by the sight of his furious haste—stood staring with the tram horses unhitched. Further on the astonished features of navvies appeared above the mounds of gravel.

His pace broke a little, and then he heard the swift pad of his pursuer, and leapt forward again. "The Invisible Man!" he cried to the navvies, with a vague indicative gesture, and by an inspiration leapt the excavation and placed a burly group between him and the chase. Then abandoning the idea of the police station he turned into a little side street, rushed by a greengrocer's cart, hesitated for the tenth of a second at the door of a sweetstuff shop, and then made for the mouth of an alley that ran back into the main Hill Street again. Two or three little children were playing here, and shrieked and scattered running at his apparition, and forthwith doors and windows opened and excited mothers revealed their hearts. Out he shot into Hill Street again, three hundred yards from the tramline end, and immediately he became aware of a tumultuous vociferation and running people.

He glanced up the street towards the hill. Hardly a dozen yards off ran a huge navvy, cursing in fragments and slashing viciously with a spade, and hard behind him came the tram conductor with his fists clenched. Up the street others followed these two, striking and shouting. Down towards the town, men and women were running, and he noticed clearly one man coming out of a shop-door with a stick in his hand. "Spread out! Spread out!" cried some one. Kemp suddenly grasped the altered condition of the chase. He stopped and looked round, panting. "He's close here!" he cried. "Form a line across—"

"Aha!" shouted a voice.

He was hit hard under the ear, and went reeling, trying to face round towards his unseen antagonist. He just managed to keep his feet, and he struck a vain counter in the air. Then he was hit again under the jaw, and sprawled headlong on the ground. In another moment a knee compressed his diaphragm, and a couple of eager hands gripped his throat, but the grip of one was weaker than the other; he grasped the wrists, heard a cry of pain from his assailant, and then the spade of the navvy came whirling through the air above him, and struck something with a dull thud. He felt a drop of moisture on his face. The grip at his throat suddenly relaxed, and with a convulsive effort Kemp loosed himself, grasped a limp shoulder, and rolled uppermost. He gripped the unseen elbows near the ground. "I've got him!" screamed Kemp. "Help! Help! hold! He's down! Hold his feet!"

In another second there was a simultaneous rush upon the struggle, and a stranger coming into the road suddenly might have thought an exceptionally savage game of Rugby football was in progress. And there was no shouting after Kemp's cry—only a sound of blows and feet and a heavy breathing.

Then came a mighty effort, and the Invisible Man threw off a couple of his antagonists and rose to his knees. Kemp clung to him in front like a hound to a stag, and a dozen hands gripped, clutched, and tore at the Unseen. The tram conductor suddenly got the neck and shoulders and lugged him back.

Down went the heap of struggling men again and rolled over. There was, I am afraid, some savage kicking. Then suddenly a wild scream of "Mercy! Mercy!" that died down swiftly to a sound like choking.

"Get back, you fools!" cried the muffled voice of Kemp, and there was a vigorous shoving back of stalwart forms. "He's hurt, I tell you. Stand back!"

There was a brief struggle to clear a space, and then the circle of eager eyes saw the doctor kneeling, as it seemed, fifteen inches in the air, and holding invisible arms to the ground. Behind him a constable gripped invisible ankles.

"Don't you leave go of en," cried the big navvy, holding a blood-stained spade; "he's shamming."

"He's not shamming," said the doctor, cautiously raising his knee; "and I'll hold him." His face was bruised and already going red; he spoke thickly because of a bleeding lip. He released one hand and seemed to be feeling at the face. "The mouth's all wet," he said. And then, "Good God!"

He stood up abruptly and then knelt down on the ground by the side of the thing unseen. There was a pushing and shuffling, a sound of heavy feet as fresh people turned up to increase the pressure of the crowd. People now were coming out of the houses. The doors of the Jolly Cricketers were suddenly wide open. Very little was said. Kempt felt about, his hand seeming to pass through empty air. "He's not breathing," he said, and then, "I can't feel his heart. His side—ugh!"

Suddenly an old woman, peering under the arm of the big navvy, screamed sharply. "Looky there!" she said, and thrust out a wrinkled finger. And looking where she pointed, every one saw, faint and transparent as though it was made of glass, so that veins and arteries and bones and nerves could be distinguished, the outline of a hand, a hand limp and prone. It grew clouded and opaque even as they stared.

"Hullo!" cried the constable. "Here's his feet a-showing!"

And so, slowly, beginning at his hands and feet and creeping along his limbs to the vital centres of his body, that strange change continued. It was like the slow spreading of a poison. First came the little white nerves, a hazy grey sketch of a limb, then the glassy bones and intricate arteries, then the flesh and skin, first a faint fogginess and then growing rapidly dense and opaque. Presently they could see his crushed chest and his shoulders, and the dim outline of his drawn and battered features.

When at last the crowd made way for Kemp to stand erect, there lay, naked and pitiful on the ground, the bruised and broken body of a young man about thirty. His hair and beard were white—not grey with age but white with the whiteness of albinism, and his eyes were like garnets. His hands were clenched, his eyes wide open, and his expression was one of anger and dismay.

"Cover his face!" said a man. "For Gawd's sake, cover that face!" and three little children, pushing forward through the crowd, were suddenly twisted round and sent packing off again.

Some one brought a sheet from the Jolly Cricketers; and having covered him, they carried him into that house.

THE EPILOGUE

So ends the story of the strange and evil experiment of the Invisible Man. And if you would learn more of him you must go to a little inn near Port Stowe and talk to the landlord. The sign of the inn is an empty board save for a hat and boots, and the name is the title of this story. The landlord is a short and corpulent little man with a nose of cylindrical protrusion, wiry hair, and a sporadic rosiness of visage. Drink generously, and he will tell you generously of all the things that happened to him after that time, and of how the lawyers tried to do him out of the treasure found upon him.

"When they found they couldn't prove who's money was which, I'm blessed," he says, "if they didn't try to make me out a blooming treasure trove! Do I *look* like a Treasure Trove? And then a gentleman gave me a guinea a night to tell the story at the Empire Music 'all—just tell 'em in my own words—barring one."

And if you want to cut off the flow of his reminiscences abruptly, you can always do so by asking if there weren't three manuscript books in the story. He admits there were and proceeds to explain, with asseverations that everybody thinks *he* has 'em! But bless you! he hasn't. "The Invisible Man it was took 'em off to hide 'em when I cut and ran for Port Stowe. It's that Mr. Kemp put people on with the idea of *my* having 'em."

And then he subsides into a pensive state, watches you furtively, bustles nervously with glasses, and presently leaves the bar.

He is a bachelor man—his tastes were ever bachelor, and there are no women folk in the house. Outwardly he buttons—it is expected of him—but in his more vital privacies, in the matter of braces for example, he still turns to string. He conducts his house without enterprise, but with eminent decorum. His movements are slow, and he is a great thinker.

But he has a reputation for wisdom and for a respectable parsimony in the village, and his knowledge of the roads of the South of England would beat Cobbett.

And on Sunday mornings, every Sunday morning all the year round, while he is closed to the outer world, and every night after ten, he goes into his bar parlour bearing a glass of gin faintly tinged with water; and having placed this down, he locks the door and examines the blinds, and even looks under the table. And then, being satisfied of his solitude, he unlocks the cupboard and a box in the cupboard and a drawer in that box, and produces three volumes bound in brown leather, and places them solemnly in the middle of the table. The covers are weather-worn and tinged with an algal green—for once they sojourned in a ditch and some of the pages have been washed blank by dirty water. The landlord sits down in an armchair, fills a long clay pipe slowly, gloating over the books the while. Then he pulls one towards him and opens it, and begins to study it—turning over the leaves backwards and forwards.

His brows are knit and his lips move painfully. "Hex, little two up in the air, cross and a fiddle-de-dee. Lord! what a one he was for intellect!"

Presently he relaxes and leans back, and blinks through his smoke across the room at things invisible to other eyes. "Full of secrets," he says. "Wonderful secrets!

"Once I get the haul of them—*Lord!*

"I wouldn't do what *he* did; I'd just—well!" He pulls at his pipe.

So he lapses into a dream, the undying wonderful dream of his life. And though Kemp has fished unceasingly, and Adye has questioned closely, no human being save the landlord knows those books are there, with the subtle secret of invisibility and a dozen other strange secrets written therein. And none other will know of them until he dies.

THE DAMNED THING

Ambrose Bierce

I

ONE DOES NOT ALWAYS EAT WHAT IS ON THE TABLE

By the light of a tallow candle which had been placed on one end of a rough table a man was reading something written in a book. It was an old account book, greatly worn; and the writing was not, apparently, very legible, for the man sometimes held the page close to the flame of the candle to get a stronger light on it. The shadow of the book would then throw into obscurity a half of the room, darkening a number of faces and figures; for besides the reader, eight other men were present. Seven of them sat against the rough log walls, silent, motionless, and the room being small, not very far from the table. By extending an arm any one of them could have touched the eighth man, who lay on the table, face upward, partly covered by a sheet, his arms at his sides. He was dead.

The man with the book was not reading aloud, and no one spoke; all seemed to be waiting for something to occur; the dead man only was without expectation. From the blank darkness outside came in, through the aperture that served for a window, all the ever unfamiliar noises of night in the wilderness—the long nameless note of a distant coyote; the stilly pulsing thrill of tireless insects in trees; strange cries of night birds, so different from those of the birds of day; the drone of great blundering beetles, and all that mysterious chorus of small sounds that seem always to have been but half heard when they have suddenly ceased, as if conscious of an indiscretion. But nothing of all this was noted in that company; its members

were not overmuch addicted to idle interest in matters of no practical importance; that was obvious in every line of their rugged
faces—obvious even in the dim light of the single candle. They were
evidently men of the vicinity—farmers and woodsmen.

The person reading was a trifle different; one would have said of
him that he was of the world, worldly, albeit there was that in his
attire which attested a certain fellowship with the organisms of his
environment. His coat would hardly have passed muster in San Fran-
cisco; his foot-gear was not of urban origin, and the hat that lay by
him on the floor (he was the only one uncovered) was such that if one
had considered it as an article of mere personal adornment he would
have missed its meaning. In countenance the man was rather pre-
possessing, with just a hint of sternness; though that he may have
assumed or cultivated, as appropriate to one in authority. For he was
a coroner. It was by virtue of his office that he had possession of the
book in which he was reading; it had been found among the dead
man's effects—in his cabin, where the inquest was now taking place.

When the coroner had finished reading he put the book into
his breast pocket. At that moment the door was pushed open and a
young man entered. He, clearly, was not of mountain birth and
breeding: he was clad as those who dwell in cities. His clothing
was dusty, however, as from travel. He had, in fact, been riding
hard to attend the inquest.

The coroner nodded; no one else greeted him.

"We have waited for you," said the coroner. "It is necessary to
have done with this business to-night."

The young man smiled. "I am sorry to have kept you," he said.
"I went away, not to evade your summons, but to post to my newspaper an account of what I suppose I am called back to relate."

The coroner smiled.

"The account that you posted to your newspaper," he said, "dif-
fers, probably, from that which you will give here under oath."

"That," replied the other, rather hotly and with a visible flush,
"is as you please. I used manifold paper and have a copy of what I
sent. It was not written as news, for it is incredible, but as fiction.
It may go as a part of my testimony under oath."

"But you say it is incredible."

"That is nothing to you, sir, if I also swear that it is true."

The coroner was silent for a time, his eyes upon the floor. The men about the sides of the cabin talked in whispers, but seldom withdrew their gaze from the face of the corpse. Presently the coroner lifted his eyes and said: "We will resume the inquest."

The men removed their hats. The witness was sworn.

"What is your name?" the coroner asked.

"William Harker."

"Age?"

"Twenty-seven."

"You knew the deceased, Hugh Morgan?"

"Yes."

"You were with him when he died?"

"Near him."

"How did that happen—your presence, I mean?"

"I was visiting him at this place to shoot and fish. A part of my purpose, however, was to study him and his odd, solitary way of life. He seemed a good model for a character in fiction. I sometimes write stories."

"I sometimes read them."

"Thank you."

"Stories in general—not yours."

Some of the jurors laughed. Against a sombre background humor shows high lights. Soldiers in the intervals of battle laugh easily, and a jest in the death chamber conquers by surprise.

"Relate the circumstances of this man's death," said the coroner. "You may use any notes or memoranda that you please."

The witness understood. Pulling a manuscript from his breast pocket he held it near the candle and turning the leaves until he found the passage that he wanted began to read.

II

WHAT MAY HAPPEN IN A FIELD OF WILD OATS

"… The sun had hardly risen when we left the house. We were looking for quail, each with a shotgun, but we had only one dog.

Morgan said that our best ground was beyond a certain ridge that he pointed out, and we crossed it by a trail through the chaparral. On the other side was comparatively level ground, thickly covered with wild oats. As we emerged from the chaparral Morgan was but a few yards in advance. Suddenly we heard, at a little distance to our right and partly in front, a noise as of some animal thrashing about in the bushes, which we could see were violently agitated.

"'We've started a deer,' I said. 'I wish we had brought a rifle.'

"Morgan, who had stopped and was intently watching the agitated chaparral, said nothing, but had cocked both barrels of his gun and was holding it in readiness to aim. I thought him a trifle excited, which surprised me, for he had a reputation for exceptional coolness, even in moments of sudden and imminent peril.

"'O, come,' I said. 'You are not going to fill up a deer with quail-shot, are you?'

"Still he did not reply; but catching a sight of his face as he turned it slightly toward me I was struck by the intensity of his look. Then I understood that we had serious business in hand and my first conjecture was that we had 'jumped' a grizzly. I advanced to Morgan's side, cocking my piece as I moved.

"The bushes were now quiet and the sounds had ceased, but Morgan was as attentive to the place as before,

"'What is it? What the devil is it?' I asked.

"'That Damned Thing!' he replied, without turning his head. His voice was husky and unnatural. He trembled visibly.

"I was about to speak further, when I observed the wild oats near the place of the disturbance moving in the most inexplicable way. I can hardly describe it. It seemed as if stirred by a streak of wind, which not only bent it, but pressed it down—crushed it so that it did not rise; and this movement was slowly prolonging itself directly toward us.

"Nothing that I had ever seen had affected me so strangely as this unfamiliar and unaccountable phenomenon, yet I am unable to recall any sense of fear. I remember—and tell it here because, singularly enough, I recollected it then—that once in looking carelessly out of an open window I momentarily mistook a small tree close at hand for one of a group of larger trees at a little distance away. It looked the same size as the others, but being more distinctly and sharply defined in mass and detail seemed out of harmony with them. It was a mere falsification of the law of aerial perspective, but it startled, almost terrified me. We so rely upon the orderly operation of familiar natural laws that any seeming suspension of them is noted as a menace to our safety, a warning of unthinkable calamity. So now the apparently causeless movement of the herbage and the slow, undeviating approach of the line of disturbance were distinctly disquieting. My companion appeared actually frightened, and I could hardly credit my senses when I saw him suddenly throw his gun to his shoulder and fire both barrels at the agitated grain! Before the smoke of the discharge had cleared away I heard a loud savage cry—a scream like that of a wild animal—and flinging his gun upon the ground Morgan sprang away and ran swiftly from the spot. At the same instant I was thrown violently to the ground by the impact of something unseen in the smoke—some soft, heavy substance that seemed thrown against me with great force.

"Before I could get upon my feet and recover my gun, which seemed to have been struck from my hands, I heard Morgan crying out as if in mortal agony, and mingling with his cries were such hoarse, savage sounds as one hears from fighting dogs. Inexpressibly terrified, I struggled to my feet and looked in the direction of Morgan's retreat; and may Heaven in mercy spare me from another sight like that! At a distance of less than thirty yards was my friend, down upon one knee, his head thrown back at a frightful angle, hatless, his long hair in disorder and his whole body in violent movement from side to side, backward and forward. His right arm was lifted and seemed to lack the hand—at least, I could see none. The other arm was invisible. At times, as my memory now reports this extraordinary scene, I could discern but a part of his body; it was as if he had been partly blotted out—I cannot otherwise express it—then a shifting of his position would bring it all into view again.

"All this must have occurred within a few seconds, yet in that time Morgan assumed all the postures of a determined wrestler vanquished by superior weight and strength. I saw nothing but him, and him not always distinctly. During the entire incident his shouts and curses were heard, as if through an enveloping uproar of such sounds of rage and fury as I had never heard from the throat of man or brute!

"For a moment only I stood irresolute, then throwing down my gun I ran forward to my friend's assistance I had a vague belief that he was suffering from a fit, or some form of convulsion. Before I could reach his side he was down and quiet. All sounds had ceased, but with a feeling of such terror as even these awful events had not inspired I now saw again the mysterious movement of the wild oats, prolonging itself from the trampled area about the prostrate man toward the edge of a wood. It was only when it had reached the wood that I was able to withdraw my eyes and look at my companion. He was dead."

III

A MAN THOUGH NAKED MAY BE IN RAGS

The coroner rose from his seat and stood beside the dead man. Lifting an edge of the sheet he pulled it away, exposing the entire body, altogether naked and showing in the candle-light a claylike yellow. It had, however, broad maculations of bluish black, obviously caused by extravasated blood from contusions. The chest and sides looked as if they had been beaten with a bludgeon. There were dreadful lacerations; the skin was torn in strips and shreds.

The coroner moved round to the end of the table and undid a silk handkerchief which had been passed under the chin and knotted on the top of the head. When the handkerchief was drawn away it exposed what had been the throat. Some of the jurors who had risen to get a better view repented their curiosity and turned away their faces. Witness Harker went to the open window and leaned out across the sill, faint and sick. Dropping the handkerchief upon the dead man's neck the coroner stepped to an angle of the room and from a pile of clothing produced one garment after another, each of which he held up a moment for inspection. All were torn, and stiff with blood. The jurors did not make a closer inspection.

They seemed rather uninterested. They had, in truth, seen all this before; the only thing that was new to them being Harker's testimony.

"Gentlemen," the coroner said, "we have no more evidence, I think. Your duty has been already explained to you; if there is nothing you wish to ask you may go outside and consider your verdict."

The foreman rose—a tall, bearded man of sixty, coarsely clad.

"I should like to ask one question, Mr. Coroner," he said. "What asylum did this yer last witness escape from?"

"Mr. Harker," said the coroner, gravely and tranquilly, "from what asylum did you last escape?"

Harker flushed crimson again, but said nothing, and the seven jurors rose and solemnly filed out of the cabin.

"If you have done insulting me, sir," said Harker, as soon as he and the officer were left alone with the dead man, "I suppose I am at liberty to go?"

"Yes."

Harker started to leave, but paused, with his hand on the door latch. The habit of his profession was strong in him—stronger than his sense of personal dignity. He turned about and said:

"The book that you have there—I recognize it as Morgan's diary. You seemed greatly interested in it; you read in it while I was testifying. May I see it? The public would like—"

"The book will cut no figure in this matter," replied the official, slipping it into his coat pocket; "all the entries in it were made before the writer's death."

As Harker passed out of the house the jury reentered and stood about the table, on which the now covered corpse showed under the sheet with sharp definition. The foreman seated himself near the candle, produced from his breast pocket a pencil and scrap of paper and wrote rather laboriously the following verdict, which with various degrees of effort all signed:

"We, the jury, do find that the remains come to their death at the hands of a mountain lion, but some of us thinks, all the same, they had fits."

IV

AN EXPLANATION FROM THE TOMB

In the diary of the late Hugh Morgan are certain interesting entries having, possibly, a scientific value as suggestions. At the inquest upon his body the book was not put in evidence; possibly the coroner thought it not worth while to confuse the jury. The date of the first of the entries mentioned cannot be ascertained; the upper part of the leaf is torn away; the part of the entry remaining follows:

"... would run in a half-circle, keeping his head turned always toward the centre, and again he would stand still, barking furiously. At last he ran away into the brush as fast as he could go. I thought at first that he had gone mad, but on returning to the house found no other alteration in his manner than what was obviously due to fear of punishment.

"Can a dog see with his nose? Do odors impress some cerebral centre with images of the thing that emitted them? ...

"Sept. 2.—Looking at the stars last night as they rose above the crest of the ridge east of the house, I observed them successively disappear—from left to right. Each was eclipsed but an instant, and only a few at the same time, but along the entire length of the ridge all that were within a degree or two of the crest were blotted out. It was as if something had passed along between me and them; but I could not see it, and the stars were not thick enough to define its outline. Ugh! I don't like this." ...

Several weeks' entries are missing, three leaves being torn from the book.

"Sept. 27.—It has been about here again—I find evidences of its presence every day. I watched again all last night in the same cover, gun in hand, double-charged with buckshot. In the morning the fresh footprints were there, as before. Yet I would have sworn that I did not sleep—indeed, I hardly sleep at all. It is terrible, insupportable! If these amazing experiences are real I shall go mad; if they are fanciful I am mad already.

"Oct. 3.—I shall not go—it shall not drive me away. No, this is my house, my land. God hates a coward....

"Oct. 5.—I can stand it no longer; I have invited Harker to pass a few weeks with me—he has a level head. I can judge from his manner if he thinks me mad.

"Oct. 7.—I have the solution of the mystery; it came to me last night—suddenly, as by revelation. How simple—how terribly simple!

"There are sounds that we cannot hear. At either end of the scale are notes that stir no chord of that imperfect instrument, the human ear. They are too high or too grave. I have observed a flock of blackbirds occupying an entire tree-top—the tops of several trees—and all in full song. Suddenly—in a moment—at absolutely the same instant—all spring into the air and fly away. How? They could not all see one another—whole tree-tops intervened. At no point could a leader have been visible to all. There must have been a signal of warning or command, high and shrill above the din, but by me unheard. I have observed, too, the same simultaneous flight when all were silent, among not only blackbirds, but other birds—quail, for example, widely separated by bushes—even on opposite sides of a hill.

"It is known to seamen that a school of whales basking or sporting on the surface of the ocean, miles apart, with the convexity of the earth between, will sometimes dive at the same instant—all gone out of sight in a moment. The signal has been sounded—too grave for the ear of the sailor at the masthead and his comrades on the deck—who nevertheless feel its vibrations in the ship as the stones of a cathedral are stirred by the bass of the organ.

"As with sounds, so with colors. At each end of the solar spectrum the chemist can detect the presence of what are known as 'actinic' rays. They represent colors—integral colors in the composition of light—which we are unable to discern. The human eye is an imperfect instrument; its range is but a few octaves of the real 'chromatic scale.' I am not mad; there are colors that we cannot see.

"And, God help me! the Damned Thing is of such a color!"

A HUMAN CHAMELEON
Newton Newkirk

He was sleeping. As I stood over his cot a nurse told me he had
come to the hospital the night before and asked to be given medical attention. He had the air and dress of a gentleman and tendered
in advance the money for his treatment. More of him than this I
did not learn.

When the nurse moved away I seated myself and, taking his hand,
felt for the pulse. As I counted the beats my eyes were on the small
hand of my watch. When I looked up his eyes were open and on mine.

"What is the pulsation, doctor?" he queried.

"One hundred and four."

"A trifle high?"

"Yes."

His voice was rich and had in it the accent of education and
refinement.

"You will find the trouble here, doctor," and he patted the right
side of his neck with a finger. Examination showed he was suffering from a small cancerous growth. I advised its removal when the
fever symptoms had subsided, to which he readily acquiesced. As
I turned to a small table and began to prescribe he reached out
and touched my arm. There was a mingled look of concern and
alarm in his face.

"Will you kindly go away for a few minutes, doctor—only a short
while—will you?"

The pitiful quaver of entreaty in his tones for the moment overcame my curiosity at his strange request. I was about to invent

some roundabout question which would bring out his reason for wanting me to withdraw, when his manner stopped me short. His hands and teeth were clenched and he strove with a mighty effort, like a man who fights off some strange spell. All the time he looked pleadingly into my eyes.

"Oh, doctor—won't you please go—for the sake of God—hasten!"

Turning quickly from my strange patient I crossed the floor and entered a large cabinet in the centre of the room in which drugs and supplies were kept. A man of medicine—especially a hospital physician—encounters numberless puzzling mental derangements in his experience and, for the time, I charged the new man's odd behavior to that side of the medical ledger. Nevertheless, my curiosity was aroused. Looking about I observed a small chink through the frame partition of the cabinet and clapped my eye to it instantly. I commanded a full view of the man I had just left. He was not more than thirty feet from me. There was a screen on either side of his cot which shut him off from the observation of other patients. He lay propped up, with his feet toward me and his hands lying on the snowy coverlet. I studied his face carefully. It was in natural repose. It was—! I winked in rapid succession to remove a blur from before my vision and looked again.

The man's head was gone!

I drew quickly back from the chink and examined it to make sure there was certainly a hole there. Then I put my eye to the opening again. The head remained missing! His hands—! They, too, were absent! Both seemed to be severed where the sleeves of his sleeping gown ended and the white coverlet began. When I looked again for the head I plainly saw the collar, but above it was neither neck nor head! Where the head should have been I saw the surface of the white pillow and the vertical iron rungs of the bed-head. Then I glanced down at myself to see if I were really the being I seemed to be. When I peeped again through the hole I beheld no longer the headless and handless man. Those members were again in place. He was looking toward the cabinet and I saw his lips frame the word "Doctor!" He was calling me.

I stopped long enough to wipe away the perspiration which had gathered on my forehead and, stepping out, walked toward him with as much of an air of unconcern as I could assume.

"Thank you," he said, simply. His very tone would have conveyed the sense of deepest gratitude if he had said "Apples." After writing out the prescription I left him.

When I had finished my rounds I examined the hospital register. My headless patient was entered in the name of Emanuel Riccardo, of Florence, Italy. I could not dismiss him from my mind and sought some pretext to visit him again that night. He was lying quite still, yet not asleep, and greeted me with a smile. I sat down and engaged him in conversation. I found Signor Riccardo the most fascinating and brilliant man I have ever met. In a short hour he took me all the way around the habitable globe, shifting the scenes east and west on the continents, or from the scent-laden atmosphere of the tropics to the frozen zones of the polar regions. I listened in rapture and left him regretfully. For the time I forgot the inexplicable occurrence of the morning, to which he made no reference. I had a natural and professional curiosity to unravel the uncanny mystery, but it was obvious that Signor Riccardo wished me not to know, and common courtesy forbade me trying to draw from him his peculiar secret.

Another time—three days later—as I sat near his cot with my back to him, writing at the stand, a peculiar quaver in his voice as he talked made me turn my eyes quickly toward him.

"Don't look at me, doctor—please—not now! " he pleaded.

He had spoken too late. My eyes were upon him as he uttered the words. His head was gone, but the voice came from where it should have been. He held up one handless arm in protest as I gazed stupidly at the headless trunk. Then the invisible fingers clutched the coverlet and pulled it completely over him. I turned away and tried to write, but my hand trembled, and laying down the pen I waited during what seemed an interminable period. I heard the clothing being adjusted behind me and when I looked around his eyes were closed. He feigned sleep, and I left him.

Two days afterward, Miss West, the nurse in charge of Signor Riccardo's ward, entered my office, white and trembling. This was an unusual manifestation on the part of a trained attendant, to whom surgery and even deaths were merely details of hospital work. The girl sank weakly into a chair and gazed at me strangely.

"Am I myself, doctor, or—is it true?"

Then she plunged on as if I could understand, and I believed I knew what was coming.

"When it happened the first time I thought I must have been deceived, but now—not ten minutes ago—when I came to his cot suddenly, the head and the hands were gone. Oh, it was dreadful!"

"You mean—?" I queried.

"Riccardo!" she gasped.

He lay quietly on the operating table with his fine, swarthy face toward the stand on which I arranged my instruments. Miss West stood with bottle and muzzle ready to administer the anaesthetic when I should give the word. He was cheerful and talked glibly. I had assured him the operation would be in no wise difficult or dangerous, which was true, and the last words which came from under the muzzle were, "I have breathed worse things—and better."

In a few minutes he was deep under, yet the nurse still held the muzzle over his nostrils as I turned to a stand to choose my instrument. I heard her try to call me, and faced about quickly. Miss West was shrinking away from the prostrate figure. She had left the muzzle lying on the face—not on the face—there was no face—nor head! The muzzle seemed to be floating in mid-air where the face should have been. The handless arms were lying at his sides.

I strove to master a nameless feeling as I advanced to the memberless figure, and lifting the muzzle, placed my hand against—against the nose, which I felt without seeing! Moving my fingers over the invisible face, I traced the chin, the moustache, the rounded cheeks, the depressions of the eyes, the forehead—and felt, as plainly as the sense of touch can convey, the thick, wavy hair of Signer Riccardo's head. Then I sought the hands and held each in turn. I could count their fingers and feel their warmth, but to my eyes I seemed to hold but air. The room was bathed in bright light, yet it was as if I felt the head and hands of a man with my eyes closed or in intense darkness. Readjusting the muzzle I waited for the strange spell to pass. The nurse stood apart, trembling, but when the head and hands began to outline themselves from apparent nothingness to visible flesh and blood, she gave her attention to administering the anaesthetic.

With the return of Signor Riccardo's head and hands he began to communicate his subconscious vagaries in speech and the first words arrested me as I stood over him, knife in hand.

"They said the curse would follow me—to my death, but I did not believe! I had rather died on that lonely island than be shunned by man and pointed out as one bewitched. Is there no cure—in the name of God—is there no help?"

A sudden thought came to me; I would question his "sleeping-self"—his *alter ego!* "There is help, Riccardo!" I said in loud, distinct tones. His face seemed to beam with a great hope, although he was yet under the influence of the drug and his eyes were closed.

"Help—for me?" he questioned, eagerly.

"Yes!"

"How?"

"You must answer my questions."

"I will!"

"What is this curse?"

"The Chameleon fever!"

"Where did it overtake you?"

"Madagascar—I was exploring the interior for diamonds—you say you can cure me?"

"Yes—what is this Chameleon fever?"

"Those who have had it are doomed to strange spells which they cannot control, during which the exposed portions of the body take on the color of the backgrounds against which they rest. This gives the flesh the appearance of having vanished altogether."

"Do you suffer while these spells last?"

"No—can you cure me?"

"I will try; now lie very still!"

In wonderment I began to operate. At the first incision I observed a structure in Signor Riccardo's skin different from anything

I had ever read of or met with in histology. When the nurse had brought me a powerful magnifying glass I examined it minutely. Instead of one secondary stratum of cuticle where I would look for the coloring matter of the skin, there were many layers, and each seemed to hold a different hue of pigment—a condition I had never met or heard of. I could understand how the exudations of vari-colored pigments from these different layers might so blend as to give the surface of the skin the complexion of surrounding objects, and thus render it invisible, like that of a chameleon. Anxious as I was to pursue this strange freak of physical structure, I discharged it to proceed with the operation.

Signer Riccardo recovered rapidly, and at the end of two weeks was ready to be discharged. As he grasped my hand at parting he looked into my eyes as if there were something he would tell me. Suddenly he seemed to think better of it.

"Good-bye, doctor!" he said, cheerily. "If I have acted strangely at times I hope you will yet think well of me. It was—something—something beyond my control—Good-bye!"

And the "Human Chameleon" pressed my hand and was gone on his wanderings. Some day I shall visit Madagascar to study that strangest of all human maladies—Chameleon fever.

MY CRANK CLIENT
Warren B. Hutchinson

The practice of my profession—I am a patent lawyer—certainly brings me in contact with more minds of a crotchety nature than it is the lot of the average man to encounter, and this, perhaps, has inclined me a little to the belief that every one of us is more or less insane on some subject. Business instinct, however, has taught me to meet all inventors with a grave face, even when their ideas seem ridiculous, for even the most unpromising client may possess something of value from both a financial and a scientific point of view.

With all my experience I should scarcely have classed as unpromising the man who followed upon the office-boy's appearance in my private room with the card of "Mr. John Robertson," one afternoon not long ago. He was a fine-looking man, about forty, with big eyes placed wide apart, a light mustache, and well dressed; his manners were easy and his appearance was that of a prosperous professional man. This rather threw me off my guard.

"You have been recommended to me," he began at once, "as a lawyer capable of handling an important matter, and discreet enough to keep it absolutely quiet for the present. I know you must be pestered by cranks and my discovery will seem so nonsensical to you, if described, that I propose to give an ocular demonstration before going deep into the matter. Now," he continued, and he looked larger than ever, "I suppose you see me?"

I replied that I was quite sure of it.

"Well," he said, "you only think you see me," and with that he began to fade from sight and was soon lost to view.

I do not think that I was frightened, but I certainly felt queer. I sat staring at the spot where he had been and concluded that I must have fallen asleep and been dreaming. I looked out of the window and even got out of my seat to assure myself that I was awake. I do not believe in ghosts, and if I had seen one it was certainly very human and mortal. All sorts of fantastic ideas ran through my head in the moment I stood there with my scattering hairs on end, and I cannot say that I felt reassured when the voice of Robertson said, "Now I suppose you will admit that you only thought you saw me." I managed to say that I would admit anything, but he continued, "Just come over to where I am sitting and take hold of me and you will see that there is nothing spiritual about me."

Of course it was foolish, but nothing would have persuaded me to make the attempt. His voice, however, sounded earthly and normal, and he said:

"Well, if you have no objection, I will try to take hold of you, but unfortunately, while I have perfected my invention to the extent of making myself invisible, it also prevents me from seeing clearly."

With that I heard him get up and knew he was groping like a blind man for me, and presently the dim outline of a hand seemed to come from nowhere and take hold of my coat. I confess that I felt like jumping out of the window and I know I trembled like a leaf.

Gradually Robertson began to reappear, and in a minute or two I beheld his form once more in the flesh.

I sank exhausted into my chair, and waited for him to speak.

He began precisely as if he had just explained a new sewing-machine, and in the oft-heard "Well, what do you think of my discovery?" I was wondering at him, and said as much. He laughed, as he continued:

"You are the first person to whom I have really shown my discovery, and you will shortly see that, like most important discoveries and inventions, it is so simple that I wonder it has not been known for ages. I did try it on my wife, but she went into hysterics, and I doubt if I ever regain my wonted place in her esteem till the invention is known and used by others. It is not entirely perfected yet, but the principle is that I am made invisible and also prevented from seeing people, yet I get glimpses of things which would never be seen by mortal vision. I wish now to find out if my discovery is patentable, and if it is advisable to patent it. I know that many great discoveries do not prove remunerative, and I come for advice as to how mine can be made profitable. I hope through you to get men and money to patent and exploit it. Now, to satisfy you that I am neither angel nor devil, but a plain citizen of good character, I will say that I am principal of the high school at Grassville, and have been for the last five years. I refer you to the postmaster there, also to J. B. Hampton, Superintendent of Schools, and the Rev. Alfred Goodfellow, to verify my statements."

He paused. "You have shown me," said I, "that you can make yourself invisible; now please explain how you do it."

"You will pardon me," he replied, "but I wish you first to look me up and see that I am what I represent myself to be. I think the matter is of such importance that we should work together with mutual confidence. I have already satisfied myself as to you, and if you think it worth while, I wish you would take time to do this, and make another appointment."

"Very well. I certainly am interested in your invention. Suppose you come here at—let me see, to-day is Tuesday—say ten o'clock Saturday. Will that suit you?"

"Perfectly; and then we will go to the bottom of the matter."

He departed, and left me in a strange state.

As he went away, the boy advised me that Mr. Dupuy had been waiting a long time to see me. I had been owing Dupuy a matter of three hundred dollars for a year, and he was getting importunate. The value of Robertson's invention at once appealed to me as it had not done before. I meant to pay Dupuy, but was not able. I dreaded to be dunned, particularly as I had promised repeatedly to pay, but I had a bright idea which I thought would relieve me of Dupuy till I could pull myself together financially, and I got rid of him after a short interview in which I promised a check in full if he would come back the following Saturday morning at ten.

Next day I went to Grassville, half expecting to find that Robertson was unknown, but learned that he was a staid, respectable citizen who was well known and had made no miraculous disappearances.

I neglected everything for the next two days and anxiously waited for Saturday and Robertson.

He was as punctual as the day. Dupuy was on hand, too. They came in together.

"Good-morning, Mr. Robertson," said I, as they entered. "I am glad to say that I find you are of the earth, earthy."

"Good; then there is no earthly reason why we should not get down to business."

"I will see you presently, Dupuy; have a chair," I called, as the door of my private office closed behind Robertson and myself.

"Mr. Robertson," I began, "you will excuse the digression, but would it be possible to make me disappear before the eyes of that man outside? There are particular reasons why I should like to do this."

"If you think it advisable to let any one see what we can do before protecting the invention, yes."

"Well, I can guarantee that no harm will come of it, for Dupuy could learn nothing of the invention, and he would never dare mention what he sees, or rather doesn't see, for he knows any one to whom he repeated it would say he was drunk or crazy."

"All right, then; I expected that you would wish to experiment a little, and so brought along a duplicate apparatus which I can attach to you and operate from a bulb in my pocket; or, if you prefer, I will apply the attachment to you, connect yours with mine, and we will both vanish."

"Very well, let us both disappear, and I will wager that there will be a third disappearance without the use of your apparatus."

Robertson opened a small bag which he had brought and took out several loops of insulated wire provided with numerous fine projections.

"I shall have to attach these temporarily," he said. "They may be seen, but will be hardly noticed. You do not see anything unusual about me, for I have the attachments inside my clothing, but the points project through slightly."

He quickly fitted a loop to each of my trouser-legs near the bottom, another around my waist, and another to my coat-collar. I began to have an inkling of how the trick was done. He then connected wires to the several loops and to some parts of his own harness, and placed himself so that I was between him and the door.

"I am ready now," he said, "but will try it and see if everything is all right," and immediately I was enveloped in a cylinder of light through which I could not see. The sensation was peculiar, but momentary, as soon as he permitted normal conditions to obtain.

"Now, when shall we obliterate ourselves?" he said.

"Can you do it rather slowly?"

"Certainly."

"Then as soon as Dupuy comes in and I begin to speak to him, let us fade out gradually. Are you ready?"

"Yes."

I signaled the boy. "Harry, show Mr. Dupuy in."

Dupuy seated himself and I said: "I believe it is three hundred and ten dollars that I owe you. Am I right?"

As I said the last three words, Dupuy, who had been fading, disappeared from my sight. I shall never forget the last glimpse I had of him as he sat there before me bolt upright, his eyes distended, his mouth open, his hair on end. Before I could begin speaking, I heard the door jerked open and knew that he had fled. I called after him, but he had left the office.

About a week after this incident, I saw him coming down Broadway, but when he saw me he bolted across the street. I am quite sure he has never mentioned what occurred, and do not believe he could be induced to come near me. I have since sent him a check.

I was mean enough to stand off several troublesome creditors in this way, but I have since paid them all. It was my only recourse, and it was well for them, for it gave me an opportunity to get my affairs in better condition and to pay them all in full. I have never heard that any of them ever mentioned what happened and I know that none of them has mentioned it to me.

As soon as Dupuy had gone, Robertson turned off the current— for by this time I understood that it was an electric phenomenon—

and we were together in the room again. I stepped to the door and asked the boy if Dupuy had left. With a very peculiar expression upon his face, he remarked that the gentleman had fairly run through the room only a moment before.

I now took up the matter with Robertson and suggested that it might be well for him to explain the invention, or discovery.

"Well," said Robertson, "I make no pretense of being an expert on matters relating to vision, but I have accepted the theory advanced by some that light-waves travel in a series of electrical impulses or oscillations, in a way similar to that in which sound is transmitted. Knowing how the transmission of sound can be prevented from going any great distance by simply making a break in the medium, it occurred to me that if I could polarize or deflect light-waves or oscillations, I should make myself invisible. I knew just enough about electricity to understand that it follows, like water, the easiest course, and therefore that if I could produce an electric current or currents of greater strength than that carrying the light-waves, and in a direction at an angle to the rays of light, such rays would therefore be deflected and my object attained.

"The next step was, of course, to provide a medium by which the transverse electric currents could be produced. From reading of the experiments in wireless telegraphy, I found that electric impulses could be made to travel through the air, and I first tried to make the current pass between terminals placed above and below my face, thinking that I might obtain the desired effect, but the result was disappointing. I then conceived the idea of providing a volatile and easily projected conductor which would serve as a medium to carry the transverse currents, and after long experiments I succeeded in discovering such a substance. The rest was easy. I, as you see, simply provide small loops, which, however, are hollow and which are insulated. They are fastened to my clothing at suitable intervals and the projections which you have noticed serve as electrical conductors and are also little jets through which my volatile conductor is forced. In my pockets are two small storage-batteries which can be connected with the several loops, and I also have a rubber vessel containing a conductor and an ordinary collapsible bulb for forcing the conductor through minute flexible tubes to the loops and out through the jets. The pressure from the bulb serves also to work the switch for turning on and off the current, and the nature of the volatile conductor is such that it does not at once mingle with the air, and so by keeping a fine spray of this material about my person, I become incased, as it were, in a mist, which also carries the electrical currents and these deflect the electric light pulsations, thus obscuring me; but the light is not shut out, and as you have seen, I appear to be contained in a translucent cylinder when the currents are on. So much for the mechanical part of the invention."

Robertson then proceeded to explain the nature of the volatile conductor, but I am not at present at liberty to make it public, for reasons which will hereafter appear.

"Now," said he, resuming, "if this is patentable, it seems to me it should be patented all over the world, which will take a good deal of money, and besides I wish to carry on further experiments, because, as I intimated to you the other day, I find that under certain conditions I see things when my invention is in use which nobody would ever see with the human eyesight, and about which I do not wish to talk much until I have given you the opportunity to see them. What do you think about the whole thing?"

"There can," I replied, "be no question that your invention is new, and also that it possesses a good deal of utility; but I have some doubts about the advisability of patenting it, and I question also whether the Patent Office or the courts would permit or sustain a patent for the invention."

"What possible objection can there be?"

"Simply upon the ground that it would be against public policy. Of course, it has already occurred to you that if this were known to a certain extent, it would prove a boon for fake mediums, who would be giving materializing séances and rob the public of its money. The thief could pick a pocket and immediately pass from sight. The murderer could easily escape. In fact, it would give criminals immunity from arrest."

Robertson's face fell, and I could see that he doubted the probability of making much money out of the invention, but I continued:

"There is, however, another side to the question, and it seems to me that you can get all the fame and we can get all the money desired without the protection of the Patent Office. Instead of making the invention a cloak for criminals, it could be used by government officers to ferret out crimes. If it were kept secret and used solely by the government, who could have the conductor made by only a few trusted people, it would enable the United States Army to march unseen to victory, for I take it that the obscurity of the individual can be overcome sufficiently to permit him to move, at least when properly guided. I see no reason why the principle cannot be applied to naval and other vessels, so that, when beset by the enemy, the vessel could be made invisible. In fact, the secret employment of this invention by the government would be of such inestimable value that I believe we can, by bringing it quietly to the attention of the right people, easily arrange to get all the money we want. I suggest that we make an arrangement to lay the matter before the Secretary of War or else the Secretary of the Navy, and we can introduce ourselves by the same means you introduced yourself to me, and be sure at least of making an impression."

We discussed the details of such an arrangement and agreed to proceed to Washington at an early date to pursue the matter on the lines I have mentioned. I then suggested to Robertson that I was consumed with curiosity to get a peep at the invisible things he had mentioned.

"To do this," he replied, "I use a little different preparation in the way of the volatile conductor from that which I now have, and I am still experimenting with the conductor, as the results so far are imperfect and unreliable; that is to say, I cannot always tell when I am going to produce the desired results, but when conditions are right I get them. As soon as I can find just what these right conditions are, I shall have solved the difficulty."

I agreed to go to Grassville on the following Monday to have Robertson experiment with me in an effort to make me see the things at which he had hinted.

I could not keep Robertson's invention from my mind. At length Monday came and I started for Grassville on time.

I had no difficulty in finding my man. It was vacation-time and he was at home. He introduced me to his wife, explaining that I was a lawyer associated with him in the finishing and exploiting of his invention. She thought the invention wonderful, but said that by it she had lost a husband, as for a long time such an ordinary affair as a wife had been of no interest whatever to him. She hoped that the perfection of the invention would restore her husband.

Robertson took me to an upper room which he used as a work-room, and we proceeded at once to business.

"Now," said he, "you will be the subject and we shall see what we shall see, but that may be nothing. I have to get both current and conductor exactly right or there is no result."

He adjusted the attachments with extra care, turned on the current, and I was half blinded by a series of flashes as if the sun had been reflected from a mirror into my eyes. He made another attempt, after a readjustment, and I was closed into the usual cell of light. We made numerous trials with no new result.

At length, after several failures, I was transported. My descriptive powers are limited and I cannot tell what I saw, but it was a new world. Like a flash it dawned on me. The light was all at once soft and yet so clear that it seemed as if I could see far out into space. I remember one beautiful morning in May after a ride through the woods and behind the hills, after climbing a sharp pitch and following a bend in the road, coming unexpectedly into the open, and seeing the whole upper valley of the Delaware bright with color and stretching away like the Land of Promise into the blue distance. It had always seemed as if nothing could be so beautiful, but what I now saw as much transcended that former scene as did that the rear view from a New York flat. The scope of vision seemed unlimited. The walls of the house seemed not to interfere with sight. But what impressed me was first the wonderful beauty, and next the fact that the most of what I saw comprised things that I had never seen or conceived, things that I could not even name.

There were living beings, and as I became accustomed to the new conditions, I was amazed and delighted to see an old scientific friend of mine who was eagerly watching the performance and smiled as he saw that I recognized him. All at once something went wrong, again I was buried in a wall of light and the next instant back with mortals. I looked blankly at Robertson. I was too much moved to speak.

Finally he said:

"Did you see anything unusual?"

"Mr. Robertson, will you be honest with me, and answer a question before I answer you?"

"I think so; go ahead."

"Are you a mortal man?"

"You are as bad as my wife. I am afraid from certain trouble that I have with my heart that I am very mortal, as the term is generally used, but I have seen enough to rob death of any terrors it ever had. I am anxious, however, before I die to leave this invention in a perfected condition. When I have seen what you have probably seen, I do not care for money. At other times I am anxious to provide for those I leave behind."

"Have you," I asked, "ever seen, when using the apparatus, people that you knew had died?"

"Yes, on many occasions."

"How do you account for it?"

"I see but one way to account for it. It must be that in our present condition we see imperfectly, are not perhaps sufficiently developed to see more than a small part of the earth, and do not yet comprehend the fact that the chief beauties have not yet been discovered. Facts and truths have always existed but we have been ages in finding out the few we have. And doubtless this discovery of mine is only one of many yet to take place, but I think it opens the door to a new world. The man who has spent his day in a coalmine knows nothing of the beauties of nature. If we should take him to a mountain-top the revelation would be akin to that you had flashed on you, and yet you probably caught but a glimpse of what may be seen. Then again, our eyes, according to the oculists, convey to the brain sight-sensations of only such things as serve as mirrors to reflect light, and obviously such things can form but a part of the things that be."

"Well," said I, "I saw an old friend of mine, apparently much interested in this performance, but I did not hear him speak. Do you think that some analogous apparatus is necessary to make us hear things not heard under normal conditions?"

"I am forced to that conclusion, and intend to try and work it out as soon as I can perfect my present invention. In my opinion, when people have seen and heard departed friends, it has been when conditions happened to prevail which are similar to those I hope to obtain at will."

We discussed these affairs at some length and gradually got back to present conditions.

Robertson instructed me in the apparatus, and told me more of the composition and manufacture of the volatile conductor. The Washington trip was arranged for; it was decided that we should go in about ten days, which would give Robertson time to make several sets of apparatus, and to carry his experiments further.

We started armed and equipped and could not resist the opportunity of having a little fun, resolved not to carry it far enough to make ourselves too conspicuous, or rather inconspicuous. We took a parlor-car at Jersey City and arranged our chairs facing each other so that we could easily converse. In a short time the conductor came along, and as he reached for my ticket, I went out, but flashed instantly back to view in time to see him straighten up and put his hand to his eyes. He looked startled, but said nothing.

As he reached for Robertson's ticket, Robertson repeated the trick, and this time the conductor straightened up with a snap, turned white and looked frightened.

"Is anything the matter?" I asked.

"I didn't know that there was, but I seem to have blind spells. I had the queerest sensation just now that I ever had in my life, and for a moment I couldn't see."

"It is probably indigestion," I said, "or perhaps you are bilious. Why don't you take something for your liver?"

We considerately refrained from any further demonstration lest we should make him really sick. We did not wish to attract too much attention, and only tested our apparatus further in the dining-car.

The waiter spread the table and brought some oysters.

"Waiter," said Robertson, as he disappeared, "these oysters are out of sight."

This disposition of Robertson's to pun was the worst thing I had seen in him.

"For de Lawd's sake!" said the darkey, and dropped the tray and soup he was bringing.

I heard the head waiter rebuke him sharply, and the darkey responded:

"Dat dar man's a hoodoo; he got de evil eye."

"Go 'long, you fool," said the head waiter, "and be more careful." But the waiter refused to serve us, even under threat of discharge.

Another came. He seemed a little nervous, and went about his work reluctantly. Finally I asked him to pass something to me, and as he did so, I obliterated myself for a minute. Well, he was the most frightened man I ever saw. He could not speak. As I came back, he managed to get away, but he refused to come near us after that.

Unfortunately, a young woman in the next seat happened to be looking at me when I disappeared, and she fainted. She was a fine-looking woman, and I would not have disappeared had I known she was looking at me.

We knew that we attracted general suspicion and ought to have stopped here, but when the head waiter timidly approached to ascertain the cause of so much confusion and alarm, Robertson faded out. This was too much. Those nearest the exit end of the car left at once without paying their bills, and every one ceased eating. The waiters were terror-stricken.

The head waiter had sufficient presence of mind to beg me to take my friend and depart.

I saw that we had made a mistake, and we paid our bill; the head waiter trembled as he took the money. I handed him a dollar each for the two discomfited waiters, though I doubt if they would touch the money.

At the hotel we were our usual selves.

I knew, of course, the necessity of a good introduction to enable a matter to be properly presented to a Cabinet officer, but resolved to make our apparatus introduce us.

I had, however, letters from different influential people to help when we got down to business.

The next morning we tested the apparatus which we wore, took a bag containing several sets and repaired to the Navy Department. I had learned that the Secretary of the Navy was in town and planned the visit so as to be reasonably sure of finding him.

To the young man who asked what he could do for us, I presented a card and said I wished to see the Secretary of the Navy on very important business.

He advised me presently that this was impossible, but that Mr. Brown would see me.

I replied that he might and might not, but that I should be glad to talk with him a moment.

The young man gave me a peculiar look and I faded out before him, remarking that he could judge for himself as to whether Mr. Brown could see me.

Of course, he was mystified, but he saw Mr. Brown, probably gave him the tip that the devil or some other imp wished to see him, and shortly presented me. I introduced Robertson and said:

"Mr. Brown, we are not cranks, as your assistant may have advised you, but come here with a most important discovery which we think should be placed at the service of the government without delay. We have no log-rolling to do, but propose to let our discovery be our sponsor. I know the manner in which all public officers are annoyed, but we ask nothing except to show what we have, and if the Secretary wishes us to depart on the instant, we will do so."

"What is the discovery?" asked Brown. "I can perhaps tell you how to bring it in the regular way before the Department, but it is impossible for you to see the Secretary."

"Do you think it is as difficult as it would be for him to see me?" said I, as I faded. Robertson faded too. Brown did not answer.

"What do you think about it?" said I, still an airy nothing.

"I don't know what to think," said he, apparently forgetting everything.

I came back and found Brown standing in open-mouthed astonishment. I saw, too, that every clerk had left his duties and was looking at me, while others were peering through the doors.

Before more could be said, a gentleman came to one of the doors to ascertain the cause of the confusion. Some one addressed him as Mr. Black, and I knew then that he was the Assistant Secretary of the Navy.

"What is the matter?" he asked.

"Mr. Black," said I, "my client here whom you cannot see"—at this he looked very knowing and I thought winked at one of the head clerks— "has a discovery or invention which it seemed to me should be at once brought without formality before the government. To save myself from the suspicion of being a crank, and you from being bored, I shall request my client to appear. Mr. Robertson, will you allow yourself to be presented?"

The big form of Robertson flashed at once to view. The faces of Mr. Black and the rest were a study.

I then faded and said: "Mr. Black, this is not a séance, and we are not wizards. Do you think anything further is necessary to make the importance of the invention manifest?"

Mr. Black is a very smart man. "Come in this way," said he, and in a few minutes we were closeted with himself and the Secretary.

To tell all that passed would be to repeat with modifications what has already been related.

I explained fully the working of the invention, and some of its uses. The latter the Secretary saw, however, before I mentioned them.

"Black," said he, "just imagine the feelings of the commander of an inferior fleet to find all at once and without warning that he was surrounded by powerful battle-ships which had dropped from a clear sky or risen from the depths, with guns in position to sink him. For if he was sighted, the battle-ships could go out of sight, steer by compass, and easily come in to him. How easy for a vessel to escape, on the other hand; or how handily big batteries could be passed."

Still I could see that he thought there must be something wrong about the matter, so I persuaded him to try the apparatus, and soon he was enthusiastic.

He turned to me sharply.

"How many people know of this invention?"

"Only myself and Robertson."

"Are you certain of this?"

"Yes."

"Haven't you applied for a patent?"

"No."

"Why?"

"Because if it were patented, foreign nations could after seeing the specifications practise the invention as well as we could, and it seemed to us that the United States government should have the sole use of the invention."

"That is right," said he. "Where are you staying?"

I mentioned the hotel.

"Well," said he, "I want you to promise me on your honor that you will neither of you make any further exhibits of this invention, that you will mention it to no one, and that you will keep reasonably close to the hotel until you hear from me."

I readily promised and we departed.

That afternoon I received a note from the Secretary asking us to meet him at a certain place the next day, and to bring our apparatus and be prepared for a full explanation.

Of course, we kept the appointment, but what was our surprise to find that we were to meet the President and Cabinet! We were at first a little embarrassed, but were greatly relieved to find that the people we met were like other men. In fact, they had great sport with the apparatus, and it of course led to all kinds of speculation.

We were delighted to find that in the opinion of all, the government should own the secret. But the difficulty lay in keeping the secret while practising the invention.

Finally the mutter was left with the Secretary of the Navy and the Secretary of War, and it was arranged that we should meet them the next morning.

This we did. The Cabinet officers were afraid that it would be difficult to keep the matter secret, but decided that it would be better to take some chances than to run the risk of losing the invention altogether. So, to make a long story short, it was arranged that Robertson should write out the formula of the conductor, which should be in the custody of the Secretary of the Navy; that Robertson and myself should give as much time as should be required to fit vessels, individuals, et cetera, with the apparatus; that we should prepare the volatile conductor when required in the presence of a government officer; that we should receive ten thousand dollars a year each for our services while in government employ; that we should receive fifty thousand dollars down, to be paid from an emergency fund; and that as soon as authority could be obtained, we should receive a million dollars for the invention.

The first part of the contract was carried out; we received our fifty thousand dollars and entered into government employ, to which most of my time is now given.

But the good fortune was too much for Robertson. Just before we were to start for home, as he was sitting talking to me, he suddenly clutched his breast, stiffened himself and died without a word.

Now comes the strangest part of the whole matter. After making the proper disposition of Robertson's remains, I went on with the government experiments. As long as the conductor we had on hand lasted, they were eminently satisfactory, but it soon gave out.

I had helped prepare it, and a government expert had also seen it prepared, but when we tried it ourselves something was wrong. We have worked at it for months without result. The officials have despaired, but I still think that Robertson was honest and only some trifling thing is necessary to make our experiments successful. I even hope to get that finer adjustment which will enable me to see him watching the experiments, as I have no doubt he does, and even to go farther and hear him explain all he knows about it.

THE WHEREABOUTS OF MR. MOSES BAILEY
James B. Nevin

The fact that Moses Bailey had not been seen for several days was not, of itself, a very peculiar circumstance.

Mose was known to possess a slight predilection for looking upon the wine when it was red, and his occasional disappearance caused no unusual comment in Belton.

When, however, it was noted that Mose had not been seen hanging around the Central Hotel for over two weeks, people began to wonder where he was. No one cared much, of course, but when a well known character just simply drops out of a community without any previous warning of his intention so to do and leaves no track or trace behind indicating when or how he left, nor when or how he expects to return, if at all—well, people will talk, and talking, grow curious—wildly curious—that's all.

The excitement grew so intense—perhaps the curiosity—that the town council seriously considered offering a reward for Moses' safe return. Upon further consideration, however, remarking the very ridiculous attitude in which this would place the community, the matter of the reward was dropped.

Mose had never been any specific benefit to Belton; in fact, it was generally conceded that he had been more of a disgrace to it than otherwise.

As for myself, I had a most important reason for wanting to know the whereabouts of Mr. Bailey. The said gentleman was indebted to me in the sum of seventeen dollars and fifty cents—an amount not to be carelessly overlooked.

Candor compels me to state here that several prominent citizens, to whom I mentioned my loss, intimated to me that it was a great pity, so far as the good of the community was concerned, that I did not make my exit at the same time Mr. Bailey made his. It appeared that I did not occupy a much higher place in the estimation of Beltonites than the mysterious Mr. Bailey.

In fact, since his remarkably clever feat of "pulling off" a real live sensation, I am rather inclined to think that Moses took precedence.

Time passed on, and, nothing being heard of Mose, I had given him up as lost, along with my seventeen fifty.

About three months after Mose was last seen in Belton I received a severe shock one day in the following communication, which reached me through the mail, bearing the local postmark:

> Dear Bill:
> I guess you are wondering what has become of me. To all intents and purposes I am a dead man, but as I have a communication to make to you which it will undoubtedly be to your interest to hear, I should be pleased to have you call at Prof. Hucksley's residence at ten o'clock next Friday evening. I can put you on the road to making a lot of very easy money. I depend upon you to keep this matter a secret, as you know you may depend upon me to do the square thing by you.
> If I remember correctly, I owe you a small sum of money. It will give me great pleasure to pay the same, when you call.
> Trusting that I may have the pleasure of seeing you upon the evening suggested above, I am
> Your friend,
> Moses Bailey.

Now this letter gave me a very creepy feeling. It was like some one talking to you from out of the grave.

At the same time I did want the seventeen fifty, and I was reasonably sure that my old friend of numerous brave enterprises of the past would not lead me into anything calculated to get me into serious trouble.

I decided to go, hear his scheme, get my money, and, incidentally, learn something of his queer conduct for the past few months—if possible.

The following Friday night, therefore, at precisely ten o'clock, I walked boldly up to Professor Hucksley's front door and rang the bell. In a few moments the door was opened and, without so much as a question being asked, I was ushered into the library, which was brilliantly lit with a cluster of incandescent electric lights.

Professor Hucksley, for he had met me at the door in person, now waved me to a chair and addressed his first remark to me as follows:

"Well, Mr. Davis, I am delighted that you did not disappoint us. Bailey will be extremely glad to see you."

"I shall certainly be glad to see Mose," I replied.

"No doubt," said the professor, giving me rather a queer look and smiling slightly.

At this moment I was startled to hear a loud guffaw right at my elbow. I jumped up and wheeled round suddenly—for it sounded very much like Bailey's laugh—when I discovered, to my intense surprise, that there was no one there.

As I stood gazing into space in the direction from which the sound had come, it seemed that I could hear a suppressed chuckle, and pattering footsteps as though some one was hastily leaving the room.

With a slight thrill of uneasiness, I turned to Hucksley for an explanation. He had vanished!

There was the chair in which he had been sitting not more than fifteen seconds before. It was empty.

Now, with all the short comings charged up to me by the Beltonites, no one has ever accused me of being a physical coward; but I am willing to admit that a mighty curious and uncomfortable feeling stole over me in the face of these very peculiar proceedings, and I began to wish that I had paid no attention to Bailey's letter—even involving, as it did, the perhaps indefinite postponement of the collection of my seventeen fifty.

However, being now in for it, I summoned all my courage and endeavored to bring my mind to bear upon the situation.

Hastily crossing over to the door, I closed and bolted it on the inside, resumed my seat, and said, in a loud tone of voice, "Very clever, very clever, Professor Hucksley; now come on, let me see my friend, and go home."

You could have cut the silence with a knife. Not the faintest sound came in response to my remark. It was getting mighty lonesome in that room.

I now began a systematic search of the apartment for the late occupant of the chair opposite mine. I looked under the bed and behind the sofa, back of the piano, and I even looked in the piano. He was not to be found. As a last resort, I got down on my knees and looked under the bookcase. No use.

Although I investigated every place where it was possible for a man to conceal himself in that room, Professor Hucksley up to this time was nowhere to be seen.

When I arose from my last named position, there sat the professor in his chair as unconcerned as though nothing had happened.

Involuntarily I glanced towards the door. It was still shut and bolted.

Very quietly I walked over to the professor and remarked, "I would regret the necessity of killing you, sir, but unless you at once conduct me either to my friend, whom I called here to see, or the front door, I shall most certainly proceed to knock your brains out."

With this I turned for an instant and picked up a heavy paper weight which I had previously noticed lying upon the table. Quick as I was, I was no match for my companion, for when my eyes almost instantaneously returned from their glance towards the table, they rested upon the gleaming barrel of a revolver held in the very steady hand of Hucksley.

"Sit down, Mr. Davis," said the professor quietly. "I know you are surprised at these seemingly strange proceedings. But, really sir, one should never be surprised at anything in these days of scientific advancement. With your permission, I will bring in your friend."

"Bring him in, if you please," I said with a shiver, for this thing had got on my nerves somehow, "and please be quick about it."

Professor Hucksley smiled, walked over and unbolted the door and left the room. In a few moments he returned as far as the door, spoke a few words to some one in a low tone of voice, and then I heard his footsteps as he passed on down the hall towards the back part of the house.

Almost instantly following the first retreating footfall of the professor, I was overjoyed to hear the well known voice of Bailey exclaim, "Well, well, Bill, I am glad to see you."

I turned, with a feeling of intense relief, to greet my old friend, but was thunderstruck to see that I was entirely alone in the room.

At this moment I felt my right hand grasped in the strong clasp of something which felt like a hand, and Mose Bailey's voice rang in my ears, saying: "Bill, this is a devil of a joint here!"

I made a lunge with my left fist in the direction of the voice, swung wildly in the air, and then rushed madly towards the front door, intent only upon getting out of this uncanny place at the very earliest possible moment.

When within about ten feet of the door I heard a sharp "click," a peal of hideous laughter, and immediately the lights went out, leaving me in total darkness.

I guess I must have fainted about this time, for the next thing I knew I was lying upon a sofa in Professor Hucksley's private sleeping apartments, while the professor was leaning over me and forcing a drink of brandy upon me.

The idea of any one forcing a drink of anything alcoholic down my throat was so ridiculous that I involuntarily smiled.

"Good," said the professor, noting the smile; "you are coming around."

"Heavens, man," I exclaimed, starting up, "what does all this mean? Have I been dreaming all these horrible things about voices and—"

"No," purred the professor soothingly, "be quiet and listen to what will presently be said to you by one who I assure you is your old friend Bailey. No matter whether you see him or not, talk to him and you will soon cease to wonder at what may now seem very strange."

At this moment Bailey's voice, coming from a point apparently not more than ten feet in front of me, addressed me, saying, "I am glad to see you, Bill, and I am quite sure you are the very man Professor Hucksley is looking for."

"I would be blamed glad to see you," I replied, for the brandy had braced up my nerves a bit, "but it seems that your voice is the only thing about you that is on exhibition today. As for my being the very man Professor Hucksley is looking for—well, you can gamble that I am not hankering after a job under him."

"Oh," replied the voice, "you simply don't know the prof—"

"Well," I snapped, "I am not sitting up nights longing for a more intimate acquaintance. What does all this mean, Mose—if you are Mose—and what is it leading to? You never threw me down in your life, and I came here upon the strength of my confidence in your doing the square thing."

"And you did right," said the voice. "I am not going back on you. After I am through talking to you, if you so choose, you are at liberty to walk out by the front door—only you are to keep secret the things you have learned here."

"Before I go, however," I rejoined, under a sudden impulse, "you will not forget the small amount of mon—"

"Certainly not," interrupted the voice; "that will be attended to in due time."

This eased my mind considerably, for money is a necessity, and I hold that it is just as well to get all that is coming to you as you go through life, as not.

"In the first place," went on the voice, coming nearer now, "I, Mose Bailey, am here by your side, in flesh and blood. You will feel my hand upon your shoulder."

I certainly did feel something on my shoulder. I also felt for the bottle of brandy which the professor had slipped under my pillow a few moments before, for that gentleman had quietly withdrawn at the starting of the conversation between Mose and myself. I assuredly did not like the queer doings in that house.

"Now, then," continued the voice, "I am here; I, Mose Bailey, to be sure—only I am invisible, and you cannot see me!"

"You are a liar," I yelled, jumping up; "this is some trick—and it is a good one, I will admit—but I am not expected to believe it, of course. I know it is some of this infernal hypnotism, or—er—er—ventriloquism, or some of those—"

"I am telling you the truth," said Mose, "only, of course, I do not expect you to grasp the idea at once. Here, feel this."

With the last words, my hand was suddenly snatched from my side by an invisible force of some kind, and directed to a point about ten inches in front of and on a level with my eyes. There it came in contact with something warm, and gradually I made out the outlines of a human nose, but I could not see the slightest sign of what I felt.

Now, as everyone in Belton knows, Moses' face is disfigured, just to the left of the left nostril, by two unsightly warts, one large and one smaller, just below it. My hand, under the guidance of the something which held it, distinctly felt those warts and convinced me, as nothing else could, that I was actually in the invisible presence of Moses Bailey.

"Well," I gasped, "what in the world—"

"Oh, you don't mind so much," said Mose, "when you get used to it. It is a bit awkward at first, of course, but the habit grows on you. I have visited Belton several times within the last few months and—really, you have no idea of the advantages of being invisible."

"Well, who would ever have thought—but how is the thing done?"

"That is Professor Hucksley's secret," said Mose. "I am getting ten dollars a week, and all I can eat, for simply allowing myself to be experimented upon. When the professor is through with me he will render me visible again, and I shall reappear in Belton not only rich in money, but rich in inside information concerning certain pious citizens—obtained by virtue of my invisible condition—which I think will be worth something to me in a financial way."

"But what have I to do with all this?" I asked, for I will confess that the experience which I was undergoing was most trying.

"For certain further experiments," he replied, "Professor Hucksley wants another subject. I told him that I was quite sure that your services could be obtained, provided you were approached in the proper manner. He requested me to place the matter before you. The rest you know. The few trifling experiences through which you were put when you first came into the house were, first, to test your nerve a little; second, to demonstrate to you the awe inspiring advantages of being invisible."

"Yes," I interposed quickly; "I want to ask a few questions about the library experience."

"The professor will answer all further questions in person," said Mose, as, at that moment, Professor Hucksley walked into the room and took a seat near me.

"My dear Mr. Davis," said the professor, handing me a cigar, and at the same time extending his case towards the invisible Bailey, "I am very anxious to secure your service for a few simple experiments."

I was not paying the slightest attention to him. I was engaged in watching a cigar apparently lift itself into space, and steady itself in air, while a match calmly arose from a nearby table, struck itself against one of the legs of the table, floated to the end of the cigar nearest me, lit the cigar, went out suddenly, and then plunged wildly into a cuspidor, where it lay very still.

I cannot describe to you the very peculiar feeling I experienced while watching that cigar smoke itself in midair.

I felt better when I heard Bailey remark to the professor that he did not like this cigar as well as some they had smoked a few days previous to this. I knew by this that Bailey was smoking this cigar, and, while he was invisible, the cigar was not. It was very curious.

"I am willing to pay you the same that I am paying Bailey," continued the professor, "if you will simply submit yourself to the same treatment. There is no danger, and you will be treated like a gentleman at all times. I calculate, after one more little test, to make the details of my discovery public. What do you say?"

"I thank you for your offer," I said, "but I must decline. I am afraid I could—"

"I am very sorry," be sighed wearily, "but I was afraid that Bailey had too high an opinion of your courage, hence the little experiments when you first came in. Well, well, it is a very simple service, and, as I was so nearly ready to make my work public, I had hoped that you would consent. I guess we can find someone else, though."

Now, I did not like the intimation concerning my lack of courage.

I began to weaken. Perhaps I was throwing away a golden opportunity and for no other reason than that it involved a somewhat novel experience.

Mose Bailey had undergone it for over three months, and, while I had no means of telling whether or not he had grown fat upon the thing, he at least appeared contented. That is to say, he did not exactly appear, in the strict sense of the term, at all; he simply said that he was contented.

"If you would allow me a little more information," I said, addressing Hucksley, "I might consider it."

"Suppose you question me," he replied, "and I will answer such questions as I feel justified in answering just now."

"Well, then, what will you do with me first?" I queried.

"Strip you," he replied, straightening up and showing great animation, "and paint every square inch of your body with a metallic preparation of mine, the exact composition of which I am not quite ready to announce at this time, after which you will be invisible."

"That's easy." I smiled. "But you can make me visible again whenever you want to?"

"Oh, yes" —enthusiastically— "I should never consider my discovery at all complete unless that feature were well understood. I simply have to ask you into my bathroom, where you will bathe in an especially prepared liquid, from whence you return quite your old self again. The chemical bath washes off the metallic paint."

"I should certainly like to know something about the nature of this remarkable discovery," I said insinuatingly.

"Well," answered the professor, "as you will learn by consulting certain technical works, distinctness of vision depends upon the accuracy with which the rays of light, diverging from all parts of a luminous object, are brought to a focus exactly at the level of the sensitive optical membrane destined to receive them. Taking that proposition as a basic law, and stripping it of all unnecessary detail, it must be true that any object not luminous in the slightest degree must be imperceptible.

"My preparation renders any object to which it is applied positively non luminous (or perhaps I should say it renders the object infinitely luminous, which is the same thing) and incapable of being made more luminous. And it does this regardless of surrounding lights.

"When a ray of light comes in contact with an object coated with my preparation, it passes through just as it would pass through a piece of plate glass, provided the object so treated be completely and absolutely covered with the preparation.

"Result," continued Hucksley, as a little red spot came in each cheek, "is transparency. Even human beings can be made invisible by my process. Why, man, the X-Ray is child's play when compared with this.

"To make it clearer," went on the professor, after a pause, "I will illustrate. I took Mr. Bailey, here, and first painted him on one side only. I found that, while I could not see him, at the same time I could not see through him. He simply appeared like a great white blot.

"I then painted him all over and stood him in front of a screen. The result was most satisfactory. When a ray of light struck him it was instantaneously conducted through him to the opposite side and released.

"The first object with which it came in contact, after being released, was the screen. The ray was immediately reflected back by the screen, through Mr. Bailey again, and the first and only impression registered in the eye was the screen."

"You cannot imagine how the success of his cherished hopes affected him," interjected Bailey. "It was really pathetic."

"Wonderful!" I gasped.

"Not more so than the effects of chloroform, the phonograph, and hundreds of other discoveries were thought to be, when first demonstrated," said Hucksley quietly.

"Perhaps not," I muttered.

"I at once washed Bailey in my other preparation," continued the professor, "and he dined with me that night not the least bit worse for wear. We have repeated the experiment many times, and Bailey has not been washed now for nearly two months—that is, not in my preparation. He really prefers to remain invisible, I think."

"I will assist you in your further experiments," I said, coming to a sudden decision in the matter, "only I cannot begin work before the end of the week. There are a few things to which I must attend."

"That will be perfectly satisfactory," responded the professor, with evident gratitude. "Come today week and all will be well. Remember, though, that I trust to your honor not to reveal one word to anyone of what you have learned here until I give you permission. Of course, if you do, I am in a position to make it extremely uncomfortable for you."

After spending an hour or more with Hucksley and the invisible Bailey, during which time I found the former to be a most charming gentleman, I arose preparatory to taking my departure. Upon reaching the front door, I remembered something that had puzzled me and inquired:

"By the way, how did you manage to disappear so completely when we were in the library?"

"Why," replied the professor, with a laugh, "that was easy—a trick, in fact. I had with me, actually in my hand, when you came in, a long bath robe which had been previously soaked in my solution. When you turned your head for a moment I just slipped it on. You could not see me when you looked around, but, of course, I was there.

"You kept me skipping around pretty lively, though, when you were searching for me. In fact, had you any idea of my real whereabouts, you would certainly have caught glimpses of my feet as I dodged you. It is almost impossible to keep entirely concealed in a bath robe, while moving about.

"Of course, when I was ready to reappear, I simply took advantage of your position, when you were looking under the bookcase, to throw off the robe."

"Your nonluminous compound is remarkable," I said solemnly.

"Yes," he replied as he bade me good night; "it represents years of patient work."

I did not hear anything from either the professor or Mose during the following week until Friday morning, when the postman handed me a letter.

> Belton, July 16th, 1897
>
> Dear Bill:
>
> You need not come to Hucksley's tonight. You will not find me there; neither will you find the professor. It took me quite a long time to see through that man, but I do at last, and very clearly.
>
> Now, in our early experiment, Hucksley was very much worried by one seemingly insurmountable obstacle in the path of complete success. Paint as he would, he could not render my mouth and eyes invisible. Of course, as long as I kept them shut, it made no difference, but what is the pleasure of being invisible if you can neither speak nor see, without giving the thing away? Then again, a man cuts a very novel figure going around with everything about him invisible except his mouth and eyes. It would most certainly cause unpleasant comment. How to get around this was the constant study of the professor for over four weeks.
>
> At last he discovered a way out of the trouble. He made me drink a quart of that stuff—and it did the work! This was just two days before you came. I was completely and absolutely invisible—eyes, mouth and all—as you know.

The morning after you left it occurred to me that I would like to resume my visible state again, for a day or so. I prepared my bath, as usual, using the proper chemicals for removing the transparency mixture and plunged in.

Upon getting out and glancing in the mirror I was surprised to see that it had had no effect upon me at all. I thought, perhaps, I had made a mistake in mixing the chemicals for the bath. I called in Hucksley and told him about it.

He looked keenly in my direction, seemed a little upset, but carefully prepared another bath for me. It was no use, the charm would not work. I could not be made visible with the bath.

Hucksley was very much worried, but told me to give him a few hours' time to study the case. The upshot of it all was, I was tearfully informed, the next day, that there was no possibility of my being made visible again while I lived. The mixture which I had taken into my stomach had so impregnated my system that I was hopelessly transparent forever!

I suggested that I swallow some of the bath mixture. I was informed that it was a deadly poison, taken internally, and could not be thought of. I, of course, prefer a transparent existence to no existence at all.

Now then, maybe I wasn't mad.

Then I thought of revenge. I cooled down, told Hucksley that I knew it was an accident and that I would forgive him. I suggested that we drink a bottle of wine on it.

Well, in the wind-up, I succeeded in getting Hucksley as drunk as a boiled owl. It was easy, the poor fellow felt so bad. Just before he fell under the table I went out and procured about a quart of the transparency mixture—we had just made some fresh and strong—and every time the professor took a drink after this, I made it half wine and half mixture. In this way I succeeded in getting about half of it down him.

After he fell under the table I stripped him and painted him good and proper. The professor is certainly out of sight today. He has the remorse so bad from his last night's jag that he is perfectly content to be invisible.

We are leaving for parts unknown tonight, so do not look for us. It is very novel. We will be compelled to steal all we eat, as we cannot buy it without exciting comment.

Hucksley says that you are at liberty to tell as much of your experience as you see fit. He says that he will never make his discovery public, as it is not complete, and besides, it is too dangerous.

Yours, etc.,

Moses Bailey.

I have never heard from them since. I have never heard anything of that seventeen fifty, either.

THE GIFT OF FERNSEED
Sir Harry Perry Robinson

I, Arthur Sayce, am now thirty-seven years of age. I was born in the United States, was educated at Utica, New York, and at Columbia College. Having taken my medical degree, I spent two years in New York hospitals, after which my next five years were passed in Europe: one year studying medicine in Berlin; two walking the hospitals of London—St. Thomas's and "Bart's;" and two in Paris—the first in private study, and the second as an *interne des hôpitaux* of the French capital.

For the last eight years I had been a practising physician in New York city, until three months ago, when I started for the North Pacific coast on a prolonged hunting trip.

In my life I have known but little sickness, and have never been subject to fits, faintings, trances, delirium, or hallucinations of any kind. It is impossible that I can have been deceived in any of the sensations which I experienced in the events that I am about to describe. However incredible the following narrative may seem, it is the simple, sober truth.

It was on May 10, late in the afternoon, that I, riding alone, arrived at the Coeur d'Alene Mission, in one of the five log cabins attached to which this story is written. The sun was already low enough in the west to be shining full in the face of the Mission. The higher slopes of the mountains beyond, now all dark with the level stretch of pines, were then snow-covered (for the snow lies late on the Bitter Roots), showing in the evening sun alternations of intense black and white. On the right wound the Coeur d'Alene

River, fringed with scattered pines, on which the ospreys had built their nests, and patches of undergrowth of thorn and hazel.

In addition to the five cabins and the Mission itself, there was a seventh building, if such it could be called, a little nearer to me, on the lower ground, an Indian teepee. On the slope to the left grazed a bunch of ponies, at sight of which my own little "buck-skin" pricked up his ragged ears, and seemed to take an interest in the proceedings for the first time since we left the fort.

We had advanced to within about a hundred yards of the build-ings before any human life appeared. Then a party of four Indian bucks, muffled in United States military blankets, came suddenly scrambling out from behind the teepee. Presumably the action of their ponies on the hill had told them that something unusual was in sight. For half a minute they stood looking at me, and I could hear their voices raised in babbling astonishment. Then they all started together towards me, on a kind of running trot. At a dis-tance of some thirty paces from me they relapsed into a walk—or rather into the shambling, half-sliding, go-as-you-please gait which serves the Indian of the prairies for a walk. When about two horse-lengths off, one of them, the oldest (and judging from the superior brilliancy of the red ochre with which the roots of his long black hair were dyed, and from the osprey feathers twisted into his locks, one holding some authority among them), darted quickly forward, and, grasping my bridle in his left hand, raised his right with a long-bladed knife gleaming in it, as if to stab me. In a moment the muzzle of my Winchester rifle, which lay across the saddle in front of me, was at his chest and my finger on the trigger. For fully two or three seconds we remained so; his arm upraised, and my rifle almost touching the blanket where it overlapped on his chest. Nei-ther moved his eyes from the other, and what wicked-looking eyes they were that I gazed at!

Suddenly the Indian dropped his arm and broke into a laugh, in which the other three joined. Then he loosed his hold of my bridle, and the whole party shambled off up the hill in front of me, chattering and cackling with laughter, all of us heading for the Mission building.

It was probably the noise which the Indians made that brought a white man (I confess that I was glad to see him) to the door of the cabin next to the Mission, while we were still some fifty yards away. As he stepped out the sun fell full upon his face, and I could see him plainly; much better, evidently, than he could see me, riding as I was with my back to the light. Dressed in the long black robe of a priest, he looked something above medium height, spare of figure, but active-seeming and hardy. His feet were cased in moccasins. The strong sunlight in his face made him droop his head forward, so that his chin rested on the heavy black cross on his breast, his eyes looking out at me from under his prominent brows. His head was partially bald, what hair he had being of a dark iron-grey. He suffered me to approach within a dozen paces, when as I dismounted, the Indians standing silently on one side, he came towards me with outstretched hands. Taking one of my hands in each of his, he kissed me on the forehead.

"Peace be with you, my son! You are welcome," he said.

This was Father Francis, of whom I had heard at the fort.

He was very cordial, with a quiet courtesy of manner, and we had not long been seated on the little stools in his cabin before I had given him a fairly detailed history of myself and of the reasons of my arrival at the Mission. He, in turn, told me, briefly, of the Mission: how he had lived for a quarter of a century among the Indians; how he had been almost alone for the last eleven months, since the Mission was deserted in the preceding June; and how the four Indians who had welcomed me so curiously had been there but a few days, having come down from the reservation ostensibly to see if the trout were beginning to run up from the lake yet, but really, as he said, more for the pure love of wandering than anything else. The eldest of the party (my friend with the osprey feathers and wicked-looking eyes) was one Tsin-shil-zaska, one of the oldest members of the Coeur d'Alene tribe, and a medicine man of no small repute. Two of the others he called respectively Good Bear and Laughing Brave. The third was named Timothy. All, he told me, spoke English fairly well; Tsin-shil-zaska in particular as well as the ordinary "cultivated" white man, and considerably better than the average of frontiersmen or of the private soldiers of the fort. These facts I subsequently verified by my own experience; and it is often the case that Indians who have learned the language from the priests, and not from trappers and miners, speak a pure and frequently a somewhat Biblical English.

When we had been sitting talking for perhaps an hour, and just as Father Francis was rising to make preparations for his evening meal, the Indian walked boldly, and, as it seemed to me, with rather an insolent air of importance, into the cabin. His three companions stood outside, peering in at the door. The father was already standing, so I arose, too, greeting the medicine man with the ordinary Western salute to Indians, "How! How!"

His reply was given with an air of rather lofty rebuke, in good if guttural English: "How do you do, my friend? You are welcome."

I smiled, partly at his implied rebuke, and partly at the statement that I was welcome, after his manner of receiving me outside.

"You did not tell me so before?" I said interrogatively.

"No. Tsin-shil-zaska tried you, whether you were a coward or not."

"And am I?"

"He cannot tell yet. A man is brave the first time, and" (with sudden emphasis) "*a coward the next. A man who is a coward the first time is always a coward.*"

Father Francis then asked him how the fish were coming up. I forget his answer, and after a few more desultory remarks the conversation dropped.

The morning after my arrival, Timothy met with an accident. He was cutting a branch from one of the thorn bushes by the river, when his knife slipped, and, with the whole strength of his arm behind it, cut a terrible gash in the poor fellow's thigh. His companions carried him into the father's cabin, where the good priest dressed the wound with a simple poultice of wild parsnip as deftly and effectively as it could have been done by the best of surgeons; declining my proffered aid on the grounds that the Indians had full confidence in him as a physician, and that his own knowledge was in fact ample for so simple a hurt.

During the operation, Tsin-shil-zaska had stood looking on with an air of supercilious contempt which exasperated me. Later in the day, when Timothy was lying on the grass by the side of the teepee, I happened to pass close by at the moment when Tsin-shil-zaska was operating upon him in his capacity of medicine man. He had removed the father's carefully placed bandages, and was going through some incantation accompanied with extravagant gesticulations. These mummeries completed, he spat upon the wound, and replaced the bandages with at least as much clumsiness as the father had used dexterity. The sight made me inwardly furious, and it was with difficulty that I restrained myself from rudely interfering then and there.

It was the custom of Father Francis to hold prayer twice daily, morning and evening, in the Mission House. These services any stranger who was at the Mission attended, as a matter of course. That evening, upon issuing from the building after service, Tsin-shil-zaska, who had preceded me, was standing close by the door, looking westward at the setting sun. My resentment was still strong within me as I stopped to ask him, rather sneeringly, how his patient prospered.

"The treatment of the good father is always successful," said he, without removing his eyes from the horizon.

"But you have taken this case out of the good father's hands. Did I not see you doctoring Timothy yourself?"

"Huh!" (The Indian never loses his guttural ejaculations.) "Tsin-shil-zaska does what he can to help the good father."

The idea of his professing to be able, with his fooleries, to give any assistance to Father Francis provoked me further. I do not know now quite how the conversation that followed ran, but it resulted, and that quickly, in my telling Tsin-shil-zaska plainly what I thought of him and his skill as a practitioner, and windup with my calling him a "quack," which he probably did not understand, and a "hypocrite," which he evidently did.

Then for the first time he shifted his eyes from the far-off landscape, and they gleamed more wickedly than ever as he fixed them on mine.

"Huh! Tsin-shil-zaska does not speak so to the Man-with-the-little-rifle." (So, as I had already learned from Father Francis, the Indians had, in reference to a 44-calibre Colt's which I carried, named me.) "He has not said that you are a hypocrite and that you know nothing. The medicine man cannot cure? Huh! The wild goat on the mountain, when shot with an arrow, knows what plant to eat to make the wounds close and the arrow fall.* The hurt beaver medicines himself. The wolf, when hunted, if given time to eat what leaves he chooses, makes himself invisible. The dog there has learned when to eat the grass to make him vomit. The birds of the air know what food will hurt them and what will do them good. Has the Indian, being wiser, learned nothing of all these? The Man-with-the-little-rifle will know better."

The next day saw me in better temper. Tsin-shil-zaska did not appear, and the statement of Good Bear that he had gone into the mountains "to find medicines" only made me laugh.

The day following I went out for a long excursion on foot up the river, taking my rifle in the hope of a shot at a bear. Deer there were in plenty, but, though no lack of "bear signs," no bear; and I returned in the middle of the afternoon, hot and tired. The whole day had been spent in climbing up hills and over crags, and scrambling through brush skirting the snow. The sun was hot (as the Pacific sun can be in May), and my shoulder was fatigued by the weight of the rifle. On my return I determined to undress and take a sponge bath in my cabin; so, having drawn a pail of water from the well and carried it inside, I moved the table into a corner, and proceeded to strip off my clothes. As I was standing "mother na-ked," sponge in hand, looking at the water, and wondering whether

* It is curious, that this same story was told centuries ago by Ælian. "The Cretans," he says, "are skilful archers. With their darts they wound the wild goats that feed upon the mountains. The goats when struck immediately go to eating the herb *dittany*. As soon as they have tasted it the dart falls from the wound."

the first *douche* would be too abominably cold, the door was suddenly pushed open, and Tsin-shil-zaska walked unceremoniously
in. I was indignant at the intrusion and the high-handed manner
of it, and at first was disposed to order the intruder out. Then,
feeling a natural bashfulness, I cast about for something where-
with to cover my nakedness. In my hand was nothing but the small
sponge, and no garment lay within easy reach. But, on reflection,
it occurred to me that my visitor was, underneath his one blanket,
but little more dressed than myself.

The Indian has, in the matter of nudity, no sense of what we
are pleased to call the proprieties, and I doubt whether the medicine man had any idea of the awkwardness which, however illogi-
cally, I could not help feeling. But subsequent events convinced
me that he had been watching me through some cranny in the log
wall—which contained plenty—and had chosen the moment of his
entrance with deliberate intent. His back was, of course, to the
light, as he entered, and even when he had shuffled close up to me
I could not see his face. When within a few feet of where I was
standing, he thrust out one arm from under the blanket.

"Tsin-shil-zaska has brought the Man-with-the-little-rifle some
medicine," he said, "that he may know the Indian has learned something."

In the hand which he extended to me was a small vial—given
him, presumably, at some time by one of the fathers—corked with
a knot of grass. The vial was almost full of a brownish liquor, of
the colour of tincture of arnica—perhaps a tablespoonful or more.
I looked at him and then at the vial.

"And what am I to do with it? Drink it?"

"Huh!" with an accent of assent. "The Man-with-the-little-rifle
will see whether Tsin-shil-zaska knows anything."

"And does Tsin-shil-zaska take me for a fool?"

The only response was a decidedly noncommittal grunt. The
question of my foolishness was an open one. The hand with the
vial was still extended to me.

"How do I know that it is not poison, and will kill me?"

"Tsin-shil-zaska does not kill. He cures people."

"But I am not sick, and need no curing."

And then silence, the Indian's strongest and favourite argument. At last he spoke: "Will not the Man-with-the-little-rifle drink? Will the man who was brave the first time *be a coward the next?*"

The wily old savage! I remembered then his curious emphasis on the phrase the day before. "So this is only to test my courage? And if it kills me?"

"Tsin-shil-zaska would not hurt a friend of the good father's. If the Man-with-the-little-rifle had come to Tsin-shil-zaska, and said, 'Drink,' he would have done so."

Again, as in the wrangle of the preceding evening, I felt that he had distinctly the advantage of me in argument. I was discomfited.

"What is it?" I asked, reaching out my hand for the vial. He let me take it readily. Holding the liquor against the light, I saw that it was semi-opaque, with small particles of fibrous matter floating in it, and slightly gummy—about as fluid as glycerine.

I took out the grass stopper, and smelled the liquor. The odour was new to me—pungent, but not strong, and very herby.

"What is it?" I asked again.

"It is precious, and Tsin-shil-zaska knows no name for it."

"But what is it going to do to me?"

"Will the Man-with-the-little-rifle drink it and learn?"

If I could only see his face! But the strong light of the door behind him made it impossible. However, I reasoned, if it had been really a dangerous drug, he would never have come to me so openly with it. At all events, it is a physician's duty to experiment with new medicines on himself, if no more convenient subject offers. I remembered Emerson's advice: "Always do what you are afraid to do!" So I walked across the cabin, laid the sponge, which I was still holding in my left hand, on the table, and returned with a tin cup. As I was about to pour the liquid into the cup, Tsin-shil-zaska reached forward and took both from me. Dipping up perhaps a wineglassful of water from the pail which was to serve as my bath-tub, he emptied the mysterious liquid into it, finally rinsing the vial out in the mixture, which he handed to me. I hesitated a moment, smelled it, sipped it, and then swallowed it in a couple of mouth-fuls, and threw the cup on one side. It had no particular taste; or rather it tasted faintly as it smelled.

"Well, what now?" I asked.

"Huh! The Man-with-the-little-rifle will soon know." And with that he gathered his blanket closer around the neck, and shuffled off.

I laughed rather angrily at myself for the ridiculousness of the whole affair, and (for I was beginning to feel chilled) ran briskly across to fetch the sponge, and returned to resume my interrupted bath. Stooping to plunge the sponge into the water, I became aware that the drug was beginning to have some effect upon me, and straightened myself up again. Yes, there was no doubt of it. I felt a distinct sensation as of incipient intoxication. I was exhilarated and slightly dizzy. I braced myself, and, planting my feet firmly, threw my shoulders back, to try to shake the feelings off. No; they only increased with great rapidity. The blood was bounding through my veins, and my spirits rose higher (for I am a sober, matter-of-fact person ordinarily) than I ever knew them to in my life. I laughed aloud at myself, and jumped into the air with very joyful-ness. Then the absurdity of my conduct struck me, and I proceeded gravely to remonstrate with myself, aloud. The next moment I had kicked the sponge up to the ceiling, and upset the pail of water over the floor—a joke which struck me as so irresistibly humorous that I was obliged to sit down on a stool and laugh, till the cabin rang again with my hysterical guffaws.

Then followed a series of sensations which I will do my best to describe accurately, for they were sensations such as no man, so I firmly believe, who has ever walked the hospitals of New York, London, or Paris has felt, either before or since.

I have spoken of dizziness. That increased in intensity with every second, and I seemed to be passing in rapid succession through all the stages of intoxication. Stories of various drinks of savage people came into my head, and I distinctly remember that the account of a native Burmese drink of which I have read some-where, which will dissolve a Martini-Henry rifle-ball in thirty sec-onds, flashed into my mind.

"And now," I maudlinly commented, "it is dissolving the Man-with-the-little-rifle himself;" and I laughed uproariously.

But the hilarity was of short duration. As the dizziness continued to increase, the cabin began to sway and the floor to heave, until I had to rock myself backwards and forwards, my head sunk on my bosom, to keep from falling off the stool. Nausea succeeded, and I made two or three ineffectual attempts to vomit, like a man in the extremity of sea-sickness.

So far, however, the sensations had not differed from those of ordinary intoxication. But now a new one mingled with the nausea and dizziness.

As I remember it, it commenced first in my extremities, but had soon distributed itself over my whole frame. There is only one word by which I can describe the process which then seemed to be going on in me—the process of *disintegration!* Every part of my body, solids and fluids, bone, blood, and tissue, was in independent and multitudinous motion, as if each tissue were resolving itself into its component cells, and each cell into its primordial atoms. It was not painful. But for the accompanying nausea and dizziness, it might have been positively pleasurable. The sensation, though intense in each member, was not to be located anywhere, but was evenly distributed from the marrow of my spine to the cuticle of my fingertips. The motion of the particles seemed to grow wilder and more rapid. My whole being seethed and boiled. It was as the ultimate dissolution of my very fabric.

Almost blind in my dizziness, I rose from the stool, and staggered to the bunk. I fell on my knees as I reached it, and then dragged myself laboriously up and on to it. The cabin rocked and swayed; the motion in me appeared to grow into—not to produce but to grow into—*sound,* horrid, tumultuous, muffled but overwhelming; a surging of chaotic but rhythmical murmurs.

Things grew indistinct before my eyes. The motion in me communicated itself to surrounding objects. Everywhere was wreck chaos, dissolution. Just before final blackness closed in on me, I remember seeing the form of Tsin-shil-zaska, almost filling the doorway. That was my last definite impression. Then came deathly nausea, retching that racked my very life, external blackness and unutterable tumult—and I lost consciousness.

When I emerged from the state of coma which ensued, it was early morning, dull and misty and grey, as I saw through the cabin door, which stood wide open. There was no difficulty in picking up the thread of memory. As soon as my consciousness returned, I found myself lying, absolutely naked, on my back. I recollected perfectly where I was, how I came there, and all the incidents of Tsin-shil-zaska's visit and the drinking of the drug.

My first serious thought was about the drug itself. What was it? Evidently a powerful narcotic. Violent in its operations, certainly; but the medicine man had given me a pretty strong dose, as my long lethargy (which must have extended over some fifteen hours) sufficiently testified. In skilful hands, and after careful experimenting to ascertain its strength, it might prove to be of considerable value. I must make Tsin-shil-zaska show me the plant.

Having arrived at which conclusion, I proceeded to raise myself on my elbow and sit up. Somehow I did not feel quite myself yet. I was perfectly conscious and had all my senses, except, apparently, one. My hearing was good, for the monotonous "see-se-se—saw-aw-aw" of a myrtle robin came at regular intervals from some tree behind the cabin, accompanied now and again by the hurried tap-tapping of a woodpecker somewhere in the further distance. I could certainly see, though there was not much to look at, the interior of the cabin, dim and dark, the door being merely a parallelogram of pearl-grey mist in the surrounding obscurity. For my sense of smell—that was excellent, as the pungent scent of moist earth which came in on the morning air, telling of rain during the night, assured me.

But I had no sense of touch! Since first consciousness returned I had been aware of a curious sensation of—what shall I say?— unsubstantiality. You know how, in the moments between sleep and waking, you lie insensible of the contact between yourself and the bedclothes, yourself imponderable, the bed beneath and the covers above you without substance. That same sensation had been present with me since my awakening, but with an infinitely greater sense of reality, for I was not now anything but wide awake. When I put my hand on the wooden side of the bunk and raised myself to a sitting posture, there had been no sensation of contact as my palm touched the wood. I reached out my fingers to the rough logs which composed the wall. It was the same. I could feel nothing. I tried my foot. Again the same.

Yet my members were not dead. The circulation appeared to be normal, for I had perfect control over all my limbs. When I raised my leg and let it fall on the bunk again, it fell quite naturally; not at all heavily or lifelessly, as in a case of ordinary perverted sensation. Still, I could not feel it strike the bed. The more I became assured that this senselessness was a fact, the more convinced I was that the drug which had caused it would be of considerable value to surgeons as an anaesthetic. I must learn its nature at once.

With this resolve, I flung my legs over the edge of the bunk, and dropped to the floor. Strange! I was certainly standing, but without sense of anything under my feet. I walked. My limbs obeyed me. My feet rested normally on the floor. There was no tendency to lose my balance; my muscles supported me perfectly; but I could feel nothing. I jumped into the air, stamped, ran a step or two— the result was the same. So I sat down to think it all over.

As I sat, it occurred to me that the room had been changed since I last saw it; and—where were my clothes?

Then it became plain to me. That miserable Tsin-shil-zaska had drugged me with deliberate intention of robbery. I remembered his coming into the cabin just before I became insensible, and doubtless he had then carried off my wardrobe. Yes, my rifle was gone, too, and my revolver. He had made a clean sweep while he was about it.

No, my saddle, with an India-rubber saddlebag attached, was left, and I could dress myself in the shirt and pair of socks which were all the change of wardrobe that I carried, and so make my way to the cabin of Father Francis, and lodge complaint against the medicine man. The table stood in the corner made by one of the side walls and the projecting end of the bunk. The bag was beneath the foot of the bunk, and therefore partly under the table. It would be easier for me to move the table than to creep under it on my hands and knees to reach the bag. So I took hold of the table to move it. I grasped it, as far as a man with no feeling in his finger-ends could grasp anything, and pulled. Not an inch did it stir. I pulled and pushed, and shook (or tried to shake), and pulled, and pushed, and shook again. It would have done as much good to have pulled, and pushed, and shaken at the Rocky Mountains. If I could only have had the satisfaction of feeling that I *was* really grasping it, that would have soothed me somewhat. But this utter numb-ness was maddening, and my wrath against Tsin-shil-zaska grew strong.

However, there was nothing for it now but to get into the lim-ited costume at my disposal as quickly as possible, and make my way to headquarters and make my complaint. So I dropped on all fours, without feeling when my hands rested on the floor, and, crawling under the table, endeavoured to grasp the bag. I say "en-deavoured," because I really could not say whether I did grasp it or not. I thought that I caught hold of it, and so far as my eyes could teach me my fingers were actually inclosing a part of it. But it was rooted as firmly as the table. If I pulled at it, my fingers simply came away from it, no matter how firm a grip I thought I had taken. They did not slip off, they simply *came away*—ceased any longer to be in contact with it. My hand was as nerveless as it was senseless. I was still tugging and gripping with what seemed a preposterous waste of energy, considering the smallness of the object that I was tugging at, but without the smallest result, when I became aware that some one had entered the cabin. My position was not dignified—my head and shoulders under the table, and the rest of my naked person protruding into the light towards the new-comer, whoever he was. So I scrambled out backwards as fast as I could, and rose to my feet. It was the Father. His back was to the light, but as I arose I saw by the motion of his head that he was looking around the room in search of something or some one; then he deliberately turned around and walked out again.

"Father! Oh! Good-morning, Father!" But he evidently did not hear me. It was very curious. If his face had not at one time been directed full towards me, I could have declared that he had not seen me. It was true that the light was dim, but a naked man, six feet and one inch in height, suddenly springing from all fours to his feet, is a fairly conspicuous object at the distance of some three paces—calculated at least to catch the eye of a man or ordinary clearness of vision.

I ran to the door, and, resting a hand on the post on either side, thrust my head out. The Father's retreating form was some ten yards from me. I called him, and called again. He kept on his way, turned into the door of his cabin, and disappeared. Certainly he did not hear me. Was he deaf as well as blind? But my voice, I was obliged to confess to myself, was weak. I called again, as an experiment. Yes, it was very weak—thin and bodiless. It was not the fault of my hearing, because the distant scream of an osprey came plainly to my ears, and a flight of Alpine grosbeaks (birds which are very plentiful about Lake Coeur d'Alene), which flew jerkily over the cabin at that moment, filled the air with twittered music.

For fully a minute I stood there wondering what I was to do. I could not feel that my hands were resting on the posts of the door, though they were visibly doing so, or I should have fallen forward on my face; nor could I feel that my feet touched the ground. Then I commenced feeling all over the door and the rough ends of the jutting logs, where they had been chopped off to leave the doorway space. How solid, and hard, and unsympathetic it all was to my numb touch and nerveless fingers!

In pure exasperation I slapped the door-post with my open hand, and a new horror dawned upon me. There was no noise when the hand came in contact with the wood. I tried again and again, and again, harder and harder; not a sound. I clapped my two hands together, but neither sound nor sense of touch told me when they met. It was very ghostly. I searched for anything that was resonant to strike. I smote the flat surface of the door. It neither trembled nor emitted any sound. I went back to the table, and struck that— slapped both palms down on it simultaneously with all my force. It was useless. When my hands reached the wooden surface on their downward course, they stopped, ceased to go any further, but the impact had not the smallest effect either on the table or on my hands.

And an unutterable terror crept into me; a hideous, indescribable feeling of unreality, as if I were out of all relation to the world around. Was it, after all, a dream? I reached out my hand to the walls, and could feel nothing. I struck the table again, and not a sound came from it. Was I in a world of shadows, or—and my heart sank as the thought came to me—was I a shadow in a world of realities? How utterly nerveless, powerless, unsubstantial, I was beside these great, black, rugged, unresponsive log walls! I called aloud, and my voice came to me thinly, as if from a distance. An ineffable hopelessness came over me, and I sank on my knees by the table, and buried my numb face on my senseless arms.

All the horrors that followed have failed to weaken the memory of that moment of overwhelming and nameless terror. As I sit now writing at that same table, and look around at these same rough walls, an echo of that feeling of hopelessness conies back to me, and I smite my clenched knuckles on the resounding board, to make sure that it rings at the stroke, and that things are realities once more.

How long that supreme sense of terror lasted I do not know; probably some ten minutes or a quarter of an hour. But slowly a feeling which had from the first been combating, and to some extent mitigating, the miseries of the situation began to possess me, and to restore me to my normal self—the feeling of professional curiosity as to the nature of the drug under the influence of which I then was. A very devil's potion it seemed. Certainly its action on me had been violent and crippling. But the stronger its properties proved, the more important its addition to the pharmacopoeia would ultimately be. As I rose to my feet from my kneeling posture, a blue jay fluttered down with a dissonant "charr-rr-rr," and perched itself, head inside the cabin, in the doorway, looking dull and bedraggled in the damp air. I raised my arm and cursed the bird in stern Anglo-Saxon, whereat it tumbled precipitately backwards, and flew clamorously headlong into the mist. Come! It was a comfort to find some external thing that would still recognise and respect my existence. I yet had some relation to the things of the world.

Walking to the door, I leaned against one of the posts and looked out. Four figures were approaching from the direction of the Father's cabin; and it was with something which was almost joy that I counted them, and knew that Tsin-shil-zaska was still at the Mission, and that I might hope to recover my properties and revenge myself.

They advanced slowly: the Father with bowed head and down-cast eyes; the Indians with heads erect and eyes gazing into the mist, as if they rested on the distant landscape beyond. They were evidently coming straight to my door, so I drew a pace or so in-side, and awaited them with a deprecatory smile, apologetic for my nudity, on my face.

The Father, after a moment's hesitation in the doorway, stepped in first, and his lips moved in murmured blessing. Tsin-shil-zaska followed. The others remained outside. I stood a yard and a half, perhaps, back from the entrance, waiting awkwardly for the good priest's salutation. But even now, sitting writing this on almost the very spot on which I stood then, and with every detail of what passed imprinted—ah, how clearly—on my memory, I cannot ac-curately describe the utter horror of the minutes which followed.

In the first place, no salutation came. The eyes of the Indian, as he entered, shifted in one rapid glance around the cabin, and then fixed themselves, not on the wall, but on the distance beyond it. Father Francis began, with an expression of deepest anxiety on his face, to search the cabin in detail with his eyes. I was standing in front of him, slightly to his left hand (what a sailor would call on his port bow), directly between him and the table where it stood pushed into the corner. His scrutiny began at the corner to his and the doorway's left, to my right, and, after resting there a moment, passed along the wall, shifting from the floor upwards to the table— and me. For fully a minute again his eyes rested on me—on my chest, dropping to my knee, passing from right shoulder to left, and from left elbow back to right. But I knew that it was not I that he was looking at—not my chest, nor knee, nor shoulder, nor elbow.

He was looking *through me* at the table, under it, up to the bunk, from one side to the other; then, following the corner post, up to the ceiling.

It is useless for me to attempt to describe the sensation of that moment of terror. People have been buried alive, conscious the whole time, and have lived to tell of it. Men have kneeled on the scaffold, awaiting the fall of the axe which never fell, and have recalled afterwards the sensations of those last moments before the joyful shout announced the reprieve. But never, as I believe now, has such mental agony been allotted to mortal man as in those moments seemed to arrest my very being. I strove to speak, but my tongue refused its office. I reached out my hand, and let it feebly fall again. Again I tried to articulate, and at last the word came:

"Father!"

But how thin, and weak, and how far away! Obviously he heard it not. Even I could hardly say whether I heard it, whether it had actually come in external waves to my ear, or whether it had simply passed to my brain over the internal currents of my nerves.

It was Father Francis who spoke:

"You have not heard the report of his rifle, my son, since he left?"

"Huh!" with negative accent.

"Yet one of you, with your keen hearing, would surely have heard it had he fired?"

"Huh!" This time in the affirmative.

And it was I of whom they were speaking as of one absent; I, who stood here so close to the Father that we could have clasped hands without either of us moving; I, who heard their every syllable, but could not make my voice heard in reply; I, present here before their very eyes, in daylight, unseen and—*invisible!* And the memory of Tsin-shil-zaska's words came back to me:

"The wolf, when hunted, if given time to eat what leaves he chooses, makes himself invisible. Has the Indian, being wiser, learned nothing of all this?"

Of the events which followed, when the first agony of the discovery of my condition had passed, my memory is vague and confused. I remember them only as a man may recall some stray shreds of the tangled visions which came to him in delirium.

Father Francis and the Indian stayed some time in the cabin, I know, the Father at intervals advancing suggestions as to my whereabouts. I know, too, that in those moments I called and prayed to them to see me. I brandished my hands in their faces; fell at their feet, and clutched the skirts of the Father's robe, which moved not as my nerveless fingers touched it. I struck Tsin-shil-zaska in the face with my clenched fist, and not so much as an eye-lid trembled. I raved and wept, and shouted in their ears, and they stood unconscious of my presence. I flung myself before their feet as they turned to go, and their feet brushed me aside, without my feeling the contact or having strength to resist. They did not so much as check in their gait. I might have been "thin as air"; apparently, to them, I was. Once, when they had traversed half the distance to the Father's cabin, I still following, and clinging, or trying to cling, to them as they went, the good priest stopped, and turning abruptly to his companion said:

"And thou, my son, knowest nothing of him?"

Gravely, sternly, searchingly, he looked the Indian in the eyes. But the other—the red scoundrel—how firmly he bore the scrutiny! Not a muscle of his face moved. He assumed no look of injured innocence. There was no over-acting. Unconcerned, imperturbable, he gazed back into and through the Father's eyes.

"Of the Man-with-the-little-rifle? Tsin-shil-zaska knows nothing of him."

"But you quarrelled with him, my son?"

"Huh!"

For an instant longer the Father looked him in the face; then turned and walked on. It was impossible to guess whether his suspicions were entirely overcome or not. I longed to tell him to go on questioning—to thrust home and spare not, and probe till he had forced the truth from the Indian's heart. But I could not. I was powerless, hopeless, substanceless.

As the day wore on and the white mist began to lift from the mountain slopes, lingering in thick flakes and scarves along the pine boughs, Father Francis organised a search expedition for me. The Indians started in a body up the river-bank, while the Father himself struck into the hills behind the Mission. I stayed behind, desolate and hopeless.

Soon after noon—a dull, sodden day it was—the Indians returned; and an hour or so later, the Father too came back. The Father spent most of the evening on his knees, coming out occasionally into the air to look and listen for any signs of me, while I would stand hopeless by his cabin door, and try again and again to make him understand that I was by his side. Late into the night his candle burned, reddening the rough inside of the cabin, and just showing the outline of the black figure that kneeled before the crucifix in prayer.

Another day came and went. The forenoon was again spent in search for me—though the Indians only started off in a perfunctory, listless way, and returned again within an hour—and all the evening and night the good priest was on his knees, praying, as I knew, for me.

For myself, I needed neither sleep nor nourishment. At night I wandered about the moonlit slope, wondering whether ghosts felt as miserable as I; or sat in the doorway of my cabin, occasionally, but rarely, throwing myself on my bunk, and lying there, longing to know how long this would last, and cursing Tsin-shil-zaska in my heart. Whatever change had come over my being, however thin and substanceless I might be (I had soon discovered that I threw no shadow), it was evident that my specific gravity was still appreciably greater than that of the atmosphere. I walked, and sat, and moved—the law of gravitation affected me—as though I were still solid and of ordinary fleshly weight. Only in relation to other substances and beings did I feel inferiority; and there were moments of solitude when I would actually forget my condition. Nor, in those first days, did it ever occur to me that my disembodiment, or etherealisation, could be anything more than a temporary affection, which would last only so long as the operation of the drug continued active.

But one day I made a discovery—curious at first, but horrible afterwards. It was on the afternoon of the third day—a variable afternoon of alternate cloud and sunshine—that I was standing in front of the Mission, in the centre of the crescent of cabins, when the five ponies, which wandered at will on the foot-hills, unhobbled, came walking in single file towards the river.

I was directly in their line of march, and as the first one approached me—a small dapple-grey, rat-like animal, with pink nose and ropy tail—I reached out my hand to its forelock. The animal at once flung its head aside and avoided my touch. Could it have been only an accident? I hurried after it, and placed myself again in its path. Again it swerved aside, and deliberately walked around me. I laid my hand on its Hank. It winced, shambled on a step or two, changed feet, and broke into a lope. The second pony had reached me by this time. The same series of experiments had a like effect, and all five were soon going at a canter towards the river.

There could be no question of it. The ponies recognised my presence. Here, as I have said, was a discovery (and now I remembered the blue jay) which might prove useful to me. At any rate, it was infinitely consoling to know that I still had some appreciable properties. It detracted something from the unutterable feeling of isolation which oppressed me, afforded me some shadow of a semblance of companionship in my solitariness, and I proceeded to make the most of it.

I have once referred indirectly to the presence of a dog at the Mission—one of the hungry, half-coyote, pariah curs which are attached to every Indian camp or caravan. When the ponies had left me, I turned my attention to this dog, which was lying on the grass beside the teepee. As I drew near, his eyes opened and his ears went back, and when I reached out my hand to pat him he drew his head away, sat up on his haunches—still keeping out of my reach—and at last got up and slunk off. He trotted a few paces around me in a half circle, and then lay down again, but evidently uneasily. I approached once more; and again he evaded me. So, for some minutes, I kept him shifting his ground, until he refused to lie down at all, but stood, tail down, waiting wearily for me to go and leave him alone. That I refused to do. Presently he grew tired of being hunted, and commenced to whimper—a low, whistling whimper at first, and then growing louder and louder. Finally, as I made a pounce at him, he fairly turned tail and fled, howling dolorously, into the teepee.

"The dogs howl with *icy* breath
When Sammaël, Angel of Death,
Takes his flight through the town."

The words of Longfellow came into my mind, and then a sudden horror seized me.

"Angel of Death!" The time since my first awakening from the coma had been divided into three stages, or periods, by three moments of supreme terror. The first was the terror of unreality, when the feeling of my lack of relationship to the substances around me had first come over me. The second was the terror of invisibility, when I first knew that Father Francis and the Indian did not see me. Next came the terror of death.

Could this be death? *Was I dead?*

Again and again, at night-time chiefly, I had thought of myself as ghost-like. But was I really a ghost? How could I deny it? What knowledge had I of the state beyond the grave, to be sure that this was not the common form of departed spirits? I thought of all the men of whom I knew, from Socrates downwards, who have believed in the presence of demons, or angels, or genii, or the spirits of dead fellow men, invisible on earth. What assurance had I that my condition was exceptional—that I was not sharing the common lot that comes to all men after death? I needed no food to support me. Perhaps it was only an ordinary, though to me unknown, poison that had been given me, and no drug of mysterious potency. But no, I thought, with sudden relief, that cannot be. Where, if so, is my body—my (how I shuddered at the thought!) corpse? The relief, however, was short-lived. Why could not Tsin-shil-zaska have hidden my body as easily as he had hidden my clothes and rifle? And I found myself actually sweeping the horizon with my eyes, to see if anywhere over the tree-tops I could see hovering the tell-tale buzzards or carrion crows, to show me where my own corpse lay.

For the first time it occurred to me with any force that perhaps my state was something more than a temporary affection, dependent upon the continued action of a drug. For the first time I thought that an eternity of this wretchedness might lie before me. How could I tell that there were not other spirits around me, invisible to me as I was invisible to living men; or, if not here on the lonely hill slope, how did I know that in the cities and haunts of men there might not be walking millions such as I? The thought was horrid in its possibility, overwhelming in its bewildering immensity.

Then I fell upon my knees on the sunlit grass, and prayed as only a man in the supremest agonies can pray. From that moment I have never ceased to be devoutly thankful for the sustaining hope which was always with me. I arose from my knees full of confidence. It was easy for me to prove by irrefutable logic that the probabilities were enormously in favour of my being dead—that I must be dead. But I never in my heart convinced myself, logic to the contrary notwithstanding. I knew inwardly that I lived still as mortals live—that the life which enabled me to move, and think, and pray, was yet, in spite of the awful change that I had suffered, the same life as had always animated me, and as now animated other men. An instinct which I could not justify to reason bore me up against my own arguments, and that instinct, implanted, or at least first developed, in those moments of prayer, alone, I believe, prevented my reason from being dethroned.

Henceforward, however, the pleasure of the mute companionship of beasts was gone. Occasionally I would stop to pat the dog or make a pony move from its path, to assure myself that I still had some hold upon the world of external things. But such experiments were ever accompanied with a chilling return of the thought of death and an echo of those agonies of doubt. I did not often try them.

So day followed day, and I still wandered about the Mission, naked in my own eyes, invisible to others, voiceless to all human ears but my own, insensible to the changes of temperature, needing neither sleep nor nourishment, and senseless and numb of touch. The Father had given up the search for me, though his eyes would wander mournfully from my cabin to the distant hills, and from there to heaven, when his lips would move in silent prayer.

How, in those days, I learned to love and honour Father Francis! And for Tsin-shil-zaska my hatred increased. He and his three companions still hung around the Mission, pretending to wait till they could take back the news that the trout had run up stream. They divided their time between sitting on the ground about the teepee and sitting on the ground by the river's bank. Occasionally, they mounted their ponies and went off, aimlessly as it seemed, for half a day's ride over the plains and foothills. Timothy was still an invalid.

I had lived thus for a week—what a week!—when I made another discovery, of more importance than the last.

It was mid-afternoon—still and hot as a Pacific coast Spring can be—the air shimmering with heat, and the last year's butterflies, which fluttered round the walls of the Mission and sat fanning their wings in the warm rays, seeming the only things moving.

I was sitting listlessly in the door of my cabin. Opposite me, the flap of canvas which made the door of the teepee was caught back with a two-pronged peg of bone, and in the shadow within, I knew, lay Timothy, alone. Drawn by idle curiosity, I crossed the intervening space and entered the tent. In spite of the open door and central hole at the apex of the roof, the air within was thick and heavy with that oppressive smell—part grease, part dirt, and part humanity—which clings to the Indian wherever he goes. In the gloom I could just distinguish the form of Timothy, stretching almost from side to side of the narrow tent. The only other contents of the place were a heap of skins and furs, scraps of dried meat, tin cups, saddles, rope, and innumerable other miscellaneous but indistinguishable things, such as the Indian loves to accumulate, which covered probably one third of the entire floor space.

Timothy was evidently asleep. There was no other seat there, so, conscious of my imponderability, but with no particular intent, I seated myself on him. As I rested on him he moved, muttered uneasily in his sleep, and then rolled round from his right side to his left, throwing me off. As soon as he was quiet, I resumed my seat. No sooner had I done so, however, than he commenced to toss again, this time suddenly, and heaving me, staggering, against the further side of the tent.

Could it be possible that he was conscious of my presence? I did not believe it, but determined to see. So, dropping on my knees by his side, I passed my hand once or twice over his face. Yes, he felt it. Drowsily he shook his head, as if to free himself from my hand, and, when I removed it, lay still again. By this time I had become excited and keenly hopeful. Again I touched his face, pressed against his side, and passed my hand over his frowsy, tangled hair. Yes, he stirred as before.

"Timothy!" I called. "Timothy! Wake up! I am here! Do you hear me? Timothy!"

Slowly his head rolled from side to side, and his lips began to move. Eagerly I bent my head to catch his words, but he made only an indistinguishable murmuring. Again I called and shook, or tried to shake him. Once more his lips moved, and brokenly among his mutterings I caught my name— "Man-with-the-little-rifle."

"Yes! Yes! Timothy," —how I was thrilling with excitement!— "the Man-with-the-little-rifle is here! He is speaking to you now! Do you hear him? Timothy!"

But the response was inaudible. Excited almost to frenzy, I called and called again, shook him, and threw myself upon him. Suddenly he reached out his arms, and, with a cry of pain, awoke. There was a startled look in his eyes, I could see in the gloom, as though he expected to find somebody there. I waited, hardly daring to breathe in my suspense. But the look died away. Evidently I was as invisible to him as ever. He pulled himself up to a half-sitting posture, and, leaning against one of the poles of the teepee, remained wide awake, with his eyes staring out through the open door into the sunlight.

Awake he was utterly unconscious of my presence, but asleep he was sensible of my touch and heard my voice. Was it possible that between human beings, when asleep, and myself there existed some such affinity as was evident between myself and brutes? Altogether incapable of making my presence felt by people when awake, was it possible that I could place myself in touch with them when asleep? So it must be; and I sat and watched Timothy, hungrily waiting for the first signs of returning somnolence, like a vulture waiting the approach of death to a wounded man. But Timothy was incorrigibly wide awake, as he reclined there, gazing with unfathomable eyes at the distant landscape. Presently the sound of cantering hoofs told that the others were returning, and I left the teepee to wait impatiently for nightfall.

Never, it seemed to me, did the sun sink so deliberately behind the horizon. When night did come, I thought the good old priest would never go to bed. How late he read! At last the volume was placed carefully aside. Then the light was extinguished, and I knew that a prolonged interval of prayer would elapse before he went to bed. I drew near, and sat in the doorway, whence, in the gloom within, I could vaguely distinguish the outline of the dark-robed figure kneeling beneath the crucifix. Sometimes the murmur of his voice reached me, fervent but low, and more than once my heart was stirred deeply as the sound of my name caught my ear. At length he rose, and was soon lying on his bed of cedar boughs, a rough and unaccommodating couch for so aged and good a head. I approached, and stood by the bunk side, waiting till the regular breathing told me that he slept. Then, with intense if suppressed excitement, I commenced my experiments.

First, I leaned over him, and whispered his name several times in his ear. Next, lightly and reverently, I passed my hand over his face and hair. After two or three such passes a certain irregularity in the breathing told me that his slumber was disturbed.

"Father! Father Francis! It is I, Arthur Sayce, your son, who speaks!"

Wearily he rolled his head from side to side; a faint murmur broke from his lips, and then—he awoke! The disappointment, when his sudden movement and the change in respiration told me that he had awaked, was intense. But there was nothing for it but to wait till sleep again asserted itself. This did not take many minutes, but to me, in my impatience, every moment of delay was irksome.

At length he slept; but, as he had awaked so easily before, I knew that it would be better to allow him to become more deeply immersed in slumber before recommencing my experiments. So I left the cabin, and sentenced myself to walk twenty times from the door to the Mission and back, before returning.

This time I was more cautious, and touched his face more carefully (for, though without any sense of touch, I could regulate my muscles perfectly) and breathed his name more lightly in his ear. Whenever he moved, I ceased—waiting breathless with fear lest he should wake; then I commenced again to touch and whisper to him as soon as the regularity of his breathing was resumed. It was a stealthy and seemed an unholy work, and more than once I started guiltily at the hoot of an owl, or the cry of a distant wolf.

"This," I thought to myself, "is how the midnight murderer feels."

Many a time he murmured indistinctly in his sleep, but it was not till the night was far advanced, after hours of striving in alternate hope and despair, that I caught the sound of my name from his lips.

"Arthur Sayce!" he murmured brokenly. "He has not returned. My son! My son! He will not come to me, but I may go to him!"

"Yes! Yes! Father, he is here; he has returned; he has come to you! It is I, Father, speaking to you now!" But he was awake again.

Once more, when he fell asleep, I exiled myself from the cabin, and resumed my old task, increased this time, by sentence of the court, to thirty turns outside. Returning, the same slow work of establishing communication with the slumbering mind commenced. By many repetitions, alternately insisting and desisting, I brought him once more to speak my name. By slow degrees, going again and again over every step of ground, and always fearful that he was on the brink of wakefulness, I told him all the story—I told him how Tsin-shil-zaska had given me a drug; and at the twentieth repetition of the fact, perhaps, the sleeper gulped, and the muscles of his throat went through the motions of swallowing in his slumbers. I told him of my sickness and of my coma, and in the responsive, uneasy tossings of head and grippings of his hand I saw that the idea of sickness and pain was with him in his sleep. I told him of my waking and of his coming to my cabin, of the discovery of my powerlessness; and as I did so, repeating each phrase many times, the name of the medicine man fell from his lips, and in the waking mutterings that followed the word "unrepentant" caught my ear.

The excitement of the narration and of the eager waiting for signs that he understood was intense. Merely as a psychical experiment, the operation was keenly fascinating; but added to that was the fact that, as I trusted, my life itself hung dependent on the experiment's success.

Again he slept, and again, with unflagging eagerness, I went through all the story, repeating and again repeating every detail of it. The final fact that I had to force upon his mind was that Tsin-shil-zaska, and he alone, as far as I knew, had possession of the secret, and from him, if from anybody, must the method of counteracting or reversing the operation of the drug be learned. How often and in how many forms I repeated that fact I do not know. But the grey light of morning came, and found me still struggling with him. Then I left him, that he might have some space of peaceful slumber, and went out into the open air to wait for day as impatiently as I had waited for the preceding night.

At the first movement inside the cabin, I returned. Father Francis was just rising. I was beside him as he stepped from his bunk, crossed the floor, and fell on his knees before the crucifix. His first sentences of prayer were audible words of thanksgiving— "In that Thou, O Lord, has esteemed my service worthy of continuance for yet another day of earth" —and of supplication for the welfare during the day of "Thy servant and those whom Thou hast allotted him to labour with, as well as for all Thy children upon earth." Then his words became unintelligible even to my strained ears, but it was with eager joy that I caught them rising again: "Strange visions, O Lord, Thou knowest have come to me in my sleep in this the past night, but I know not whether they were of Thee, and sent as of old when Thou spakest to Thy servants in dreams and symbols, as also not seldom in later times. If in truth Thy laws have been broken, and one of Thy children has had the life which Thou gavest him taken from him contrary to Thy will, and if Thou hast appointed me as a minister to rebuke the offender, Thou knowest, O Lord, that Thy servant is waiting to do what Thou dost command."

Again his voice became almost inaudible.

Breathless with eagerness, I endeavoured to catch the murmured syllables, but it was useless. How I longed for the power, only for one moment, to tell the Father that what he had heard in his sleep was true, to urge him to follow the clue thus given to him! But it was futile wishing, and, weary and desperate, I turned into the open air again, as the Father rose from his knees.

I waited anxiously for the first meeting or the Father and the medicine man. It came after the morning prayer, when the sun was a-glitter on the mountain peaks, though the Mission lay yet in shadow. On issuing from the building, the Father called Tsin-shil-zaska to him, and with him re-entered the cabin. For some moments both stood silent: the Father keeping his eyes fixed on the ground; the Indian, with frowsy hair and blanket muffled round his chin, gazing into vacancy. At length the Father raised his eyes and looked at the Indian, while I stood trembling by.

"Tsin-shil-zaska, my son, I have had strange dreams during the night."

"Huh!" And there was a whole monograph of scepticism condensed into the monosyllable.

"Once more I must ask thee: thou knowest naught of him who is lost?"

"Of the Man-with-the-little-rifle? Huh!" This time in the negative and with one slow shake of his head.

"In my dreams, I thought thou knewest of the manner of his death; nay, that thou hadst the power to produce him again."

"Tsin-shil-zaska has no power to bring the dead to life. The good Father is a greater medicine man than he."

"When didst thou last see him?"

"The good Father was with the Man-with-the-little-rifle last before he went away. Tsin-shil-zaska might ask the good Father whether he knows anything of him."

"My son," said Father Francis, "thou knowest that I have never unjustly accused any one—that I have quarrelled with none and done no man wrong. Thou knowest that I would rather love thee than hate, and if thou canst show me that my suspicions are unjust it will be gladness and joy to me."

The Indian's face remained utterly without expression during this appeal.

"The good Father has no cause for his suspicions. Tsin-shil-zaska has done no wrong."

Again there was silence. The Father looked anxiously at him for some seconds; then—

"I trust it is so, my son. If thou hast done any wrong, be sure that the Lord will convict and punish thee."

With that he moved away to the farther end of the cabin. Then for the first time a gleam of expression came into the Indian's eyes—only one flash, but a flash of such malignity and hatred as I have never seen in human eyes before or since. A moment later he shuffled out of the cabin.

That day formed another epoch in my period of exile from the world. Then arose the fourth terror, which held a longer sway than any of its predecessors. This was the terror of murder.

After the events of the preceding night, the strain and mental agonies of those hours of darkness, I was possessed with a strange restlessness all day. It was a curious feeling—feverishness, perhaps, if a man without blood could be obnoxious to fever; intense nervousness, if nervousness could attach to a being that was nerveless.

The Indians had shambled off afoot in the morning, and the place was lonely even to me, accustomed as I was now to the supreme isolation of my condition. About midday I, for the first time since the drinking of the drug, left the Mission, and wandered aimlessly towards the river. The stream was running brimful and muddy with the melted snow from the mountains. Most unlike a trout stream it looked, as it hurried past in thick eddies and rapids, flecked with bubbles. Reaching the bank, I turned down stream, following the winding water through patches of woodland, and beds of purple iris, and round smooth lawns of grass. Arriving at one unusually dense patch of woodland and brush, I found it necessary to leave the stream, and skirt the edges of the thicket. When I was half-way round, the sound of voices from the other side of the intervening brush caught my ear. These, as I approached, resolved themselves into the rhythmic cadence of an Indian chant—the rising and falling of that simple song without words which is common to all the Northwestern Indians: "Hi-yi-yi-yi-ya-ha-ha-ha-hi-yi!" and so on in endless strophes of "Hi-yi-yi!" and antistrophes of "Ha-ya-ya!" On rounding the end of the woodland, I came upon the party from which the song proceeded—my friend and enemy, Tsin-shil-zaska, and his two satellites. Just now all three were revolving in a common orbit round the same centre. From a distance I could not see what that centre was; but on approaching I found it to be a simple stake, some four feet high, driven into the ground, on the top of which a dead scarlet-crested woodpecker was impaled. Whether the woodpecker was an accidental victim, or whether the old bird of augury still has for the red man of the North-west any supernatural properties I do not know. However, there Picus lay, or hung, evidently the central figure in a solemn ceremonial.

It was a dance which was new to me, and I have a suspicion that it was invented for the occasion by Tsin-shil-zaska. Their blankets were thrown aside, and all were, except for a waistcloth, from the sides of which depended the straps by which the leggings, which reached a little above the knees, were supported, entirely naked. They were revolving, each equidistant from the other, in a circle, some ten feet in diameter, of which the impaled woodpecker was the centre. Their attitudes and gestures were the same, and those which are adopted by, I believe, all Indians in their solemn dances: the knees slightly bent; the bronze body leaned a little forward, as if in eager, stealthy march upon some enemy; the head erect, and turning stiffly and in jerks from side to side; the left hand pressed upon the groin; the right upraised, as if about to stab with the large knife which each held in his fingers. "Hi-yi-yi-yi! Hi-ya-a-a! Ya-ha-ha-ha!" and so on, and so on—*da capo* and *ad libitum*. Each sang without reference to the time of the others, and moved his feet, raising them at each step very high, and planting them flat and firmly, only to the cadence of his own voice. At intervals, Tsin-shil-zaska, who was evidently coryphaeus, would, in addition to his regular revolution in the common orbit, make a quick second-ary revolution on his own axis—turning round on his heels as if suspecting some enemy behind, and quickly resuming his place in the circle, to recommence hi-yi-ing with renewed vigour.

For fully a quarter of an hour I watched them treading their weary round; then Tsin-shil-zaska quickened his step. The others followed suit. Quicker and quicker they revolved, till all were fairly on the run. Meanwhile their voices were rising, and the chant grew faster and wilder, till at length it culminated in that strange yelp-ing noise into which all Indian chantings resolve themselves in the crisis of a dance. They brandished their right arms around their heads. The heads themselves turned rapidly from side to side. Keenest excitement was on every face. The yelpings rose higher and higher yet; faster and more furious grew the dance, till sud-denly, with one demoniacal howl in unison, all three sprang on the poor woodpecker with uplifted knives. A sudden stab from Tsin-shil-zaska's hand loosened the bird from the stake, and it dropped to the ground. In an instant all were on their knees beside it, and in rapid succession the three knives were plunging into the mangled body—so rapidly that it seemed a wonder that none stabbed a com-rade by mistake. For half a minute, perhaps, they were on their knees, each stabbing as fast as his muscles would work, and throw-ing into every stroke the strength of a death-thrust.

It was unutterably horrible and savage to watch. I felt my own being thrill with excitement, and the muscles of my hands twitched responsively as the Indians stabbed. When they rose from the ground, a few small shreds of bloody flesh and a litter of feath-ers—red and green and grey—were all that remained of the sacred bird.

It was a very Dance of Death. Whether or not anything as to the meaning of what I had witnessed had yet formed itself in my mind, I cannot say. I knew that it made me shudder; that it was horrid—the condensed expression of all the bloodthirstiness of savage nature; and, vaguely, that it had somehow a terrible significance. It was not long before I knew what that significance was.

After a moment's rest, Tsin-shil-zaska proceeded to gather up the feathers and fragments of flesh in his hands. Advancing to the edge of the swollen river, which was not ten paces distant, he scattered them over the water, to be swirled away into eddies as soon as they touched the stream. This action he accompanied with the low chanting of what I knew must be a curse. Most of it was unintelligible to me, being in his native tongue, but twice the words "good father" caught my ear, and made me shudder. Ceasing, he turned round, took half a pace towards the Mission, and stood, the knife clasped in his right hand at the level of the thigh, the left foot forward as if about to make a spring, and every muscle in his body strained and rigid. The other two at once caught the spirit of the pose, and, similarly grasping their knives, threw themselves into the same attitude, facing in the same direction. A yell broke from Tsin-shil-zaska's lips. He raised his knife as if to strike, and all three started to run abreast towards the Mission. At first I thought they were really about to "run amuck" to the Father's cabin, and murder him in their present frenzy. But after some ten paces they halted, brandished their knives, with a ferocity that was indescribable, in the air, in the direction of the invisible buildings, gave one yell, and suddenly relapsed into perfect Indian apathy.

It was awful to see the completeness with which they controlled themselves. A moment before, fierce as wolves savage with the lust of blood; and now, with their bronze skins still flashing in the sun from the perspiration which the excitement and exercise had forced from their pores, unconcerned and listless as if after a day of idleness.

I did not wait by the river, but started at once for the Mission. There was no longer the shadow of a doubt in my mind as to the significance of what I had witnessed. The ferocity of the final feint in the direction of the Mission could not be misunderstood, even if the repetition of the Father's name in Tsin-shil-zaska's curse had not already given the cue. That a murder, and a murder of the most revolting kind, was about to be committed I knew, without any argument or the necessity of putting my knowledge into words. The medicine man was, of course, the instigator of the horrible conspiracy, with no possible motive for his crime but malice and jealousy, with perhaps a touch of fear, awakened by the Father's reference to his vision, lest his disposition of myself should be discovered. The dance, with its bloody symbolism—whether improvised or of traditional observance on such occasions, I could not guess—was undoubtedly intended to give to the crime some semblance of religious sacrifice in the minds of the other two. All this I realised without formulating my apprehensions into words, as I ran, in dazed, staggering haste, back to the Mission.

Arrived at the Father's cabin, I found him seated on a stool, lost in meditation, with his eyes fixed upon the ground, his hands folded in his lap. I threw myself kneeling at his feet, rested my elbows on his knees, and gazed in an agony of supplication and despair into his eyes. If I could but tell him! If by the lightest sign I could only make known my presence to him, then it might be that in some way I could put him on his guard! If it were only night-time, when I could speak to him in his sleep! But I thought with terror that before another night came it might be too late, and I would only be able, having witnessed his murder, to implore, in the perhaps more perfect communication of invisible with invisible spirit, his forgiveness.

Was it quite impossible to establish a means of correspondence with his waking mind? All my life I have had the supremest contempt for what I have considered the charlatanry of spiritualism, and mind-reading, and "Christian science;" but in those moments of agony, how I wished that I had given even the smallest study to the methods which I had been so quick to despise!

Kneeling before him, I gazed with all my soul into the great grave eyes which, at a distance of scarcely a foot, looked through mine, and struggled to project some impulse of my mind into his. If ever man was enabled to influence and inform the mind of another, surely I, I thought, in the intensity of my endeavour, can influence him. Striving my utmost, contracting my brows to concentrate my gaze the more perfectly, drawing my eyes closer and closer to his, I watched with tingling anxiety every light and shade that flitted across his face. Sometimes serene in quiet meditation, then ruffling under the passing shadow of troubled thought, then again placid and smooth as if sunlit with the light of piety, I watched his eyes, as one may watch the surface of the lake on a day of fickle cloud and sunshine. More earnestly still I attempted to compress my whole being—heart and thought—into my gaze, and to force my mind into communion with his, trying to cut my attention from wandering even so far as to recognise the changes of expression on his sad, sweet face.

Whether or not I influenced him, certainly he was influencing me. I felt myself drawn more near and yet more near to him; my very life seemed to merge and lose itself in the soft light of his eyes; a sense of dependence came over me—of oblivion. I ceased to realise my own corporeal individuality, and felt drawn by those eyes into a clearer, purer atmosphere than I was used to move in. My mind was wrapped, engulfed, in his. A sense of quiet and of holy awe to which I was a stranger came over me. I knew that his temper was absorbing mine, or rather infusing itself into me. With an effort I strove to undazzle my sense, and with my heart as much as with my lips I murmured, "Murder!" And it seemed to me as if it were he who murmured it, not I—or at least that our two beings murmured it as one.

Suddenly his brow contracted. His eye darkened, as if some thunder-cloud obscured the light. His lips moved. The charm was broken, and my mind freed itself from his. Hastily he rose and paced to the door; then returned, and gazing for a moment, with clasped hands, at the crucifix where it hung against the rough log wall, in the further shadow of the little cabin, dropped on his knees beneath it in prayer.

"O Lord! I know not whether these presentiments, so often recurring, are sent of Thee, or whether they are but the unworthy forebodings of a fearful heart. Thy will be done, O Lord! In the days past, Thine arm has upheld me in the presence of death, when the knives were already lifted against me, and Thy goodness has softened the savage hearts. Lord, Thou knowest that Thy servant awaits Thy bidding, and that if it be Thy pleasure that I should now die by the hand of violence I am willing to suffer. But I pray Thee, O Lord, that this act be not laid to the charge of him who does it. Of Thy infinite mercy, I beseech Thee to pardon him "

And here his voice became inaudible. I *had* influenced him! At least I had been able, however dimly, to warn him of the danger which impended; but I knew, and sickened at the knowledge, that he would take no steps to avoid what was coming, but would meet it resignedly as a manifestation of His will.

The rest of that day was terrible to me, as one long waking nightmare. But at last the time for the evening service arrived. The Father, who had been on his knees in prayer since mid-afternoon, entered the Mission building. The Indians came up the hill, with their long shadows in front, and followed him into the sacred edifice. There they sat, silent, expressionless, indifferent, while the man whom they were about to murder prayed for them! Perhaps they did not hear him, or surely his gentle words must have softened their hearts. His prayers were short. Doubtless he felt the mockery of it all. His words were chiefly a supplication in behalf of the three visible members of his congregation; a hope that they might be blessed and purified, and made to live in the way of peace and gentleness, forgetting more and more the untaught manners of their fathers, and leading with every day a life of greater humanity and mercy. They submitted passively to be prayed for, never changing countenance, and, when he ceased, rose and shuffled down the aisle, shutting the sunlight out of the door as they stepped into the open air. The Father remained, as usual, a few minutes on his knees, and then passed out with bowed head. The Indians were waiting outside for his customary evening greeting, which was given with greater earnestness than usual, and which they acknowledged doggedly, and with a brief, ungracious-sounding murmur of response. Their faces did not change—the same stolid, expressionless features, and the eyes fixed on the further dusk of the evening.

It was all, to me, inexpressibly pathetic and very terrible.

The Father lingered in his cabin doorway for one last look at the now half-hidden sun, and I thought that I saw "in his eyes the foreknowledge of death." Very deep and sad the eyes were, while the whole cabin, his face, his very robe, and the hillside beyond, were flushed with rose-colour. Turning, he went into the cabin. The Indians shuffled off, their three figures black and large against the sky.

The Father was soon again upon his knees, and I sat crushed and weary in the doorway. The last tinge of rose almost faded from the western sky. The song of the meadow-lark and the osprey's shrill scream ceased, and the night-hawks wheeled overhead. The mist hanging over the river shut out all the landscape. Once the Father rose, and paced up and down his cabin; and when he stopped in the doorway I rose, and laid my hands on his shoulders, endeavouring to bring my mind once more into communication with his, to piece out the imperfect warning of the afternoon. But it was useless. His eyes were looking up to heaven, "filled with the sacred imagination of things which are not," and I knew that his mind was on a plane to which I could not climb—holy and unapproachable in its serenity. It awed me, and I soon desisted. As I sat down again a strange dizziness came over me, causing sudden hope to thrill through me. But it passed, though I sat with head thrown back and muscles relaxed, inviting it to return.

Darkness fell. The Father prayed on. Hours passed—nine o'clock—ten—eleven. My strained ears had as yet heard no sound from the direction of the teepee. At last the Father rose, and lit a small remnant of candle, which was placed on a shelf just below the crucifix, so that that only caught any light, the kneeling figure below and the bunk being in complete darkness. Looking out into the night, I gave a sudden start. Something moved there in the further, faint candlelight. Yes, there were figures approaching—one—two—three; and I knew that the supreme hour had come.

But once more the dizziness was on me. This time the fit did not pass away so quickly; and what followed is all indistinct in my memory. I can remember Tsin-shil-zaska entering the cabin. I rose, and followed him in. I saw the Father standing and facing the Indian. Then sinking on my knees behind and almost touching the latter, as he stood beside the table, I swooned.

When I recovered consciousness, it was to suffer again all the internal rackings, the nausea, and the dizziness that had beset me after the drinking of the drug. Through them I was dimly conscious of a certain hopefulness—hope that this second agony might mean that the potion had exhausted itself. But hope was soon blotted out again by physical pain.

Brokenly, as if from a distance, voices reached me. A movement in the blanket just before my face suddenly attracted my attention. The Indian's right arm had dropped stealthily down, and the long blade of the knife that I had seen twice before protruded from under the folds to within a few inches of my cheek. Again the fit came over me, and I sank lower to the ground, resting with my knuckles on the sawdust floor; and as the paroxysm passed, a new fact came dimly to me: I became aware that I could feel a sensation of weight upon my hands—a sensation to which I had long been a stranger.

Hope? Yes. I was hopeful in a vague, weary way. Everything was strange and unreal. I knew that I was becoming myself again; that my flesh gained substance once more. I knew that my horrid trance was ending; but I knew also that murder was about to be committed before me, and above all was the sense of intense sickness and great physical pain. I knew what was going on—knew it acutely; but I did not seem to care.

The Indian fumbled the handle of the knife in his fingers; and I heard his voice:

"Tsin-shil-zaska has not the power to bring the dead to life, but he can make the living dead."

The crisis had arrived. I saw the fingers moving nervously on the knife handle, as if preparing for the final grip. A few seconds more and all would be too late. Clearly, as in a burst of light, it all came to me. Had I strength? I knew not, but with a sudden spring I had clutched the murderer's hand in both of mine. The left grasped his wrist. The right wrenched the knife from his unsuspecting fingers. I jumped to my feet. He turned quickly to confront me. The candle, long apparently dead, shot up into sudden brilliancy, and a gleam of terror came into his eyes, as he saw who it was that faced him. In a quick movement of fear he raised his left arm, and with it the blanket from his breast, and I drove the knife with all my strength into his heart.

We fell together to the ground. Neither had uttered a sound. Then, as I lay, came the nausea again—deathly retching; everything swam around me; my head seemed bursting; then blackness, and once more I was unconscious.

When I awoke it was afternoon, as was evident from the sun-light which shone aslant in at the open door, throwing a long, pointed patch of yellow across the floor. I was in the Father's cabin, lying on the bunk, with a blanket thrown over me. I knew at once that I was again as other men are. Father Francis kneeled by my side.

"Father!"

"My son!"

"Can you see me?"

"Assuredly, my son!"

With a long sigh of relief I turned on my side, and gazed out of the open door at the sunlit landscape, my whole being filled with a sense of dreamy pleasure, such as one feels between sleep and waking—an inexpressible contentment. There was no alloy what-ever in the pure enjoyment of the sensation of newfound life.

THE SHADOW AND THE FLASH
Jack London

When I look back, I realize what a peculiar friendship it was. First, there was Lloyd Inwood, tall, slender, and finely knit, nervous and dark. And then Paul Tichlorne, tall, slender, and finely knit, nervous and blond. Each was the replica of the other in everything except color. Lloyd's eyes were black; Paul's were blue. Under stress of excitement, the blood coursed olive in the face of Lloyd, crimson in the face of Paul. But outside this matter of coloring they were as like as two peas. Both were high-strung, prone to excessive tension and endurance, and they lived at concert pitch.

But there was a trio involved in this remarkable friendship, and the third was short, and fat, and chunky, and lazy, and, loath to say, it was I. Paul and Lloyd seemed born to rivalry with each other, and I to be peacemaker between them. We grew up together, the three of us, and full often have I received the angry blows each intended for the other. They were always competing, striving to outdo each other, and when entered upon some such struggle there was no limit either to their endeavors or passions.

This intense spirit of rivalry obtained in their studies and their games. If Paul memorized one canto of "Marmion," Lloyd memorized two cantos, Paul came back with three, and Lloyd again with four, till each knew the whole poem by heart. I remember an incident that occurred at the swimming hole—an incident tragically significant of the life-struggle between them. The boys had a game of diving to the bottom of a ten-foot pool and holding on by submerged roots to see who could stay under the longest. Paul and

Lloyd allowed themselves to be bantered into making the descent together. When I saw their faces, set and determined, disappear in the water as they sank swiftly down, I felt a foreboding of something dreadful. The moments sped, the ripples died away, the face of the pool grew placid and untroubled, and neither black nor golden head broke surface in quest of air. We above grew anxious. The longest record of the longest-winded boy had been exceeded, and still there was no sign. Air bubbles trickled slowly upward, showing that the breath had been expelled from their lungs, and after that the bubbles ceased to trickle upward. Each second became interminable, and, unable longer to endure the suspense, I plunged into the water.

I found them down at the bottom, clutching tight to the roots, their heads not a foot apart, their eyes wide open, each glaring fixedly at the other. They were suffering frightful torment, writhing and twisting in the pangs of voluntary suffocation; for neither would let go and acknowledge himself beaten. I tried to break Paul's hold on the root, but he resisted me fiercely. Then I lost my breath and came to the surface, badly scared. I quickly explained the situation, and half a dozen of us went down and by main strength tore them loose. By the time we got them out, both were unconscious, and it was only after much barrel-rolling and rubbing and pounding that they finally came to their senses. They would have drowned there, had no one rescued them.

When Paul Tichlorne entered college, he let it be generally understood that he was going in for the social sciences. Lloyd Inwood, entering at the same time, elected to take the same course. But Paul had had it secretly in mind all the time to study the natural sciences, specializing on chemistry, and at the last moment he switched over. Though Lloyd had already arranged his year's work and attended the first lectures, he at once followed Paul's lead and went in for the natural sciences and especially for chemistry. Their rivalry soon became a noted thing throughout the university. Each was a spur to the other, and they went into chemistry deeper than did ever students before—so deep, in fact, that ere they took their sheepskins they could have stumped any chemistry or "cow college"

professor in the institution, save "old" Moss, head of the department, and even him they puzzled and edified more than once.
Lloyd's discovery of the "death bacillus" of the sea toad, and his
experiments on it with potassium cyanide, sent his name and that
of his university ringing round the world; nor was Paul a whit behind when he succeeded in producing laboratory colloids exhibiting amoeba-like activities, and when he cast new light upon the
processes of fertilization through his startling experiments with
simple sodium chlorides and magnesium solutions on low forms
of marine life.

It was in their undergraduate days, however, in the midst of
their profoundest plunges into the mysteries of organic chemistry, that Doris Van Benschoten entered into their lives. Lloyd met
her first, but within twenty-four hours Paul saw to it that he also
made her acquaintance. Of course, they fell in love with her, and
she became the only thing in life worth living for. They wooed her
with equal ardor and fire, and so intense became their struggle for
her that half the student-body took to wagering wildly on the result. Even "old" Moss, one day, after an astounding demonstration in his private laboratory by Paul, was guilty to the extent of a
month's salary of backing him to become the bridegroom of Doris
Van Benschoten.

In the end she solved the problem in her own way, to everybody's
satisfaction except Paul's and Lloyd's. Getting them together, she
said that she really could not choose between them because she
loved them both equally well; and that, unfortunately, since poly-
andry was not permitted in the United States she would be compelled to forego the honor and happiness of marrying either of
them. Each blamed the other for this lamentable outcome, and the
bitterness between them grew more bitter.

But things came to a head enough. It was at my home, after
they had taken their degrees and dropped out of the world's sight,
that the beginning of the end came to pass. Both were men of
means, with little inclination and no necessity for professional life.
My friendship and their mutual animosity were the two things that
linked them in any way together. While they were very often at my

place, they made it a fastidious point to avoid each other on such visits, though it was inevitable, under the circumstances, that they should come upon each other occasionally.

On the day I have in recollection, Paul Tichlorne had been mooning all morning in my study over a current scientific review. This left me free to my own affairs, and I was out among my roses when Lloyd Inwood arrived. Clipping and pruning and tacking the climbers on the porch, with my mouth full of nails, and Lloyd following me about and lending a hand now and again, we fell to discussing the mythical race of invisible people, that strange and vagrant people the traditions of which have come down to us. Lloyd warmed to the talk in his nervous, jerky fashion, and was soon interrogating the physical properties and possibilities of invisibility. A perfectly black object, he contended, would elude and defy the acutest vision.

"Color is a sensation," he was saying. "It has no objective reality. Without light, we can see neither colors nor objects themselves. All objects are black in the dark, and in the dark it is impossible to see them. If no light strikes upon them, then no light is flung back from them to the eye, and so we have no vision-evidence of their being."

"But we see black objects in daylight," I objected.

"Very true," he went on warmly. "And that is because they are not perfectly black. Were they perfectly black, absolutely black, as it were, we could not see them—ay, not in the blaze of a thousand suns could we see them! And so I say, with the right pigments, properly compounded, an absolutely black paint could be produced which would render invisible whatever it was applied to."

"It would be a remarkable discovery," I said noncommittally, for the whole thing seemed too fantastic for aught but speculative purposes.

"Remarkable!" Lloyd slapped me on the shoulder. "I should say so. Why, old chap, to coat myself with such a paint would be to put the world at my feet. The secrets of kings and courts would be mine, the machinations of diplomats and politicians, the play of stock-gamblers, the plans of trusts and corporations. I could keep my hand on the inner pulse of things and become the greatest power in the world. And I—" He broke off shortly, then added, "Well, I have begun my experiments, and I don't mind telling you that I'm right in line for it."

A laugh from the doorway startled us. Paul Tichlorne was standing there, a smile of mockery on his lips.

"You forget, my dear Lloyd," he said.

"Forget what?"

"You forget," Paul went on— "ah, you forget the shadow."

I saw Lloyd's face drop, but he answered sneeringly, "I can carry a sunshade, you know." Then he turned suddenly and fiercely upon him. "Look here, Paul, you'll keep out of this if you know what's good for you."

A rupture seemed imminent, but Paul laughed good-naturedly. "I wouldn't lay fingers on your dirty pigments. Succeed beyond your most sanguine expectations, yet you will always fetch up against the shadow. You can't get away from it. Now I shall go on the very opposite tack. In the very nature of my proposition the shadow will be eliminated—"

"Transparency!" ejaculated Lloyd, instantly. "But it can't be achieved."

"Oh, no; of course not." And Paul shrugged his shoulders and strolled off down the briar-rose path.

This was the beginning of it. Both men attacked the problem with all the tremendous energy for which they were noted, and with a rancor and bitterness that made me tremble for the success of either. Each trusted me to the utmost, and in the long weeks of experimentation that followed I was made a party to both sides, listening to their theorizings and witnessing their demonstrations. Never, by word or sign, did I convey to either the slightest hint of the other's progress, and they respected me for the seal I put upon my lips.

Lloyd Inwood, after prolonged and unintermittent application, when the tension upon his mind and body became too great to bear, had a strange way of obtaining relief. He attended prize fights. It was at one of these brutal exhibitions, whither he had dragged me in order to tell his latest results, that his theory received striking confirmation.

"Do you see that red-whiskered man?" he asked, pointing across the ring to the fifth tier of seats on the opposite side. "And do you see the next man to him, the one in the white hat? Well, there is quite a gap between them, is there not?"

"Certainly," I answered. "They are a seat apart. The gap is the unoccupied seat."

He leaned over to me and spoke seriously. "Between the red-whiskered man and the white-hatted man sits Ben Wasson. You have heard me speak of him. He is the cleverest pugilist of his weight in the country. He is also a Caribbean negro, full-blooded, and the blackest in the United State;. He has on a black overcoat buttoned up. I saw him when he came in and took that seat. As soon as he sat down he disappeared. Watch closely; he may smile."

I was for crossing over to verify Lloyd's statement, but he restrained me. "Wait," he said.

I waited and watched, till the red-whiskered man turned his head as though addressing the unoccupied seat; and then, in that empty space, I saw the rolling whites of a pair of eyes and the white double-crescent of two rows of teeth, and for the instant I could make out a negro's face. But with the passing of the smile his visibility passed, and the chair seemed vacant as before.

"Were he perfectly black, you could sit alongside him and not see him," Lloyd said; and I confess the illustration was apt enough to make me well-nigh convinced.

I visited Lloyd's laboratory a number of times after that, and found him always deep in his search after the absolute black. His experiments covered all sorts of pigments, such as lamp-blacks, tars, carbonized vegetable matters, soots of oils and fats, and the various carbonized animal substances.

"White light is composed of the seven primary colors," he argued to me. "But it is itself, of itself, invisible. Only by being reflected from objects do it and the objects become visible. But only that portion of it that is reflected becomes visible. For instance, here is a blue tobacco-box. The white light strikes against it, and, with one exception, all its component colors—violet, indigo, green, yellow, orange, and red—are absorbed. The one exception is *blue*. It is not absorbed, but reflected. Therefore the tobacco-box gives us a sensation of blueness. We do not see the other colors because they are absorbed. We see only the blue. For the same reason grass is *green*. The green waves of white light are thrown upon our eyes."

"When we paint our houses, we do not apply color to them," he said at another time. "What we do is to apply certain substances that have the property of absorbing from white light all the colors except those that we would have our houses appear. When a substance reflects all the colors to the eye, it seems to us white. When it absorbs all the colors, it is black. But, as I said before, we have as yet no perfect black. *All* the colors are not absorbed. The perfect black, guarding against high lights, will be utterly and absolutely invisible. Look at that, for example."

He pointed to the palette lying on his work-table. Different shades of black pigments were brushed on it. One, in particular, I could hardly see. It gave my eyes a blurring sensation, and I rubbed them and looked again.

"That," he said impressively, "is the blackest black you or any mortal man ever looked upon. But just you wait, and I'll have a black so black that no mortal man will be able to look upon it— *and see it!*"

On the other hand, I used to find Paul Tichlorne plunged as deeply into the study of light polarization, diffraction, and interference, single and double refraction, and all manner of strange organic compounds.

"Transparency: a state or quality of body which permits all rays of light to pass through," he defined for me. "That is what I am seeking. Lloyd blunders up against the shadow with his perfect opaqueness. But I escape it. A transparent body casts no shadow; neither does it reflect light-waves—that is, the perfectly transparent does not. So, avoiding high lights, not only will such a body cast no shadow, but, since it reflects no light, it will also be invisible."

We were standing by the window at another time. Paul was engaged in polishing a number of lenses, which were ranged along the sill. Suddenly, after a pause in the conversation, he said, "Oh! I've dropped a lens. Stick your head out, old man, and see where it went to."

Out I started to thrust my head, but a sharp blow on the forehead caused me to recoil. I rubbed my bruised brow and gazed with reproachful inquiry at Paul, who was laughing in gleeful, boyish fashion.

"Well?" he said.

"Well?" I echoed.

"Why don't you investigate?" he demanded. And investigate I did. Before thrusting out my head, my senses, automatically active, had told me there was nothing there, that nothing intervened between me and out-of-doors, that the aperture of the window opening was utterly empty. I stretched forth my hand and felt a hard object, smooth and cool and flat, which my touch, out of its experience, told me to be glass. I looked again, but could see positively nothing.

"White quartzose sand," Paul rattled off, "sodic carbonate, slaked lime, cutlet, manganese peroxide—there you have it, the finest French plate glass, made by the great St. Gobain Company, who made the finest plate glass in the world, and this is the finest piece they ever made. It cost a king's ransom. But look at it! You can't see it. You don't know it's there till you run your head against it.

"Eh, old boy! That's merely an object-lesson—certain elements, in themselves opaque, yet so compounded as to give a resultant body which is transparent. But that is a matter of inorganic chemistry, you say. Very true. But I dare to assert, standing here on my two feet, that in the organic I can duplicate whatever occurs in the inorganic.

"Here!" He held a test-tube between me and the light, and I noted the cloudy or muddy liquid it contained. He emptied the contents of another test-tube into it, and almost instantly it became clear and sparkling.

"Or here!" With quick, nervous movements among his array of test-tubes, he turned a white solution to a wine color, and a light yellow solution to a dark brown. He dropped a piece of litmus paper into an acid, when it changed instantly to red, and on floating it in an alkali it turned as quickly to blue.

"The litmus paper is still the litmus paper," he enunciated in the formal manner of the lecturer. "I have not changed it into something else. Then what did I do? I merely changed the arrangement of its molecules. Where, at first, it absorbed all colors from the light but red, its molecular structure was so changed that it absorbed red and all colors except blue. And so it goes, *ad infinitum*. Now, what I purpose to do is this." He paused for a space. "I purpose to seek—ay, and to find—the proper reagents, which, acting upon the living organism, will bring about molecular changes analogous to those you have just witnessed. But these reagents, which I shall find, and for that matter, upon which I already have my hands, will not turn the living body to blue or red or black, but they will turn it to transparency. All light will pass through it. It will be invisible. It will cast no shadow."

A few weeks later I went hunting with Paul. He had been promising me for some time that I should have the pleasure of shooting over a wonderful dog—the most wonderful dog, in fact, that ever man shot over, so he averred, and continued to aver till my curiosity was aroused. But on the morning in question I was disappointed, for there was no dog in evidence.

"Don't see him about," Paul remarked unconcernedly, and we set off across the fields.

I could not imagine, at the time, what was ailing me, but I had a feeling of some impending and deadly illness. My nerves were all awry, and, from the astounding tricks they played me, my senses seemed to have run riot. Strange sounds disturbed me. At times I heard the swish-swish of grass being shoved aside, and once the patter of feet across a patch of stony ground.

"Did you hear anything, Paul?" I asked once.

But he shook his head, and thrust his feet steadily forward.

While climbing a fence, I heard the low, eager whine of a dog, apparently from within a couple of feet of me; but on looking about me I saw nothing.

I dropped to the ground, limp and trembling.

"Paul," I said, "we had better return to the house. I am afraid I am going to be sick."

"Nonsense, old man," he answered. "The sunshine has gone to your head like wine. You'll be all right. It's famous weather."

But, passing along a narrow path through a clump of cotton-woods, some object brushed against my legs and I stumbled and nearly fell. I looked with sudden anxiety at Paul.

"What's the matter?" he asked. "Tripping over your own feet?"

I kept my tongue between my teeth and plodded on, though sore perplexed and thoroughly satisfied that some acute and mysterious malady had attacked my nerves. So far my eyes had escaped; but, when we got to the open fields again, even my vision went back on me. Strange flashes of vari-colored, rainbow light began to appear and disappear on the path before me. Still, I managed to keep myself in hand, till the vari-colored lights persisted for a space of fully twenty seconds, dancing and flashing in continuous play. Then I sat down, weak and shaky.

"It's all up with me," I gasped, covering my eyes with my hands. "It has attacked my eyes. Paul, take me home."

But Paul laughed long and loud. "What did I tell you?—the most wonderful dog, eh? Well, what do you think?"

He turned partly from me and began to whistle. I heard the patter of feet, the panting of a heated animal, and the unmistakable yelp of a dog. Then Paul stooped down and apparently fondled the empty air.

"Here! Give me your fist."

And he rubbed my hand over the cold nose and jowls of a dog. A dog it certainly was, with the shape and the smooth, short coat of a pointer.

Suffice to say, I speedily recovered my spirits and control. Paul put a collar about the animal's neck and tied his handkerchief to its tail. And then was vouchsafed us the remarkable sight of an empty collar and a waving handkerchief cavorting over the fields. It was something to see that collar and handkerchief pin a bevy of quail in a clump of locusts and remain rigid and immovable till we had flushed the birds.

Now and again the dog emitted the vari-colored light-flashes I have mentioned. The one thing, Paul explained, which he had not anticipated and which he doubted could be overcome.

"They're a large family," he said, "these sun dogs, wind dogs, rainbows, halos, and parhelia. They are produced by refraction of light from mineral and ice crystals, from mist, rain, spray, and no end of things; and I am afraid they are the penalty I must pay for transparency. I escaped Lloyd's shadow only to fetch up against the rainbow flash."

A couple of days later, before the entrance to Paul's laboratory, I encountered a terrible stench. So overpowering was it that it was easy to discover the source: a mass of putrescent matter on the doorstep which in general outlines resembled a dog.

Paul was startled when he investigated my find. It was his invisible dog, or rather, what had been his invisible dog, for it was now plainly visible. It had been playing about but a few minutes before in all health and strength. Closer examination revealed that the skull had been crushed by some heavy blow. While it was strange that the animal should have been killed, the inexplicable thing was that it should so quickly decay.

"The reagents I injected into its system were harmless," Paul explained. "Yet they were powerful, and it appears that when death comes they force practically instantaneous disintegration. Remarkable! Most remarkable! Well, the only thing is not to die. They do not harm so long as one lives. But I do wonder who smashed in that dog's head."

Light, however, was thrown upon this when a frightened housemaid brought the news that Gaffer Bedshaw had that very morning, not more than an hour back, gone violently insane, and was strapped down at home, in the huntsman's lodge, where he raved of a battle with a ferocious and gigantic beast that he had encountered in the Tichlorne pasture. He claimed that the thing, whatever it was, was invisible, that with his own eyes he had seen that it was invisible; wherefore his tearful wife and daughters shook their heads, and wherefore he but waxed the more violent, and the gardener and the coachman tightened the straps by another hole.

Nor, while Paul Tichlorne was thus successfully mastering the problem of invisibility, was Lloyd Inwood a whit behind. I went over in answer to a message of his to come and see how he was getting on. Now his laboratory occupied an isolated situation in the midst of his vast grounds. It was built in a pleasant little glade, surrounded on all sides by a dense forest growth, and was to be gained by way of a winding and erratic path. But I have travelled that path so often as to know every foot of it, and conceive my surprise when I came upon the glade and found no laboratory. The quaint shed structure with its red sandstone chimney was not. Nor did it look as if it ever had been. There were no signs of ruin, no debris, nothing.

I started to walk across what had once been its site. "This," I said to myself, "should be where the step went up to the door." Barely were the words out of my mouth when I stubbed my toe on some obstacle, pitched forward, and butted my head into something that *felt* very much like a door. I reached out my hand. It *was* a door. I found the knob and turned it. And at once, as the door swung inward on its hinges, the whole interior of the laboratory impinged upon my vision. Greeting Lloyd, I closed the door and backed up the path a few paces. I could see nothing of the building. Returning and opening the door, at once all the furniture and every detail of the interior were visible. It was indeed startling, the sudden transition from void to light and form and color.

"What do you think of it, eh?" Lloyd asked, wringing my hand. "I slapped a couple of coats of absolute black on the outside yesterday afternoon to see how it worked. How's your head? you bumped it pretty solidly, I imagine."

"Never mind that," he interrupted my congratulations. "I've something better for you to do."

While he talked he began to strip, and when he stood naked before me he thrust a pot and brush into my hand and said, "Here, give me a coat of this."

It was an oily, shellac-like stuff, which spread quickly and easily over the skin and dried immediately.

"Merely preliminary and precautionary," he explained when I had finished; "but now for the real stuff."

I picked up another pot he indicated, and glanced inside, but could see nothing.

"It's empty," I said.

"Stick your finger in it."

I obeyed, and was aware of a sensation of cool moistness. On withdrawing my hand I glanced at the forefinger, the one I had immersed, but it had disappeared. I moved and knew from the alternate tension and relaxation of the muscles that I moved it, but it defied my sense of sight. To all appearances I had been shorn of a finger; nor could I get any visual impression of it till I extended it under the skylight and saw its shadow plainly blotted on the floor.

Lloyd chuckled. "Now spread it on, and keep your eyes open."

I dipped the brush into the seemingly empty pot, and gave him a long stroke across his chest. With the passage of the brush the living flesh disappeared from beneath. I covered his right leg, and he was a one-legged man defying all laws of gravitation. And so, stroke by stroke, member by member, I painted Lloyd Inwood into nothingness. It was a creepy experience, and I was glad when naught remained in sight but his burning black eyes, poised apparently unsupported in mid-air.

"I have a refined and harmless solution for them," he said. "A fine spray with an air-brush, and presto! I am not."

This deftly accomplished, he said, "Now I shall move about, and do you tell me what sensations you experience."

"In the first place, I cannot see you," I said, and I could hear his gleeful laugh from the midst of the emptiness. "Of course," I continued, "you cannot escape your shadow, but that was to be expected. When you pass between my eye and an object, the object disappears, but so unusual and incomprehensible is its disappearance that it seems to me as though my eyes had blurred. When you move rapidly, I experience a bewildering succession of blurs. The blurring sensation makes my eyes ache and my brain tired."

"Have you any other warnings of my presence?" he asked.

"No, and yes," I answered. "When you are near me I have feelings similar to those produced by dank warehouses, gloomy crypts, and deep mines. And as sailors feel the loom of the land on dark nights, so I think I feel the loom of your body. But it is all very vague and intangible."

Long we talked that last morning in his laboratory; and when I turned to go, he put his unseen hand in mine with nervous grip, and said, "Now I shall conquer the world!" And I could not dare to tell him of Paul Tichlorne's equal success.

At home I found a note from Paul, asking me to come up immediately, and it was high noon when I came spinning up the driveway on my wheel. Paul called me from the tennis court, and I dismounted and went over. But the court was empty. As I stood there, gaping open-mouthed, a tennis ball struck me on the arm, and as I turned about, another whizzed past my ear. For aught I could see of my assailant, they came whirling at me from out of space, and right well was I peppered with them. But when the balls already flung at me began to come back for a second whack, I realized the situation. Seizing a racquet and keeping my eyes open, I quickly saw a rainbow flash appearing and disappearing and darting over the ground. I took out after it, and when I laid the racquet upon it for a half-dozen stout blows, Paul's voice rang out:

"Enough! Enough! Oh! Ouch! Stop! You're landing on my naked skin, you know! Ow! O-w-w! I'll be good! I'll be good! I only wanted you to see my metamorphosis," he said ruefully, and I imagined he was rubbing his hurts.

A few minutes later we were playing tennis—a handicap on my part, for I could have no knowledge of his position save when all the angles between himself, the sun, and me, were in proper conjunction. Then he flashed, and only then. But the flashes were more brilliant than the rainbow—purest blue, most delicate violet, brightest yellow, and all the intermediary shades, with the scintillant brilliancy of the diamond, dazzling, blinding, iridescent.

But in the midst of our play I felt a sudden cold chill, reminding me of deep mines and gloomy crypts, such a chill as I had experienced that very morning. The next moment, close to the net, I saw a ball rebound in mid-air and empty space, and at the same instant, a score of feet away, Paul Tichlorne emitted a rainbow flash. It could not be he from whom the ball had rebounded, and with sickening dread I realized that Lloyd Inwood had come upon the scene. To make sure, I looked for his shadow, and there it was, a shapeless blotch the girth of his body, (the sun was overhead), moving along the ground. I remembered his threat, and felt sure that all the long years of rivalry were about to culminate in uncanny battle.

I cried a warning to Paul, and heard a snarl as of a wild beast, and an answering snarl. I saw the dark blotch move swiftly across the court, and a brilliant burst of vari-colored light moving with equal swiftness to meet it; and then shadow and flash came together and there was the sound of unseen blows. The net went down before my frightened eyes. I sprang toward the fighters, crying:

"For God's sake!"

But their locked bodies smote against my knees, and I was overthrown.

"You keep out of this, old man!" I heard the voice of Lloyd Inwood from out of the emptiness. And then Paul's voice crying, "Yes, we've had enough of peacemaking!"

From the sound of their voices I knew they had separated. I could not locate Paul, and so approached the shadow that represented Lloyd. But from the other side came a stunning blow on the point of my jaw, and I heard Paul scream angrily, "Now will you keep away?"

Then they came together again, the impact of their blows, their groans and gasps, and the swift flashings and shadow-movings telling plainly of the deadliness of the struggle.

I shouted for help, and Gaffer Bedshaw came running into the court. I could see, as he approached, that he was looking at me strangely, but he collided with the combatants and was hurled headlong to the ground. With despairing shriek and a cry of "O Lord, I've got 'em!" he sprang to his feet and tore madly out of the court.

I could do nothing, so I sat up, fascinated and powerless, and watched the struggle. The noonday sun beat down with dazzling brightness on the naked tennis court. And it *was* naked. All I could see was the blotch of shadow and the rainbow flashes, the dust rising from the invisible feet, the earth tearing up from beneath the straining foot-grips, and the wire screen bulge once or twice as their bodies hurled against it. That was all, and after a time even that ceased. There were no more flashes, and the shadow had become long and stationary; and I remembered their set boyish faces when they clung to the roots in the deep coolness of the pool.

They found me an hour afterward. Some inkling of what had happened got to the servants and they quitted the Tichlorne service in a body. Gaffer Bedshaw never recovered from the second shock he received, and is confined in a madhouse, hopelessly incurable. The secrets of their marvellous discoveries died with Paul and Lloyd, both laboratories being destroyed by grief-stricken relatives. As for myself, I no longer care for chemical research, and science is a tabooed topic in my household. I have returned to my roses. Nature's colors are good enough for me.

THE FACE OF AIR
George L. Knapp

I

The *Nancy Hanks* was a schooner of 250 tons; a tramp schooner, owned in part by her captain, Ezra Hawkins. She left New York on her last voyage September third, 1871, bearing a miscellaneous cargo for Pernambuco. Something over two weeks later she was sighted in latitude 24 degrees, 31 minutes N., longitude 65 degrees, 40 minutes W. This was a good bit out of her normal and proper course, as a glance at the map will show. But being out of course was the least remarkable thing about the *Nancy Hanks* that fine September day.

She was empty! She had left New York with a crew of nine men, besides captain and mate; and the captain's wife had accompanied him on the voyage. But captain, wife, mate, and crew had vanished. When sighted, the schooner was yawing, backing, filling; steering herself in an erratic fashion, which at once excited remark on board the ship *Aurora*, which happened to be the sighting vessel. A hail brought no answer; and a boat was sent to the schooner in charge of the second mate of the *Aurora*. Everything aboard the *Nancy Hanks* was found in proper shape, except her people—and they were not found at all. The log was written to within two days of the date of this visit. The crew's weekly wash was spread to dry on deck. A sewing machine, with a hem still under the needle, was found in the captain's cabin. There was no sign of violence or struggle. There had been no serious storm for weeks, nor did the vessel bear any marks of bad weather. Most amazing of all, a full complement of boats seemed to be present; and though doubts were cast on this conclusion later, I still believe it to be correct. But the officers and crew and the woman who had started the hem on the sewing machine *were gone!*

The *Aurora* put a prize crew aboard the *Nancy Hanks*, with orders to keep the ship in sight. A squall parted the two vessels; and the next day, when the *Aurora* again sighted the *Nancy Hanks*, the *Nancy Hanks* was again empty! This time, there could be no doubt on the boat question. The prize crew had taken no boat—but the prize crew was gone.

So much of the story is known to all the world. One farther chapter of the uncanny tale is likewise, public property. By dint of good luck, much manoeuvring, and offers of high prize money, a second prize crew was induced to go aboard the schooner, this time with orders to take her to the nearest port. The second prize crew went aboard the schooner, trimmed her sails, pointed her nose to the west—and from that moment the *Nancy Hanks* disappears from the records of the seas. She was never seen again. Three crews within three weeks had shipped on that eerie schooner; and their fate and that of their ship have remained mysteries—until now.

For I was one of the second prize crew that went aboard the *Nancy Hanks*; and the story of what befell us there will explain the fate of those who went before us.

In all the accounts thus far written of the affair the *Aurora* is described as a small sailing ship, bound for the Barbadoes with a cargo consisting of flour, salt meats and cement. This description is only partly true. The *Aurora* was a sailing ship, to be sure; but she was not intending to touch at Barbadoes if she could help it; and her cargo contained no more provisions than enough to provide the crew against emergencies. She was really a filibustering ship, carrying the arms, ammunition and leaders designed to overturn the despotism then prevailing in Venezuela, and substitute an equally obnoxious despotism in its place. She was likewise carrying some human reenforcements to the revolutionary cause; and of these I was one.

I was then a youngster of twenty; with a boundless capital of health and strength, a fair allowance, I hope, of courage; but destitute of money, trade, or profession. I came of a dwindling Southern family that had lost everything in the war. My father was killed at Gettysburg; my mother died a few months after the close of the war; and some time before setting out on the uncanny voyage whose story is here to be told I had lost my last near relation, an aunt. My efforts in the youthful enterprise of seeking my fortune had so far brought little but experience, and I was literally down to my last dollar when I met two of the men who were to be my companions on the *Nancy Hanks*.

It was a rather unusual introduction. The young man who has been temporarily worsted in the world's tussle, and is not yet ready to accept final defeat, gravitates toward trouble as naturally as water runs down hill. Whether this is a preservative instinct, urging youth toward murky waters as offering security; or whether it is merely a surly defiance of the ordinary laws of prudence, I have never been able to decide. In my own case it seemed to be the latter. Enough that on a sweltering August night in 1871 I was sulking down one of the toughest streets in the lower part of New York. I have forgotten what street it was—if, indeed, I ever knew—but it was one which a local gang of toughs had chosen for a midnight promenade. They were drunk and I was surly; and the natural result was a free-for-all fight. I had muscle plus in those days; and more than one of the gang must have carried vivid reminders of the country lad they tried to do. But, in spite of my strength, I was down on my back, fighting in savage silence with both feet and one hand, and hugging the smallest of my antagonists to my breast as a partial shield with the other hand, when help arrived. I heard a hoarse roar, an exclamation in some foreign tongue, a thud of feet on the pavement, a sound of blows; and suddenly the gang was gone. Someone was helping me to my feet. My head was still buzzing from a vicious kick.

"Thank you, officer," I remember saying; for I took it as a matter of course that my helper was a policeman. There was a laugh in the same hoarse tone that had been a rescue signal. My eyes cleared a bit, and my legs grew steadier. "Where's your uniform?" I enquired stupidly; and then, as another laugh answered me, my jarred brain cells came back to something like their normal function, and I was able to take a look at the men before me.

One was a bullet-headed, bull-necked, bull-chested fellow of about medium height, with thick arms, big hands, and a weathered oak face. Even a landsman like myself could mark him for a sailor; and there was a look of truculent authority in his face which told of accustomed command. The other man, the one who was steadying me by the arm, was taller; lean, wiry, graceful in spite of a certain stiffness which very likely I did not notice till later; and with an indefinable foreign air which I am sure was one of my very first impressions of him.

"You are all right," the taller man was saying. I can hear yet the curious, unfamiliar intonation with which he uttered the colloquial words. The hoarse tones of the bull-necked sailor broke in once more.

"What makes your head so hard, kid? You ain't got any sense to pad it with, that's a cinch, or you wouldn't be buckin' these gangs lone-handed this time o' night. Say, does your mother know you're out?"

"My mother is dead," I answered with the literalness of a man whose thoughts are still woolly. The seaman roared again with laughter. His tall companion spoke with the grave courtesy which I was to know so well and love so much.

"There, mein sohn, there! Your head, it is dizzy yet. Come, so."

"We'll get him some poison," said the sailor roughly, but not at all unkindly. The man with the foreign accent assented, and I was too woozy to resist, even had I wished to do so. A couple of minutes found the three of us in the saloon of a worthy gentleman who was making an honest living by breaking the law; and my throat was tingling with the bite of something which merited the sailor's phrase, "poison." Whatever it was, it pulled me together for a moment, and I began to take stock of my companions.

The sailor, indeed, was too easily classified to need a second glance. The other man I could not classify at all. There was pride and breeding in the high cut, half melancholy face, in the carefully waxed, straw-yellow mustache, in the long, half-shut grey eyes that peered so thoughtfully into my own. There was martial training, surely, in the poise of those shoulders; yet it was a martial air quite different from that with which I was so familiar at home. I remembered the foreign accent, and wondered if he were not a foreign soldier; but the gold braid which I had been taught to associate with the European army officer was conspicuous by its absence; and no one could look at the man for a moment and think him a private in the ranks. He pushed aside his glass, half empty, and I noticed the aristocratic taper of his hands and the sinewy strength of his wrists.

"You are a stranger in this city, nicht war?" he asked.

"Yes," I answered. "You're German," was my next remark. The tall man nodded, still studying me with a thoughtful air.

"What for a living do you do?"

"Nothing," I retorted shortly. "There's nothing to do."

"From the South you are?"

"South Carolina." I remember wondering how he guessed.

"You have no trade?"

"No."

"And your family?"

"I have none."

"And—you will the question pardon, it is a friend who asks. And the money, you have it plenty?"

"Oh, plenty." I turned out my pockets. They held a fifty-cent "shinplaster," three dimes, a nickel, and four copper pennies.

I can see the sorry assortment yet. I arrayed it with a boy's half drunken bravado on the table before us. "Plenty of money, lots of it," I repeated foolishly.

The grey eyes twinkled as they looked into mine.

"It is a fortune," said the tall man gravely. "It is wealth, particularly when with youth and courage it is allied. You must be my guest for the night, so far as she is left. In the morning we will talk about—many things." The seaman flashed a look of enquiry at the tall man, who answered with a slight nod as he rose. "Oh, I had forgotten," he exclaimed. "You have not my name. Permit me to introduce myself as Rudolph Steinmetz, at your service, and this, my friend, is Mr. Rogers, mate of the good ship *Aurora*."

"Second mate," corrected the bull-necked man.

"My name is John Harkness," I announced. We shook hands gravely.

I suppose there were orders given and instructions passed, but I do not remember them. I was young, tired, somewhat battered up, and quite unaccustomed to ardent spirits, and the fusel oil cocktail I had drunk had by this time begun to fog such sense as the kicking had left me. All I recollect is Steinmetz bidding me goodnight in a room to which I have no remembrance of going, and telling me that he would see me on the morrow.

II

I had been awake some minutes the next morning before realizing that I was in a strange place. The realization brought me upright in bed with a swing, and the sudden movement informed me that I had a morning-after headache fit for the oldest rounder in the land. Physical pain claimed precedence over curiosity. There was a washstand in the room, and a dirty pitcher, which proved to be full of cold water. A liberal sousing partly remedied the headache, and as I dried my tousled hair the events of the night before came back to me bit by bit. I remembered them in inverse order; the grave, kindly humour of a strange man with grey eyes and long yellow mustache; a disreputable looking table with some few coins atop; the taste of villainous liquor; a hoarse roar, a thump of running feet; and then the brain wires snapped into circuit again, and the whole weird night rose clear before me.

It was weird enough, in all conscience; a baffling, puzzling section of a life that seemed not my own; but it gave me a sense of exhilaration, not of dread. I had tasted the sweets of adventure; I had nothing to lose and perhaps much to win; and I had met a man and a situation both of which aroused my boyish curiosity to the full. I dressed quickly—no great merit when one has been put to bed with his shirt on—and whistling blithely, opened the unlocked door, and went out to a boy's kingdom of mystery.

A "he-chambermaid" met me in the hall with the word that my breakfast was waiting. He conducted me to the dining-room, just a shade less dingy than the bedroom and the hall, and seated me before the greasy ham and eggs and muddy coffee which in those days was the all but universal American morning meal. "Mister Rogers an' the Dutch duke'll be in purty soon," he declared, and went out. It took me some moments to realize that Rogers was the hoarse-voiced seaman of the night's adventure, but the phrase "Dutch duke" fitted itself to the trim figure of Steinmetz on the instant.

Rogers was the first to appear.

"Hello, kid," he greeted. "How's that cast iron cocoanut of yourn this morning?"

"Good as new," I answered. Rogers spat at a knot in the floor six or eight feet away, missed, tried again with better success, swore genially, and replied:

"I guess that ain't no lie, kid. If I had a crew with heads like yourn, it ain't no little belayin' pins that'd keep discipline. Now, say. The duke'll be here in a minute to talk to you."

He paused, plainly expecting a reply. Not knowing what reply would serve, I tried a bluff.

"Let him come," I said placidly. "I'm willing."

Rogers looked at me in something very like admiration.

"Say, kid," he said. "I guess your gall's as hard as your nut. Now, look here. We've got a little private business on foot, an' Steiny wants to let you in on it. The old man's willing, see, provided you can keep your mouth shut. Tight shut. Understand?"

The last word was whipped out in a menacing tone, with the lower jaw thrust forward, and the brows drawn down in a scowl. But I declined to be frightened. When one is twenty years old, six feet high, has nothing to lose, and owns far more muscle than brains, he is entitled to a certain indifference to threats. I answered curtly:

"No. I don't understand. And I think you'd better leave it to the duke to explain. When will he be here?"

I shoved back from the table as I spoke, and crossed my legs indifferently. Rogers favored me with a long stare, and this time there was no disguising the admiration in looks and tone.

"You'll do, kid. You're all right. I'll tell the old man you're all right. Say, if I had your cheek—" He shook his head as one who thinks unutterable things, spat again at his chosen target, hit it in the bull's eye, informed me that the duke would be in pretty soon, and went out.

Anyone who recalls his own boyhood will understand the pleased anticipation with which I settled down to wait for Steinmetz. Private business; business in which secrecy was essential; and a "Dutch duke" coming to talk with me on the subject. He could not come too soon. Was it smuggling they were up to? Free trade was an hereditary dogma in our family. Was it filibustering? Walker was my childhood's hero. Was it—Good Heavens! was it piracy? The thought sent a shiver over me, but only for a moment. Steinmetz was no pirate; of that I was certain. On the whole, filibustering seemed the most probable occupation of my new friends; and if they needed another pair of hands in that business, they were welcome to mine.

The arrival of Steinmetz put an end to my speculations.

"Good morning, my squire of the hard head," he said, offering his hand with a grave courtesy fit for a president's greeting. It was not especially flattering to think that one's headpiece attracted attention for no other reason than its impenetrability, but I had no inclination to quarrel with Steinmetz. Instead, I shook hands with a sudden awkwardness very different from my cool impudence when dealing with Rogers.

"Do you feel equal to a business talk this morning?" enquired Steinmetz.

"Perfectly," I replied.

"Then let us to my room go," said the "Dutch duke," and led the way. I followed. As we left the street door I saw a seedy looking individual turn and go inside with a sailor's roll. It might have been fancy, but I would have sworn the ragged sailor was on guard to keep me from leaving before Steinmetz came.

Steinmetz was lodging in a house somewhat less run down at the heel than the one in which I had spent the night. He had a big, cheerful-looking room on the top floor, with ample windows looking out over the nearby buildings and the bay, flowers on the window ledge, a good-looking rug on the floor, and a huge, imposing-looking bed in the corner. Only at later visits did I become aware that the bed was a bad imitation of the colonial style I had once known at home, that the window plants were cheap and badly cared for, that the roofs nearby were cluttered with the odds and ends of light housekeeping, and that the rug had seen many better days before finding its way to this particular apartment. At present it seemed like a glimpse of another world to a lad in my condition and temper. A big Maltese cat, miaowing cheerfully, greeted us as Steinmetz swung open the door.

"Permit me to introduce Señor Gato," said Steinmetz, stooping and lifting the cat. "Señor Gato, my new friend, Mr. Harkness. That is right, that is a good omen." For the cat had hopped cheerfully to my shoulder, and was already caressing my cheek with his big, rough tongue. I was almost as fond of cats as of dogs and horses, and to me likewise it seemed a good omen.

"He has the best of cat blood in him, though perhaps too many kinds," said Steinmetz, pointing to a part of the animal's coat that told of a mixed ancestry. "It has damaged his pedigree, but I think it has improved his looks. That is not so unusual, nicht war? And you," he went on with a sharp, soldierly ring to his voice, "you have good blood too, yes?"

Had anyone else asked me that question I might have felt insulted or tempted to boast. Now, most luckily, I did neither.

"My father was a gentleman and a soldier," I answered quietly. "I hope not to disgrace him, in spite of the situation in which you found me last night. By the way, I have forgotten to thank you for your timely coming."

He waved away the thanks with a gesture which implied that little things of that sort were commonplaces in his life—as doubtless they were. "It was last night that made me know you for a gentleman. A gentleman whose finances are not so prosperous as once. Is it not so?"

I reddened as I remembered my foolish display of the night before. "I am down and out so far as money is concerned," was the only answer to make. Steinmetz nodded soberly.

"A heart full of courage and a pocket empty of money, nicht war? So. There have many worse combinations been known. But you would like money, if it could fairly come?"

"Of course."

"Good. Then listen, and if you do not approve, forget. I trust you. You have heard of revolutions?"

"Plenty of them." Evidently my guess at filibustering was not far wrong.

"Do you know where the revolutionary centre of the world, it is located?"

"South America," I ventured at a hazard. Steinmetz shook his head as at an expected error.

"New York," he corrected. "Two blocks in this checkerboard city, and you have of every Spanish-American revolution the beginnings. I know. Well, would you like to help make revolutions?"

"I would if I could do it with you." There could not have been a better answer, though of that I took small heed. The blond head bowed with pleasure as Steinmetz spoke again.

"I thank you. You shall go with me. You shall be my son-at-arms—I have no other. Now hear."

I heard. It took hours for the telling of details, but the main outlines were sketched in two crisp, inverted-English sentences.

A ship, the *Aurora*, was loading with arms and ammunition to be sent to the revolutionary party of Venezuela. Steinmetz had been commissioned at a handsome salary to secure the arms, see that they were useful as well as threatening, and help in the details of getting them away. He was likewise offered a generalship in the revolutionary army, but he meant to have a close hand look at the noble forces before accepting. For the present he wanted my help, since the revolution-purveyors with whom he was dealing had to be watched at every point to keep them from selling sawdust for gunpowder. For the future, if he accepted that generalship in the revolutionary army, I might have a commission under him. To my protestations that I knew nothing of military matters Steinmetz answered that any white man could learn fast enough to keep well ahead of his coffee-colored followers. The pay was fair. The danger was just enough to add spice to the adventure and the mystery. Is it necessary to repeat a boy's response to such a lure?

III

I was now fairly enlisted in the noble business of manufacturing revolutions, but my duties for a time were the reverse of arduous. I would accompany Steinmetz on his marketing trips, listen while he chaffered with the dealers in second-hand arms, laugh over the many languages which he pressed into service at times to tell the dealers what he thought of them and of the wares they offered; and finally, when the purchases were made, I would camp with them till nightfall, to see that they were not changed by the honest merchants before being packed to send to the ship. The ammunition we packed in barrels labelled "cement," or "flour"; the muskets and rifles were crated as "agricultural machinery"; the hospital supplies, on which Steinmetz insisted, bore the innocent indorsement of "salt meat." I forget how the revolvers were disguised and labelled. Steinmetz was a conscientious revolutionist, and I doubt if ever a patriot cause got more for its money than did the noble junta that convened in the back streets of New York to "liberate" Venezuela.

I met the officers of the *Aurora* the day after the interview with Steinmetz. The captain was a veteran of the war, named Somers. To most youngsters of to-day the word "veteran" connotes a grizzled individual with a cane and a bronze button; a man full of romantic stories of the past, but with little connection with the busy work of the immediate hour. Captain Somers was the reverse of this ideal. He was scant thirty years of age, without a grey hair in his head or an unsound cell in his body; and, though he had entered the Union navy a volunteer, he had absorbed much of the man-of-war trimness, decision, and iron discipline. He was engaged in a business which some highly respectable governments rank as piracy; and which at the best is grossly illegal. Yet he never strutted as does the traditional bandit, nor skulked like one who fears the law. He seemed to know every policeman and plain clothes operator in the lower half of New York, and I am convinced that they knew him for just what he was. But they did not let their information rest heavy on their minds. It was Captain Somers' business to so manage his affairs that a policeman might conceivably remain ignorant of their nature; and, this done, it was the policeman's business to look the other way when a dray-load of second-hand rifles was being crated and delivered. The minions of the law and the captain of the filibustering ship understood each other perfectly.

The first mate of the *Aurora*, *the* mate, as he is always called, was a silent, capable Yankee of the old school, a graduate both of the whaling ship and the steam frigate. I never really knew him, but I could not help knowing his efficiency, and, in a grim sort of way, his kindliness as well. The sailors liked him, feared him, and never talked about him. He was a bachelor, considerably older than his captain; and I was told that he had bought and paid for a Connecticut farm. For all I know, he may be living on that farm today, managing his pigs and poultry in the same quiet, effective fashion with which he managed his ship.

The second mate, Rogers, was of different stuff altogether. He could do nothing without a tremendous noise, though much of what he did was very well done. He had an assortment of metaphors that would make the fortune of any literary man who could get them through the mails, and he could swear with a vivid force and variety which I have never heard equalled. He had several acts of unusual courage to his credit; he was ranked as a terror, even among the bucko mates of the dwindling American merchant marine. Yet, somehow, I never felt perfect confidence in him. However loud his talk, however strenuous his actions, one always wondered what he would do if loud talk were at a discount, and conditions demanded something more than the ability to haze an insubordinate sailor. Perhaps a conversation between Captain Somers and Steinmetz will set the second mate before you better than words of mine.

"That d—d fool Rogers," said the captain. "He'd try to walk over hell on a rotten rail if anyone dared him to."

"He would start," agreed Steinmetz. "And then in the middle he would lose his head and fall off. Mr. Start-and-Not-Finish Rogers. Yes." Captain Somers laughed appreciatively, and the subject was changed. But I was to remember the words later.

It was Steinmetz, of course, who made the greatest and most permanent impression on my boyish imagination; who roused in me the hero worship which is half a young man's capital in life. There is nothing cleaner and finer, nothing more wholly unselfish than a boy's whole-hearted admiration of his hero; and Steinmetz was a hero to fit a lad's fondest dreams. He was literally a man without a country; a man who had fought under every flag but his own. He belonged to the older Germany, the pre-Prussian Germany, the Germany of dreams rather than of drill masters; of philosophies rather than of factories. He had taken a dozen useless wounds in the abortive revolutions of 1848, and then, when the iron beak of the Prussian eagle had torn to tatters the dream of a free Federation, Steinmetz had escaped to become a wanderer on the face of the earth. He had no capital but his sword, but that had brought him a living for more than twenty years. There may be a Spanish-American state so small and so peaceful that it had not seen Steinmetz' blade in action, but I doubt it. He was a fair shot, a deadly swordsman, a man of great strength and utterly unconscious courage. The corpses must have been thick in his track at times, and yet he had the gentleness of a child toward those he loved.

"Why did you fight for the Yankees in the war?" I asked him one day. That was a rather sore point with me, and perhaps I was trying, unconsciously, to check my rapidly growing love for the man.

"Because the Yankees for the once were right," he answered. "You will see it some day. I have fought for so many bad causes, in so many foolish wars. You must not grudge me the pleasure of for once giving my sword to something good."

"But why fight for bad causes?" I countered.

"One must eat," he answered gravely. "It is an unfortunate habit, but I acquired it early. You have the same, I perceive, nicht war?"

I flushed, and well I might, for I had eaten enough for four men, and Steinmetz had just annexed the bill. I am sure no thought of that was in his mind, however. He went on, still gently:

"Who knows for certain when he does good or bad? There is no way of telling. I do good to myself when I fight to make a living, and I fight fair. If these heroes of the coffee colour want to play revolution, why should I not help their play? I help them to get it over more quickly, and I do not let them torture each other so much. Besides, it is all but for the moment. Some day this big-boy country of yours will step in and swallow Cuba, swallow Mexico, swallow everything to the Caribbean, and perhaps beyond. We may be paving the way for that swallow with our little revolutions."

"You didn't like it when Prussia swallowed your principality," I answered, smiling at his mixed metaphors.

"That is because I am not Prussian. The greatest meal to the greatest eater, so. Shall we walk?"

We walked. Also, that night we closed the deal for the last arms and ammunition, and the following day saw the stuff safely aboard the *Aurora*. After which Steinmetz and I sat down to enjoy ourselves while the "patriots" who were paying our expenses wrangled over the division of spoils not yet secured, and worked their debating society overtime to decide questions that could only be settled by a strong man at the critical moment. For such is the way of coffee-coloured revolutions.

IV

The urge of action is in our blood, and no man, at least of our restless race, can escape his strenuous destiny. Yet age is teaching me that the moments which we recall with the most unalloyed satisfaction are seldom the moments of greatest activity. Rather are they the times when we drift with the stream of events, idle as the driftwood beside us; or make ourselves lotus eaters on enchanted islands of our own wills. My life has been a pleasant one in the main, but there is little of it on which memory dwells so lovingly as on those days of waiting in New York. The prospect of being denounced and arrested never entered my mind, though I am convinced it must have troubled Steinmetz quite a bit. Our work for the time was done, our immediate needs were provided for, we were not even put to the trouble of deciding on the next move. It was ours for a time to be content with the mere living; and for my part I was more than content.

By day I sat mainly in Steinmetz' rooms, playing with Señor Gato, and listening to the soldier's tales of fortune's whims in the four corners of the earth. I have no authority but his own for some rather remarkable stories, but, for me, that is authority enough. He was not a man one could disbelieve. By night we would wander through the city, already great, though with little of its present Titanic splendour; or take a boat and row out over the river or bay. If we went on foot, we went alone, or sometimes Captain Somers or Mr. Rogers would accompany us part of the way. If we took a boat, our unfailing companion was Señor Gato; perched on a thwart, miauwing sociably now and then, and at intervals jumping down to rub against his master's leg or mine, and assure us of his undying affection. He was the only cat I ever knew who had no apparent fear of water, and almost the only cat of my acquaintance with the dog loyalty to persons, rather than the usual feline fondness for places.

Steinmetz planned to take the cat with him on the *Aurora*, and, in case we stopped in Venezuela, the captain would pilot Gato back to New York. "I want my friends with me as long as possible," said the soldier. "All my friends," he added, looking up at me. "I have not so many."

One night in our wanderings we ran across another ugly gang of toughs; or, for all I know, it may have been the same gang. The experience was very different, however. Steinmetz ordered the crowd to one side, an ugly protuberance in his coat pocket backing the quiet menace of his tone, and then the gang leader, a hulking scamp of about my own age, fought it out with me. The combat was one-sided, I was probably the heavier and certainly far the stronger. Steinmetz smoked quietly through the fray, and when it was over we walked past the beaten thug and his friends without once looking around. This was a trying performance for me, but Steinmetz was as placid as a summer morning.

"Lucky you had that revolver," I said when we had gone a little distance.

"Revolver? I have none. The—what do you call it, bluff?—the bluff was just as good as the gun for that canaille."

"What a poker player you would make I" I exclaimed.

"I would rather play revolutions," he answered. "Donnerwetter! What a muscle you possess!"

"It is nothing."

"It is much. Have you given it the training? Do you fence?"

"A little," I answered. "But I'm afraid I shouldn't have much chance with you."

"You would have no chance with me," he said soberly. "I am the second best swordsman in the world." It was a mere statement of statistical fact, as if he were naming the second largest steam engine.

"Who is the first swordsman?" I queried.

"Monstery," was the reply. "He can take a sword out of my hand as easily as I could take one out of yours. He did it in Mexico, and a prisoner made me, and then he killed a guard who was giving me abuse. He is German, too; Hohenzollern by the left hand."

And the rest of that night was occupied in recounting the bits of unwritten history thus brought to the surface.

The days of waiting passed all too quickly and at last came the order for us to go aboard. We went aboard, and waited there in idleness for another twenty-four hours. Then a pompous individual in a long cloak was ushered aboard with elaborate pretense of secrecy, as though a plainclothes policeman were not at that very moment taking observations from the wharf. Rogers winked at me as he caught my enquiring look, the cloaked individual was hustled below; and then the deck rang with orders and echoed with dizzying metaphors as Rogers translated the captain's instructions to the crew. A little puffing tug dragged us out, as a terrier might pilot a pig by the ear; the sails were shaken out and braced to their places, conjured there, it seemed to me, by the second mate's incantations; and we were off on the voyage which some of us were destined to leave forever unfinished.

I am no sailor, a fact which will become increasingly apparent in these pages. But I think there are few experiences to stir a young

man's blood more than his first voyage at sea. This was my first
voyage. I was sailing for the Spanish Main on a mission as lawless,
though not as cruel, as any foray which my ancestors, perchance,
had made in those same waters. Up to the very moment that the
tug let us go, I was, or thought I was, an unreconstructed rebel, a
faithful devotee of the Lost Cause. But as we made our way down
that bay, through the shipping, I felt that, after all, I was leaving
home, and shamefacedly blessed the fortune which in my own despite had made this my country. The wind was fair; the tide, of
course, was with us. The hour was near to sunset, and it seemed
almost as if the great city were setting with the sun. Our boat was
sea kindly to a degree. Landsman though I was, the swing of the
open water brought only exhilaration, unmixed with

> "That dreadful heaviness of heart,
>   Or rather, stomach, which, alas! attends
>   The youthful voyager."

It may be proper to say that I have felt that heaviness since,
and know how great was my initial mercy.

I was taking a last look at the fading city when Steinmetz came
up with Señor Gato on his shoulder. Behind him was the steward,
with a tray and some glasses. Steinmetz took one and handed me
the other.

"To the Brotherhood of Revolutionists," he said gravely. "May
its noble members never lack for lands to save and tyrants to over-
throw. Drink!"

We clinked glasses and drank, while Señor Gato intimated that
it was really impolite of us not to offer him something, too.

Rogers was bustling about the deck, volleying out orders which
were salted and spiced with the queerest profanity to which I have
ever listened. Some of it was downright Shakesperian in its sweep
and scope; but none of it, alas! will bear transference to paper. We
listened and watched for a time, and then I brought up more immediate business.

"Who's His Nibs in the long cloak?" I enquired.

Steinmetz shrugged his shoulders with a French grace of gesture.

"He is one who will liberate his fatherland—aber nicht. He is one whose heart beats warmly for his oppressed people and an office. He is the reincarnation of Napoleon, and the superior to Bismarck. He will tell you so later, if you let him. At present he is below, casting up his dinner instead of his noble sentiments." Steinmetz dropped his careful English and swore roundly in the German-Spanish mixture to which he always resorted when his soul was really disturbed. Presently he returned to my own tongue.

"If I had known that pigdog were to be on hand to spoil things, I would for another revolution have looked," he said whimsically.

"Is he so bad as that?"

"He is an ass, a schweinhund, a—what you call spoil-plot. He is a black-and-tan ape, without so much sense as my Gato, nor so much good blood in him, either. It was agreed that Martinez should come, and then, after we are aboard, this mongrel comes instead." Steinmetz concluded his estimate of José Maria Manuel Gonzales with some more German remarks.

"Do you think he will spoil the expedition?"

"I think he will do nothing else. He brings an order from the junta to go to the mouths of the Orinoco, where there is fever even in winter, and the insects eat you alive. Captain Somers doesn't care, he has only to unload the arms. But me I do not choose my son-at-arms shall die of fever to please the whim of a black-and-tan patriot," he concluded, laying a hand on my shoulder. "We will back to New York go in the *Aurora*. If this schweinhund is too troublesome, I shall ask Captain Somers to put us ashore at St. Thomas or Barbadoes."

The wind hummed in the rigging, and the vessel rose and fell in long, easy swings to the rhythmical pulse of the ocean. I had never dreamed that a ship made so much noise, nor was it till later that I learned this was a special prerogative of wooden vessels. The sun was down, but the western sky was fairly aflame with red and orange lights. Six bells were struck, six high, piercing notes that vibrated through the ship. A negro sailor forward took the bell for a keynote, and began a deep sea chanty in one of those rich tenor-baritone voices of which his race has so many; a voice that seemed throbbing with feminine overtones. I do not recall a single word of his song; yet no picture of my life is clearer with me than the one the *Aurora* presented in that evening glow.

The steward brought us something to eat on deck. After a time we went below. But the sounds from José Maria's cabin next door, where the patriot was bringing up his meal for re-examination, were not encouraging, and, taking our blankets, we beat a retreat to the deck. It was a bit cold, but, running before the wind as we did, there was nothing of the bone-searching chill one feels on the deck of a driving steamer. Rogers came to us, told us we were ruining the ship's discipline, went to the captain with the matter, and doubtless received an order to let us do as we pleased; for he came back and chatted pleasantly with us in the intervals between remarks to the sailors.

It must have been well past midnight when I went to sleep. Steinmetz had been in the land of dreams for at least two hours.

V

And now for some days the course of the *Aurora* was monotonously smooth. Not that the ocean made an easy path for us, or greeted us with smiles. The weather was the raw, lowering sort which I have since learned to look for on the North Atlantic, the winds were light and variable, and our progress was slow. But there was no storm, no danger, no excitement. The most imaginative romancer would be troubled to weave a thrill out of our life those first days, and I am no romancer at all, but an old man, telling as plainly as he may the story of his youth. There was one constant source of surprise to me—the amount of work which the officers found for the crew to do. Morning, noon, and night there was always something. It might be cleaning the decks, which were kept spotless; it might be bracing the ropes, of which there was such an unaccountable number. It might be and was many things, but it was always something; and never for a moment did that crew seem idle. No, I must make one exception to that statement, there was a very little loafing allowed in the anchor watch, at the end of the day; though what was accounted leisure by those sailors would be reckoned hard work enough by many a laborer ashore.

And quite as surprising as the amount of work there was to do was the amount of abuse it took to get that work done. I was familiar with plantation life, I had seen eight hundred negroes working on a cotton crop under none too gentle overseers. But never did I hear such language ladled out to human beings as on the *Aurora*, and never had I known words so frequently backed—and preceded—by blows. The first mate, indeed, cursed his men only in moderation, and but once did I see him resort to force. But Rogers— His simplest order was accompanied by a perfect gale of curses and epithets, and when anything difficult was to be done the gale took on the proportions of a hurricane. The first day out the negro sailor whose voice I had so much admired the night before made some blunder—my ignorance of the sea kept me from knowing just what it was. Rogers leaped at him like a panther, and calling him names of which a "flat-nosed son of a chimpanzee" was the mildest, knocked him down and fairly kicked him across the deck. The fellow got up and scrambled in a frightened way to his task, while Rogers delivered an oration on the sins of sailors in general and of black sailors in particular.

Steinmetz turned to me at the first lull in the storm of words, and pointed to the flag which had been run up to salute a passing vessel.

"The flag of the free," he said. "On land and sometimes, yes. But on sea she is the flag of the bucko mate. Your country much needs an Uncle Tom's Cabin of the sea."

"Don't other countries need it just as much?" I asked. Steinmetz smiled at my jealous defence of the land my father had died trying to repudiate, and answered: "All need it, yes, aber, the need of the United States, she is greatest. On a British ship they do not do things so."

But I remember arguing the matter until Steinmetz called the captain to give testimony as to the superior hazing abilities of Yankee mates.

There was this justification for the barbarity of Rogers and the quiet but incessant "working up" of the mate, that ours was a hard crew to handle. We had more men than we needed at sea, because it would take something of a force to land our little ready-made revolution when we came to the appointed place. A couple of our men were "Souwegians," two or three were Portuguese from the Azores, and these were capable and not insubordinate sailors. For the rest, ours was a crew of city wharf rats, navy sweepings, Cuban mixed bloods, and negroes, partly from the South and partly from the West Indies. Besides the officers and myself, there was just one American in the ship, and he had taken to the water a year or two previous to avoid complications about a little matter of a Five Points murder. Every man in the crew must have known that our mission was illegal, and that the ship was a floating arsenal. In a case like this it was plainly the business of the officers to see that the men had no time to plot mischief. I am bound to say that they performed this duty thoroughly.

We loafed southward, at first through grey seas and under lowering skies; but in a couple of days the clouds were gone, and the sea took on that brilliant blue which is the despair of painters. The Gulf Stream tossed us choppily for a space, and let us pass. The low, flat, crooked islands of Bermuda sprawled invitingly to starboard for the better part of a day as we lolled by, but we did not stop. British governors have an impertinent habit of asking questions of the ships which visit their ports, and we had no notion of going on the witness stand if we could help it. Day by day the sun mounted higher; night by night the pole star sank lower; and the sea life around us grew more abundant with every lazy league. Once a tramp steamer stormed past us to the north, bringing back for a moment memories of the strenuous hurry we had left behind, and now and then we would sight a white-winged sailing ship. But for the most part the ship was alone with the sea and the sky; a little world swimming in a blue void of its own; a world where bucko mates licked reluctant seamen into order; where a tall soldier of fortune told wondrous tales of adventure to a worshipping boy; or played with a cat while the boy read aloud from the "Ancient Mariner," truest and saltiest of all the poems of the sea. It was a veritable voyage of dreams.

And then, almost as suddenly as the scene shifting in a theatre, the dream ended and the nightmare began.

I had gone to my berth after breakfast to make up a little of the sleep lost the night before. How long I slept is uncertain, perhaps a couple of hours. I awoke with a feeling of some excitement in the air, and a sharp exclamation which reached me from the deck testified that the feeling was correct. I hurried to the deck. Everyone whose duty did not compel his presence elsewhere was crowded to the port rail, staring at a vessel less than a mile away. I took my place beside Steinmetz and stared with the rest.

The vessel was schooner rigged, and was probably somewhat smaller than the *Aurora*. So much even my landsman's eye could tell, though I could see nothing to account for the evident excitement of my companions. The schooner was approaching us in the light wind, with most of her sails set, and each moment the view of her grew clearer. I had just begun to feel a vague sense of something lacking when, without warning, the schooner swung with a curious, irresponsible lurch, and fairly turned her back on us. Through the glass which Steinmetz handed me I could read the name across her stern. It was the *Nancy Hanks*.

"Well, what do you know about that?" queried Rogers, anticipating a popular vaudeville question by some dozen or score of years. He shook his head as if in answer to his own enquiry, and the mate spoke:

"Steering herself! Nobody at the wheel! Nobody on lookout! Nobody nowhere! Wall, I swan!"

"The Flying Dutchman she is, nicht war?" said Steinmetz. Up forward I saw a Portuguese cross himself at the ominous name, but the mate answered calmly:

"You're the only Dutchman in these parts, an' I ain't seen you fly. The *Nancy Hanks*. She left a week or ten days ahead of us."

The captain put down the glass and spoke with naval curtness.

"Mr. Rogers, take a boat and go aboard that schooner. Find out what's the matter with her. Take Mr. Steinmetz with you." I looked a request at him, received a nod for answer, and jumped for the boat.

It would be very thrilling, just now, to tell how a presentment of coming doom hung over us on our way to the strange vessel. But, unfortunately, it would not be true. While the boat was being launched the mate had made a suggestion which seemed quite probable to us all. He surmised that the *Nancy Hanks*, like ourselves, was engaged in a contraband trade, and that on the near approach of a warship in the night or in a fog the crew had mistakenly fancied themselves discovered, and had taken to the boats. We were wondering how much we could get out of the owners for salvage, and whether this little windfall could be managed without hindering our revolutionary schemes. The boat came skilfully along side, and Rogers sprang aboard with the agility of a cat. Steinmetz was next, and I followed Steinmetz. Rogers was standing, a puzzled frown deepening on his forehead as he stared about.

"Look at the boats," he commanded.

"Aren't they all right?" was my idiotic question. Rogers swore impatiently, but without the vivid personal application he would have used in talking to a sailor.

"That's just the trouble. They're all right—and they're all here!"

"Then the crew must be sick below," said Steinmetz, sniffing the air as if he expected it to tell him the story of a pestilence. The puzzled frown of Rogers changed to a scowl of alarm, but Steinmetz turned quietly aft, and went down to the cabin. I followed, and this time it was Rogers who brought up the rear. There were no sick men below. There were no dead men. There were no men at all; there was no smell of sickness, no sign of disorder. There was nothing, just nothing; and somehow that nothing was more daunting than many an evil sight would be. There were three staterooms, fitted up rather better than is the rule on vessels of the size of the *Nancy Hanks*, but all three were empty. Before us stood a sewing machine, with a hem still under the needle. Steinmetz pointed to it, uttering many German exclamations before he took pity on me and spoke in English.

"The Flying Dutchman," he said again. "But where is the Dutchman's crew?"

I had no answer to make. Rogers was already turning the leaves of the log. A sharp exclamation from him made us turn quickly.

"This log's posted to two days ago," he said, looking at us in utter bewilderment. "What the devil does this thing mean?"

"Suppose at the other papers you look," suggested Steinmetz. "I will to the forecastle go. We may find something there."

We went to the forecastle, passing the knob of the galley without looking in. The forecastle was as empty as the cabin!

"Der galley," said Steinmetz next, and by this time I knew that the Teutonic particle was a sign of strong excitement. "Der galley of der cook. He will amidships be, we have passed him." Again he led the way, and again I followed at his heels.

The galley was as empty as the forecastle or the cabin, but hardly as commonplace. A large wooden cage was lashed in one corner. It was much too large to be the cage of a bird, even of a cockatoo; and there was nothing to tell what had occupied it nor that it had been occupied at all. Anyway, it was empty now, and the door was open. I inspected it fruitlessly for a moment, and lifted my head to find Steinmetz peering closely at something written on the galley walls.

"What is it?" I asked.

"Du lieber Gott! I would like to know what it is!" exclaimed Steinmetz. "'Das Gesicht von Luft,'" he read slowly, and then halted over the translation. "The Sight—no, it must be the Face—The Face of Air."

"The face of air?" I repeated blankly. Steinmetz was bending to some more writing, and as I spoke he gave another German exclamation.

"Goethe!" he replied to my look and question. "Goethe! On the walls of a cook, his galley!" One would think from Steinmetz' tone that this was a mystery compared to which the empty schooner was a commonplace puzzle. He read off a German couplet, and translated it with a swift sureness very different from his halting rendition of the first inscription. It was the one which in my English translation of Goethe is given thus:

"'Tis thus at the roaring loom of Time I ply,
And weave for God the garment thou seest Him by."

Underneath this, still in German script, were words which
Steinmetz translated slowly once more, as if he could not be sure
that he had caught their meaning:
"'I—the garment—have dissolved in air.'"
"The fellow was daffy on air," was my irreverent remark. "But
what in thunder does it mean?"
"I do not know. 'The Face of Air.' A garment dissolved in air.
And Goethe. Goethe, in the original German, in the galley of the
cook of a Yankee hooker! Du lieber Gott! The cook is the key to
this mystery!" He shook his head gloomily.
    We came out to find our boat's crew huddled together forward,
making low remarks and shaking their heads. In a moment Rogers
came up from the cabin, shaking *his* head. It seemed to be the official
gesture of our little party.

                                    VI
    When we got back to the *Aurora* and Rogers made his report
the captain's answer was to take the boat and go to the schooner
himself. He was gone two hours, during which time Rogers frequently expressed a firm conviction of his ultimate condemnation
if he understood the thing, and Steinmetz smoked gloomily, and
spat German quotations by the yard. At the end of this time the
captain returned, with a brisk, business-like air. "You're wrong
about the boat," was the first thing he said. "There *is* a boat gone,
an' that changes the whole shebang. It's just as the mate put it up,
I guess. They're in a line of private business, an' something come
too close, an' they got nervous an' bolted. When a fellow's running
contraband, it doesn't pay to get scared too soon. They've lost a
good schooner, and we've found one."
    This oration was purposely pronounced in the hearing of the
crew, and had an excellent effect. Captain Somers had earned a
reputation which made his words carry weight, and in the light of
his matter-of-fact sentences, the mystery seemed to shred away

and disappear. I remember thinking it queer that a man should take his wife along if he were running arms through a blockade, but I did not speak. The bo'sun was ordered to take a crew of four men and go on board, and he moved with an alacrity which showed that he, at least, had no thought of troubles awaiting him. He was one of the Souwegians, and a capable sailor; but his little crew contained four of the laziest and most worthless men in the ship. I suppose this was managed by the mates, who took this means of shifting their burdens to the bo'sun.

Down in the cabin Captain Somers was not quite so sure of himself.

"It's a queer business, but there's no use gettin' crazy about it," he declared. "Rogers missed one thing, the cook died five days ago. They found him dead in his galley."

"Dead or alive, that cook is the key to this mystery," said Steinmetz, shaking his head. "You laugh, may you keep on laughing; but I tell you it is so."

"Do you think his ghost came back and drove the crew overboard?" laughed the captain. The German gave his head an obstinate toss.

"I do not know what I think. But the cook is the heart of the puzzle, and not any smuggling business. 'The Face of Air!' Goethe, in a cook's galley, and on a Yankee hooker! That is more strange than a deserted vessel, my friend."

"How did you find out about the boat?" I ventured to ask.

"Been towing one astern," was the brief reply. "Besides, it's common sense. A crew ain't going to swim ashore when they've plenty of boats."

"Why didn't they take the log?" mused the mate. "An' how'd they come to have so big a crew?"

"How do we come to have one?" countered the captain, ignoring the first and most difficult question.

"Do her papers show any queer cargo?" This was my question, and the captain and mate joined in a laugh.

"Ours don't, my son," said the captain. "We're loaded with cement an' plows an' stuff."

We thrashed the matter over for a time before the "black-and-tan patriot" sent his servant to ask for a private confab with the captain. Then Steinmetz and I adjourned to the deck and continued the discussion of the puzzle there. The two vessels slipped southward through the warm water, the schooner being palpably the better sailor of the two. When I expressed wonder that she had got no farther on her course Rogers broke in to tell me that she had stopped at Bermuda. I recall my relief at finding a solution to even this tiny part of the mystery.

The conference between Captain Somers and José Maria Manuel Gonzales came to nothing. Being strictly private, the steward brought us a full report of it the moment it was over. José Maria wanted to set the schooner adrift, partly for superstitious reasons, partly, no doubt, for sheer contrariness, and the captain naturally did not see it that way. Late in the afternoon Steinmetz was called to the cabin for another confab. From my post on deck I could hear their voices, though not their words, which indeed were hardly necessary to understanding. I heard the captain's dictatorial tone, heard an evident approval from Steinmetz, heard a shrill spitting of mixed up language from the Venezuelan, and then a resounding smack. I knew what had happened as well as though I had been present. José Maria Manuel Gonzales had gone too far, and Steinmetz had slapped his face. After a few minutes' silence the tall German joined me on deck.

"Well," I enquired, "did you cuff him up to a peak?"

"How did you know?" he countered, and then swore in German without waiting for an answer. Presently he laughed. "It simplifies matters, at all events," he said. "Tomorrow we go, you and I, aboard the schooner of mystery and make sail for a Yankee port. They may land their own guns."

"Are you going to give it up?" I exclaimed. The boyish disappointment of my tone must have hurt him, but he gave no sign beyond unusual gentleness.

"It is giving us up," he explained. "I did not want to go to be eaten by insects on the Orinoco, as you know. Now, it would be idle for me to go anywhere with this fellow. Whatever I did would be wrong, and he would find a way to leave his knife in our backs, in some manner. If I leave now, he may get on with the captain; at least, the chance there is. The schooner of mystery, mein lieber kind, is providential. We will drink to the cook's health aboard her to-morrow. Du lieber Gott! Between a cook who quotes Goethe and a black-and-tan waiter who tries to run revolutions, I prefer the cook."

"You seem very sure that the cook is the key to the mystery?" The sun had set while we talked, and a bank of storm clouds was showing in the west. I peered off as I spoke through the mixed twilight and moonlight to where the schooner lolled on the sea a couple of miles ahead. The wind had failed utterly, and the sea was rolling in long, metallic-looking swells.

Steinmetz answered thoughtfully, following my gaze the while.

"It saves energy to think so. Here is a mysterious ship that by a mysterious cook has been inhabited. That those two mysteries should be connected it is natural to think, nicht war? Otherwise, we should have to hunt for two explanations instead of one."

"We may solve it when we get aboard," I suggested.

"And we may not. Ah, there is Señor Gato. Gato, can you smell a cook's ghost?" We sat for a time, puzzling over the schooner, petting the cat, and exchanging views on the nature and permanence of the Caribbean "republics." The bank of clouds climbed higher and higher, then seemed to stop climbing, and rolled over the water towards us in a blackish-grey mass. To me it was awe-inspiring enough, to the sailors and even to Steinmetz it was just an ordinary squall. It was the first mate's watch, I remember, and vivid was my admiration for the way the men made the canvas snug under his direction. Then the squall struck with a shower of chilly rain, and we went to our berths.

I was up at daybreak next morning to find the sky clear as ever, though the sea running a bit more roughly in an easterly wind. Rogers was on deck, and I took advantage of a moment's lull in his sulphurous rhetoric to ask where the schooner was.

"Lost her in the night," was the brief answer, as he turned to stir the stumps of a negro sailor by the pure power of anathema.

"Pick her up to-day, most like," he added, as he saw my disappointed look. For, boy fashion, I was now as eager to quit the *Aurora* as I had formerly been reluctant.

We nosed through the water for some hours, keeping a sharp lookout for the schooner. When we went to breakfast it was noticeable that José Maria was not present. The wind was light and puffy, but enough to keep us going, and to stir the sea to more action than we had been accustomed to for some days. Steinmetz sat placidly on deck, petting Señor Gato, and occasionally quoting German poetry, which I took to be somehow related to the verses scrawled up in the schooner's galley. A little before noon we heard the cry "Sail, ho!" from the lookout. The *Aurora* altered her course to meet the sail, pointing closer into the wind than a landsman would dream possible. I remember we were eating our dinner on deck when the lookout declared that the sail was the *Nancy Hanks*, headed to meet us.

"Sighted us first," said the taciturn mate. "I hope so," said Steinmetz enigmatically. Rogers opined that the bo'sun and the crew he had with him couldn't sight anything.

The two vessels continued to approach each other rapidly. A hush fell over the *Aurora*, broken at last by the voice of the captain as he flung a crisp order to the man at the wheel. "I'll give that bo'sun something to think about in a minute," he added savagely; for the schooner was driving towards us as if to invite a collision. And then, all at once, the whole ship's company cried out in amazement. Just as she had done on the previous day, the *Nancy Hanks* swung around with a lubberly lurch, her sails slatted viciously as they caught the breeze at this new angle; she heeled well over for an instant, righted herself, and paid off before the wind again. But in that brief space every eye and glass on the *Aurora* had been trained on the wheel of the *Nancy Hanks*—and had found no steersman!

The captain put down his glass and stared for a minute with naked eyes at the schooner. Then he snapped out a few orders, and the *Aurora* came around with a cow-like motion, very different from the quick lurches of the schooner. A boat was lowered.

Steinmetz and I followed the captain, in response to his quick order, and in a few minutes we were pulling once more towards the schooner of mystery. But this time there was no speculating as to salvage on the way.

VII

When we came alongside the schooner Captain Somers first made sure that his navy Colt was loose in its holster, and then went over the vessel's rail as if he were boarding an enemy. No enemy was in sight, however.

The little expanse of deck was empty of friend or foe. Somers swept one quick look up and down the deck, called to a sailor to take the wheel, and then, drawing his revolver, plunged into the forecastle, telling us to wait. A moment later he reappeared.

"Empty," was all he said, and ran aft to dive into the cabin. This time I followed, but Steinmetz turned to the galley, as if to him this were the one point worth searching.

Captain Somers poked head and gun simultaneously into one of the tiny staterooms. I did as much for one on the other side. Both were vacant. I drew back, searched the third stateroom with the same result, and turned back to the captain. He was holding the open log, and as I came up he pointed without speaking to a scrawling entry:

"Sept. —. Took charge of schooner *Nancy Hanks* with orders to keep *Aurora* in sight. Squall coming. Reefed—"

It broke off just like that; no period, no sign that the entry was finished, no anything. As I stared the captain stooped and picked up something from the floor. It was a pen.

We came up without a word and joined Steinmetz. He was examining something at the foot of the foremast. For a moment the captain stood, looking at the boats; then he went up to them, as if nothing but his sense of touch would convince him that they were real. He made the round twice while I watched him. Whatever doubt there may have been on the boat question before, this time there was none. The prize crew was gone; but the prize crew had not taken a boat.

When the captain had made sure of this astounding fact he looked at me as if he would stare me into giving him an explanation of the thing. Steinmetz left the foremast and came near. The captain spoke in a low tone. "Is there something on this vessel that drives men overboard?" he demanded.

"Is there something on this vessel which the garment of flesh dissolves in air?" retorted Steinmetz. "I have something found by the foremast which is queer." He led the way and pointed. It was a piece of broken crockery.

"That's nothing," said the captain. "Some duffer dropped it."

Without answering, Steinmetz pointed to the foremast about three feet above the deck. There was a slight dent in the tough wood, and in the dent were sticking two or three tiny slivers of crockery. It was not much, but it was decisive. The bowl or cup or whatever it was had been flung against the mast.

Captain Somers called to two of the sailors, and ordered them to open the hold. For the next hour the little party of us searched that schooner till it seemed as if a rat could hardly have escaped our inspection. And the search ended as it began, in nothing. The captain at last motioned Steinmetz and myself to the cabin.

"What do you make of this?" he demanded, his hand on the sewing machine as he spoke. Steinmetz shook his head.

"I make of it nothing," he replied slowly. "It is a mystery. And the cook who quotes Goethe is the key to that mystery. More I cannot say."

"But the cook is dead, man," expostulated the captain.

"And the schooner is empty," retorted Steinmetz. He repeated thoughtfully the German couplet scrawled in the galley. I said nothing. The captain pondered for a space.

"Look here!" he exclaimed at length. "The Spaniards know there's a lot of smuggling arms from America to Cuba, don't they?"

"It is possible they have learned it by this time," returned Steinmetz with grave irony. "Well?"

"Well, they don't like it. That is possible, too," added the captain, grinning at his own parody of Steinmetz's words. "And Spain has a navy, hasn't she?"

"It goes by the name of a navy."

"It's enough of a navy for what I'm thinking of. Now suppose Spain has got a gunboat or two in these waters, watching for smugglers. Suppose she thinks the *Nancy Hanks* is running arms, or maybe knows it. Is there anything to hinder a gunboat catching a schooner like this?"

"She hasn't caught us yet," I ventured, as Steinmetz offered no reply.

"She may," retorted the captain. "And suppose she thinks it would throw a bigger scare into others of the same line of business to take the crew out and just let the vessel drift than to sink or capture the ship. Wouldn't that explain it?"

"A war balloon would explain it so much better," said Steinmetz. "A war balloon, with a steam engine, that could drive against the wind and pick men off the decks with a lasso. That would the perfect explanation be. Make your gunboat a balloon, Herr captain."

"Laugh if you want to," said the captain. "It doesn't strike me as so much of a laughing matter. But here! It must be something from the outside, else we'd be jumping overboard, too."

"Give us time," murmured Steinmetz.

"Besides, we've raked the old hooker with a fine-tooth comb, and there ain't nothing wrong aboard her."

"'Das Gesicht von Luft,'" quoted Steinmetz. "The Sight of Air. The Face of Air. That might be aboard."

"Oh, h—l!" exclaimed the captain disgustedly.

"Aber," continued Steinmetz after a pause. "There is the practical question. You do not want the salvage on so fine a schooner to lose. That is well. I want to get back to New York for another revolution to look, and to have no more companionship with my black-and-tan Napoleon of the proclamations. That also is well. So. You furnish the men to navigate this vessel, and I the guard will be. We will take her to the nearest port, which will be Nassau, and I will keep watch for the danger. If it comes from the outside, we will try to greet it. If it comes from the inside, so, it will find us interested. And you can divide the salvage with me; for now I have an heir, I must begin a fortune to accumulate." He looked across at me with whimsical affection.

354 A Spectrum Unseen

"Will you do it?" asked the captain.

"I will wait with the steersman," returned Steinmetz. "My son-at-arms can bring me Señor Gato and the baggage in the boat that brings the crew. Then we can say good-bye."

"We won't say good-bye," I retorted. "If there's any fun going on this old hooker, I want my share. I'm not afraid of ghosts."

Steinmetz frowned thoughtfully, then smiled. I could see he was balancing the respective dangers of the trip in the schooner and the voyage to the Orinoco. The captain put in a word which decided him, and saved me the trouble of argument.

"If both of you go, there'll be less trouble getting a crew."

"All well," agreed Steinmetz. "It will a better crew want than the first one, however."

"I'll get you the best we have," said the captain.

We returned to the *Aurora*, leaving Steinmetz and a steersman aboard the schooner. An hour or so later I put off once more for the *Nancy Hanks*. On my shoulder sat Señor Gato, balancing himself nonchalantly to the swing of the boat; in the stern sat Rogers, looking as if he wished himself a thousand miles away, and trying to cover his uneasiness by scowling and cursing at the rowers. We boarded the schooner, the boat's crew returned to the *Aurora*, there was a general hail and farewell, and the two vessels separated for the last time. The *Aurora* swung back on her southward course. The *Nancy Hanks* turned west by southwest for the Bahamas.

VIII

Before going farther with this history, it will be well to pause a moment and run over the list of persons now making a temporary home in the *Nancy Hanks*. Steinmetz the reader knows already, and Rogers, and even as the historian of the party I need no farther introduction. Besides us three and Señor Gato, who was not the least in dignity of our party, there were four sailors. Captain Somers had kept his word and sent us the best he could get, but the best was nothing to cause an officer to boast. One, the steersman who had stayed aboard with Steinmetz, was one of the three Portuguese of whom I have spoken. Doubtless he had a name, but it was so seldom used that I never learned it; he was simply the Portugee, and by far the best sailor and best man of our little crew. One was a huge negro, who claimed Jamaican birth, British citizenship, and the privileges of a Union navy veteran. Privately I doubted if he ever saw Jamaica, and I am sure that his services under Farragut were confined to the cooking and demolishing of provisions. A third was my friend of the Five Points, sea name McCarthy; a likeable, truculent rascal, who feared nothing that he could see, and walked in mortal dread of the invisible. He stood barely five and a half feet above sea level, but he had already thrashed the big negro twice on our voyage, and then fairly grovelled in fear that the black would put the hoodoo on him. Last was a Cuban mixed-blood, Garcia by name; a moderate seaman, but full of the dangerous temper that comes from the mating of Latin blood and black.

All four of the men were used to salt water, though the Portugee was the only first-class sailor among them. All looked on the voyage with superstitious dread. All had come aboard in response to the captain's judicious mingling of offers of big prize money with ridicule of those who feared to take the chance. Rogers himself was in no better case than the sailors before the mast. He had been tricked into saying that he could manage the voyage, no matter what the mystery, and then was given no chance to back out.

And here were seven men mured in a little schooner from which two crews had already disappeared in four days. Is it strange that we felt a bit uneasy as the *Aurora* dropped below the horizon and left us the sole inhabitants of the visible world? For my part, I confess to a sinking at the heart which I had never felt before, and seldom since. It was not a presentiment of doom, though one needs but little superstition to translate it as such. It was merely the natural dread of the unknown, especially when the veil of the unknown has been lifted just far enough to show that something of unwonted power and fearsomeness lies behind.

Rogers, Steinmetz and myself divided the three staterooms between us. Rogers' kit was carried to his room by the negro, and then master and man went on deck immediately. Steinmetz came into my cubby hole, sat down on the edge of the bunk, and lifted a humorous grin to me.

"In the language of your country, we are in for it," he remarked.

"We are," I returned. "And we don't know what *it* is."

"True," he replied with a shrug of his shoulders. "Aber, we shall probably see. I have been thinking of our trip." He stopped, fished a cigar out of his pocket, lighted it, puffed in silence a few moments. I did not speak. Presently he went on:

"The success of this, our voyage, on the landsmen depends. The Herr Captain Rogers is scared till about the gills he is white. The men are scared, and they know the captain is scared. If a mermaid poked her head up on one side of the ship and said 'Boo!' our captain and crew over the other side would go splash."

He stopped to puff again. I ventured a feeble joke. "Well," I said, "do you think mermaids are thick in these parts?"

"They are at least as thick as the heroes in our crew," he retorted. "That would not be a large population. Aber, the point is that you and I must bring this venture through."

"How?"

"One of us must always be on deck. One of us must furnish the moral stamina for the noble crew, and one must a backbone be for the gallant captain. We must watch and watch stand with the rest."

"That is easy," I answered.

"It is doubtless the easiest part of our task," said Steinmetz. "Let us go up."

We went on deck. The weather had thickened while we were below and, though there was no fog, the sharp outline of the horizon was blurred, and a leaden tinge was beginning to show in the blue of the sea. Off on the starboard bow some sea creature was playing and tossing the spray. But the distance was too great to identify it with the naked eye, and by the time I had brought the glass the play was over. The Portugee was still at the wheel. The other three members of the crew were on deck—idle. Knowing Rogers' fondness for sailor hazing as I did, it struck me that this sudden tenderness to the little crew boded anything rather than good.

McCarthy was staring fixedly over the port quarter, and I loafed over to see what occupied his attention. It was a shark, one of the largest I have ever seen. We must have been making five or six knots an hour, but the shark seemed hardly to move as he kept our pace.

The dorsal fin of him cut the water like the black flag of a submarine pirate.

"He's a big one, isn't he?" I remarked, for the sake of making conversation. McCarthy spat thoughtfully into the water before answering.

"An' he wants to grow bigger. He's waitin' for his supper."

"For his supper?"

"Yep. That's what he's waitin' for."

It took me a full minute to catch the fatalistic notion which prompted the statement, and to realize that to McCarthy this voracious attendant was a messenger of doom.

"We'll see if we can't give him a supper of lead," I answered when at last I grasped the fellow's meaning. I went back to the cabin, and brought up one of the rifles we had transshipped. It was a 44 Winchester, with a soft nosed bullet, and I judged it should make even a shark lose interest in eating. The brute was not thirty feet away. I aimed just forward of his dorsal fin and fired. It could hardly have been a miss, but it might have been for all the shark seemed to care. I could not see that he even flirted his tail.

"See?" said McCarthy, in the tone of a priest confuting a sceptic. I saw, but judged it best not to say so.

"I must be out of practice," was my only rejoinder. "Better luck this time." I drew a bead on the glassy eye of the monster, just below the surface, held it till I felt as sure of the destination of the bullet as if I were to place it there with my fingers, and fired again. This time I scored. There was a wild boiling of the water for a second, and then just vacancy. The shark was gone, and I thought he left a streak of blood behind him.

"'At supper, not where he eats, but where he is eaten,'" quoted Steinmetz behind me. McCarthy shook his head as if he regretted the passing of the brute.

"What makes you so glum, Mac?" I asked in a low voice, for I did not wish the other sailors to hear. Steinmetz heard the question and turned away, evidently thinking that McCarthy would talk more freely to me alone. McCarthy looked around, lowered his own voice, and made answer:

"I wisht I'd never heard of this old hooker!"

"But why?" I persisted. "She seems a comfortable ship to me."

"Comfortable," said McCarthy gloomily. "Comfortable. Well, mebbe. There's two crews before us didn't seem to find her so."

"Oh, they." I waved my hand as if the other crews really did not matter. "The first crew got scared at a Spanish patrol and took to the boat. The next one got nutty or drunk and jumped overboard. You know what a good for nothing bunch they were."

"I ain't so sure about the boat," argued McCarthy.

"Then what do you think did happen to them? Did they go in swimming and forget to come back?"

The fellow shook his head reproachfully as though my levity were little short of sacrilege. Then he took another tack.

"There's heaps more things in the sea than most folks knows of. That fellow, now," he jerked his thumb to indicate the vanished shark; "he ain't the only thing that likes man meat."

"Well, what are the others?"

McCarthy looked cautiously around again, and dropped his voice still lower.

"There's sea sarpents! You can laugh if you want to, but I've seen 'em. Lots of men's seen 'em. They could swallow a man like pie."

"I suppose the nigger's been stuffing you with this and trying to sell you a charm on the strength of it. Eh?"

McCarthy did not deny the impeachment, but he stuck to his guns.

"There's somethin' got 'em. An' the same somethin's goin' to try to get us. I wisht I'd never seen this bloody old hooker!" He went forward at an order from Rogers.

Steinmetz had been talking to the man at the wheel. It was contrary to all rules of good seamanship, of course; but Rogers seemed to have dropped all rules the moment he came to the *Nancy Hanks*. Presently the German left the wheel and came forward. He had something to tell me, but discouraged my questions with a look easy to interpret. We stood, talking about nothing for a few minutes. Señor Gato rubbed against my leg and purred, and then, getting no encouragement, strolled away. A moment later a sudden noise made me look around.

"Look at the cat! Look at the cat!" I cried out.

Señor Gato was standing, back humped, tail inflated, the shapely outlines of him lost in a fluffy ball about three times his normal size. The breeze was on our quarter, and even as I cried out I noticed that the cat was looking up wind. There was nothing in that direction but Garcia, and the cat did not seem to be looking at him. But Rogers fell foul of the mulatto on the instant.

"What have you been doing to that cat?" he roared. The mixed blood shrugged his shoulders.

"I no do nothing to heem. I no toucha heem witha tena foot steeck. Zat Gato, heem one damn hoodoo!"

"It isn't Garcia," I said in a low voice to Rogers. Steinmetz motioned with his hand and the Cuban drew aside, so that the wind of him could no longer come to the cat's nostrils. Still Señor Gato continued to glare, uttering the most eerie yowls I ever heard, even from the throat of a cat, and spitting softly as if to punctuate his plaint.

"What is it, Señor?" said Steinmetz soothingly, coming forward and stooping over his pet. The cat looked round, took heart from the approach of his master, and began to advance up wind with little, mincing steps, spitting furiously every half inch, and raising a caterwaul fit to scare a stone image. He had progressed in this manner for perhaps three or four feet, when suddenly his long-drawn yowl changed in the middle to a heaven-splitting shriek, and Señor Gato, dignity thrown to the winds, made for the foremast as if seven devils were after each of his nine lives. Not until he reached the cross-trees did he venture to turn and glare back at the deck, and resume his cattish discourse on the evils of the world.

"Now, what in the world was that?" demanded Rogers, and his voice was husky with awe. My own throat felt too dry to speak at all. Steinmetz was quartering the deck up wind from where the cat had stood, poking with his sword as a blind man pokes with a stick. Garcia came nearer and touched his greasy forelock, for cap he had none.

"'Scuse me, please, but wot I tell you? Zat Gato, heem one damn hoodoo. Heem devil cat. Le diablo come to give heem orders. Heem see diablo, zat w'y heem spit an' yowl."

"Shut your jaw!" shouted Rogers, and one could see how he welcomed the chance to abuse some tangible thing of flesh and blood. "You'll see the devil, too, if you don't clew up that tongue! Get forward, you Roman-nosed chocolate drop!"

Garcia went forward. Steinmetz turned from his quest, smiling with his lips, though his eyes showed his utter bewilderment. The big negro had been installed as cook, and he now came to tell us that supper was served. From the fact that he was able to speak, I judged he had been below during the most mysterious part of the proceedings, and so it proved. I rescued Señor Gato from the foremast, for he quite refused to come down at our calling, and together we went to the meal.

IX

"What were you looking for?" I asked Steinmetz when we were seated.

He shook his head and waited till the negro was out of the room before replying.

"I do not know. And I did not find it, so it does not matter."

Rogers ate in silence for a time; in silence as to speech, I mean; for his revictualling process was anything but noiseless. Then he looked up with a question:

"Recollect that cage in the galley?" I nodded. Steinmetz showed by his face that he knew what Rogers had in mind, so the mate addressed his next remark to me. "It's gone," he said.

"Gone?" I repeated incredulously.

"Gone," he repeated. "Gone," he said again when the negro had left the cabin once more. "I don't like this business. I don't like it for a cent."

"Maybe the other crew thought it was a hoodoo and threw it overboard."

"And who threw them overboard?" he countered. "They're gone, as much gone as the cage. They didn't take no boats, and we didn't see the tracks where they was walkin' on the water. There's just one place for 'em to go, an' that's to the bottom."

"But why should they go there?" I asked. Rogers did not answer, perhaps because Steinmetz signalled to him that the negro was waiting in the passage. Rogers called the fellow, sent him on some errand which I have forgotten, and then brought up the subject which I fancy had been at the back of all our minds.

"I wonder what killed the first cook."

"The log only says he was found dead," replied Steinmetz. Rogers grunted as one who has heard an improbable story before.

"He might have had too much belayin' pin before he was found. Same as that coon'll get if he sneaks 'round in that passage any more," he added in a louder tone. There was a swift scurrying of feet, and the mate went on:

"Anyhow, the cook's dead. An' he's the only man that's known to have died aboard this schooner. An' now there's something hauntin' the cursed hooker that scares cats into fits, an' makes men tumble overboard. What do you make of that?"

"I don't make a ghost of it, if that's what you're driving at," I responded. Steinmetz fed Señor Gato a bit of gravy-soaked bread, and spoke with judicial gravity.

"The talk of a ghost is foolishness, like the talk of a devil cat."

"And like the talk of a sea serpent," I added, repeating Mc-Carthy's speculations for their benefit. For the first time since coming to the schooner, Rogers laughed. But it was not a very hearty laugh, and he stopped it to say:

"Well, you can poke fun at all these ideas, but what's your own?"

"I have none," I answered, after waiting a moment for Steinmetz to speak. "I have no doubt there's a perfectly simple explanation of the whole business, if we could just find it."

"Simple explanation!" exclaimed Rogers. He got no further. From above came a slap and the sound of an oath, a strange, whining squeak, and then a yell of frank terror and the pad-pad of bare feet in rapid flight. Rogers seemed to negotiate the route to the deck in a single twisting movement, and Steinmetz and myself were not far behind.

McCarthy was standing, half way between the two masts, his fists clenched, and looking about him as if for something to strike. The big negro was huddled in a heap against the lee rail, his arms clasped over his eyes, and whimpering softly. The man at the wheel was looking up at the main mast with wide eyes of panic. I followed the direction of his look. The mast was perfectly normal, the sails were drawing just as before; but up near the crosstrees a loose end of rope was shaking violently, irrationally, as if the spirit of St. Vitus had got into the inanimate thing. I whipped out my revolver, but did not shoot. There was nothing to shoot at. Above, below, at each side of the rope, there was absolutely nothing in the nature of a living creature in sight. The rope stopped its movements as if it had seen me draw the gun. I circled the mast cautiously, looking up the while, but could see nothing other than the perfectly normal gear of a sailing schooner. Suddenly I became aware that Rogers was speaking.

"A simple explanation!" he was saying. "A perfectly simple explanation! Oh, sure! You!" he roared at McCarthy. "What's the matter with you?"

"Somethin' touched me," said McCarthy stupidly, as if the touch had sent his wits wool gathering. "I ain't hurted none, but somethin' touched me."

"You'll feel something else touch you if you throw any more fits on this deck," stormed Rogers. "Here, you black whelp! What's eating you?"

"Voodoo!" said the negro softly. He uncovered his eyes, and rolled them about him as only a frightened negro can. Rogers caught him by the throat and shook him violently. He seemed hardly to feel it.

"What touched you?" I asked McCarthy.

"I—I don't know, sir." The truculent man-fighter seemed to shrink and shiver. "It was soft, an' it went down my hand like that—" he made a caressing motion.

"An' then I looked down, an' there wa'n't nothing there at all!" His voice rose to something like a shriek. "I hit at it, an' it run into the coon. He felt it, too."

"Did it hurt you?" asked Steinmetz.

"No, sir."

"Was it warm or cold?"

"I don't rightly know, sir."

"A simple explanation!" Rogers dwelt on the words as if they were a personal affront. "A simple explanation, perfectly simple! Oh, h—l, yes!"

"Let us see what we can discover," said Steinmetz.

We beat the deck like a thicket from stem to stern. We went down to the forecastle and explored that. We went to the galley and solemnly inspected the place where the cage had been and was not, and where the German script still mocked us with its riddle. We stared at the masts, and with many misgivings and a chilliness at the spine which was more than uncomfortable I climbed first one and then the other. We quizzed the crew. And we were as empty of explanations at the end of our work as at the beginning of it. Rogers summoned us to the cabin.

"What are we going to do about this?" he demanded brusquely.

Steinmetz lifted his eyebrows in polite surprise.

"I was not aware there was anything to do about it." he said. The mate scowled gloomily.

"The men won't stand for much more of this sort of thing," he said at length.

"The men will have to stand for it if you do your duty," exclaimed Steinmetz sharply. "They are not of our voyage the masters. Do you ask them whether they will clean the deck or reef the sails?"

"That's different," said Rogers sullenly.

"Not unless you yourself the difference make," said Steinmetz. "I came on this schooner to sail to Nassau. To Nassau we will sail."

"The men'll take to the boats if we leave 'em up there alone," argued Rogers.

"They will not be alone," snapped Steinmetz. "Donnerwetter, be a man once!"

Rogers straightened up and glared for a moment, but the eyes which met him were well accustomed to glaring. In a moment the mate dropped his truculent look, though he still sat straight. "That is better," went on Steinmetz. "John and myself, we will take watch and watch with you. There is no danger, except to cowards."

"The other crews thought there was danger," said Rogers.

"They may have found it in the boat or in the ocean," was the answer. "With all the mystery, no man has met harm while he has stuck to this vessel. It is running away that is dangerous—and I will see that the danger is not lessened," he added significantly.

Rogers turned after a moment and went on deck. I received a few instructions from Steinmetz and followed, while the soldier turned in, carefully carrying Señor Gato to the stateroom with him.

I have often wondered since why the very aimlessness and harmlessness of the happenings did not guide us to the truth. I have often wished we had both turned in that night and left the mate and the crew to run away if they liked. They would have done it, past a doubt; but it would have been better for at least one of us if they had. We could doubtless have worked the schooner to land somehow. But wishes, like regrets, usually come too late; and as for guessing at the truth, it was hard enough to realize it when proven.

I took a good strategic position near the galley, where I could keep both wheel and fo'c'sle hatch under surveillance, and began my watch. I was careful likewise to so place myself that no one could get at me from the rear, for I had my doubts about the means Garcia might take to get away from the neighbourhood of his "devil cat." If Rogers knew my opinion of him, he gave no sign. Our first introduction had taught him the strength of my muscles and the hardness of my skull, and he knew that I was even better armed than himself. He came over and began to talk with me about a former voyage; but neither of us felt any interest in the topic, and, in spite of my efforts, it was soon dropped. Rogers strolled away, and I was left to enjoy the night alone. I have seldom seen a more beautiful one. There was just enough haze to weave a royal robe for the moon—a robe with a silver train that glimmered across the waves. The Portugee at the wheel might have been a bronze statue most of the time, for he hardly turned a spoke. I grew intolerably sleepy, and paced the deck to keep awake. But the ship remained as peaceful as the night.

Eight bells struck, and Rogers went below, after giving a few orders to McCarthy, who relieved the Portugee at the wheel. I remained on deck, intending to call Steinmetz later; but he heard the changing watch and came up immediately, leaving Señor Gato below. I made my brief report, and then for a while we paced the deck together, commenting in low tones on the curious voyage. It must have been a full hour before I went below. Rogers stuck his head out of his cabin as I came, and looked at me wonderingly.

"When did you go up?" he asked.

"I haven't been down," was my answer. Rogers looked mystified.

"I'm sure I heard somebody in your bunk," he said. "Is Steinmetz—"

He broke off suddenly. The nameless fear had gripped both of us once more. I drew my revolver, and swung open the door of my tiny cabin. The evil-smelling lamp in the passage cast a yellow light on the berth, a light that swung grotesquely with the rolling of the ship. The little room was empty.

"I heard something, I'll swear I did," insisted Rogers. We both stepped inside. "Beg pardon," said Rogers, for no reason that I could see, though I was too puzzled to ask questions.

"Do you leave your blankets in that shape?" enquired Rogers after a moment, pointing to a rather disorderly crumple near the foot. He put his hand down as if to rearrange the covers, and jumped back so sharply that he nearly knocked me down.

"It's—it's—*warm!*" he gasped.

With an effort, I stooped and felt. The mate was right. A circle of the blankets, something over a foot in diameter, was distinctly warm to the touch. It was such a mark as a terrier might leave, after curling up on his master's bed. Then I laughed foolishly in sudden relief.

"Why, the cat, of course!"

Rogers shook his head.

"Cat's fastened in the other berth. Been there ever since I come down."

I turned to Steinmetz' room and looked. Again the mate was right. The door was shut, and inside lay Señor Gato, curled up snugly on his master's bunk. I went back to my own room and touched the blankets again. They were still warm, though less so than the moment before. Plainly it could not have been the cat. I stooped and put my nose to the covers. There was an odor, a very perceptible odor; but for the life of me, I could not tell what it was. Rogers followed my example, sniffed for a moment, and then we both stood straight.

I can see that scene yet; I have relived it more than once in my dreams. I can see the tiny cabin, the narrow bunk, the slightly disarranged blankets. I can see the yellow light swing back and forth to the roll of the ship, feel again the effort with which my unpractised legs met the roll, and see Rogers, yellow pale in the yellow gleam, looking about him with sick eyes of fear. I can smell the evil lamp, and through its reek I can catch once more the pungent odor of that warm spot on the blankets. And always with the scene comes back the grotesque phrase in which Steinmetz summed up the combative but unreliable seaman: "Mr. Start-and-Not-Finish Rogers."

It seemed ages before he spoke. In reality, it was probably two minutes. He hesitated as if the fear of being laughed at had not quite given place to the stronger terror which was overmastering him.

"The—the cook. The one that's dead, you know. Do—do you suppose?"

"No!" I answered sharply, and then I thought of another tack, and grinned broadly. "Would a ghost leave a warm spot on the blankets?" I demanded.

It was the logic of unreason, and therefore it worked. "That's so," said Rogers, in a less awe-struck tone. "That's so. A—a ghost wouldn't be warm, would it?" He considered a moment. "And a cook couldn't curl up that small, could he?"

"Of course not," I answered promptly.

The coming and going of ideas in Rogers' mind was almost a visible process. His brow cleared, then clouded again, and, once more looking about him, he asked:

"Do you suppose—it could have been something—something from the sea?"

"The blankets aren't wet," I replied soberly, stooping once more to feel them. Rogers looked at me as if he believed there might be something other than bone in my hard head.

"That's so, too. I never thought of that, either. Say, you're all right, not to laugh at a fellow. But what do you suppose it was?"

"The cat, of course," I insisted. "The door wasn't fast, it swung open with the roll of the ship. Old Gato came in to see his pal, waited a while, got tired and went back, and another roll shut the door. That's what you heard, and we're a pair of fools to be scared. And now I'm going to bed."

"Not—not there?" demanded Rogers incredulously as I started to undress.

"Where else?" I retorted. Boyish bravado would have carried me through now, but it seemed good policy to show Rogers an in- difference which I was far from feeling. He stared at me for a mo- ment, and then with a more confident step went back to his larger room across the passage. I was asleep in five minutes.

X

It was still dark in the cabin when I awoke, though my sleep seemed to have been of the usual length. Someone had put out the lamp, but the smell of stale kerosene smoke was still thick on the air, and the air itself had a sticky feeling which I could not under- stand. I dressed hurriedly by the sense of touch, went on deck, and saw what had caused the untimely darkness. The schooner was wrapped in a thick, white blanket of fog, fog so thick that one could not see twenty feet ahead of him. The mainmast towered ghostly in the gloom; the foremast I could not see at all. Voices oddly muffled came out of the fog, and water from the yards and sails drummed unevenly on the deck. Moving shadows crossed back and forth through this darkness visible, and soon, by the knobby loom of the galley, I made out a taller shadow coming my way. It was Steinmetz.

"Have you seen Señor Gato?" was his instant question.

"No," I answered. "Isn't he with you?"

"He is gone," said Steinmetz, shaking his head. "That chocolate scamp has thrown him overboard. Du lieber Gott! I have half a mind to send him along for company!"

"Let us make sure," I suggested, and we went together to make a quick search of the cabins. They showed no Gato. Steinmetz had already drawn the fo'c'sle, and had called back and forth along the deck. Señor Gato was gone, but there was still a question as to the manner of his going. I told my friend of the warm spot on the blankets the night before. He listened intently.

"And it was too big a warm place for the cat?" he inquired. "You are sure of that, very sure?"

"Perfectly sure. I didn't say so to Rogers, because there was no use adding to his scare, but I took a rough measurement of the place with my hands."

"It would be hard to enlarge that same scare," said Steinmetz. "In the phrase of your good country, he is scared stiff. So are they all. And now this verdamnt fog! Soon if we do not look out a ship without a crew we shall be. They could get a boat overboard and slip away without our knowledge now."

"They wouldn't dare, in this fog."

"Panic dares all things. There was trouble in the fo'c'sle last night, also."

"What was it?"

"Their clothes were moved, piled in a heap. So much I gathered out of their frightened lies. At first they laid it to each other, and the little Irishman slugged the big negro—the Portugee pried them apart. The negro says he never touched the clothes, and now McCarthy believes him."

"I wonder they dared to undress."

"They won't dare it again. My boy," and Steinmetz took my arm, and looked around very carefully at the white blackness before continuing, "of all the voyages on which I ever sailed, this the most mysterious is. If we had a man in command, we could weather it. Now—"

The pause was more eloquent than speech. I tried to face the problem squarely, but I got small comfort from the inspection. There was professional knowledge on board the *Nancy Hanks*; and there was courage of the sort to face the unknown. But the two qualities were hopelessly divorced. Those who would dare could not do; and those who could do would not dare. If the tension once reached the breaking point—and it seemed barely short of that now—Rogers would go with his panic-stricken crew; and nothing could save the voyage from disaster. Nay, I suppose it would have been mutiny for Steinmetz and myself to resist any order the mate in his terror might give; but, to be frank about it, that phase of the difficulty was the least of our troubles.

We were pacing the deck as we talked and pondered. The fog seemed thicker than ever. We had reached the forward limit of our beat and were ready to turn, when from a shadowy hummock on the port side, a smaller shadow seemed to separate itself. It moved, lengthened, and a ghostly, misshapen hand outlined itself in the fog; a hand such as one sees in evil dreams; a hand that reached and clutched. Long fingers opened, and closed, and opened again; and a thin shred of an arm seemed to connect them with the deeper shadow below. And then, it vanished. It did not withdraw, did not fade. One moment, it was; and the next, the fog parted, and the hand was not.

We stood as if petrified for a moment, and then with a tigerish bound which went far to explain his triumph in arms, Steinmetz sprang for the place where the hand had been. It seemed impossible that anything could move quickly enough to evade him, but he merely stumbled over the coil of rope which was the shadowy hummock, and brought up against the rail. He groped with his arms, clutching frantically, and catching nothing more substantial than the thinning mist. He plunged his hand into the hollow of the coil of rope, but it was empty. He straightened up, swearing in German, and struck his forehead with his open hand. The fog was lifting and shredding away. Looking aft, I could see the foremast and the galley, and near the galley Rogers and the black cook were standing with their heads very close together. Rogers started and turned away as we looked.

"See?" muttered Steinmetz. The wheel came into view, with Garcia in charge of it. The cook started to enter the galley, stopped stumbling as one who has brought up against an unexpected barrier, jumped back with a yell; and then—

Out of the galley came a plate. It whizzed through the air, missed the cook's head by a foot, and went over the side. A second plate smashed against the rail; a cup caught the negro squarely in the face; a light kettle clattered to the deck; and then, as a third plate struck him amidships, the black gave a scream like the squeal of a horse in mortal agony, and bolted. He dived—there is no other word for it—down the fo'c'sle hatch.

As the negro ran forward Steinmetz bounded aft and, drawing his sword as he ran, plunged into the galley. The eruption of dishes stopped. Steinmetz poked sharply around with his sword with no result, then whirled and clutched at something which I could not see. The grip was fruitless, but he emerged from the galley with a look of dawning triumph on his face—a look that turned to rage as he glanced aft. One of the boats was gone from its place. I sprang to the side and looked over. The boat had been lowered, and was lying alongside; and even in that hurried glimpse I could see that she was roughly provisioned for a voyage.

"Thought you would leave us, eh?" demanded Steinmetz, his bare sword flashing within an inch of the face of the cowering mate. "Aber, you won't. Get those fellows from the fo'c'sle up. You go with him," he added to me. "I have it now! Gott! The face of air! Get them up!"

"Come!" I yelled in the mate's ear, and plunged into the fo'c'sle ahead of him.

The negro was cowering in the farthest corner, moaning prayers to deities which his ancestors had brought from the Congo. The Portugee and McCarthy stood petrified at our sudden entry. They had been packing a kit. McCarthy held a candle, and this and the glimmer from the hatch furnished the sole light in the place. It was plain that the men and Rogers had joined in planning the desertion of the ship.

"Tumble up!" commanded Rogers, but there was no heart to the order. "The Dutchman thinks he's got the thing. Come on up."

The negro stopped moaning long enough to look around. McCarthy stooped and set the candle in a wire loop at the end of a bunk before speaking. "Ain't we goin', after all?" he demanded.

"Not yet," I answered, when Rogers failed to speak. "Go on deck as the mate tells you." The nigger buried his face in his arms again, and, seeing that he did not mean to obey, I crossed the fo'c'sle, and caught him sharply by the ear. "Here, you!" I exclaimed. "Get on deck!"

And in a breath came the climax. Even as I yanked the shivering black by the ear, I heard a scream from the Portugee, a groan from Rogers, an oath from McCarthy. I dropped the negro and looked around, and my hair rose on my head as I saw the candle flit across the fo'c'sle. It was not thrown as the dishes were thrown; it moved as if carried by a child, a child unsteady on his legs. It went to a bunk, stopped a moment, and started on to another.

I whipped out my revolver and fired. It was a clean miss, but the candle dropped to the floor, and in a second I followed it. The fist of the huge negro struck me on the back of the head, and his feet trampled me as he led the headlong rout for the deck. "A ghost carrying candles!" I heard McCarthy shriek, and then, with difficulty, I scrambled to my feet and made after the crazy sailors.

"Get back!" roared Steinmetz, and I reached the deck in time to see the stampeded mob halt for a second before the flash of his sword. We might have won yet, had we not forgotten Garcia. I saw him leap from somewhere near the wheel, and his knife gleamed through the air and sunk almost to the hilt under Steinmetz' upraised arm. The soldier sank to the deck, still holding his sword, and the sailors leaped for the boat. I had to run aft to get a shot, and Garcia was on the rail when my bullet reached him. He sprang up standing, clasping one hand on his stomach and the other over his kidneys, stood there for an interminable second, and then with a sort of tired sigh, pitched head-first to the water.

The others had already gained the boat, but they halted before the menace of my revolver.

"Come back, you curs!" I yelled, and whatever authority my voice may have lacked was supplied by the gun. They hung irresolute. "Come back and get Steinmetz or I'll blow your heads off!" I repeated.

The Portugee dropped his oar. "Eet is right," he said. He crossed himself, muttering, and climbed back aboard. It took a direct threat to bring Rogers, but he came.

"I am finished!" gasped Steinmetz as we stooped to raise him. "But there is no need to go. I the mystery have solved. The Face of Air—" He broke off and his features set with the pain of our moving him, and then he pointed forward. A thin line of smoke was coming up the fo'c'sle hatch. The candle had done its work.

The smoke settled any doubt I may have had on the course to pursue. Carefully as we might, we lowered Steinmetz to the boat, followed ourselves; and then the men grabbed their oars and pulled frantically away from the ship. At perhaps a hundred feet distant I gave the order to stop till we could care for my companion. Again I had to use direct threats to bring Rogers to compliance; but the Portugee once more set the example of obedience and helped my clumsy efforts to remove the knife and bandage the wound of my companion. The smoke column grew larger each second, rising straight in the still air.

A shrill, whining yelp, a sound like the cry of a child half frightened and half distressed came from the haunted schooner. A rope, flapping loose from the foremast, tightened suddenly in grotesque jerks, as if some creature were climbing it; then suddenly swung loose again. At the same instant there was a splash in the water ten or twelve feet from the side of the vessel, and a widening, V-shaped wake pointed our way.

And then, at the crest of a little wavelet, I saw a Thing like a big air bubble in the water; a bubble that moved and squirmed like a land creature swimming; a bubble with misshapen legs, and hairy body, and weird, half human looking feet. A cry went up from the boat's crew, but not a man retained wit enough to think of his oars.

Steinmetz caught the hand with which I was trying to stanch his bleeding and pulled himself to a sitting posture. McCarthy snatched something from the bottom of the boat and threw it at the Thing. It fell short, and the tough longshore fighter, his truculent courage all gone, dropped on his knees and screamed to me to shoot.

"Shoot, man, shoot! and Mother of God bless the bullet!" he yelled. I raised my pistol and fired. The bullet went high, and the Thing dived.

"The Face of Air! The Face of Air!" cried Steinmetz.

A Face of Air it was, and the face of an African ape as well. There was the bushy beard, from which real air bubbles detached and floated to the surface; the crest of hair that simulated a high forehead; a caricature of a man shaped of air by some grisly joker of the sea. As in a dream, I seemed to see the explanation of the whole ghastly voyage; but understanding brought no relief from horror. The head disappeared above the surface, and the wake came nearer. I fired again, and that shrill, whining yelp told that the bullet had found its mark. An arm shot above the water, was outlined for a moment in dripping spray; disappeared; and then the head sank and became horribly visible once more. The long arms lashed the water, and hands like the one we had seen in the fog swept the Thing nearer. I fired again, but it still came on. A hand shot up once more, a spray struck me in the face, a wet patch appeared on the edge of the boat; and then, almost touching the Thing, I fired my last shot. There was no more outcry; but the pitifully crooked legs stretched out helplessly, the Face of Air showed once more in the water; and with staring eyes still fixed on us, sank from sight.

We pulled a little further, for the flames were now raging on the schooner, and stopped again to do what we might for my master-at-arms. It was a hopeless case from the first. He died within an hour, and we buried him over the side at sunset. Two days later we were picked up by some Bahama wreckers. I forget what story Rogers told to account for our condition, but it was accepted. Once in a seaport, we scattered. There was no need to pledge each other to secrecy. Two dead men, an abandoned schooner, and nothing to explain these things but a tale which no jury would believe—these were better guarantees of silence than many oaths.

It was years before I followed the back track of that mysterious cook who scrawled fragments of Goethe on the walls of his galley. I learned that he was a substitute, taken on at the last moment, when the cook originally engaged failed for some reason to appear. The cage was covered when he appeared at the shipping office, and he would not allow anyone to touch it. Casting farther, I found that an old German chemist, long believed to be mad, disappeared from his lodgings about the time of the sailing of the *Nancy Hanks*. When I made sure that this old chemist likewise had a mysterious cage in his quarters, the identification was complete enough for me. What the old chemist did is easy to tell. How he did it remains—and I hope will continue to remain—a mystery. He found some way of decolourizing the luckless ape, and of reducing its tissues to the same refractive index as that of air. This done, the creature would be invisible under ordinary conditions; but in the water or in a fog would come into sight. So long as the old chemist lived he kept his ghostly pet safe. He died; perhaps he spent his last effort lifting the cage door; at any rate, the invisible ape was at large. After that, the catastrophe. Sailors' superstitions magnified the horror and the weirdness of the ensuing events, but I am not superstitious, and I protest that an angry tiger would be less daunting than the harmless, viewless mischief of that ghostly Thing.

I like to think that the first crew escaped in a boat from the haunted schooner, and that events like those which happened to us kept their lips sealed. For the four rapscallions whom we first put aboard the *Nancy Hanks* I have no hope, and no very great regret; though the bo'sun who led them deserved better followers, and a fairer fortune. As the record stands, at least six men, and all too probably eighteen, were driven to their death by a Thing that never meant them harm; were sacrificed to the wizard dream of a crazy chemist. To this day it costs me a serious effort to visit the monkey department of a menagerie. The pungent smell brings back a memory of tiny cabins and rolling floors, and shifting yellow lights, and frightened men staring at an empty bunk; and the creatures in the cages call up the picture of that other creature in the water, that Thing, with the Face of Air.

FROM THE DARKNESS AND THE DEPTHS
Morgan Robertson

I had known him for a painter of renown—a master of his art, whose pictures, which sold for high prices, adorned museums, the parlors of the rich, and, when on exhibition, were hung low and conspicuous. Also, I knew him for an expert photographer—an "art photographer," as they say, one who dealt with this branch of industry as a fad, an amusement, and who produced pictures that in composition, lights, and shades rivaled his productions with the brush.

His cameras were the best that the market could supply, yet he was able, from his knowledge of optics and chemistry, to improve them for his own uses far beyond the ability of the makers. His studio was filled with examples of his work, and his mind was stocked with information and opinions on all subjects ranging from international policies to the servant-girl problem.

He was a man of the world, gentlemanly and successful, about sixty years old, kindly and gracious of manner, and out of this kindliness and graciousness had granted me the compliment of his friendship, and access to his studio whenever I felt like calling upon him.

Yet it never occurred to me that the wonderful and technically correct marines hanging on his walls were due to anything but the artist's conscientious study of his subject, and only his casual mispronounciation of the word "leeward," which landsmen pronounce as spelled, but which rolls off the tongue of a sailor, be he former dock rat or naval officer, as "looward," and his giving the long sounds to the vowels of the words "patent" and "tackle," that induced me to ask if he had ever been to sea.

"Why, yes," he answered. "Until I was thirty I had no higher ambition than to become a skipper of some craft; but I never achieved it. The best I did was to sign first mate for one voyage—and that one was my last. It was on that voyage that I learned something of the mysterious properties of light, and it made me a photographer, then an artist. You are wrong when you say that a searchlight cannot penetrate fog."

"But it has been tried," I remonstrated.

"With ordinary light. Yes, of course, subject to refraction, reflection, and absorption by the millions of minute globules of water it encounters."

We had been discussing the wreck of the *Titanic*, the most terrible marine disaster of history, the blunders of construction and management, and the later proposed improvements as to the lowering of boats and the location of ice in a fog.

Among these considerations was also the plan of carrying a powerful searchlight whose beam would illumine the path of a twenty-knot liner and render objects visible in time to avoid them. In regard to this I had contended that a searchlight could not penetrate fog, and if it could, would do as much harm as good by blinding and confusing the watch officers and lookouts on other craft.

"But what other kind of light can be used?" I asked, in answer to his mention of ordinary light.

"Invisible light," he answered. "I do not mean the Röntgen ray, nor the emanation from radium, both of which are invisible, but neither of which is light, in that neither can be reflected nor refracted. Both will penetrate many different kinds of matter, but it needs reflection or refraction to make visible an object on which it impinges. Understand?"

"Hardly," I answered dubiously. "What kind of visible light is there, if not radium or the Röntgen ray? You can photograph with either, can't you?"

"Yes, but to see what you have photographed you must develop the film. And there is no time for that aboard a fast steamer running through the ice and the fog. No, it is mere theory, but I have an idea that the ultraviolet light—the actinic rays beyond the violet end of the spectrum, you know—will penetrate fog to a great distance, and in spite of its higher refractive power, which would distort and magnify an object, it is better than nothing."

"But what makes you think that it will penetrate fog?" I queried. "And if it is invisible itself, how will it illumine an object?"

"As to your first question," he answered, with a smile, "it is well known to surgeons that ultraviolet light will penetrate the human body to the depth of an inch, while the visible rays are reflected at the surface. And it has been known to photographers for fifty years that this light—easily isolated by dispersion through prisms—will act on a sensitized plate in an utterly dark room."

"Granted," I said. "But how about the second question? How can you see by this light?"

"There you have me," he answered. "It will need a quicker development than any now known to photography—a traveling film, for instance, that will show the picture of an iceberg or a ship before it is too late to avoid it—a traveling film sensitized by a quicker acting chemical than any now used."

"Why not puzzle it out?" I asked. "It would be a wonderful invention."

"I am too old," he answered dreamily. "My life work is about done. But other and younger men will take it up. We have made great strides in optics. The moving picture is a fact. Colored photographs are possible. The ultraviolet microscope shows us objects hitherto invisible because smaller than the wave length of visible light. We shall ultimately use this light to see through opaque objects. We shall see colors never imagined by the human mind, but which have existed since the beginning of light.

"We shall see new hues in the sunset, in the rainbow, in the flowers and foliage of forest and field. We may possibly see creatures in the air above never seen before.

"We shall certainly see creatures from the depths of the sea, where visible light cannot reach—creatures whose substance is of such a nature that it will not respond to the light it has never been exposed to—a substance which is absolutely transparent because it will not absorb, and appear black; will not reflect, and show a color of some kind; and will not refract, and distort objects seen through it."

"What!" I exclaimed. "Do you think there are invisible creatures?"

He looked gravely at me for a moment, then said: "You know that there are sounds that are inaudible to the human ear because of their too rapid vibration, others that are audible to some, but not to all. There are men who cannot hear the chirp of a cricket, the tweet of a bird, or the creaking of a wagon wheel.

"You know that there are electric currents much stronger in voltage than is necessary to kill us, but of wave frequency so rapid that the human tissue will not respond, and we can receive such currents without a shock. And I know"—he spoke with vehemence—"that there are creatures in the deep sea of color invisible to the human eye, for I have not only felt such a creature, but seen its photograph taken by the ultraviolet light."

"Tell me," I asked breathlessly. "Creatures solid, but invisible?"

"Creatures solid, and invisible because absolutely transparent. It is long since I have told the yarn. People would not believe me, and it was so horrible an experience that I have tried to forget it. However, if you care for it, and are willing to lose your sleep tonight, I'll give it to you."

He reached for a pipe, filled it, and began to smoke; and as he smoked and talked, some of the glamor and polish of the successful artist and clubman left him. He was an old sailor, spinning a yarn.

"It was about thirty years ago," he began, "or, to be explicit, twenty-nine years this coming August, at the time of the great Java earthquake. You've heard of it—how it killed seventy thousand people, thirty thousand of whom were drowned by the tidal wave.

"It was a curious phenomenon; Krakatoa Island, a huge conical mountain rising from the bottom of Sunda Strait, went out of existence, while in Java a mountain chain was leveled, and up from the bowels of the earth came an iceberg—as you might call it—that floated a hundred miles on a stream of molten lava before melting.

"I was not there; I was two hundred miles to the sou'west, first mate of one of those old-fashioned, soft-pine, centerboard barkentines—three sticks the same length, you know—with the mainmast stepped on the port side of the keel to make room for the centerboard—a craft that would neither stay, nor wear, nor scud, nor heave to, like a decent vessel.

"But she had several advantages; she was new, and well painted, deck, top-sides, and bottom. Hence her light timbers and planking were not water-soaked. She was fastened with 'trunnels,' not spikes and bolts, and hemp rigged.

"Perhaps there was not a hundredweight of iron aboard of her, while her hemp rigging, though heavier than water, was lighter than wire rope, and so, when we were hit by the back wash of that tidal wave, we did not sink, even though butts were started from one end to the other of the flimsy hull, and all hatches were ripped off.

"I have called it the back wash, yet we may have had a tidal wave of our own; for, though we had no knowledge of the frightful catastrophe at Java, still there had been for days several submarine earthquakes all about us, sending fountains of water, steam bubbles, and mud from the sea bed into the air.

"As the soundings were over two thousand fathoms in that neighborhood, you can imagine the seismic forces at work beneath us. There had been no wind for days, and no sea, except the agitation caused by the upheavals. The sky was a dull mud color, and the sun looked like nothing but a dark, red ball, rising day by day in the east, to move overhead and set in the west. The air was hot, sultry, and stifling, and I had difficulty in keeping the men—a big crew—at work.

"The conditions would try anybody's temper, and I had my own troubles. There was a passenger on board, a big, fat, highly educated German—a scientist and explorer—whom we had taken aboard at some little town on the West Australian coast, and who was to leave us at Batavia, where he could catch a steamer for Germany.

"He had a whole laboratory with him, with scientific instruments that I didn't know the names of, with maps he had made, stuffed beasts and birds he had killed, and a few live ones which he kept in cages and attended to himself in the empty hold; for we were flying light, you know, without even ballast aboard, and bound to Batavia for a cargo.

"It was after a few eruptions from the bottom of the sea that he got to be a nuisance; he was keenly interested in the strange dead fish and nondescript creatures that had been thrown up. He declared them new, unknown to science, and wore out my patience with entreaties to haul them aboard for examination and classification.

"I obliged him for a time, until the decks stank with dead fish, and the men got mutinous. Then I refused to advance the interests of science any farther, and, in spite of his excitement and pleadings, refused to litter the decks any more. But he got all he wanted of the unclassified and unknown before long.

"Tidal wave, you know, is a name we give to any big wave, and it has no necessary connection with the tides. It may be the big third wave of a series—just a little bigger than usual; it may be the ninth, tenth, and eleventh waves merged into one huge comber by uneven wind pressure; it may be the back wash from an earthquake that depresses the nearest coast, and it may be—as I think it was in our case—a wave sent out by an upheaval from the sea bed. At any rate, we got it, and we got it just after a tremendous spouting of water and mud, and a thick cloud of steam on the northern horizon.

"We saw a seeming rise to the horizon, as though caused by refraction, but which soon eliminated refraction as a cause by its becoming visible in its details—its streaks of water and mud, its irregular upper edge, the occasional combers that appeared on this edge, and the terrific speed of its approach. It was a wave, nothing else, and coming at forty knots at least.

"There was little that we could do; there was no wind, and we headed about west, showing our broadside; yet I got the men at the downhauls, clewlines, and stripping lines of the lighter kites; but before a man could leave the deck to furl, that moving mountain hit us, and buried us on our beam ends just as I had time to sing out: 'Lash yourselves, every man.'

"Then I needed to think of my own safety and passed a turn of the mizzen gaff-topsail downhaul about me, belaying to a pin as the cataclysm hit us. For the next two minutes—although it seemed an hour, I did not speak, nor breathe, nor think, unless my instinctive grip on the turns of the downhaul on the pin may have been an index of thought. I was under water; there was roaring in my ears, pain in my lungs, and terror in my heart.

"Then there came a lessening of the turmoil, a momentary quiet, and I roused up, to find the craft floating on her side, about a third out of water, but apt to turn bottom up at any moment from the weight of the water-soaked gear and canvas, which will sink, you know, when wet.

"I was hanging in my bight of rope from a belaying pin, my feet clear of the perpendicular deck, and my ears tortured by the sound of men overboard crying for help—men who had not lashed themselves. Among them I knew was the skipper, a mild-mannered little fellow, and the second mate, an incompetent tough from Portsmouth, who had caused me lots of trouble by his abuse of the men and his depending upon me to stand by him.

"Nothing could be done for them; they were adrift on the back wall of a moving mountain that towered thirty degrees above the horizon to port; and another moving mountain, as big as the first, was coming on from starboard—caused by the tumble into the sea of the uplifted water.

"Did you ever fall overboard in a full suit of clothes? If you did, you know the mighty exercise of strength required to climb out. I was a strong, healthy man at the time, but never in my life was I so tested. I finally got a grip on the belaying pin and rested; then, with an effort that caused me physical pain, I got my right foot up to the pinrail and rested again; then, perhaps more by mental strength than physical—for I loved life and wanted to live—I hooked my right foot over the rail, reached higher on the rope, rested again, and finally hove myself up to the mizzen rigging, where I sat for a few moments to get my breath, and think, and look around.

"Forward, I saw men who had lashed themselves to the starboard rail, and they were struggling, as I had struggled, to get up to the horizontal side of the vessel. They succeeded, but at the time I had no use for them. Sailors will obey orders, if they understand the orders, but this was an exigency outside the realm of mere seamanship.

"Men were drowning off to port; men, like myself, were climbing up to temporary safety afforded by the topsides of a craft on her beam ends; and aft, in the alleyway, was the German professor, unlashed, but safe and secure in his narrow confines, one leg through a cabin window, and both hands gripping the rail, while he bellowed like a bull, not for himself, however—but for his menagerie in the empty hold.

"There was small chance for the brutes—smaller than for ourselves, left on the upper rail of an over-turned craft, and still smaller than the chance of the poor devils off to port, some of whom had gripped the half-submerged top-hamper, and were calling for help.

"We could not help them; she was a Yankee craft, and there was not a life buoy or belt on board; and who, with another big wave coming, would swim down to looward with a line?

"Landsmen, especially women and boys, have often asked me why a wooden ship, filled with water, sinks, even though not weighted with cargo. Some sailors have pondered over it, too, knowing that a small boat, built of wood, and fastened with nails, will float if water-logged.

"But the answer is simple. Most big craft are built of oak or hard pine, and fastened together with iron spikes and bolts—sixty tons at least to a three-hundred-ton schooner. After a year or two this hard, heavy wood becomes water-soaked, and, with the iron bolts and spikes, is heavier than water, and will sink when the hold is flooded.

"This craft of ours was like a small boat—built of soft light wood, with trunnels instead of bolts, and no iron on board except the anchors and one capstan. As a result, though ripped, twisted, broken, and disintegrated, she still floated even on her beam ends.

"But the soaked hemp rigging and canvas might be enough to drag the craft down, and with this fear in my mind I acted quickly. Singing out to the men to hang on, I made my way aft to where we had an ax, lodged in its beckets on the after house. With this I attacked the mizzen lanyards, cutting everything clear, then climbed forward to the main.

"Hard as I worked I had barely cut the last lanyard when that second wave loomed up and crashed down on us. I just had time to slip into the bight of a rope, and save myself; but I had to give up the ax; it slipped from my hands and slid down to the port scuppers.

"That second wave, in its effect, was about the same as the first, except that it righted the craft. We were buried, choked, and half drowned; but when the wave had passed on, the main and mizzenmasts, unsupported by the rigging that I had cut away, snapped cleanly about three feet above the deck, and the broad, flat-bottomed craft straightened up, lifting the weight of the foremast and its gear, and lay on an even keel, with foresail, staysail, and jib set, the fore gaff-topsail, flying jib, and jib-topsail clewed down and the wreck of the masts bumping against the port side.

"We floated, but with the hold full of water, and four feet of it on deck amidships that surged from one rail to the other as the craft rolled, pouring over and coming back. All hatches were ripped off, and our three boats were carried away from their chocks on the house.

"Six men were clearing themselves from their lashings at the fore rigging, and three more, who had gone overboard with the first sea, and had caught the upper gear to be lifted as the craft righted, were coming down, while the professor still declaimed from the alley.

"'Hang on all,' I yelled; 'there's another sea coming.'

"It came, but passed over us without doing any more damage, and though a fourth, fifth, and sixth followed, each was of lesser force than the last, and finally it was safe to leave the rail and wade about, though we still rolled rails under in what was left of the turmoil.

"Luckily, there was no wind, though I never understood why, for earthquakes are usually accompanied by squalls. However, even with wind, our canvas would have been no use to us; for, water-logged as we were, we couldn't have made a knot an hour, nor could we have steered, even with all sail set. All we could hope for was the appearance of some craft that would tow the ripped and shivered hull to port, or at least take us off.

"So, while I searched for the ax, and the professor searched into the depths under the main hatch for signs of his menagerie—all drowned, surely—the remnant of the crew lowered the foresail and jibs, stowing them as best they could.

"I found the ax, and found it just in time; for I was attacked by what could have been nothing but a small-sized sea serpent, that had been hove up to the surface and washed aboard us. It was only about six feet long, but it had a mouth like a bulldog, and a row of spikes along its back that could have sawed a man's leg off.

"I managed to kill it before it harmed me, and chucked it overboard against the protests of the professor, who averred that I took no interest in science.

"'No, I don't,' I said to him. 'I've other things to think of. And you, too. You'd better go below and clean up your instruments, or you'll find them ruined by salt water.'

"He looked sorrowfully and reproachfully at me, and started to wade aft; but he halted at the forward companion, and turned, for a scream of agony rang out from the forecastle deck, where the men were coming in from the jibs, and I saw one of them writhing on his back, apparently in a fit, while the others stood wonderingly around.

"The forecastle deck was just out of water, and there was no wash; but in spite of this, the wriggling, screaming man slid head-first along the break and plunged into the water on the main deck.

"I scrambled forward, still carrying the ax, and the men tumbled down into the water after the man; but we could not get near him. We could see him under water, feebly moving, but not swimming; and yet he shot this way and that faster than a man ever swam; and once, as he passed near me, I noticed a gaping wound in his neck, from which the blood was flowing in a stream—a stream like a current, which did not mix with the water and discolor it.

"Soon his movements ceased, and I waded toward him; but he shot swiftly away from me, and I did not follow, for something cold, slimy, and firm touched my hand—something in the water, but which I could not see.

"I floundered back, still holding the ax, and sang out to the men to keep away from the dead man; for he was surely dead by now. He lay close to the break of the topgallant forecastle, on the starboard side; and as the men mustered around me I gave one my ax, told the rest to secure others, and to chop away the useless wreck pounding our port side—useless because it was past all seamanship to patch up that basketlike hull, pump it out, and raise jury rigging.

"While they were doing it, I secured a long pike pole from its beckets, and, joined by the professor, cautiously approached the body prodding ahead of me.

"As I neared the dead man, the pike pole was suddenly torn from my grasp, one end sank to the deck, while the other raised above the water; then it slid upward, fell, and floated close to me. I seized it again and turned to the professor.

"'What do you make of this, Herr Smidt?' I asked. 'There is something down there that we cannot see—something that killed that man. See the blood?'

"He peered closely at the dead man, who looked curiously distorted and shrunken, four feet under water. But the blood no longer was a thin stream issuing from his neck; it was gathered into a misshapen mass about two feet away from his neck.

"'Nonsense,' he answered. 'Something alive which we cannot see is contrary to all laws of physics. Der man must have fallen und hurt himself, which accounts for der bleeding. Den he drowned in der water. Do you see?—mine Gott! What iss?'

"He suddenly went under water himself, and dropping the pike pole, I grabbed him by the collar and braced myself. Something was pulling him away from me, but I managed to get his head out, and he spluttered:

"'Help! Holdt on to me. Something haf my right foot.'

"'Lend a hand here,' I yelled to the men, and a few joined me, grabbing him by his clothing. Together we pulled against the invisible force, and finally all of us went backward, professor and all, nearly to drown ourselves before regaining our feet. Then, as the agitated water smoothed, I distinctly saw the mass of red move slowly forward and disappear in the darkness under the forecastle deck.

"'You were right, mine friend,' said the professor, who, in spite of his experience, held his nerve. 'Dere is something invisible in der water—something dangerous, something which violates all laws of physics und optics. Oh, mine foot, how it hurts!'

"'Get aft,' I answered, 'and find out what ails it. And you fellows,' I added to the men, 'keep away from the forecastle deck. Whatever it is, it has gone under it.'

"Then I grabbed the pike pole again, cautiously hooked the barb into the dead man's clothing, and, assisted by the men, pulled him aft to the poop, where the professor had preceded, and was examining his ankle. There was a big, red wale around it, in the middle of which was a huge blood blister. He pricked it with his knife, then rearranged his stocking and joined us as we lifted the body.

"'Great God, sir!' exclaimed big Bill, the bosun. 'Is that Frank? I wouldn't know him.'

"Frank, the dead man, had been strong, robust, and full-blooded. But he bore no resemblance to his living self. He lay there, shrunken, shortened, and changed, a look of agony on his emaciated face, and his hands clenched—not extended like those of one drowned.

"'I thought drowned men swelled up,' ventured one of the men.

"'He was not drowned,' said Herr Smidt. 'He was sucked dry, like a lemon. Perhaps in his whole body there is not an ounce of blood, nor lymph, nor fluid of any kind.'

"I secured an iron belaying pin, tucked it inside his shirt, and we hove him overboard at once; for, in the presence of this horror, we were not in the mood for a burial service. There we were, eleven men on a water-logged hulk, adrift on a heaving, greasy sea, with a dark-red sun showing through a muddy sky above, and an invisible thing forward that might seize any of us at any moment it chose, in the water or out; for Frank had been caught and dragged down.

"Still, I ordered the men, cook, steward, and all, to remain on the poop and—the galley being forward—to expect no hot meals, as we could subsist for a time on the cold, canned food in the storeroom and lazaret.

"Because of an early friction between the men and the second mate, the mild-mannered and peace-loving skipper had forbidden the crew to wear sheath knives; but in this exigency I overruled the edict. While the professor went down into his flooded room to doctor his ankle and attend to his instruments, I raided the slop chest, and armed every man of us with a sheath knife and belt; for while we could not see the creature, we could feel it—and a knife is better than a gun in a hand-to-hand fight.

"Then we sat around, waiting, while the sky grew muddier, the sun darker, and the northern horizon lighter with a reddish glow that was better than the sun. It was the Java earthquake, but we did not know it for a long time.

"Soon the professor appeared and announced that his instruments were in good condition, and stowed high on shelves above the water.

"'I must resensitize my plates, however,' he said. 'Der salt water has spoiled them; but mine camera merely needs to dry out; und mine telescope, und mine static machine und Leyden jars— why, der water did not touch them.'

"'Well,' I answered. 'That's all right. But what good are they in the face of this emergency? Are you thinking of photographing anything now?'

"'Perhaps. I haf been thinking some.'

"'Have you thought out what that creature is—forward, there?'

"'Partly. It is some creature thrown up from der bottom of der sea, und washed on board by der wave. Light, like wave motion, ends at a certain depth, you know; und we have over twelve thousand feet beneath us. At that depth dere is absolute darkness, but we know that creatures live down dere, und fight, und eat, und die.'

"'But what of it? Why can't we see that thing?'

"'Because, in der ages that haf passed in its evolution from der original moneron, it has never been exposed to light—I mean visible light, der light that contains der seven colors of der spectrum. Hence it may not respond to der three properties of visible light—reflection, which would give it a color of some kind; absorption, which would make it appear black; or refraction, which, in der absence of der other two, would distort things seen through it. For it would be transparent, you know.'

"'But what can be done?' I asked helplessly, for I could not understand at the time what he meant.

"'Nothing, except that der next man attacked must use his knife. If he cannot see der creature, he can feel it. Und perhaps—I do not know yet—perhaps, in a way, we may see it—its photograph.'

"I looked blankly at him, thinking he might have gone crazy, but he continued.

"'You know,' he said, 'that objects too small to be seen by the microscope, because smaller than der amplitude of der shortest wave of visible light, can be seen when exposed to der ultraviolet light—der dark light beyond der spectrum? Und you know that this light is what acts der most in photography? That it exposes on a sensitized plate new stars in der heavens invisible to der eye through the strongest telescope?'

"'Don't know anything about it,' I answered. 'But if you can find a way out of this scrape we're in, go ahead.'

"'I must think,' he said dreamily. 'I haf a rock-crystal lens which is permeable to this light, und which I can place in mine camera. I must have a concave mirror, not of glass, which is opaque to this light, but of metal.'

"'What for?' I asked.

"'To throw der ultraviolet light on der beast. I can generate it with mine static machine.'

"'How will one of our lantern reflectors do? They are of polished tin, I think.'

"'Good! I can repolish one.'

"We had one deck lantern larger than usual, with a metallic reflector that concentrated the light into a beam, much as do the present day searchlights. This I procured from the lazaret, and he pronounced it available. Then he disappeared, to tinker up his apparatus.

"Night came down, and I lighted three masthead lights, to hoist at the fore to inform any passing craft that we were not under command; but, as I would not send a man forward on that job, I went myself, carefully feeling my way with the pike pole. Luckily, I escaped contact with the creature, and returned to the poop, where we had a cold supper of canned cabin stores.

"The top of the house was dry, but it was cold, especially so as we were all drenched to the skin. The steward brought up all the blankets there were in the cabin—for even a wet blanket is better than none at all—but there were not enough to go around, and one man volunteered, against my advice, to go forward and bring aft bedding from the forecastle.

"He did not come back; we heard his yell, that finished with a gurgle; but in that pitch black darkness, relieved only by the red glow from the north, not one of us dared to venture to his rescue. We knew that he would be dead, anyhow, before we could get to him; so we stood watch, sharing the blankets we had when our time came to sleep.

"It was a wretched night that we spent on the top of that after house. It began to rain before midnight, the heavy drops coming down almost in solid waves; then came wind, out of the south, cold and biting, with real waves, that rolled even over the house, forcing us to lash ourselves. The red glow to the north was hidden by the rain and spume, and, to add to our discomfort, we were showered with ashes, which, even though the surface wind was from the south, must have been brought from the north by an upper air current.

"We did not find the dead man when the faint daylight came; and so could not tell whether or not he had used his knife. His body must have washed over the rail with a sea, and we hoped the invisible killer had gone, too. But we hoped too much. With courage born of this hope a man went forward to lower the masthead lights, prodding his way with the pike pole.

"We watched him closely, the pole in one hand, his knife in the other. But he went under at the fore rigging without even a yell, and the pole went with him, while we could see, even at the distance and through the disturbed water, that his arms were close to his sides, and that he made no movement, except for the quick darting to and fro. After a few moments, however, the pike pole floated to the surface, but the man's body, drained, no doubt, of its buoyant fluids, remained on the deck.

"It was an hour later, with the pike pole for a feeler, before we dared approach the body, hook on to it, and tow it aft. It resembled that of the first victim, a skeleton clothed with skin, with the same look of horror on the face. We buried it like the other, and held to the poop, still drenched by the downpour of rain, hammered by the seas, and choked by ashes from the sky.

"As the shower of ashes increased it became dark as twilight, and though the three lights aloft burned out at about midday, I forbade a man to go forward to lower them, contenting myself with a turpentine flare lamp that I brought up from the lazaret, and filled, ready to show if the lights of a craft came in view. Before the afternoon was half gone it was dark as night, and down below, up to his waist in water, the German professor was working away.

"He came up at supper time, humming cheerfully to himself, and announced that he had replaced his camera lens with the rock crystal, that the lantern, with its reflector and a blue spark in the focus, made an admirable instrument for throwing the invisible rays on the beast, and that he was all ready, except that his plates, which he had resensitized—with some phosphorescent substance that I forget the name of, now—must have time to dry. And then, he needed some light to work by when the time came, he explained.

"'Also another victim,' I suggested bitterly; for he had not been on deck when the last two men had died.

"'I hope not,' he said. 'When we can see, it may be possible to stir him up by throwing things forward; then when he moves der water we can take shots.'

"'Better devise some means of killing him,' I answered. 'Shooting won't do, for water stops a bullet before it goes a foot into it.'

"'Der only way I can think of,' he responded, 'is for der next man—you hear me all, you men—to stick your knife at the end of the blood—where it collects in a lump. Dere is der creature's stomach, and a vital spot.'

"'Remember this, boys,' I laughed, thinking of the last poor devil, with his arms pinioned to his side. 'When you've lost enough blood to see it in a lump, stab for it.'

"But my laugh was answered by a shriek. A man lashed with a turn of rope around his waist to the stump of the mizzenmast, was writhing and heaving on his back, while he struck with his knife, apparently at his own body. With my own knife in my hand I sprang toward him, and felt for what had seized him. It was something cold, and hard, and leathery, close to his waist.

"Carefully gauging my stroke, I lunged with the knife, but I hardly think it entered the invisible fin, or tail, or paw of the monster; but it moved away from the screaming man, and the next moment I received a blow in the face that sent me aft six feet, flat on my back.

"Then came unconsciousness.

"When I recovered my senses the remnant of the crew were around me, but the man was gone—dragged out of the bight of the rope that had held him against the force of breaking seas, and down to the flooded main deck, to die like the others. It was too dark to see, or do anything; so, when I could speak I ordered all hands but one into the flooded cabin where, in the upper berths and on the top of the table, were a few dry spots.

"I filled and lighted a lantern, and gave it to the man on watch with instructions to hang it to the stump of the mizzen and to call his relief at the end of four hours. Then, with doors and windows closed, we went to sleep, or tried to go to sleep. I succeeded first, I think, for up to the last of consciousness I could hear the mutterings of the men; when I awakened, they were all asleep, and the cabin clock, high above the water, told me that, though it was still dark, it was six in the morning.

"I went on deck; the lantern still burned at the stump of miz-zenmast but the lookout was gone. He had not lived long enough to be relieved, as I learned by going below and finding that no one had been called.

"We were but six, now—one sailor and the bos'n, the cook and steward, the professor and myself."

The old artist paused, while he refilled and lighted his pipe. I noticed that the hand that held the match shook perceptibly, as though the memories of that awful experience had affected his nerves. I know that the recital had affected mine; for I joined him in a smoke, my hands shaking also.

"Why," I asked, after a moment of silence, "if it was a deep-sea creature, did it not die from the lesser pressure at the surface?"

"Why do not men die on the mountaintops?" he answered. "Or up in balloons? The record is seven miles high, I think; but they lived. They suffered from cold, and from lack of oxygen—that is, no matter how fast, or deeply they breathed, they could not get enough. But the lack of pressure did not trouble them; the human body can adjust itself.

"Conversely, however, an increase of pressure may be fatal. A man dragged down more than one hundred and fifty feet may be crushed; and a surface fish sent to the bottom of the sea may die from the pressure. It is simple; it is like the difference between a weight lifted from us and a weight added."

"Did this thing kill any more men?" I asked.

"All but the professor and myself, and it almost killed me. Look here." He removed his cravat and collar, pulled down his shirt, and exposed two livid scars about an inch in diameter, and two apart.

"I lost all the blood I could spare through those two holes," he said, as he readjusted his apparel; "but I saved enough to keep me alive."

"Go on with the yarn," I asked. "I promise you I will not sleep to-night."

"Perhaps I will not sleep myself," he answered, with a mournful smile. "Some things should be forgotten, but as I have told you this much I may as well finish, and be done with it.

"It was partly due to a sailor's love for tobacco, partly to our cold, drenched condition. A sailor will starve quietly, but go crazy if deprived of his smoke. This is so well known at sea that a skipper, who will not hesitate to sail from port with rotten or insufficient food for his men, will not dare take a chance without a full supply of tobacco in the slop chest.

"But our slop chest was under water, and the tobacco utterly useless. I did not use it at the time, but I fished some out for the others. It did not do; it would not dry out to smoke, and the salt in it made it unfit to chew. But the bos'n had an upper bunk in the forward house, in which was a couple of pounds of navy plug, and he and the sailor talked this over until their craving for a smoke overcame their fear of death.

"Of course, by this time, all discipline was ended, and all my commands and entreaties went for nothing. They sharpened their knives, and, agreeing to go forward, one on the starboard rail, the other on the port, and each to come to the other's aid if called, they went up into the darkness of ashes and rain. I opened my room window, which overlooked the main deck, but could see nothing.

"Yet I could hear; I heard two screams for help, one after the other—one from the starboard side, the other from the port, and knew that they were caught. I closed the window, for nothing could be done.

"What manner of thing it was that could grab two men so far apart nearly at the same time was beyond all imagining.

"I talked to the steward and cook, but found small comfort. The first was a Jap, the other a Chinaman, and they were the old-fashioned kind—what they could not see with their eyes, they could not believe. Both thought that all those men who had met death had either drowned or died by falling. Neither understood—and, in fact, I did not myself—the theories of Herr Smidt. He had stopped his cheerful humming to himself now, and was very busy with his instruments.

"'This thing,' I said to him, 'must be able to see in the dark. It certainly could not have heard those two men, over the noise of the wind, sea, and rain.'

"'Why not?' he answered, as he puttered with his wires. 'Cats and owls can see in the dark, und the accepted explanation is that by their power of enlarging der pupils they admit more light to the retina. But that explanation never satisfied me. You haf noticed, haf you not, that a cat's eyes shine in der dark, but only when der cat is looking at you?—that is, when it looks elsewhere you do not see der shiny eyes.'

"'Yes,' I answered, 'I have noticed that.'

"'A cat's eyes are searchlights, but they send forth a visible light, such as is generated by fireflies, und some fish. Und dere are fish in der upper tributaries of der Amazon which haf four eyes, der two upper of which are searchlights, der two lower of which are organs of percipience or vision. But visible light is not der only light. It is possible that the creature out on deck generates the invisible light, and can see by it.'

"'But what does it all amount to?' I asked impatiently.

"'I haf told you,' he answered calmly. 'Der creature may live in an atmosphere of ultraviolet light, which I can generate mineself. When mine plates dry, und it clears off so I can see what I am doing, I may get a picture of it. When we know what it is, we may find means of killing it.'

"'God grant that you succeed,' I answered fervently. 'It has killed enough of us.'

"But, as I said, the thing killed all but the professor and myself. And it came about through the other reason I mentioned—our cold, drenched condition. If there is anything an Oriental loves above his ancestors, it is his stomach; and the cold, canned food was palling upon us all. We had a little light through the downpour of ashes and rain about mid-day, and the steward and cook began talking about hot coffee.

"We had the turpentine torch for heating water, and some coffee, high and dry on a shelf in the steward's storeroom, but not a pot, pan, or cooking utensil of any kind in the cabin. So these two poor heathen, against my expostulations—somewhat faint, I admit, for the thought of hot coffee took away some of my common sense—went out on the deck and waded forward, waist-deep in the water, muddy now, from the downfall of ashes.

"I could see them as they entered the galley to get the coffee-pot, but, though I stared from my window until the blackness closed down, I did not see them come out. Nor did I hear even a squeal. The thing must have been in the galley.

"Night came on, and, with its coming, the wind and rain ceased, though there was still a slight shower of ashes. But this ended toward midnight, and I could see stars overhead and a clear horizon. Sleep, in my nervous, overwrought condition, was impossible; but the professor, after the bright idea of using the turpentine torch to dry out his plates, had gone to his fairly dry berth, after announcing his readiness to take snapshots about the deck in the morning.

"But I roused him long before morning. I roused him when I saw through my window the masthead and two side lights of a steamer approaching from the starboard, still about a mile away. I had not dared to go up and rig that lantern at the mizzen stump; but now I nerved myself to go up with the torch, the professor following with his instruments.

"'You cold-blooded crank,' I said to him, as I waved the torch. 'I admire your devotion to science, but are you waiting for that thing to get me?'

"He did not answer, but rigged his apparatus on the top of the cabin. He had a Wimshurst machine—to generate a blue spark, you know—and this he had attached to the big deck light, from which he had removed the opaque glass. Then he had his camera, with its rock-crystal lens.

"He trained both forward, and waited, while I waved the torch, standing near the stump with a turn of rope around me for safety's sake in case the thing seized me; and to this idea I added the foolish hope, aroused by the professor's theories, that the blinding light of the torch would frighten the thing away from me as it does wild animals.

"But in this last I was mistaken. No sooner was there an answering blast of a steam whistle, indicating that the steamer had seen the torch, than something cold, wet, leathery, and slimy slipped around my neck. I dropped the torch, and drew my knife, while I heard the whir of the static machine as the professor turned it.

"'Use your knife, mine friend,' he called. 'Use your knife, und reach for any blood what you see.'

"I knew better than to call for help, and I had little chance to use the knife. Still, I managed to keep my right hand, in which I held it, free, while that cold, leathery thing slipped farther around my neck and waist. I struck as I could, but could make no impression; and soon I felt another stricture around my legs, which brought me on my back. Still another belt encircled me, and, though I had come up warmly clad in woolen shirts and monkey jacket, I felt these garments being torn away from me. Then I was dragged forward, but the turn of rope had slipped down toward my waist, and I was merely bent double.

"And all the time that German was whirling his machine, and shouting to strike for any blood I saw. But I saw none. I felt it going, however. Two spots on my chest began to smart, then burn as though hot irons were piercing me. Frantically I struck, right and left, sometimes at the coils encircling me, again in the air. Then all became dark.

"I awakened in a stateroom berth, too weak to lift my hands, with the taste of brandy in my mouth and the professor standing over me with a bottle in his hand.

"'Ach, it is well,' he said. 'You will recover. You haf merely lost blood, but you did the right thing. You struck with your knife at the blood, and you killed the creature. I was right. Heart, brain, und all vital parts were in der stomach.'

"'Where are we now?' I asked, for I did not recognize the room.

"'On board der steamer. When you got on your feet und staggered aft, I knew you had killed him, and gave you my assistance. But you fainted away. Then we were taken off. Und I haf two or three beautiful negatives, which I am printing. They will be a glorious contribution to der scientific world.'

"I was glad that I was alive, yet not alive enough to ask any more questions. But next day he showed me the photographs he had printed."

"In Heaven's name, what was it?" I asked excitedly, as the old artist paused to empty and refill his pipe.

"Nothing but a giant squid, or octopus. Except that it was bigger than any ever seen before, and invisible to the eye, of course. Did you ever read Hugo's terrible story of Gilliat's fight with a squid?"

I had, and nodded.

"Hugo's imagination could not give him a creature—no matter how formidable—larger than one of four feet stretch. This one had three tentacles around me, two others gripped the port and starboard pin-rails, and three were gripping the stump of the mainmast. It had a reach of forty feet, I should think, comparing it with the beam of the craft.

"But there was one part of each picture, ill defined and missing. My knife and right hand were not shown. They were buried in a dark lump, which could be nothing but the blood from my veins. Unconscious, but still struggling, I had struck into the soft body of the monster, and struck true."

SISTER HANNAH
Charles Loring Jackson

I passed the year after my graduation from College in the Law School, although I had no intention of practising law or, for that matter, any other profession. The truth was I had a wild notion that some little knowledge of the law might help me in the management of my property; but long before the end of the year I got that bee out of my bonnet, and also found without the slightest question that the law was not for me, or I was not for the law.

Even in the early spring I began to talk of the coming vacation as my last, "because I must take up the serious business of life in the autumn," or at any rate come to a decision whether I should take up any business at all, or knock about the world for a year or two.

On the whole I inclined to the idea of plunging into work, as I found this added a decided zest to my plans for this "last" vacation. So I put a great deal of time and thought into trying to find the most attractive way of spending it, and in the end decided to take a journey on horseback through northern New England.

Rather to my surprise there was no hitch in my plans; and the journey began quite as pleasantly as I had hoped, except for the country inns. How I did suffer from them! At that time they had reached their very lowest ebb and were marvels of shabbiness and discomfort, because the stagecoaches had vanished long ago, and motor cars were not heard of till many a year afterward.

By far the worst I came across was in an unfrequented part of New Hampshire far from any railroad. That morning, in spite of a

black and threatening sky, I had left quarters with nothing to rec-
ommend them, and pushed on, paying no attention to little spurts
of rain, until about noon the scattered showers changed into a soak-
ing downpour, and drove me to take refuge in the public house of
a little village. The stale rancid smell which met me in the doorway, would have driven me out again, if the rain pelting on my
back had not convinced me that in such a storm it was better to
make even a port like this.

What a hole it was! I shudder even now when I think of those
meals— Well! the less said about them the better! And then that
long dreary afternoon in the close fetid bar! Time after time I decided I must get out of it, only to glance at the streaming windows,
and realize a start might land me in nearly as bad quarters (there
could not be worse) with the added misery of a thorough ducking.
As to the bed—one look at it was enough, and I passed the whole of
that wretched endless night perched on a hard, uncompromising
wooden chair. How I longed for the sunrise! And, when at last it
came, what a relief it was to look out on a bright morning washed
clean by last night's rain. I had begun to doubt if anything could
ever be clean again.

I was glad enough to shake off the dust of the inn, so far as it
was possible; and, as I rode down the village street beneath its arch-
ing elms, I breathed in great draughts of the clear clean air to try
and drive the fustiness out of my lungs. My horse had evidently
fared much better than I, and after such light work the day before
was in uproarious spirits, so, when a boy with a drum came out of
one of the last houses in the village, he laid back his ears, arched
his back, and broke into a spanking gallop. I, too, was quite ready
for a scamper, so I gave him his head, and we must have run nearly
a quarter of a mile before he shied at nothing, so far as I could see,
and getting into a mud puddle slipped, and fell, throwing me
against a stone wall with such force that I was completely stunned.

When I came to myself, I was dimly conscious of some one
bending over me, and faintly heard a woman's voice, as if at a great
distance, saying:

"We ought to carry him into the house."

And the muffled answer:

"No! Elizabeth. No! We can't do that."

"But Mehitable," said the first voice, "it seems as if he were kinder sent to us by Providence. We must take him in. We cannot let him lie here."

The other sighed deeply.

"Well! If you say so, I suppose we must, so call Ann and—"

Here I dropped off again and must have been unconscious a long time, as, when at last I came to my senses, I found I had been put to bed. As I opened my eyes, a most attractive old lady got up from a rocking-chair nearby, and told me that I must not try to talk, as I had had a serious accident, but I was in good hands, and would be well taken care of.

There was no doubt about the accident. My left arm had been broken, and an injury to my head was, I believe, even worse, although I was never entirely clear as to its nature, but suspect I understood it quite as well as the village doctor. If, however, the doctor left much to be desired, I was most fortunate in my kind hostesses, the Misses Hastings, for I could not have fallen upon more devoted care, or more comfortable quarters.

Their father, as I heard later, had been the beloved physician of this whole region, and after his death, now almost twenty years ago, his daughters had come to this retired house about a quarter of a mile from the village, and had lived here ever since. In the long hours I passed in bed I often speculated on the reason for this. It certainly was very inconvenient in many ways, especially as the two dear old ladies were the great people of the place. They visited the poor and the sick, presided at choir practice, managed the church sewing society, and in all other ways were the undisputed leaders of the village activities. Why then should they prefer to carry on all this business at arm's length, instead of living in the village itself?

The part of Lady Bountiful suited them to perfection; and, when they spoke of "the villagers" in a tone, which implied "the tenantry," if I felt inclined to smile, it was a kindly smile, as this innocent pride added a last quaint touch to their gracious and charming personalities. I, at least, had reason to be grateful to it, for, when I had offered to relieve them of the burden of my presence, as soon as I could be moved, Miss Elizabeth had said:

"No! The villagers are very good people, and would do their best for you, but none of them know how to take care of a gentleman. You will stay here."

I was only too glad to do so, as it was not at all likely that I should be so comfortable with one of "the villagers," even at the very best, and, when I thought of that perfectly impossible tavern, I shuddered to think what the worst might be.

Later, however, when I thought I was well enough to travel as far as the nearest town, where decent quarters might be found, I offered once more to go away, rather, I confess, as a matter of form than with any idea that my offer would be accepted, so imagine my disappointment, when Miss Mehitable thanked me, and said she thought I had better go! This was a cruel blow, but it brought its own remedy in the shape of a relapse, which sent me back to bed for nearly a week; and after that they would not hear of my leaving them, until I was entirely well.

Getting well was far from unpleasant. While I was confined to the house, I could enjoy the beautiful views from the windows, and the thought of the delightful walks in the woods they promised later, while before I grew strong enough, there would be long lazy days in the garden at the back of the house. This had a tantalizing air of mystery, since it was cut off from the outside world by a solid fence nearly fifteen feet high. What could be the need of such a fence? Once, when I asked Miss Elizabeth about it, she seemed much more embarrassed than the occasion called for, and after a great deal of hesitation at last could find nothing better to say than "We are fond of our privacy."

When I was well enough to go into the garden it appeared its only door opened from the house, and was locked; and, the key could not be found for half an hour, and then only after a decided flurry in the household. The garden itself, after I succeeded in getting through its defenses, was very pleasant—full of clove-pinks, sweet Williams, larkspurs, southern wood, and such old-fashioned plants arranged with a delicate grace and even a sportive fancy most unlike the primness, I should have expected from the Misses Hastings, but I could not see why either these flowers, charming as they were, or the fruit, of which there was but little, should need such exaggerated protection, for, even if they had been much better worth stealing, there were no thieves in this idyllic region.

The next time I asked to go into the garden, the key was not to be found; and, as I saw that for some unexplained reason my visits to it were unwelcome to my kind hostesses, I did not try again; and afterwards when I was able to take longer walks, I ceased to regret the fenced-in garden.

At about this time I made the acquaintance of "the villagers," and became a lion for the first and last time in my life. The coming of a stranger was more than an event, it was an adventure in their quiet secluded lives, and they made such good use of it that I was nearly swamped with invitations.

Among the first of these was one from Miss Sims, the village mantua-maker. To my great delight there were many of these quaint old-fashioned words common in our village. She received me in great state, wearing her black mitts until we sat down to tea; and after I had done what justice I could to her eight sorts of cake and other delicacies, and we had nearly finished, she suddenly fired the question at me:

"What do you think of the Misses Hastings' sister Hannah?"

"Their sister Hannah!" said I. "What do you mean? Have they got a sister?"

"Yes they hev," said she. "Hain't you seen her yet?"

"Seen her? You don't mean to say she is at home. But that is too absurd! There is not a soul in the house, but Miss Mehitable, Miss Elizabeth, and Ann."

"Do tell!" said she. "Well! I did hear as Hannah was kep' powerful close, but I had no idee it was so close, as all that comes to."

Here I realized that, supposing the Misses Hastings had a secret, it was not for me to pry into it; and I tried to turn the conversation, but it was no use until Miss Sims had told me everything she knew. This was little enough, and stripped of guesses and exaggerations came to this: The suppositious Miss Hastings, about twenty years old, was a half-sister of my two friends, and had always lived in the greatest seclusion, her very existence being concealed as far as possible. Miss Sims herself, had never seen her, but the few who had said she was "uncommon hahnsome."

As I walked home that night I did my best not to think of this possible secret, but the more I tried the more I dwelt upon it, and I could not help remembering many things which might show that there was someone else in the house beside the two old ladies and their hard-featured Yankee servant Ann. For instance, more than once I had heard someone walking about in the upper story when I was sure that all the acknowledged members of the family were downstairs. Then, too, every evening after dark one of the three women took a long walk; and, when I had offered my escort to one of the ladies, it had been refused with great embarrassment. Further—and this was the most striking thing I had noticed—one day I found on the sitting-room table a strange work box, very different from the prim business-like box of either of the ladies, or the capacious ark with which Ann did the family mending. This was dainty, almost coquettish, and I felt sure must belong to a charming young girl. While I was looking at it, Miss Elizabeth came in, and after a second or two of half-frightened hesitation succeeded in finding an obviously transparent pretext for calling my attention away from the box, hid it behind her back, and then scuttled out of the room entirely forgetting her usual quiet primness.

I spent most of that night and the next day in thinking of the possible Sister Hannah, and all the time my conscience kept insisting that I ought to go away, before I intruded further; but it was so hard to leave the dear old ladies and such pleasant quarters, that I was still trying to find an excuse for avoiding this unpleasant duty, when a decision was forced on me.

The next afternoon I started on one of the long walks, now my principal amusement, but, as the day was close and sultry, and my arm unusually painful, after walking a few minutes I gave it up and went home again. The sitting room looked so cool and inviting that I turned into it, and had reached the middle of the room, before I realized I was not alone. Seated in a rocking chair by the shaded window was a young girl, and, although I saw only her back, her graceful slender figure in its well-fitting blue dress, and her thick coil of yellow hair made a most attractive picture. On the window-sill at her elbow stood the work-box. This then was the mysterious Sister Hannah; but, as I realized this, I saw also that if possible, I ought to escape before she found out I was there, and in trying to do this I must have made noise enough to attract her attention, for she sprang from her chair, turned toward me—and vanished!

I could not believe my eyes! She was gone, absolutely gone!

I ran to the window—no one!

As I stood gazing at the empty chair in blank astonishment, I heard a stifled little laugh from the other side of the room, and the door was shut gently.

What did it mean?

Could I possibly have imagined the whole thing? But no! It was too vivid and detailed for that, and, besides, there by the window still lay the telltale work-box.

What did it mean?

This question I asked myself over and over again all the after-noon, and was as far from an answer as ever, when I went down to tea. There the sight of Miss Mehitable and Miss Elizabeth reminded me of my obligations to them, and I was thoroughly ashamed that I could have forgotten them even for a minute. My only excuse was that the strangeness of my experience had driven everything else out of my head.

They seemed to be quite aware I had something to tell them; but I was kept silent by the fear that I might hurt their feelings, if I spoke without the most careful preparation, and, therefore, as soon as tea was over I bade them good night without a word about the encounter of the afternoon, to their very evident disappoint-ment. I vowed to myself, however, they should have an explana-tion the first thing in the morning, and was only sorry that they would have to wait till then.

That night after I had carefully planned what I meant to say to the two old ladies, I lay awake a long time thinking disconsolately that this explanation would undoubtedly drive me away from these friends, who had become so dear to me, and a good deal to my surprise I found my thoughts were also dwelling continually on that graceful little figure and mass of yellow hair, and that I could not bear the thought of going away without seeing them again.

Next morning at breakfast, when I said I had something important to tell them, they showed no surprise, and after the meal—I, at least, had little appetite for it—they ushered me into the awful, but somewhat musty stateliness of the parlor, and there, after we were seated, I said:

"By accident I seem to have come upon a secret of yours and have decided the only thing for me to do is to go away at once. I mean to start today for the nearest town, and I am now well enough to reach it without danger to my health."

"Thank you!" said Miss Mehitable. "Elizabeth and I knew you would act in the kindest and most considerate way. I cannot tell you how sorry we are to have you go, but really, we can find nothing else to do."

So, after telling them how I hated to say goodbye, I went upstairs to pack.

Packing with a broken arm is slow work at best, but it becomes slower than slow, when after putting each of your belongings into the valise you sit for half an hour brooding over the bad luck, which obliges you to go away, so it was within half an hour of the noon dinner time when at last I got it done, and came downstairs. The door of the parlor was open, and there sat the Misses Hastings with an air of flurried importance. They called to me to come in, and Miss Mehitable, now and then catching her breath a little as she spoke, told me:

"Elizabeth and I have been talking it over, and she says it seems as if Providence had kinder sent you to us, so (I hope it is wise) we have decided to tell you about our dear Sister Hannah."

Here is the story and I wish I could give it in her words: Their father, when he was already an old man, married as his second wife a girl several years younger than his daughters; and then after a few months of happiness their misfortunes began. A paralytic stroke changed Dr. Hastings from a hale old man into a feeble invalid; and, when they were beginning to get over this blow, and the birth of a child should have brought back happiness to them, it turned out instead an even greater misfortune, for, when Miss Mehitable laid the baby in the cradle, it vanished completely. While they were staring at the empty cradle in blank amazement, the shrieks of the young mother called them to her side. The shock had been too much for her, and she fell into convulsions, which ended in her death less than half an hour later. This double loss prostrated Dr. Hastings with a second attack so alarming that his daughters had no time or thought for anything else.

About three hours later, while they were still working over him, they were startled by hearing a child cry. Miss Mehitable followed the sound, and it led her to the chamber where the body of the young mother lay. As the noise came from the cradle she put her hands into it, when she felt the child, although she could not see the slightest sign of it. To hush the pitiful crying she picked up the invisible baby, laid it across her knee, and then saw it, for, while its back was like that of any other child it was entirely invisible when looked at from in front.

The girl had never lost this strange peculiarity; and, as they had no wish to expose her to the talk of the villagers, after the death of their father, who followed his wife in less than a week, they built this house farther from prying eyes than their old home in the village street, and had brought her up here in absolute secrecy, themselves attending to her education to the best of their ability, as Miss Mehitable said bridling a little. This, I was sure, had left nothing to be desired, as the two ladies were perfect examples of the cultivated New England gentlewoman.

Miss Hannah was now eighteen, and of late they had begun to doubt, whether such a lonely existence was good for her, and to wish that she might have some companions more suited to her age than three old women.

Then my accident had thrown me into the family, but, even in the face of what seemed a direct interposition of Providence, they could not make up their minds to tell the secret, which they had

guarded so jealously through all these years. In fact, after I had
seen her, it took a great deal of discussion and much hesitation,
before they could decide to introduce me to their sister, and ask
me to stay, as long as I wished, so that she might have some youthful companionship.

After I had accepted this invitation with perhaps too much eagerness, Miss Elizabeth left the room and, coming back presently said:

"Let me introduce you to my sister, Hannah."

I bowed, although I could see no one, and a low sweet voice
said: "I suppose I must turn around, if you are to see me."

And at once that well-remembered, graceful back came into
sight from the empty air before me. We sat down, and after the
first natural stiffness had worn off, the time before dinner passed
in pleasant talk.

There was something very touching in her voice. It was quiet
and sweet, with even a little humorous appreciation of the oddity
of the situation, but penetrating and coloring it all was a strong
tinge of pathos showing that the strange fate, which cut her off
from her kind, was always present in her thoughts. She was cheerful, often even merry, but this was all thrown into relief, like sunlight striking across clouds, by that background of pathetic isolation.

After this the time went only too quickly. The long days in the
fenced-in garden were most delightful in the warm summer
weather. We talked for hours in the old-fashioned arbor, for it was
impossible to satisfy her eager curiosity about the great world she
had never seen; or, when, tired of sitting still, we set to work on
the flowers, I became the learner and caught from her that love of
gardening, which has been one of the greatest pleasures of my life;
or again, if our spirits boiled over, we chased one another round
the flower beds, like a couple of children.

In the walks after dark I now acted as her escort; in fact, there
was hardly an hour from morning till night when we were not together, so it was not surprising that after a week of this delightful
life I found I was deeply in love with Hannah. What though I had
never seen her? Do you have to see a bobolink to love it?

As soon as I realized my feelings, I spoke to her sisters. At first surprise overwhelmed all other feelings.

"What! That child!"

But this at once gave place to delight at my news; and so I entered upon the great happiness of my life.

There was nothing to prevent me from settling down in the farmhouse after our marriage, but it was necessary to arrange my affairs in Boston, before I cut loose from it forever, so after a fortnight of paradise I reluctantly said good-bye to Hannah, and travelled to Boston—a really terrible journey.

Beside making my arrangements there I went to Cambridge to call on my best friend, Professor Tane, who early in my college course had rescued me from a serious trouble with the dean; and, what was more to me, had succeeded in getting me out of a rather bad set, in which I had become entangled.

As I had no secrets from him, I told him the great news, and gave him an invitation from the Misses Hastings to come back with me for a visit. He was very glad to accept it, as his plans for the summer having miscarried, it had looked as if he would be obliged to pass the whole vacation in Cambridge.

When he was introduced to Hannah, he bowed to entirely the wrong part of the room to our great amusement, Hannah's merry laugh bubbling out with the rest. This broke the ice completely, and the evening passed most pleasantly.

After tea I gave Hannah several pieces of jewelry that had belonged to my mother. Among them there was one in particular—a necklace of spar beads—which would suit her to perfection, if she looked as my imagination pictured her. How I wished I could see if it really was as becoming, as I thought! She liked it as much as I did, and was so delighted with it, for she had a young girl's fondness for jewels, that she put it on and wore it the whole of the evening.

After the ladies had gone to bed, we went out on the porch for a smoke, and Professor Tane congratulated me most heartily.

"You are a very lucky fellow!" said he. "Miss Hastings is perfectly charming; but what an astonishing thing this partial invisibility is! It seems incredible. In fact, before I saw her, I thought you were trying to play off some huge practical joke on me, although it seemed hard to reconcile it with your state of mushy happiness; and even when I have seen her, or rather have not seen her, I find it hard to believe my senses. It is certainly most interesting, and"— after a pause— "I wonder if I may have found the explanation for it."

At this I was all attention.

"Did you notice," he went on, "that when she wore those spar beads you could see them?"

"Why!" said I, "why yes! I believe I did see them in an indistinct sort of way."

"I saw them plainly," said he.

And then he launched out into a long explanation, which at the time I thought I understood perfectly, but now that I try to repeat it, I find much of it is very misty. It seems that this spar (I think he called it fluor-spar) has the power of changing the color of the light, which falls upon it. For instance, it turns white light to purple, and this makes pieces that are really white look purple. Now, as we could see the beads when Hannah was wearing them, Professor Tane thought that she might give off from in front only invisible light, which in passing through the beads was turned into visible light.

Invisible light was a strange idea to me. It seemed like a contradiction in terms, but Professor Tane told me that sunlight contains a good many more of these invisible, ultraviolet rays, than of the visible ones. (That word ultraviolet has stuck in my memory anyway!) When I asked how they knew there was such a thing as invisible light, he said one way was by letting it fall on this spar, which made it into visible light, and another was by photographing it.

"So," said he, "if Miss Hannah does give off ultraviolet rays,"—

"We can photograph her!" shouted I.

"Oh! You have taken in that idea, have you?" said he. "Of course we can, that is, if my explanation is the right one, but there are so many weak spots in it that I would not crow till we see if it works."

Fortunately it was easy to test it, as he had brought his photographic kit with him, and we agreed the experiment should be tried the first thing in the morning.

I got the Professor out of bed at a perfectly unearthly hour, and sent the exciting news to the ladies by Ann, whose work always began at daybreak. They soon joined us, and we waited with the utmost impatience, till the light became strong enough. Hannah was as eager as any of us, for she, poor girl, felt an intense curiosity to know what she looked like.

When at last the moment arrived, there arose the difficulty of focussing the camera upon her, but the Professor was equal to the occasion. He made a pile of books on a table beside her, focussed the machine on that, and then swung it around, until it covered the chair, on which she was sitting.

I shall never forget our excitement, as we crowded round the Professor in the closet we had converted into a dark room, anxiously craning our necks to get a glimpse of the plate, nor how simply interminable the development of that plate seemed, although it could not have taken more than a few minutes. At last the image appeared, but what a disappointment! There was an excellent picture of the chair, but not the least sign of Hannah.

This blow, which destroyed his theory, seemed to crush Professor Tane. He stared at the plate in a dazed sort of way a minute or so, and then struck himself a tremendous blow on the forehead.

"I ought to resign my professorship," said he. "I am not fit to teach chemistry in a primary school."

"Why! What is the matter?"

"Matter enough! Glass absorbs the ultraviolet rays, so none of them could get through the lens."

"Then we must give it up?"

"O no! Not at all! They pass easily through quartz, and luckily I happen to have a very good quartz lens."

"Oh! Let us try it at once!" we all cried, but he answered sadly:

"It is in Cambridge."

However, he was certainly most obliging, for after only one day of rest he took that terrible journey again; and came back as soon as he could have the quartz lens fitted to his camera, so that our suspense lasted only a few days.

Then came the sitting as before, and the endless waiting, while he developed the plate, but even that was done at last, and for the first time we all saw Hannah. There she sat, or rather half of her, for the Professor had turned the camera a little too far, but that was no matter, as here was the proof that we could photograph her, and before night we had a great many good pictures, and knew how she looked almost as well as if we could see her in the ordinary way.

How can I describe her demure, pathetic charm, lighted by a gleam of fun playing in her eyes? But why should I try? No words could make you see her, or bring before you her fresh sweet New England beauty.

That evening, as we were smoking on the porch, I congratulated Professor Tane on the confirmation of his theory, and he certainly did seem pretty well pleased with himself.

He then told me that we could come even nearer to making Hannah visible, as there were several other things, which like the spar change invisible into visible light, and, as some of them are taken up by water, if we bathed her face and dress in them, we ought to be able to see her actually.

I was so delighted at this that I jumped up, and shook his hand vigorously, but I suppose my raptures must have been too much for him, as he at once spoilt my pleasure by telling me that the best we could do would be to make her bright sky blue, or vivid parrot green.

In spite of this, however, I decided that we ought to try the experiment, because the little knowledge of law I had picked up in the Law School was proving, if not a dangerous, at least an uncomfortable thing. I learned then that a marriage to be legal must take place in the presence of witnesses, but would this be the case when the witnesses could see only part of Hannah?

This doubt was absurd, I imagine, but, as we could not be too careful, we made up our minds after some discussion to try to make Hannah visible on the wedding day. Good-natured Professor Tane offered to go to Boston again to get the things that we needed, but we were not inhuman enough to ask him to start at once, so he passed a pleasant week at the farmhouse, and then ventured once more on that most repulsive journey.

Before he started for Cambridge, he said to me:

"You will not want to have the villagers chattering about your bride, as they certainly will, if you have the village minister, so why wouldn't it be a good plan to get my classmate, Forrest, to marry you? He has a parish in Nashua, and, as he is unmarried, there will be no danger that the secret will leak out through him."

I was amused that he should have learned already to speak of the villagers as we do, but I must say, too, that I thought he need not be jeering at women all the time, even if he is such a confirmed old bachelor.

Two days before the wedding, when Professor Tane came back with his pleasant friend, Mr. Forrest, he was in high feather, for he told us a new chemical—Magdala red—had been discovered, which would make a very good flesh color, and he had been lucky enough to get some of it for Hannah's face and hands. So all the next morning he was very busy making this wash for Hannah, and two others, in which Ann was to soak the wedding dress and veil.

Of course, I was not allowed to see her until the ceremony, but, when she came into the parlor my fears of legal difficulties vanished completely, for you could see her, I must confess a little vaguely and indistinctly, but she was visible without the slightest question. I cannot say much for the flesh color, of which Professor Tane was so proud. I should call it a pale brick red, but then it looked much better for her face and hands than the sky blue of the dress, or the bright yellowish green of the veil.

It was a great pleasure really to see her, but I have never repeated the experiment, although Professor Tane was kind enough to give me a good supply of each of the washes. To tell the truth the effect was a trifle ghastly, and beside I do not want to run any risk of hurting my wife's complexion.

These proofs of Professor Tane's theory were enough for me, but evidently they did not satisfy him, for some years later, when the Roentgen rays were discovered, he came to me with a new one, which, he said, explained some facts in Hannah's case that were not in harmony with his first theory. I took little interest in it, however, for even if I could have understood it, I feel that Hannah is far too sacred to be made an object of study.

Since our marriage my life has run on quietly, but most happily in the farmhouse. I have devoted myself to photography, and have probably the finest quartz lenses in the world, so that now my collection of over three thousand photographs of Hannah makes me nearly as familiar with her, as if I could see her always.

None of our children, I am happy to say, take after their mother, but I noticed that, when the older children asked "Where is Mamma?" our second girl, Lizzie, could always point her out. This led me to ask Professor Tane to examine her eyes, and he found that she could see the ultraviolet rays, which was a most fortunate discovery for her, as she had always been nearly blinded by the sunlight, and no wonder, poor child, since for her it was more than twice as bright as for the eyes of us common people. The trouble was remedied by spectacles made of window glass, which cut off the ultraviolet rays, and with these she can bear the sun as well as any one.

So my life glides away. People may wonder how I can bear to be so entirely cut off from all the rest of the world, but I do not miss it, for Hannah is all the world to me.

Coachwhip Publications

COACHWHIPBOOKS.COM

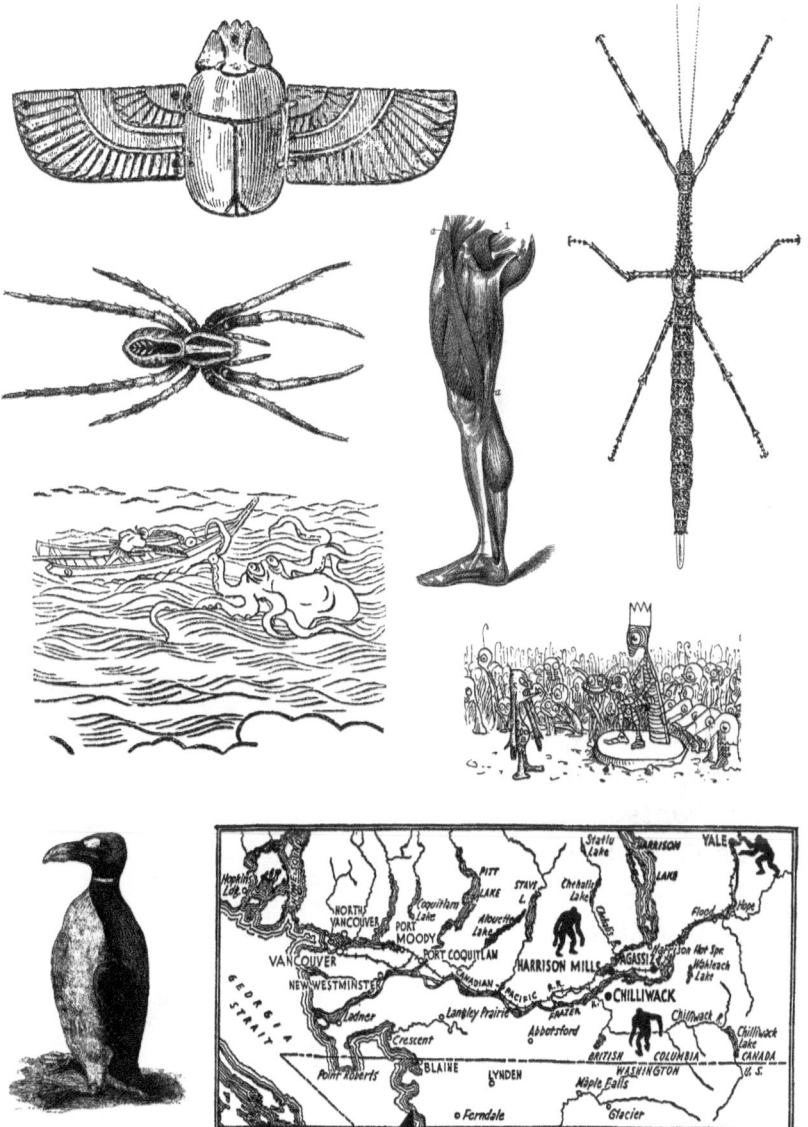

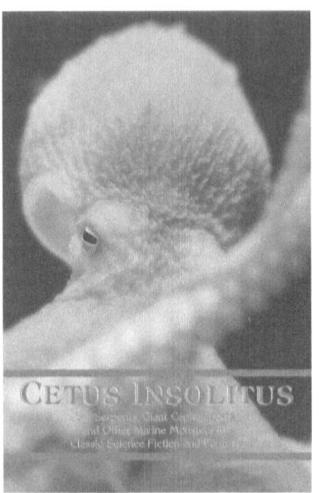

CETUS INSOLITUS:
Sea Serpents, Giant Cephalo-
pods, and Other Marine Monsters in Classic Science Fiction and Fantasy

ISBN 1-930585-66-7

26 stories, 391 pp.

FLORA CURIOSA:
Cryptobotany, Mysterious
Fungi, Sentient Trees, and
Deadly Plants in Classic
Science Fiction and Fantasy

ISBN 1-930585-56-X

20 stories, 337 pp.

Coachwhip Publications

CoachwhipBooks.com

SAURIA MONSTRA:
Dinosaurs, Pterosaurs, and
Other Fossil Saurians in
Classic Science Fiction and
Fantasy

ISBN 1-930585-77-2

14 stories, 1 novel, 413 pp.

INVERTEBRATA ENIGMATICA:
Giant Spiders, Dangerous
Insects, and Other Strange
Invertebrates in Classic
Science Fiction and Fantasy

ISBN 1-930585-65-9

30 stories, 396 pp.

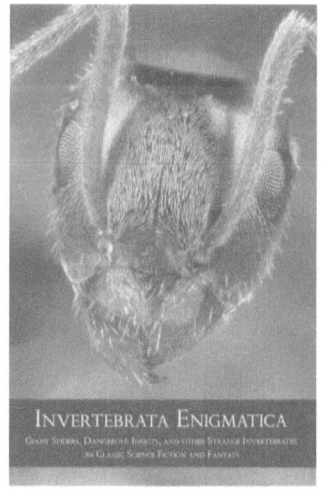

www.ingramcontent.com/pod-product-compliance
Lightning Source LLC
Chambersburg PA
CBHW020635020726

47494CB00001B/207